KT-559-224
29 MAR 2019
BRISTOL CITY LIBRARIES
WITHDRAWN AND OFFERED FOR SALE
Please return/renew this item by the last date shown on this label, or on your self-service receipt.
To renew this item, visit www.librarieswest.org.uk or contact your library
Your borrower number and PIN are required.
LibrariesWest
4 4 0047059 2

Why YOU love Nancy Revell

'A cracking saga set in the North East of England during World War 2. I LOVED it and became totally immersed and involved in the story. Can't wait to read the next book in the series'

'Reading this, I was drawn into the story. I felt I was there in those streets I know so well. This series of books just get better and better; a fantastic group of girls who could be any one of us if we were alive in the war. Could only give 5 STARS but worth many more.'

'What a brilliant read – the story is so good it keeps you wanting more . . . I fell in love with the girls; their stories, laughter, tears and so much more'

'How wonderful to read about everyday women, young, middle-aged, married or single all coming to work in a man's world. The pride and courage they all showed in taking over from the men who had gone to war. A debt of gratitude is very much owed'

'The shipyard saga goes on and with each book I want to read more! This book was so intriguing and with surprises as well. I can't wait for the next book!!'

'This is a book that lets the reader know the way our ancestors behaved during the two world wars. With strength, honour and downright bravery . . . I for one salute them all and give thanks to the author Nancy Revell, for letting us as readers know mostly as it was'

'Marvellous read, couldn't put down. Exciting, heart rendering, hope it will not be long before another one. Nancy Revell is an excellent author'

'I have now read all of the Shipyard Girls books – I was absolutely enthralled. I laughed, cried and rejoiced with each and every character'

'Each book, at some point, has had me lying wide-eyed in my bed wondering, and caring, questioning what's going to happen next? Thank you Nancy, as if I could be any more proud of my hometown'

'The lives of the young women welders and their families are once again beautifully and sympathetically portrayed.'

What the reviewers are saying...

'Well-drawn, believable characters combined with a storyline to keep you turning the page'
Woman magazine

'The author is one to watch'
Sun

'A riveting read is just what this is in more ways than one'
Northern Echo

'Researched within an inch of its life; the novel is enjoyably entertaining. A perfect way to spend hours, wrapped up in the characters' lives'
Frost magazine

'We're huge fans of Nancy's Shipyard Girls saga, and this is as emotional and gripping as the rest'
Take a Break

'This is a series that has gone from strength to strength . . . The cleverly weaved secrets and expert plotting had me hooked! 5* Genius'
Anne Bonny Book Reviews Blog

'There is a bit of everything within its pages – drama, heartache, happiness, sadness and the odd dash of humour . . . I absolutely loved this heart wrenching and extremely realistic saga series. A brilliant 5 out of 5*'
Ginger Book Geek Blog

'I adored this book! It is very well written and has a fabulous story! I loved how the past was brought back to life in the pages. Five stars from me – very highly recommended!'
Donna's Book Blog

'Heartfelt, pacy and gutsy, I adore it already and will no doubt be devouring the rest of the series with just as much enthusiasm'
Fiona Ford, author of *Christmas at Liberty's*

Also available by Nancy Revell

The Shipyard Girls
Shipyard Girls at War
Secrets of the Shipyard Girls
Shipyard Girls in Love
Victory for the Shipyard Girls

Courage of the Shipyard Girls

Nancy Revell

arrow books

1 3 5 7 9 10 8 6 4 2

Arrow Books
20 Vauxhall Bridge Road
London SW1V 2SA

Arrow Books is part of the Penguin Random House group
of companies whose addresses can be found at
global.penguinrandomhouse.com

First published in Great Britain by Arrow Books in 2019

www.penguin.co.uk

A CIP catalogue record for this book is available
from the British Library

ISBN 9781787460843

Typeset in 10.75/13.5 pt Palatino
by Integra Software Services Pvt. Ltd, Pondicherry

Printed and bound in Great Britain by Clays Ltd, Elcograf S.p.A.

To Suzanne Brown and all the members of Soroptimist International of Sunderland.

Happy 80th Birthday to an inspiring organisation!

Acknowledgements

Thank you to postmaster John Wilson and Liz Skelton and the rest of the lovely staff at Fulwell Post Office; Linda King, Norm Kirtlan and Philip Curtis at the Sunderland Antiquarian Society; journalist Katy Wheeler at the *Sunderland Echo*; news editor Stephen McCabe and team at 103.4 Sun FM; presenter Lisa Shaw and producer Jane Downs at BBC Radio Newcastle; onscreen journalist Julia Barthram at ITV News; Jenny Needham, features editor at the *Northern Echo*; Waterstones in Sunderland; researcher Meg Hartford; Jackie Caffrey, of Nostalgic Memories of Sunderland in Writing; Beverley Ann Hopper, of The Book Lovers, as well as 'Team Nancy' at Arrow: publishing director Emily Griffin, editor Cassandra Di Bello, my wonderful literary agent Diana Beaumont, and, of course, my parents, Audrey and Syd Walton, and husband, Paul.

Thank you all for your ongoing support and endless enthusiasm for the Shipyard Girls series.

There is no living thing that is not afraid when it faces danger.
The true courage is in facing danger when you are afraid, and
that kind of courage you have in plenty.
L. Frank Baum, *The Wonderful Wizard of Oz*

Prologue

On the last day of June 1942, a young woman in Sunderland stepped out of her front door on her way to work at one of the town's biggest shipyards – J.L. Thompson & Sons. It was a quarter to seven in the morning, but the sun was already up and proving that this day, like the one before, was going to be hot and sweaty.

The young woman, who was wearing a colourful headscarf and denim overalls, with a boxed gas mask and haversack slung over her shoulder, was leaving at the same time the postwoman was making her early-morning deliveries.

If an outsider was watching, they would rightly presume the two women knew each other by the ease of their greeting.

The postwoman handed the young woman an envelope, lingering for a short moment, which was unusual for her as she was not one to idle. She touched the young girl's arm gently before going on her way.

Tearing open the envelope, the young woman stood stock-still as she read the few paragraphs that had been typed onto the single sheet of paper. Passers-by would have observed that she stood and read it for longer than was needed.

For a moment it looked as though she was going to turn and go back into the house from which she had just come, but she didn't.

Instead, she reached into the top pocket of her overalls and pulled out what appeared to be a ring and put it on her left hand. As she did so, the letter she had just received in the post floated freely to the ground, and a short blast of air swept it under an oncoming tram.

The young woman didn't make any attempt to chase after the piece of paper that had escaped her grasp, but instead stepped onto the pavement and joined the throng of chattering, flat-capped workers all heading towards the shipyards that lined the banks of the Wear.

If anyone had looked at the face of the woman with the ruby engagement ring on her finger, they would have seen tears rolling down her cheeks unchecked.

But nobody noticed, so nobody asked if she was all right, and she walked in her hobnailed boots to the ferry that would take her to her place of work.

A place of work where people *would* spot that she had been crying, and would ask her why and comfort her – just as the young man who had given her the ruby engagement ring knew they would.

Chapter One

The letter floated to the ground before a gentle breeze lifted it up again at the exact time a tram was trundling down the length of Tatham Street.

Like the first draw of a fire as it catches, the letter was sucked under the metal belly of the carriage and disappeared from view.

By the time the tram had screeched its way past number 34, the letter had been unceremoniously spat out again into the still morning air, and after another brief flutter it landed by the side of the road.

The letter's near demise did not go unnoticed, though. For two minutes earlier, at the exact time Polly had been leaving for work and had bumped into the postwoman, Maud Goode had been having her usual early-morning tussle with the heavy blackout curtains that adorned her bedroom window.

'Mavis!' Maud kept her sight focused on the letter now languishing in the gutter across the road from where she and her sister lived above the sweet shop they jointly owned.

'Mavis!' Her tone was different to the one she normally adopted to wake her sister. This morning her voice was serious. Urgent. Lacking its usual annoyance that she was, as always, the first to rise.

'What's the matter?' Mavis's voice was croaky with sleep.

'Something's wrong.' Maud tightened the cord of her dressing gown around her ample waist and hurried out of the bedroom. In a matter of seconds, she had made it down the narrow staircase and out the front door. Bumping into a couple of shipyard workers, Maud ignored their apologies as well as their look of surprise at seeing her cross the road in just her nightclothes and slippers, her pink plastic curlers still in her hair.

Having made it to the other side, Maud was forced to wait until a double-decker bus had crunched through its gears and passed before she could bend down and pick up the letter, now smudged with dirt.

Shoving it straight into the pocket of her robe, Maud looked left, then right, before making her way back to the house.

'I'm in the kitchen,' Mavis shouted out, hearing the front door clash.

Walking into the scullery, Maud saw that her sister was making a big pot of tea.

'What's wrong?' Mavis asked again as her sister pulled out a chair and sat down at the kitchen table.

Maud didn't reply but reached into her pocket and retrieved the letter, her plump hands straightening the thick sheet of crumpled paper out on the wooden tabletop. The kettle started to whistle and Mavis poured steaming hot water into the ceramic teapot.

'Young Polly ... ' Maud looked up at her sister. 'She just got this.' Her eyes dropped to the letter now spread out in front of her.

'Poor bairn went white as a ghost. I thought she was going to go back inside, but she didn't. She got something out of her pocket and then just walked off down the street. Looked like she was in a trance.'

Mavis brought the teapot over and placed it on the table. She stirred before pouring out two cups, adding milk and half a teaspoon of sugar to each.

'Go on then,' she said, nodding across to the letter. 'What's it say?'

Chapter Two

Fifteen minutes later Maud and Mavis had got themselves dressed and were standing at the front door of number 34.

Maud looked at her younger sister.

'You do it,' she said.

Mavis took the letter.

They both took a deep breath and Maud knocked.

As soon as Agnes opened the door she knew something was wrong. The early hour of the day, and the faces of 'the two old maids', as they were known, told her that this was not a social visit. Agnes was still in her nightdress and had been in the kitchen, setting the breakfast table for the rest of the household, having seen her daughter off to work with her usual packed lunch.

'Sorry to call this early,' Mavis began before hesitating, not wanting to relate what she had to say out on the street.

'Come in.' Agnes opened the door wide. Tramp and Pup were by her feet, looking up at the unexpected visitors. 'Go through to the kitchen. I've just put a brew on.'

As Agnes followed the two sisters down the hallway, Arthur came out of his bedroom.

'Everything all right?' he asked. He was dressed for the day, bar his tartan slippers.

Agnes shook her head. 'I don't know.'

Arthur followed Agnes into the kitchen and said a polite 'Good mornin'' to the sisters as they sat down at the table while Agnes poured the tea.

'We're really sorry to come here like this.' Mavis paused. 'And I hope you don't think we've stuck our noses in where they're not wanted.' Another pause. 'But Maud here,' a quick look at her sister, 'saw Polly leave the house this morning. Just as she was leaving she bumped into the postwoman, who gave her this.'

Mavis put the letter on the table next to her cup of tea.

'Maud says that Polly read the letter and turned white as a sheet.'

Another look at Maud, who nodded.

'Maud thought she was going to come back here, but she didn't. She just dropped the letter and walked off.'

'In a trance,' Maud added, gravely.

'I hope you don't mind … but Maud was concerned … So she went and got the letter.'

The two sisters looked at each other.

'We thought we should bring it to you straight away.'

Mavis handed the letter to Agnes, who immediately unfolded it, sat down and started to read.

It didn't take her long.

When she finished, she looked at Arthur, who was perched on the chair next to her. She took his hand and squeezed it gently.

'I'm sorry, Arthur,' she said, tears in her eyes, as she handed him the letter.

Holding it at arm's length, Arthur started to read.

Commander Bridgman
Royal Navy
Gibraltar

21st June 1942

Dear Miss Elliot,

May I be permitted to express my own and the squadron's deepest sympathy with you in reporting that your fiancé Petty Officer (Diver) Tommy Watts has been declared missing.

Petty Officer Watts was a most proficient underwater diver for the clearance unit and his loss is deeply regretted by us all. Your fiancé's effects have been collected and will be forwarded to you in due course.

You may be aware that many of those classified as 'missing' are eventually reported prisoner of war, and I hope that this may give you some comfort in your anxiety.

Once again please accept the deep sympathy of us all.

Yours very sincerely,
Commander Bridgman

Miss Pollyanna Henrietta Elliot
34 Tatham Street
Sunderland
County Durham

By the time Arthur finished reading, his hands were shaking.

He looked up at Maud and Mavis.

'Yer did right ta bring the letter here.'

He then looked at Agnes.

'I think we need ta find Pol, make sure she's all right?'

Sensing the urgency in Arthur's voice, Maud and Mavis stood up. No one had touched their tea.

'We're so sorry,' Mavis said.

Her sister nodded.

'If there's anything we can do, just ask.'

And without further ado, the sisters left, shutting the front door quietly behind them.

'We did the right thing,' Mavis said to Maud, linking arms with her as they stood on the pavement.

'I want to go and light a candle. Say a prayer,' Maud told her sister, who nodded her understanding.

And so the pair turned right and started the short walk to St Ignatius Church.

Mavis wasn't a believer, but she was glad of the fresh air, and didn't mind sitting in the pews while her sister begged the Lord above to save yet another soul that this war looked likely to have taken.

Agnes got changed quickly.

By the time the town hall clock struck eight, she and Arthur were heading towards the ferry landing.

'Yer don't tink she'll have done anyting stupid, do yer?' The Irish in Agnes's voice was strong, as it always was when she was either worried or angry. She looked at Arthur as they crossed the Borough Road and started heading down to the south docks.

'Polly won't have done 'owt daft,' Arthur reassured her. 'She's got a good head on her that one ... She'll have gorra hell of a shock, though. There's no doubting that.'

'Yer tink she'll have gone ta the yard?' Agnes asked, unsure.

'I'd wager a bet that's where she's gone.' Arthur stuck his hand in his pocket to pay the ferryman but was waved on. Everyone who worked on the river knew Arthur. His years working for the Wear Commissioner as a deep-sea diver afforded him a free pass.

'If she's not at Thompson's, we'll find her. Dinnit worry, Agnes. She'll be all right. Or as all right as can be.'

As they looked across at the shipyards, coal drops and timber stores that lined the riverbanks, Arthur offered up his own silent prayer. Unlike Maud, though, Arthur's invocation was to his wife, Flo, who he believed would look after 'their Tommy' on this side as well as the next.

'This bloody war!' Agnes couldn't stop the fury that had been building up in her since she'd read the words of Tommy's commander.

'And that bloody letter!' She turned her head to look at Arthur. 'It just doesn't make sense. Is he missing? Is he a prisoner of war?' She paused. 'Or do they *really* tink he's dead?'

As soon as the words were out of her mouth she regretted them. She squeezed Arthur's gnarled hand again, which was gripping the side of the old steamer, presently heaving its way across an uncannily calm River Wear.

Arthur let out a long sigh.

'God only knows. Sounds like they've got no idea themselves. They should knar soon enough if our Tommy's been taken prisoner o' war, but yer just dinnit knar. They didn't exactly tell us much about where, or when, or *how* he went missing.' Anger was now creeping into Arthur's voice. 'Poor Polly, she's not gonna knar where she is. Her head'll be all over the shop.'

Chapter Three

Polly was aware of the hustle and bustle as she made her way to J.L. Thompson & Sons, the place she had been working at for almost two years now. She could smell the familiar odour of burning tobacco mixed with the salty air, particularly pungent this morning due to a low tide and the warm weather. She felt the gentle bob of the *W.F. Vint* as the screw steamer made her tired way across to North Sands, and she heard the excited squawking of the seagulls circling above.

Stepping off the ferry and walking up the embankment, she found herself being jostled by her fellow workers, and felt the weight of their bodies pressing into her as the usual bottleneck formed at the clocking-on cabin. She saw her hand reaching out to grab the white board on which her number, 111, had been scrawled in pencil by the young timekeeper, Alfie, along with her start time. And as she walked into the yard, she looked about her, as if for the first time. The world was now very different from the one she had known only yesterday.

'All reet, pet?'

Polly looked to see Jimmy the head riveter standing with his squad, a young apprentice burner stoking up a smouldering metal brazier. She felt her mouth widen and pull itself into the semblance of a smile and her hand rise up by way of a response.

Making her way around a mound of thick chains next to a crane, Polly looked up to see the driver sitting in the small steel cabin, watching the early-morning sun making its slow ascent over the endless expanse of the North Sea. He seemed to be enjoying the stillness before the start of the day's shift.

It wasn't until she saw her friends – the yard's squad of women welders – chatting and drinking tea at their work station that Polly's fractured mind started to understand what she had just learnt. She felt in her pocket for the letter, before remembering she had let it go.

In the corner of her eye she caught the glint of diamonds. She looked down and touched her little ruby ring.

Looking up again she saw Dorothy, who was wrapping her thick chestnut-coloured hair into a turban, expertly done so that not a wisp was visible.

Angie was chatting to Rosie, who was smiling and laughing at something her young welder was telling her.

And Martha, who had her hand to her forehead to shield her eyes from the sun's glare, was inspecting a warship that had just docked.

It took Polly a moment to realise that one of their team was missing: Gloria. Then another moment to recall that she had told them yesterday she would be in late.

'Yeh! Here she is! At long bloody last!' Dorothy shouted out, having spotted her workmate walking towards them.

'Hurry up! We've got loads of goss to tell you!'

It wasn't until Polly was near that they all realised there was something very wrong. They had spent the best part of ten hours a day, six – sometimes seven – days a week with each other for the past twenty-three months. They had got to know just about everything there was to know about one another, but most of all, they could read each other as well as if they'd been friends their entire lives.

And this morning they all knew instantly that Polly was not herself.

'Oh my goodness, Polly.' Rosie strode over to her workmate. 'What's happened?'

Dorothy, Angie and Martha formed a semicircle around Polly, their eyes filled with genuine concern.

Polly looked at their worried faces but didn't speak.

'Come and sit down.' Martha took Polly's arm and pulled her forward, manoeuvring her over to a stack of wooden pallets.

Polly allowed herself to be guided to the makeshift seating.

Dorothy told Angie to get Polly a cup of tea, before sitting down next to her.

'What's happened, Pol?' Dorothy asked.

'Is it Tommy?' Rosie asked tentatively, as Angie handed Polly a tin cup of steaming hot tea.

Polly nodded.

'Wot's happened to him?' It was Angie, who had never met Tommy, having joined Rosie's squad later than the rest. She still felt that she knew him, though, having had endless discussions with Dorothy, the two of them agreeing that the romance between their workmate and the shipyard's dock diver beat all the made-up love stories they'd ever seen acted out on the silver screen.

Rosie bobbed down on her haunches so that she was looking straight at Polly.

'Have you had a telegram?'

Polly shook her head.

'That's good.' Martha stared down at Polly as her large frame cast a shadow across the women, shielding them from the sun's early morning rays.

Rosie looked up at Martha and then back at Polly.

'That's good, eh? No telegram?'

Again Polly nodded. Slowly.

'No telegram,' she said, her voice shaky. 'But a letter. From his commander.'

The women didn't move, so intent were they on hearing what Polly had to say.

'He said,' she continued, 'that Tommy's "missing". Might be a prisoner of war … Might be … ' Polly's voice trailed off.

The women were quiet. They were all thinking the same. *Might be dead.*

'Did the letter say anything else?' Rosie gently coaxed.

'Not really. Just that they sent their sympathies … and that they were going to send his things back to me.'

There was a morbid silence.

'Drink yer tea,' Angie cajoled. 'Do yer want a biscuit? Martha's got some of her mam's home-made ginger nuts.'

Polly shook her head, but took a slurp of tea.

Rosie looked at the clock on the side of the admin offices and saw they only had a few minutes to go before the klaxon sounded out and then there would be no chance of hearing themselves think, never mind talk.

'Do you want to go for a cuppa in the canteen?'

'No.' Polly shook her head. 'I just want to work.'

Rosie looked at Polly's ashen face and wondered if it was a good idea.

Reading her thoughts, Polly looked around at the women.

'I'm all right, honestly. I just want to get on and work. I need to do something.'

'All right,' Rosie said, 'but if you feel funny, or light-headed, you must say. Promise?'

'I promise,' Polly agreed, handing Angie's tin teacup back to her and getting off the wooden pallets.

As she did so the horn blared.

Rosie looked at Martha and cocked her head over to Polly, now collecting her helmet and welding rods from the nearby shed they used to store their equipment. Martha nodded her understanding and went over to Polly.

Rosie, Dorothy and Angie followed Martha and Polly up the metal gangplank and onto the main deck. One of the ship's gun mountings needed welding.

The three women looked at Polly and Martha and then back at each other.

Even if they could have been heard, there was no need to put into words what they were thinking and feeling.

By the time Agnes and Arthur arrived at the main gates of Thompson's it had gone half eight.

It had been many years since Agnes had ventured over to North Sands. In fact, she couldn't remember the last time she had been here. There had never been the need, until now.

As Agnes started to walk through the main entrance, determined to find her daughter, to make sure she had, in fact, gone straight to work, she heard a voice from above calling out to her.

'Madam! Madam! Sorry, but you can't just go in there!'

As Agnes was looking around to see where the voice came from, she felt Arthur's bony hand on her arm.

'Yer need a pass, Agnes,' he explained. 'Let's ask the young lad here,' he pointed up to Alfie in the timekeeper's cabin, 'and see if Polly's clocked on today.'

As they walked towards the cabin, Agnes felt overwhelmed by the intensity of sound – the constant clashing and clanging of metal. She could almost feel the thudding in her head. How on earth Polly stood this day in, day out, she had no idea. Her hatred for the yards and for her daughter's working there seemed to be gaining momentum by the second.

If Polly hadn't got a job here, then she would never have met Tommy, and if she hadn't met Tommy, she wouldn't now be looking at a lifetime of heartache – for there was no doubt in Agnes's mind that Tommy would not be coming back.

'Young laddie!' Arthur put his hands around his mouth and shouted up to the cabin window, but there was no one there.

A few seconds later he felt a hand on his shoulder.

It was Alfie.

He looked at Arthur and then Agnes.

'Can I help you?' he shouted.

Agnes and Arthur nodded energetically.

'Do yer know if Polly Elliot has clocked on this mornin'?' Agnes asked.

Alfie put his hand to his ear. He hadn't caught a word.

'Polly Elliot!' Arthur stepped nearer to the young lad and shouted in his ear.

Alfie's face immediately lit up and he nodded.

'Aye,' he said, looking across the yard. Turning to the old man and the middle-aged woman, he pointed to a metal grey warship that was docked by the quayside.

'There!' he shouted. 'There she is!'

Agnes and Arthur squinted into the sun. It took them both a moment to adjust their vision and focus on the ship's top deck before they could see five overall-clad figures working closely together. It was clearly the women welders and they recognised Polly instantly by the red headscarf she'd had since starting work at the yard. She was next to Martha and they were both on the top of what looked like a huge gun mount. Martha was easily recognisable by her size and her short hair that meant she had no need of a turban. Both women were hunched over a flickering live weld that Agnes thought looked like a small, sparkling waterfall. It was almost pretty.

'She's all right. Or as all right as she can be.' Agnes nudged Arthur. 'Come on. Let's go home. She won't want us fussing about her. Not with everyone about, gawking.'

Arthur shook the young lad's hand and mouthed 'Thank you' before guiding Agnes back down the embankment and onto the waiting ferry, now relatively empty after the rush of the early-morning shift.

As the ferry churned water and they made their way back across to the south side, Agnes kept her eyes on Thompson's. She could no longer see the women, but she could see the warship they were working on.

'I wish I'd never let her start work there,' Agnes said. 'I should have put me foot down. If her da had been about he'd never have let her.'

Arthur looked at Agnes. She rarely mentioned her husband.

'I dinnit think wild horses would have stopped her working here,' Arthur said. 'Even if your Harry had still been here. Yer've got yerself a very headstrong daughter there, Agnes Elliot.' Arthur smiled at the woman who had shown him nothing but kindness since first meeting him. 'Takes after her ma.'

They were silent for a few moments, looking out at the river life, and listening to the rhythmic lapping of the greeny-grey water against the hull. Neither of them said anything, but, having seen Polly hard at work and surrounded by her workmates, they were both more than aware that this was now her life, whether Agnes liked it or not.

As they neared the docks, Agnes turned to Arthur.

'This is just the start, isn't it?' Agnes said.

'Aye, it is,' Arthur agreed sadly.

'It's going to change her,' Agnes said.

Arthur's voice was low. 'Aye, it will.'

Chapter Four

As soon as the blare of the klaxon sounded out dead on midday, Rosie pushed up her metal mask and looked at Martha and Polly, who were doing the same.

'Come on,' she shouted to Dorothy and Angie, who had been doing flat welds on the platform on which the huge cannon-sized guns had been mounted.

'Let's have our lunch on the bridge today, there's some shade there.' Rosie wiped sweat off her brow. They'd all been working like troopers this morning. Polly had shaken her head when she'd suggested a mid-morning break and, in a show of solidarity, Martha, Dorothy and Angie had also declined and soldiered on.

'How you feeling?' Rosie asked, as they all rummaged around in their bags, unwrapped sandwiches and poured tea from their flasks.

Polly tried to force a smile.

'I'm all right,' she said, but she sounded and looked anything but.

There was a moment's quiet. An uncertainty as to what to say.

Martha leant forward. For once she wasn't tucking into her sandwiches as though she had been starved for a week.

'There's still hope, you know.' Her eyes were focused on Polly. 'He might not be dead.'

All the women stared at Martha, shocked at her bluntness.

'I know … I know,' Polly agreed, but her tone and the undisguised sorrow pouring from her eyes betrayed her true feelings.

An unnatural quietness fell on the squad, and the absence of the usual incessant chatter and verbal jousting created a void that was filled with a great communal sadness.

The silence was broken a few minutes later by the sound of Gloria's arrival.

'Cooeee!'

They all turned automatically at the sound of their workmate's excited voice and watched as she hurried across the gangplank and onto the main deck. She was waving what looked like an official document in the air with unreserved glee.

'I'm free!' she shouted out as she strode towards them. 'Free as a bird!' She let loose a guttural laugh.

'Free of that bastard!'

As she ducked under one of the machine guns, she declared:

'I am now officially – and unashamedly – a divorcee!'

But as soon as she was near enough to clock the faces of her workmates, she dropped her arm and slowed her pace.

'What's happened? What's wrong?' she asked, the sing-song voice now gone, her tone laced with panic. She saw Rosie, Martha, Dorothy and Angie turn their gaze to Polly.

'What's happened?' This time the question was directed at Polly. 'Is it Tommy?'

Polly nodded and Gloria immediately strode over to her friend, wrapped her arms around her and held her close.

'He's been declared missing.' Polly's voice was shaky. 'They don't know if he's dead or alive, or a prisoner of war.'

Gloria hugged Polly hard.

'Oh, my poor girl. I'm so sorry. So sorry.'

And then the dam burst and tears erupted from Polly, her body heaving with great sobs.

For a good while the women watched sadly, with tears in their own eyes, as Polly sobbed her heart out into the folds of Gloria's overalls. Her juddering body held tightly by the strong arms of the squad's mother hen. The tight embrace not easing but holding her fast, showing her that she was supported. They would not let her fall.

And when there were no more tears, Polly let her head rest on Gloria's chest, closed her eyes and let the sun fall on her face.

When she opened them again, Rosie gently urged her to eat, telling her she had to keep her stamina up, otherwise she would be no good and wouldn't have the strength to weld. It was what Polly needed to hear and so they all sat and ate their lunch and drank their tea, even though it was the last thing any of them felt like doing.

And then they went back to work, but before they did so, they all gave Polly a hug, each one telling her that they were there for her. The deep sincerity in their voices showed the depth of feeling they had for their friend.

'You sure you don't want me to come with you?' Rosie asked.

It was the end of the shift and Polly had told them that she wanted to go and tell Ralph, the head dock diver, about Tommy being declared missing. Afterwards she would tell Stan the ferryman, who had known Tommy since he was a young lad.

'No. Thanks anyway. I'd rather see them on my own.'

'You sure you want to do it now?' Gloria asked.

Polly nodded, picking up her haversack.

'They thought—' Polly corrected herself. 'They *think* the world of Tommy. I'd hate for them to hear it from anyone else. Besides, I'd rather get it over with.'

'I'll tell yer mam yer gonna be a bit later than normal,' Gloria said.

Polly was just turning away when Hannah came running over.

'Polly, I'm so sorry.' She flung her stick-like arms around her former workmate. 'Martha has just told me.'

'Thanks, Hannah,' Polly said.

'We're here for you,' Hannah said, her small, pale hands taking hold of Polly's and squeezing them with surprising strength. 'But you mustn't give up hope. Promise me you won't give up hope on your Tommy? You don't know for certain what's happened to him.'

Polly looked down at Hannah, their 'little bird'. She knew that she also carried a weight of worry on her slender shoulders. She too had no idea if those she loved were alive or dead, or were somewhere between the two, languishing in some godforsaken labour camp.

'Promise?' Hannah repeated.

'Promise,' Polly agreed.

The women watched with heavy hearts as Polly trudged to the other side of the yard where she knew the divers were presently working on a frigate they hoped to fix without it having to be brought into the dry dock.

'See you all tomorrow,' Hannah said sadly, as she headed back over to the drawing office where Martha and her 'friend boy' Olly were waiting for her.

'Do yer think Polly will be all reet, miss?' Angie asked as they started to make their way over to the main entrance.

'Let's hope so, Angie,' Rosie said. 'It's like what Hannah just said. She's got to have hope, until she knows either way.'

Rosie took a deep breath.

'Anyway, what are you two up to tonight?' She looked at Dorothy and back again at Angie.

'Gannin to the Ritz, miss,' Angie said.

'Well, go 'n have some fun,' Gloria said. 'Tell us all about it tomorrow. No more gloomy faces. For Polly's sake, yeh?'

'Aye, we will, Glor,' Angie said as Dorothy hooked arms with her and they both walked off, though without the usual spring in their step.

Rosie and Gloria were quiet as they made their way down the embankment to the ferry landing.

Rosie walked over to the docking cleat and sat down.

'God, I'm knackered,' she admitted. 'What a day, eh?'

Gloria sighed and nodded sadly.

'But at least you're now a properly divorced woman,' Rosie said, looking up at her friend.

'I know. In different circumstances I might have felt tempted to go and paint the town red with Dorothy and Angie. Or at least dragged you all to the Admiral for a celebratory drink,' she added.

'Well, I think we should do something to mark the occasion later in the week,' Rosie mused. 'I mean, that man has been the bane of your life. I think we were all nearly as happy as you when he signed up and was sent to Portsmouth.'

'Yes, thanks to your Peter,' Gloria said, watching Rosie undo her turban.

'What's that?' Gloria pointed to a dried petal that had fluttered out of the folds of Rosie's headscarf.

Rosie spotted and grabbed it just before it landed on the ground.

'Ahh.' A smile as wide as any Gloria had ever seen on her friend's face suddenly appeared.

Rosie held her hand up to show Gloria the dried petal. 'Oh, Gloria, I wasn't going to say anything. Didn't know if I should, to be honest. You know, with all this "careless whispers" talk.' Rosie looked around as if to check no one was earwigging in on their conversation. The ferry landing had started to fill up with fellow workers, but none looked remotely interested in the two women, or in what they were talking about.

'And, of course,' Rosie continued, 'there was no way I was going to say anything after Polly's awful news.' She paused for a moment, not sure whether she should really be telling anyone about the letter she had received that morning.

'Go on,' Gloria egged her on.

'Well,' Rosie said, lowering her voice. 'I'd just left the house this morning when I saw the postwoman coming towards me, waving a letter in the air. I was surprised because I don't really get any post unless it's from Charlotte – and I've only just had another begging letter from her.' Rosie rolled her eyes and Gloria chuckled. They all knew of the present stand-off between Rosie and her little sister over the issue of whether or not she should be allowed to come back home to live.

'I knew it wasn't from Charlotte, though, as soon as I looked at the envelope.' Rosie paused for the second time. 'Not unless she had somehow got herself over to the south of France!'

Gloria's eyes widened. 'What? The postmark was French?' She whispered the question.

Rosie nodded. Her eyes were sparkling with excitement.

'The south is unoccupied, so they're still able to get post out,' she explained.

Gloria had moved nearer to hear Rosie, entranced by this latest turn of events.

'So, what did the letter say?' she asked, her attention momentarily distracted by the approaching ferry.

Rosie stood and picked up her haversack. 'Well, it wasn't a letter as such.' She paused. 'When we were saying our goodbyes at the train station, Peter said he would try and get word to me that he was all right.'

Gloria's face looked confused as they turned to board the ferry bumping gently against the wooden landing posts.

'So, if there wasn't a letter in the envelope ... ?' Gloria left the question hanging in the air as they both paid their fares and made their way down to the far end.

'Petals,' Rosie turned to Gloria and whispered. 'He'd filled the envelope with dried petals. Petals from a bunch of *pansies*.'

Slowly comprehension showed on Gloria's face. She smiled. 'Ahh, I get it. Yer wedding bouquet?'

'Yes!' Rosie said. Her face looked vibrant. 'We'd had this discussion at the time about the bouquet. He said I should have kept it, you know, pressed the flowers as a memento?'

Gloria nodded.

'But I said it was better that two brides made use of the bouquet rather than just the one, which is why I gave it to a young couple who were due to get married after us.'

Gloria listened. Rosie hadn't mentioned this act of kindness when she had told them all about her ad hoc wedding to Peter.

'When I gave the young ATS bride the flowers I whispered something to her, and Peter, forever the nebby-nose,' Rosie chuckled, 'asked what I'd said to her, and I told him what the florist had told me – that the pansy meant you are always thinking of someone.'

'Oh, Rosie,' Gloria sighed, 'that really is so incredibly romantic.' Tears came into her eyes for the second time that day. 'I'm so chuffed fer yer.' Gloria looked at her friend and saw how happy those dried petals had made her. It was a joy to see, especially after the sadness of the day.

'I felt like I was walking on air this morning when I came into work,' Rosie admitted. 'I felt like the happiest woman on the planet. Like I could have built an entire ship with my own bare hands.' They both laughed.

'But then,' Rosie's voice dropped, 'Polly arrived and my heart could have broken for her. I really felt for her ... but I felt really guilty as well. There was me, all happy that I'd heard from Peter and there was Polly – devastated.'

The ferry arrived at the south docks and Gloria and Rosie hopped onto the landing and started up the bank to the main road.

'Well, yer daft if yer feel guilty about getting some good news, Rosie. I can see why you wouldn't want Polly to know about yer petals, even if yer could tell her, but you've no reason to feel *guilty* about it. God, there's so much bad news about these days we've got to really make the most of any good news we get. Bloody enjoy it, that's what I say!'

Rosie smiled. She knew Gloria was right. 'Anyway, talking of good news, we've got your divorce to celebrate.'

Gloria laughed. 'It's a sad state of affairs when getting a divorce is a call for celebration.'

'Not when it's from someone like Vinnie,' Rosie said.

The women's laughter was bittersweet as they said their goodbyes and went their separate ways.

Chapter Five

Twenty minutes later Gloria was pushing Hope back home in her pram. Every time she made the short journey up Tatham Street and across the Borough Road to her flat, she was thankful she no longer lived on the Ford Estate on the other side of town. Not just because it meant she didn't have to schlep five miles to and from work every day, but because the little basement flat that had once been Rosie's home signified the start of her new life.

Her new *divorced* life.

Four months previously she had left her old marital home, and all the awful memories that went with it, and she had never looked back.

Of course, she had hoped to have been starting her new life with Jack and Hope as a family, but that was not to be. Not for the moment anyway. But at least, Gloria thought as she carefully bumped the pram down the half-dozen stone steps to her front door, Jack was alive – even if she hadn't seen him for nearly six months.

'Ahh, home sweet home,' Gloria said as she opened the front door, manoeuvred the pram inside, and hauled Hope out. As soon as she did so, though, Hope let out an ear-splitting cry.

'Now, why did I just know that was going to happen?' Gloria spoke her thoughts. 'A perfect angel for yer lovely aunty Bel, but a little devil for yer auld ma. Let's just see if a nice bottle of milk will do the trick.'

Gloria was heading towards her little kitchenette, a screaming Hope in her arms, when she heard a knock on the door.

She went to answer it.

'Helen! How lovely to see you!' Gloria had to speak loudly to be heard over Hope's crying, which seemed to be getting louder and more demanding by the second.

As soon as Helen saw her little sister's scrunched-up red face, her hands automatically went out to take her.

Closing the door behind her and watching Helen gently kiss Hope's thick mop of black hair, then gently jig her up and down, Gloria caught her breath. Seeing Hope and her big sister together made her heart swell.

'I'm sorry I haven't been able to come round before now,' Helen said as she did a slow lap of the small living area. She wanted to explain why, but couldn't. Her head had been all over the shop this past week since turning up unannounced and meeting her sister for the first time.

Gloria went into the kitchen and put the kettle on.

'Don't worry,' Gloria reassured her. 'That door's always open. You just come whenever you want. There'll always be two people who are more than happy to see you. Particularly this one.' Gloria looked over to her daughter who was now like a kitten in Helen's arms.

'You fancy a cuppa? I know I'm parched,' Gloria said.

'Yes, please.' Helen's voice was soft with barely the hint of a north-east accent.

Gloria headed into the kitchen, conscious of not fussing over Helen and steamrolling her with a load of questions:

How was she feeling?

Had she got a message to that no good Theodore that she was expecting his child?

She knew Helen must be beside herself. It might not be that unusual for young women of Helen's standing to find themselves in the family way, but if they did, then they'd be racing down the aisle faster than the speed of light while they still had the semblance of a waist.

Helen, however, didn't have that option.

After making the tea she took it through to the lounge on a little tray, put it on the coffee table and poured out two cups.

'You fancy a sandwich? Or some biscuits with yer tea?' Gloria asked.

Helen's face blanched and she shook her head vehemently.

Gloria laughed.

'Morning sickness in the evening then?'

'More like morning, afternoon and evening sickness.' Helen smiled, but Gloria thought she looked incredibly sad, as well as very tired.

'Let me take little Miss Muffet off yer,' Gloria volunteered.

'That's all right. I don't mind,' Helen said.

Gloria got up, went back into the kitchen and made up a bottle of milk.

'Here you are.' She handed the bottle to Helen, who gently cajoled her baby sister into drinking the milk.

Gloria laughed. 'Please feel free to come 'n visit any time. If yer hadn't come around I know fer a fact that little 'un would still be screaming her head off – 'n if I'd tried to give her that bottle she would have batted it away like she was trying to swat a fly.'

Helen chuckled.

'So,' Gloria's face became serious, 'how yer feeling? About everything?'

Helen looked at Hope.

'She's getting tired now,' she said, purposely avoiding answering Gloria's question, not because she didn't want to answer, but because she really had no idea how she was feeling – about anything. Her emotions seemed all over the place. One minute she felt completely serene, the next as though she was hurtling down the rabbit hole and seeing only darkness at the end.

'You haven't told Dad have you?' Helen looked up, her eyes finding Gloria's for the first time, hoping she would be able to tell if she was lying.

'Like I told yer last week, if you don't want me to tell yer dad, then I won't.' Gloria's voice was firm. She had spoken to Jack on the phone a few days after Helen's impromptu visit and she'd had to bite her tongue more than once.

'And you definitely won't tell any of the other women, will you?'

'Of course I won't. Like I said before, it goes without saying. This is your business 'n no one else's.'

'It's just … ' Helen hesitated. 'I know what Mum found out … About your workmates. All their secrets.' She looked at Gloria. She felt awful for having to do this, but it was the only way she knew for certain that Gloria would keep schtum. 'I know about Dorothy's mother's bigamy, Angie's mam's lover, and Martha … ' Helen let her voice trail off. She didn't need to go into any more detail about what else her mother's private eye had found out. 'I'll keep your friend's secrets if you keep mine.'

Gloria looked at Helen.

'Yer don't have to blackmail me to make sure I keep my mouth shut, Helen. If I say I won't tell anyone, then I won't. I'm a woman of my word. Are we clear on that?'

Helen nodded.

'No more threats?' Gloria added.

Helen blushed.

'I know what it's like to be fodder fer the local gossip-mongers,' Gloria said. 'I am, after all, a middle-aged woman who's not only had a baby when most other women my age are becoming grandparents, but I also dared to kick my husband of twenty years out of the marital home.

'But,' she added hesitantly, 'busybodies with nothing better to do than stick their noses into other people's business are one thing – yer dad is another.'

She looked at Helen and saw anger flash across her face, but still she persevered. 'I don't know why yer won't tell him?'

'Why *would* I tell Dad?' Helen snapped back. Her change in mood unsettled Hope, who started to wake up and was blinking at her sister with large green-blue eyes.

'He doesn't care about me any more.' Helen dropped her voice to an almost whisper.

'Why do you think that?' Gloria asked, genuinely perplexed. 'Yer dad adores you. He always has done and always will.' Gloria paused, not wanting to sound accusatory, but needing to say what she had wanted to say for a good while.

'To be honest,' Gloria took a deep breath, 'yer dad's more than a little hurt you haven't written to him.'

Helen opened her mouth in disbelief. Feeling Hope begin to wriggle about, she stood up and started walking round the room, swaying Hope in her arms, trying to keep her calm when she herself felt like exploding.

'I might have written to Dad if he'd bothered to write to me!' Her voice was low but furious. 'To have sent me just one letter!' Helen let out a bitter laugh. 'A postcard even! I'd have been over the moon with just a few words scrawled on the back of a photograph of the Clyde! But nothing! Not a single word.'

Gloria stared at Helen.

'I don't understand,' she said. 'Yer dad's been writing to yer every week. Sometimes more. He's been so worried. He thinks yer hate him.'

Gloria was quiet for a moment, trying to fathom a reason why Helen had not been getting Jack's letters. He must have written dozens since Miriam had banished him to Glasgow at the start of the year.

Helen stopped walking.

'I don't believe it!' Her voice was barely audible, her piercing green eyes showing the sheer incredulity she was feeling. The penny had not just dropped, but clunked down heavy and hard.

'That bloody postbox.' Helen's voice was breathless.

Gloria got up and took Hope.

'Come and sit down, Helen. You've gone as red as a beetroot.'

Helen sat down in the armchair but leant forward, her back rigid, her hands clasped as though she wanted to strangle someone.

'Tell me,' Gloria asked. 'What postbox?'

'Mum got a little postbox put up just outside the front door. Said she was sick of the new postwoman ramming mail through the letter box as if she was stuffing a chicken … I thought it was just Mum being Mum. I didn't even think … Didn't even think to ask for a key … God, I should have guessed.' Helen was shaking her head.

'What? You think Miriam's been taking yer dad's letters?' Now it was Gloria's turn to sound completely stupefied.

'I don't *think*,' Helen said. 'I know!'

Helen's mind scanned the past six months, how her mother had often complained about the new postwoman's timekeeping. She had thought it was just her mother's way – to moan about any kind of service, be it from a restaurant, a shop or, in this case, the GPO.

Helen stood up.

'Sorry, Gloria, I'm going to have to go.' She stepped over to where Gloria was sitting with Hope and bent down to give her little sister a kiss on the cheek.

Gloria opened her mouth to object, but Helen was already picking up her handbag and gas mask by the front door.

'Can I ask you a favour?' Helen said.

'Course you can.' Gloria stood up carefully so as not to wake Hope, who was now fast asleep.

'Tell Dad I've not been getting his letters, but please tell him not to pick up the phone and have a rant at Mum.' Gloria nodded. Helen clearly knew her dad well, as that would be the first thing he would want to do on finding out what Miriam had done.

'I want to deal with this my way.' She took a deep breath and opened the front door. 'And, if it's all right with you, can you ask him to send his letters here from now on?'

'Of course,' Gloria said. She wanted to say so much more, but she could see that there was no stopping Helen. 'Drop by in a few days. I'll try and speak to yer dad tomorrow, get him to send a letter straight away.'

Suddenly, as Helen started to make her way up the steps, a thought occurred to Gloria.

'Yer don't want to give him a call yerself, do you? He'd be over the moon to hear from yer?'

Helen shook her head. 'I couldn't. He'd know something was wrong.' She instinctively smoothed down her dress. She wasn't showing, but it wouldn't be long before she was.

'He's going to have to know.' Gloria kept her voice soft.

'I know,' Helen said, 'but not yet. I just need some more time.'

And with that she turned and left.

Gloria heard the sound of Helen's high heels on the pavement as she hurried down the street.

Chapter Six

As soon as Helen reached the top of the steps she immediately turned right and started striding along the busy Borough Road. If she hadn't felt so nauseous, she would have run, in spite of her two-inch-high Mary-Jane shoes.

How could you?! How could you do something like this?! She wanted to scream at her mother – would, in fact, scream at her mother when she reached the Grand.

Turning right into Frederick Street, Helen continued her march. By the time she had reached St Thomas's Street, though, her energy levels were depleted and she had to stop and steady herself against an iron railing.

'Are you all right, my dear?' The question came from an elderly, well-dressed gentleman who had been walking behind. He gently rested a hand on her back. Helen straightened and swallowed air as she found this stopped the dry retching and sometimes, but not always, prevented her from actually being sick.

'Yes, thank you.' Helen's words were clipped, causing the man to remove his hand and carry on his way.

Helen stood for a moment and waited for the nausea to pass. Looking across to the other side of the street, with its plush three-storey terraces that housed both families and businesses, she spotted the gleaming bronze plaque of the doctor's surgery she had visited a week ago.

She forced herself to carry on walking, away from the memory of that afternoon, away from the vivid recall of those twenty minutes she had spent in the doctor's consultation room. Minutes that had forever altered the course of her life.

She picked up her pace but knew it was pointless. She would never forget.

After a hundred yards or so another wave of queasiness forced Helen to stop again. She took in a deep gulp of air. She could feel her heart beating fast and her legs felt shaky. A wave of anger rose up along with the bile that had reached the back of her throat.

If her mother had not intercepted her father's letters, she doubted very much she'd be in the hellish predicament in which she now found herself. She would have known that her father had not forsaken her for his new family – that he did still love her.

And if she had known that, if she had been in contact with him, perhaps even gone and visited him in Glasgow, then there was a good chance she would not have become involved with Theodore.

The reason she had flung herself so readily into Theo's arms was because of her father's perceived rejection of her. She had been so desperate for love. So desperate to escape her reality and leave behind everything she had ever known. Theo being Theo, had, of course, seen her neediness – her vulnerability – and taken full advantage of it.

In many ways, just like her mother had.

Both had only been concerned with their own needs.

Neither had given two hoots about her.

Well, no more, Helen told herself. *No one would ever do that to her again. As long as she drew breath.*

As Helen reached Bridge Street, she stopped. She would have loved more than anything to have continued to stomp the few hundred yards to the Grand, to march through the foyer and up the first flight of stairs to where she knew her mother would be. But Helen knew she couldn't. Not there, in such a public place. She couldn't risk others hearing and knowing her business. She still had her self-respect, if nothing else.

Having made her decision, Helen felt herself deflate as exhaustion took over.

Seeing a tram squeal to a stop a few yards up the road, she dredged up her last bit of energy and hurried to catch it.

It had become a habit since she had been forced to use public transport to go up to the top deck and look out at the Wear and observe the general hubbub of street life, but this evening she simply didn't have it in her so she grabbed the first empty seat she saw. It was next to a woman about her mother's age, who kept turning around to chat to her daughter and granddaughter in the seats behind. The happy family unit annoyed Helen instantly and she got up and moved to the back of the tram, next to an old man who smelled of stale sweat and tobacco. It was the lesser of two evils.

Why couldn't she have a mother like the one she could still see at the front of the tram?

What normal mother, Helen kept asking herself, *tries to keep a father and daughter apart?*

As the tram trundled along Dame Dorothy Street, she reran the awful scene in the Grand, where she had gone after finding out that not only was she pregnant, but that Theodore was married. But instead of being there for her in her hour of need, her mother had reviled and rejected her – *had even slapped her in the face.*

Still, Helen mused bitterly, she really shouldn't have been so surprised by her mother's reaction. She had always been completely self-centred – devoid of any kind of love for anyone other than herself.

As the tram slowed to a stop, Helen got off and walked the few hundred yards along the perimeter of Roker Park to her home on the corner of Park Avenue. It was a lovely evening, but all Helen wanted to do was get home and fall into bed.

When Helen walked through the gate and saw the post-box at the bottom of the stone steps, she could have happily taken a sledgehammer to it – had she had the strength.

She should have guessed. She should have thought it odd that her mother had, all of a sudden, become obsessed with the post. Helen wished, more than anything, that she hadn't been so ready to believe her mother's lies – that she'd had more faith in her father and hadn't been so quick to believe that all he was bothered about was his lover and his new baby daughter.

Putting the key in the front door and stepping onto the terracotta-tiled floor, Helen knew that her pregnancy was going to be the talk of the town. Jack Crawford's daughter – Mr Havelock's granddaughter – with a bun in the oven and no ring on her finger.

And when that happened, her father *really* would not want to see her.

What a mess.

Chapter Seven

Bel and Polly stood in the hallway.

'If you can't sleep, or you wake up in the middle of the night and want a bit of company, just come up and get me. All right?' Bel told Polly as she gave her a big hug. She wished, more than anything, that she could somehow lessen her best friend's heartache, but she knew she couldn't. No one could.

'I know nothing anyone says is going to make you feel any better, so I'm not going to say anything, other than I'm here for you – night or day. Especially night.' Bel knew more than most that grief always struck the hardest when you were at your weakest and when you were most alone – usually around three o'clock in the morning. She had called it her 'haunting hour' when she had been in the throes of a deep and very angry depression after being given the news that her husband, Teddy, had been killed in action.

'Thanks, Bel.' Polly clung to her sister-in-law for a short while, before going into her bedroom and closing the door.

She made it to the bed just as her body gave up and all her energy dissolved in one fell swoop.

Grabbing the pillow, she pressed it against her face. It was all she could do to muffle her grief.

Her whole body juddered as she silenced the sound of her heartbreak.

Walking back into the kitchen, Bel was greeted by three tense and extremely sad faces. Agnes, Arthur and Joe were sitting around the kitchen table, their half-eaten suppers languishing on their plates. Even Tramp and Pup looked up at her with forlorn expressions from their spot by the hearth.

'You'll keep a good eye on her, pet, won't yer?' Arthur stood up and shuffled over to the sideboard, from where he retrieved a bottle of whisky. 'You'll tell us if there's need fer worry?' They all knew Arthur's daughter had killed herself, unable to face life after her husband, Tommy's father, had been killed in the First War. 'Yer never knar what's really gannin on inside of someone's head.'

'I will, Arthur.' Bel forced a smile.

Arthur put the bottle on the table and got out four glass tumblers.

'Just put a splash in my cup,' Agnes told Arthur as she went to top up the teapot.

'Same for me too, please, Arthur,' Bel said, pouring a little milk into her and Agnes's cups.

Arthur did as asked, before splashing good measures into two glasses and handing one to Joe.

'Cheers, Arthur.' Joe held up his glass, and waited for Agnes to add tea to the caramel-coloured swirl of milk and whisky.

'May this war be won. And quickly,' he said.

'Aye,' Arthur nodded, taking a large gulp.

No one needed to say anything, but it was Tommy they were really toasting. And the life they all believed had been lost.

They sat quietly for a while.

When Joe saw that Bel had finished her tea, he downed the rest of his Scotch.

'Do yer fancy a little walk before I do my night shift?' he asked.

'That sounds nice,' Bel said, pushing her chair back.

Joe stood up and grabbed his walking stick.

'See you all in a while,' he said as Bel gave Arthur a quick hug and a kiss on the cheek. She knew the old man didn't like to be fussed over, but she felt for him. He and Tommy shared a special bond, closer even than most fathers and sons.

Bel knew that his heart, along with Polly's, must be breaking.

'Mowbray Park?' Joe suggested when they stepped out onto the pavement.

Bel nodded, squinting against the evening sun that was still surprisingly radiant and hot.

Joe took Bel's hand as they walked down Tatham Street and turned left into Murton Street. The news that Tommy was missing had hit them all hard but in different ways. Joe's thoughts had immediately gone to Teddy. There was not a day that went by when he didn't think about his twin brother, although he had refused to mourn his death. War had given Joe a different perspective on life, and he'd been adamant that those who had murdered his brother would not have the added scalp of his grief.

'You thinking about Ted?' Joe asked Bel as they side-stepped an elderly woman who was on her hands and knees whitewashing her front doorstep.

'Yes.' She looked at Joe. 'You?'

Joe nodded.

'Do you think Tommy's dead?' Bel asked.

Again Joe nodded.

'I reckon so.'

Bel felt tears prick her eyes.

When they reached the top of the street they turned the corner into Laura Street. Halfway down the road they both automatically looked to their right as they passed a house with a distinctive green door.

'Remember?' Joe asked.

Bel nodded and smiled. It was the house where they had taken refuge in the middle of an air raid. They had been cooped up in the cupboard underneath the stairs for hours while the town's Victoria Hall had been reduced to rubble just a few hundred yards up the road. As the bombs had devastated their town, Bel had opened up for the first time about the grief and the anger festering inside her about Teddy's death. It was only then, after she had unburdened herself to her brother-in-law, that Bel had slowly started to climb out of the dank well of desolation that had held her captive. And as she had started to glimpse the light of life once again, her love for Joe had also blossomed.

'Let's walk up to the top of the park,' Joe suggested.

The adjoining Winter Gardens were a sorry sight, having been recently pockmarked with a forty-foot crater. The rest of the park, though, was still unspoilt and peaceful.

'Why do I feel there's a reason you wanted to go for a walk?' Bel asked.

Joe spotted a wooden bench and led them both to it.

'You can read me like a book,' he said. His words sounded jokey but his face looked serious.

They sat down and Joe turned to Bel.

'I feel there's been something on yer mind this past week,' he said gently. 'Is there anything yer want to tell me? Anything yer want to talk about?'

Bel sighed. 'And *you* can also read *me* like a book.'

'I just feel something's bothering yer?' Joe asked. 'I wondered if it's because yer've not managed to fall yet?'

Bel squeezed Joe's hand.

'Well, there's that.' She looked at Joe's big, rough hands. 'It's coming up to eight months since we got married ... ' She didn't need to say more.

'Yer know,' Joe said, turning his head to look at Bel, 'I'm happy either way. I'd love to have a bab with yer, but it won't be the end o' the world if that never happens. I've got you 'n Lucille. I'm the luckiest man alive.'

'I know,' Bel said. 'And I know I shouldn't say this – I know that I should just be happy to have you and Lucille and the life we have, but it *will* feel like the end of the world to me if I can't have any more children. I know that sounds selfish. Especially with what's just happened to Polly … But there's something inside of me that just craves another baby. I can't help it.'

Joe put his arm around Bel and pulled her close. 'Yer know, I honestly think this is just a little glitch. And that this time next year yer'll be as big as a barrel.'

They both chuckled.

'Oh, I hope so,' Bel said.

They both sat, momentarily lost in their own thoughts, until a young mother walked past them, pushing a pram, a little parasol protecting her baby from the sun's rays.

'See, no escape,' Bel laughed, and sat up so she was looking at Joe.

'There was actually something I wanted to tell you,' she said. 'That's been bothering me this past week. More than not falling pregnant.'

'Go on,' Joe encouraged.

'You know how much I've been haranguing Ma to tell me about my real dad?'

'Aye.' Joe was now listening intently. He'd been out a lot this week with Major Black and the Home Guard, but he had noticed that Bel hadn't been on Pearl's back as much, if at all. In fact, the two had been almost nice to each other.

'Well, when you were out last week, Ma came in from the pub between her shifts and said she wanted to go for a walk. Just the two of us. She had even arranged for Maisie to come and take Lucille up the town for a treat.'

Joe nodded. 'The new doll?'

Bel nodded.

'We walked all the way to Backhouse Park. We stopped outside one of the big posh houses.' Bel paused. For a moment she was back there, walking along Glen Path, her ma fagging away, unusually nervous.

Joe was looking intently at his wife. 'And?'

'And ... ' Bel hesitated. 'And that's when Ma told me who my da was.'

Joe could see Bel's eyes had suddenly filled with what looked like anger.

'Who?' Joe asked.

Bel decided to just come out and say it.

'*Charles Havelock.*'

'Mr Havelock? *The* Mr Havelock?' Joe repeated.

Bel nodded.

'I don't understand.' Joe's face showed his confusion. 'Did they have some sort of affair?'

Bel didn't answer.

'God, last time I saw him at one of the ship launches he looked like he was on his last legs. He's ancient. Must be twice yer ma's age.'

'Exactly,' Bel said. 'He is. Ma started work as a scullery maid for Mr and Mrs Havelock after she'd had Maisie and had her adopted out.'

'I'm guessing ... ' Joe paused, trying to choose his words properly, ' ... that he took advantage of her?'

'Well, that's one way of putting it,' Bel said tersely. 'Ma tried to make out they had some brief love affair – that she'd put a stop to it because of his wife, who she liked by the sounds of it – and then after she left, she found she was pregnant with me.'

Joe was quiet.

'Ma was only fifteen at the time,' Bel said. 'Mr Havelock must have been in his fifties.'

Joe was genuinely shocked. He had always assumed that Bel's father was some sailor or spiv who had diddled off as soon as he'd realised Pearl was in the family way. What he was hearing now was so much worse.

'It was awful, Joe,' Bel said, tears stinging her eyes again. 'We were standing there, Ma trying to make out that it'd been some doomed love affair, and me almost believing her – and then a big black posh car pulled into the driveway and out stepped Mr Havelock.'

Bel sat back but kept a hold of Joe's hand.

'She hadn't said who it was. Just that it was the master of the house. I couldn't believe it. It took me a few seconds to work out who it was. I've never seen him in the flesh – just in photos in the local paper.' Bel took a deep breath. 'He looked so old and frail. And then his daughter, Miriam – you know, the one Jack's married to?'

Joe nodded.

'Well, she got out of the car. And his granddaughter – Helen.'

Bel didn't need to ask if Joe knew Helen; the whole of the Elliot household had been well aware of who Helen was after she had tried to nab Tommy off Polly.

Joe blew out air. This was the last thing he expected to hear when he'd asked Bel to go for a walk.

'Blimey, Bel. How do you feel about all this? It's a lot to take on board.'

'I know. I think it's taken this past week for it to really sink in.'

'So,' Joe said, 'just to make sure I've got this straight. Mr Havelock. *The* Mr Havelock.' Joe paused. '*Forced himself* on yer ma, and got her pregnant. With you?'

Bel nodded.

'Did Pearl ever tell him?'

'God, no!' Bel said. 'I think that was the first time Ma had seen him in the flesh since she worked for him. You should have seen her. She went as white as a ghost. She was shaking ... It was awful. I've never seen her like that before. Ever.' Bel could feel the anger that had been simmering inside her since that day come to the boil. 'That man ... That man, who everyone thinks is the bee's knees because of all his so-called charitable work, has no idea that he got Ma pregnant and that he's got another daughter. And that we live just a few miles apart!'

'Bel, I'm so sorry. This must be awful for you.' Joe knew just how determined Bel had been to find her real father. She could never have guessed that this was what she would unearth.

'So,' Bel laughed a little bitterly, 'it looks like I've got another sister. Or rather, half-sister. Miriam Crawford. And that Helen,' her voice rose, '*is my half-niece*.'

Joe put his arm back around Bel and kissed her forehead.

'What yer gonna do?' he asked.

'I've thought about it, but there's not a lot I really can do, is there? It's not as if I want to have any kind of relationship with the man. And I can't exactly go up to one of the town's richest and most important men and accuse him of raping my ma and then tell him that I'm the result.'

Joe pulled Bel closer.

'I just can't shake this feeling of anger,' Bel admitted.

They were both quiet.

'There's a big part of me that wishes I'd listened to your ma. She kept saying in that quiet way of hers that sometimes it's best to let sleeping dogs lie. But I didn't. I kept prodding, and now I can't stop thinking about it.'

Joe didn't say anything; it worried him how this would affect Bel in the long run. Mr Havelock was a high-profile man. It would not be easy for Bel to forget him, even if she wanted to. He just needed to sneeze and there'd be something in the paper about it.

And then there were his daughter and granddaughter. Miriam and Helen. They were both permanent fixtures in the lives of Bel's friends, albeit not necessarily welcome ones.

Joe wondered, though, even if Bel *could* sweep all of this under the carpet and forget about it, would she choose to do so?

And it was that which gave Joe the most cause for concern.

Chapter Eight

A week later

Tuesday 7 July

'Come in!'

Helen sat behind her desk, a cigarette smouldering in the steel ashtray in front of her.

'Goodness, Rosie, for once come all the way into my office!' Her voice had an edge of exasperation to it. '*Please* don't stand in the doorway. I'm not going to bite, you know?'

Rosie wasn't so sure and fought the urge to say so as she stepped over the threshold of the small, windowless room.

'And will you please sit down. This may take a little time and I don't want to crane my neck up at you while we discuss what we've got to discuss.'

Rosie did as she was told and sat herself down.

'And what is it we have to *discuss*?' Rosie asked, looking round the room; she couldn't believe how organised and tidy it looked. Helen had obviously been spring-cleaning.

'Well, first of all I'm putting in a big order and want to know if you and your squad need anything. I know you were hankering after a new welding machine.'

Rosie perked up. She was forever fixing the one she had, which was well and truly on its last legs.

'Well, yes, that would be great if we could.'

Helen scribbled on her notepad, before stubbing out the cigarette that Rosie noticed had not been smoked and instead had simply burnt itself down to the butt.

'And is there anything else you need that would increase productivity?'

Rosie looked a little puzzled.

'You know,' Helen said impatiently, 'anything else that will help you increase your squad's work output?'

Rosie sat up straight, annoyed by Helen's curtness.

'A couple of extra women welders would help no end!'

Helen pursed her lips. 'You're lucky to have the ones you've got,' she bit back. 'Especially as you've managed to keep Martha … '

Helen pushed her chair back as though she was getting ready to stand up.

'So? Is that it? Nothing else?'

Rosie panicked and wracked her brains before quickly reeling off a list of things she knew she probably wouldn't get, but it was worth a try.

'Well,' Helen said, 'I'll see what I can do.' She looked at Rosie, trying hard not to stare at the light smattering of scars across her face. Still, they hadn't stopped her finding a man who loved her enough to marry her, even if, from what she'd heard, he was quite a bit older than her.

'I need your lot back on *Brutus* this afternoon. The Ministry of War Transport want her ready for launch by the middle of January, at the latest, so it's going to be all hands on deck.' Helen felt a stab of regret that she would not be working at the yard then. Her due date was, ironically, around the same time.

'If we keep on going the way we are,' she added, 'we're looking at setting a new production record this year, which, to be honest, is pretty amazing, all things considered.'

'That's fantastic news!' Rosie was genuinely over the moon.

'Hence,' Helen said, 'the wish list.'

For the briefest moment there was no friction between the two women. There was no denying that they disliked each other intensely, but they had a shared passion for the shipyards, and the town's shipbuilding heritage, which they were both incredibly proud to be a part of.

Helen stood up, causing Rosie to do the same.

'Right, well, I'll tell you when the order's in,' Helen said.

As Rosie turned to leave, Helen couldn't stop herself asking:

'Oh and Rosie, I don't suppose there's been any more news about Tommy Watts, has there?'

Rosie shook her head sadly.

'I'm afraid not.'

After Rosie had gone Helen sat back down and forced herself to keep her emotions in check. When Rosie had come to tell her and Harold the news about Tommy last week, she had nearly burst into tears. Thankfully she had managed to keep it bottled up, but as soon as she had got home that evening, she'd cried her eyes out. Mrs Westley, the cook, had sat with her in the kitchen and given her a big cuddle while she too had cried almost as much as Helen, having known Tommy from his visits to the house as a little boy.

If only, Helen kept thinking. If only she had managed to win his heart. If she had done, she would never have let him go. He'd have been there now, alive and well. With her.

And if she *had* succeeded in getting the only man she had ever truly loved, her own life would have been so very different from what it was now.

As Rosie left the admin building and made her way across the yard, she couldn't shake the feeling that Helen seemed different somehow.

Seeing her squad in their usual place by the quayside, Rosie had to smile. Dorothy and Angie were sitting on the wooden bench and, by the looks of it, were regaling the rest of the women with either their latest shenanigans or some yard gossip.

As soon as the pair spotted Rosie they shouted out in unison:

'She's back!'

Gloria, Polly, Martha, Hannah and Olly all turned around.

'So?' Dorothy demanded. 'What did the Wicked Witch of the West want?'

Rosie grabbed her holdall and perched herself on an upturned crate.

'Well,' she said, rummaging around for her sandwiches and tea flask, 'she wasn't so much the Wicked Witch of the West today, more the Wizard of Oz ... ' She purposely let her voice trail off.

There was a general rumpus from the women all demanding to know what Rosie meant.

'It would seem,' Rosie said, putting them out of their misery, 'that we're finally getting a new welding machine! And some other bits and pieces too.'

'How come?' Martha asked.

'Helen wants to see the yard hit an all-time production record,' Rosie explained.

'So she's sussed out that we'll get more done if we actually have equipment that works!' Dorothy rolled her eyes.

'*So,* when *we* hit the target *she* can take all the glory,' Polly said, her tone cynical. She and Helen had pretty much hated each other from first clapping eyes on one another, or rather from the moment Tommy had clapped eyes on Polly and scuppered any chance Helen might have had of bagging Tommy for herself.

'That's about the sum of it.' Rosie poured tea into her tin cup.

'I have to say, though,' she added, 'there seems to be something different about Helen.'

'What do you mean? *Different*?' Gloria asked.

'I dunno.' Rosie thought for a moment. 'Can't really put my finger on it.'

'I agree with Rosie,' Hannah chipped in. 'We saw her this morning going over to talk to one of the foremen in the platers' shed, didn't we, Olly?'

Olly nodded.

'And when one of the men wolf-whistled her, she stopped dead in her tracks. What's that expression? If looks could kill?'

'Eee.' Angie jumped down from the bench and stretched her back. 'She normally loves being ogled at.'

'And not only that,' Dorothy chipped in, 'she's always strutted about the yard like she's sex on legs, swinging her hips about like a pendulum, *wanting* the blokes to leer at her – preferably with their tongues hanging out.'

There was a general murmur of agreement.

'Perhaps she's started to get a bit of sense. Growing up a bit,' Gloria said.

'There she goes again,' Dorothy looked over at her workmate and made a face, showing her irritation, 'defending the woman who has brought nothing but trouble and strife to all of our lives.'

'Yeh, look what she did to Hannah,' Martha said. 'She nearly finished her off, making her do the hardest jobs. Working her to the bone.'

'But, in a funny way,' Hannah squeezed her friend's arm, knowing how protective she was of her, 'I'm glad she did. Otherwise I wouldn't be training to be a draughtsman—'

'—and then we wouldn't have got to know each other,' Olly butted in, taking hold of Hannah's hand and making her blush.

Dorothy rolled her eyes again.

'Well, Hannah, you might well be feeling all loved-up and able to forgive and forget, but I know she's still got my card marked for grassing her up to Ned's wife.'

Olly looked puzzled.

'Helen told everyone that I was seeing some plater called Ned when she was trying to split me and Tommy up,' Polly said, her resentment clear to hear.

'And she very nearly succeeded!' Dorothy exclaimed.

'Until thankfully,' Polly added with increasing ire, 'Dorothy told Ned's wife and she came and gave Helen a right old earbashing – right here in front of everyone in the middle of the yard.'

'Anyway,' Rosie jumped in, wanting to change the subject, knowing Polly's resentment towards Helen had increased tenfold since Tommy had been declared missing, 'what were you all yapping about before I got here?'

'My divorce,' Gloria said. 'Or rather divorce in general.'

'Ah,' Rosie said, taking a bite of her sandwich.

'Aye,' Angie chipped in. 'Glor here was telling us that you have to prove that yer other half is either violent or mad – like a *proper* fruit loop – or has buggered off and not come back for years!' She paused. 'Anyways, we're gannin to celebrate at the café that miserable auld woman runs up from the docks.'

Rosie shook her head, but didn't reprimand Angie. Vera was, if truth be told, a rather grouchy old woman, but Rosie had a soft spot for her. As did Peter.

'I told Bel to come along as well,' Gloria said, 'when I dropped off Hope this morning.'

'I think she was glad of the invite,' Polly said. 'She's going a bit stir-crazy in the house at the moment – keeps saying she feels like her life is all about other people's babies and laundry. The emphasis being on *other people's babies*.' They all knew about Bel's failure to fall pregnant.

Polly looked across at Gloria.

'Of course, that excludes Hope. She's like family now.'

As they gathered up their equipment and started to head over to *Brutus* in the dry dock, Rosie caught Polly looking over to where Ralph and his team were climbing down to the pontoon by the quayside. Her heart went out to her workmate. *Poor Polly.* Everywhere she looked there were reminders of Tommy. They had all tried to reiterate Hannah's words that she mustn't give up hope, but Rosie knew that deep down, none of them truly believed that Tommy was still alive.

Chapter Nine

As they all made their way to Vera's café, the women were full of chatter.

'So, it's tonight you two are seeing what may well be your new digs?' Rosie asked.

She looked at Dorothy and Angie, who were walking next to her, their arms linked.

'Aye, miss,' Ange said, looking unusually sombre, 'we're gannin there right after here.'

'Why the serious face, Angie?' Gloria asked, catching up with them. 'I thought you'd be excited. You two. Yer own flat. Getting yer independence.'

Dorothy sighed loudly.

'You would think, *wouldn't you*? No more doing all the chores cos her mam's always out. No more dodging her dad when he's in a one.'

Dorothy looked at Rosie and Gloria and pulled a face she hoped reflected her exasperation.

'No.' She paused for effect. 'Ange here is worried that George's lovely flat – the rent for which, I hasten to add, is very reasonable – is going to be *too posh*.'

Gloria chuckled, thinking that anything George owned was likely to be pretty posh. George *was* posh.

'Just go 'n see it, Angie. See what yer think of it. Where's the flat again?'

'Foyle Street.' Angie looked at Gloria with eyes that pleaded for understanding. 'All the houses along there look git grand. Right la-di-da.'

'There do seem to be a lot of rich families living along that street,' Rosie chipped in, 'but that doesn't mean they won't be nice.' Rosie did wonder, though, how the residents might react to two dirt-smeared, overall-clad women shipyard workers being their new neighbours.

'If it *is* posh,' Gloria said, 'would that really be so terrible? Better than living in some dump, eh?'

Angie nodded. She always listened to Gloria.

'Here we are!' Hannah's voice sang out as they reached the glass-panelled front door of the café, covered, like all the other windows in the town, with large crosses of brown tape.

'It says "Closed",' Polly said as she and Martha caught up and they all gathered outside on the pavement.

'That's because,' Hannah said, 'my aunty Rina and' – she lowered her voice and looked at Angie – 'that "miserable auld woman"' – they all laughed at Hannah's skill at taking off the north-east accent in spite of the fact she still had a slight Czechoslovakian accent herself – 'have closed the café especially for us. So we can have the whole place to ourselves for Gloria's celebrations.'

Olly opened the door and held it back like a proper gentleman.

As soon as Gloria walked in she was greeted by Hannah's aunty, who threw her arms in the air and hurried over to embrace her, giving her a kiss on both cheeks.

'Congratulations!' she said, a big smile spreading across her face.

Vera came bustling up behind her.

'I dinnit think *congratulations* are exactly in order, Rina!'

'Phat!' Rina waved her hand dismissively at her boss. 'Vera, my dear, these days any kind of good news is worthy of a celebration. And *getting shot*, as you would say, of some ne'er-do-well husband, is, I think you would agree, good news. Yes?'

Vera huffed, shuffled back to the counter and started filling two big brown ceramic teapots with boiling water from her copper urn.

'I see Rina's settling in well, then,' Rosie whispered to Gloria, who chuckled. They had visited the café a few times since Hannah's aunty had started work there, but as it was always busy, they had never seen the two women interact much. Hannah had told them that they seemed to rub along well, much to Gloria's surprise. She'd had her doubts when she and Rosie had secretly gone to ask Vera if she would employ Rina after hearing that her one-woman credit drapery business was itself in the hock and Hannah was working all hours to keep a roof over their heads.

'Hiya!' The door opened and the little bell tinkled as the front of a grey Silver Cross pram butted its way into the cafeteria.

Olly hurried over to hold the door open.

'Hi, Bel.' He smiled down at Hope, who was sitting up looking as bright as a button. 'She looks like she's ready for the party,' he laughed.

'I know, she's been full of it today.'

'Ahh, how's my cheeky little Charlie been today?' Gloria came over, hauled Hope out of the pram, and perched her on her hip.

'This little one has had quite an eventful day today, haven't you?' Bel cupped Hope's chubby face in her hands, causing her to squeal with excitement.

'How's that?' Gloria asked.

'Well, she managed a little stagger down the hallway just before we came here, didn't you?' Bel ruffled Hope's thick mop of black hair.

Gloria's heart dropped. *She* wanted to be the one to see her daughter's first faltering steps.

'I think it was because she was excited about seeing her mammy,' Bel added, sensing Gloria's disappointment.

'Ahh. It's my goddaughter!' Dorothy shouted over.

Gloria turned round to see everyone's faces light up on seeing Hope.

'I'll take her, Gloria,' Bel offered. 'You enjoy the party.'

Before she had time to answer, Bel had taken Hope.

'No Lucille this evening?' Gloria asked.

'No, she was shattered when she came in. She's been out with Maisie and my ma all afternoon.'

Bel raised Hope into the air, making the little girl squeal with laughter.

'I can't believe I'm going to say this.' She lowered Hope back down. 'But those two have been a godsend lately. They've helped out no end with Lucille.'

Gloria was surprised to hear Bel praise her half-sister as well as say something about her mother that was *not* derogatory.

'Cor! Look!' Angie's eyes were out on stalks.

Rina smiled as she brought out a large, three-tiered cake. Everyone sat down around a couple of tables that had been pushed together and covered with a white tablecloth.

'I feel like it's my birthday!' Gloria was taken aback by the cake, which was beautifully decorated with delicately crafted roses. She wondered how the two women had managed to produce such a magnificent cake in these times of rationing.

As if in answer to her question, Vera announced:

'We've Rosie's friend Lily to thank fer some o' the ... how d'ya say it ... *harder to come by* ingredients.'

'And it was a joint effort,' Rina said in her perfect King's English. Anyone who didn't know her would never have guessed that this was not her mother tongue. 'I baked the cake, and Vera here did the wonderful, very intricate decorations.'

Everyone looked at Vera's gnarled, arthritic hands as she carefully manoeuvred the two teapots from her tray onto the table.

Going back into the kitchen, Vera returned with a huge knife and handed it to Gloria.

'Do I get to make a wish 'n all?' Gloria exclaimed.

Everyone laughed and Vera and Rina sat down with the women to enjoy the fruits of their labour.

As Gloria went to plunge the knife into the middle of the cake and cut the first slice, Dorothy and Angie couldn't contain themselves.

'Pretend it's Vinnie!' they both cackled, causing their workmates to roll their eyes.

Vera tutted her disapproval.

After Gloria had sliced up the cake and Martha played waitress and handed out the plates, there was a comfortable silence, punctuated by the occasional 'Delicious!' and the licking of fingers.

'Eee,' Gloria spoke up, 'I just want to say a really big thank you to Vera and Rina. This is really lovely. I wish I could repay yer both somehow, but unless yer need anything welding, I'm not sure I can!'

Rina laughed.

'It was our pleasure,' she said, nudging Vera, who forced a smile but was actually trying to think of anything that she might indeed need welding.

'And,' Gloria added, looking round at her workmates, 'I want to thank you all fer being such a huge support. I know fer a fact if I hadn't started at Thompson's 'n made friends with yer all, I'd still be trapped in a marriage made in hell.'

Gloria tried to lighten her voice as she could feel herself becoming emotional. She looked across at Hope, who was being fed cake by Bel and looked in seventh heaven.

'So,' Polly asked, taking a quick sip of her tea, 'I hate to even say that man's name, but I'm guessing you've not heard anything from Vinnie?'

'No, thank God,' Gloria said. 'And I don't want to either.'

'Do Gordon and Bobby know you've got divorced?' Martha asked.

'They're Gloria's sons,' Hannah whispered to her aunty, who was sitting next to her.

'They've no idea,' Gloria said. 'I want to tell them myself. Face-to-face. God willing.'

'Do yer think they'd be upset?' Angie asked, swallowing her last chunk of cake.

'Nah,' Gloria said, 'I think they'd be shocked, but not upset. Neither of them really got on with their dad.' It was on the tip of Gloria's tongue to add that it had been because of Vinnie and his explosive temper that her boys had joined the navy well before the outbreak of war.

'I'm just so glad that Peter's old friend down in Portsmouth got Vinnie to sign the divorce papers before they set sail,' Gloria added.

The women all looked at Rosie. They knew not to ask if she'd had any news about Peter as Gloria had told them that what he was doing was all very hush-hush, and it was unlikely Rosie would hear anything from her new husband unless it was bad news.

'Eee, do you all know about that Sylvia from admin?' Dorothy perked up.

'No, but I think we're gonna now,' Martha chuckled.

'Was she the one Helen kept having a go at because she was making spelling mistakes?' Hannah asked.

'That's the one,' Dorothy said. 'Well, she's gone! Left. Packed the job in. Didn't even work her notice.'

'What, because of Helen?' Gloria asked, concerned.

'No, although she probably would have done if she'd stayed much longer.' Dorothy glared at Gloria. 'No, her entire family have upped sticks and moved out to the country. They got bombed-out back in May – you know, the one that killed that poor couple in their air raid shelter in Fulwell, behind the Blue Bell?'

Everyone nodded sadly.

'Well, Sylvia's home was badly damaged and they've been living with relatives, but by the sounds of it, it's been a right squash and they've had enough. Muriel from the canteen said the family just up and left. Moved out to a village near Middleton.'

'Right out in the sticks!' Angie chipped in.

'So, I wonder what they're going to do about replacing her?' Rosie asked.

'Well, whoever they take on better be a good speller, otherwise they'll be feeling the sharp end of Helen's tongue,' Polly said.

Dorothy suddenly looked up at the clock on the wall above the entrance to the kitchen. It was ten past seven.

She nudged Angie.

'We should be going soon. We said we'd be at the flat at half past.'

Angie's face dropped.

'We need to help with the clearing-up first,' she said, standing up and stacking the plates.

'Get yourselves away,' Rina said, just as Vera was handing Dorothy a tray.

'Yes, go on, yer don't want to keep George waiting,' Gloria said, taking the tray off Vera.

'I'll do the dishes,' Polly said.

'I'll give you a hand,' Bel said, finally giving Hope back to Gloria.

'Go on then, get yourselves off – and say hi to George,' Rosie said as Dorothy and Angie made for the door. 'Tell him I'll see him later.'

'And don't worry about it being too posh, Ange!' Gloria shouted after them as the door jangled shut.

Quarter of an hour later the plates, cups and saucers had been washed and dried and put away and everyone was getting ready to leave.

'I can't thank yer both enough,' Gloria said. 'I really can't.'

'Actually, Gloria,' Rina's voice was low so that their conversation could not be overheard, 'it's *you and Rosie* that really need to be thanked.'

Gloria shuffled Hope onto her other hip.

'Why's that?'

'For getting me this job,' Rina said.

Gloria was just opening her mouth to deny having any involvement in the matter when Vera butted in.

'I didn't tell her, if that's what yer thinking. Rina's not daft. Neither's that niece of hers.' The three women glanced across at Hannah, who was presently chatting away to Polly.

'They worked it out,' Vera explained.

'If you and Rosie hadn't got me this job,' Rina continued, 'I'd still be tearing my hair out trying to keep my little business afloat. And failing miserably … And Vera here,' Rina looked down at her boss, who was half her size and almost twice as wide, 'would still be run ragged and working herself into an early grave.'

Vera put her hands on her hips, and pressed her lips together, but didn't object to the veracity of her new employee's words.

Rina stepped forward, took Gloria's free hand and clasped it for a short moment.

'It won't be forgotten,' she said. 'Nor what you have all done for my niece.'

Gloria was again just about to say something when Polly shouted over.

'We're off now!'

Rosie came over and gave Vera a big hug.

'Aye, all of yer, bugger off!' Vera said. 'Leave me in peace.'

Everyone shouted their thanks and their goodbyes as Vera shooed them all away and closed the shop door, pulled down the blind and turned the lock.

As she shuffled her way through the café and towards the stairs out the back that led up to her living quarters, she allowed herself the slightest of smiles.

'Rina said *thanks*.' Gloria kept her voice low as she spoke to Rosie, who was walking next to her, leaning into the pram and adjusting Hope's little sun hat.

The rest of their party were walking ahead.

Rosie looked at Gloria.

'She'd worked it out. Or rather Hannah had,' Gloria explained, casting a look ahead at their 'little bird' walking next to Martha. Just behind them was Rina, who was chatting away to Olly, and behind them were Polly and Bel, also deep in conversation.

'I thought Hannah might have guessed,' Rosie mused. 'Remember the way she looked at us both when she was telling everyone how Vera had approached her aunty in the street that day and offered her a job?'

Gloria nodded.

'I suppose we should have known she'd have guessed, with the café being yours and Peter's regular meeting place.' She thought for a moment. 'I'm amazed Rina and Vera get on so well, though. I couldn't see it happening myself. I mean, yer really couldn't get two more different people.'

They both chuckled.

'Talk about chalk and cheese.'

'I know,' Rosie said, 'but I think it's *because* Rina's so different that it works so well. Vera couldn't have abided anyone like herself.'

Gloria laughed out loud.

'She's a rare one, isn't she?'

'She is,' Rosie agreed.

They walked for a while in silence. Rosie thinking about Peter and the many hours they had spent in the café, chatting away, drinking tea and falling in love. Gloria about all the things she wanted to say, but couldn't.

'Now, we just need to make sure Dorothy and Angie take this flat,' Gloria said, still keeping her voice low.

Rosie agreed.

'Definitely. I was thinking about Dorothy's mam, with all this divorce talk.'

'I know,' Gloria said. 'When we were chatting earlier on, I kept looking to gauge Dorothy's reaction, but I didn't pick up anything. Makes me think she doesn't know her mam is – what do you call it again? A bigam—'

'Bigamist,' Rosie said. 'Either that or she's very good at keeping a secret. Have you noticed she rarely talks about her mum or her stepfather? And she never mentions her real dad.'

Gloria nodded. 'But it's Angie that I worry about most. I know her dad's not quite in the same league as Vinnie, but he's still got a short fuse on him.'

'And a fuse that will explode if he finds out his wife is having it off with someone else.'

All of a sudden Rosie's head turned as a bus passed them.

'Oh, there's the number seven!' Rosie squeezed Gloria's arm. 'See you all tomorrow!' she shouted out as she ran across the road.

Everyone chorused their goodbyes as the bus headed for Villette Road passed and Rina, Hannah, Martha and Olly hurried off to catch it.

Gloria was also just about to say her farewells, having reached the corner of Tatham Street, when she suddenly remembered something.

'Oh, Bel, I almost forgot to give you this.' Gloria rummaged around in her haversack and pulled out a box of soap powder. Since it had been rationed back in February, Gloria knew that Bel and Agnes had been pushed to make do with the paltry amount they had for the growing piles of laundry they were taking in.

'Oh, thanks, Gloria. That really is much appreciated. Here, let me give you some money for it.' Bel went to open her handbag.

'Don't you even dare suggest it,' Gloria tutted loudly. 'Not when you've refused to take a penny for looking after this little one for nearly a year now.'

Bel leant in and gave Hope a kiss on the cheek. 'I can't believe she's nearly one.'

'Me neither,' Gloria said, watching how tender Bel was with Hope. It had never bothered Gloria before, but lately she had started to feel more than a little uncomfortable when she'd seen how much Bel adored Hope.

And also how much Hope clearly adored Bel.

'So, it sounds like it's all hands on deck at the moment at work?' Bel asked Polly as they turned to walk down Tatham Street.

'Even more so than normal,' Polly said. 'Was Rosie telling you that the yard's on track to hit a thirty-six-year tonnage record?'

Bel nodded. 'And Olly was saying that they've taken on more women at the yard?'

'They've had to,' Polly said. 'Looks like all the yards have. Not just here but everywhere. Like Arthur says, it's simple maths. If we're going to stand a chance of winning this war we need to be able to build at least as many ships as are being destroyed.'

'And now it looks like they're in need of more clerical staff as well?' Bel tried to make her question sound as casual as she could.

'Looks that way,' Polly said.

'Clerical just really means filing and typing up letters?' Bel asked.

'Yeh, I think so,' Polly said, but her mind was drifting. All she wanted to do now was have a wash, force some food down, and go to bed so she could think about Tommy and nurse her breaking heart.

Chapter Ten

'George, *mon cher*!'

Rosie looked up from the ledger on hearing Lily's less than dulcet tones sounding out down the hallway of the bordello. Pushing her chair away from the large cherry-wood desk that she spent most of her evenings hunched over, she strode across the plush, carpeted reception room that was now her office.

Stepping out into the hallway, Rosie caught George taking Lily into his arms and giving her the tenderest of kisses. Rosie felt herself blush. It was very rare to see the pair in such an intimate embrace. Lily liked to keep her hard, seemingly unsentimental veneer in place at all times.

Rosie turned to go back into the office, but her presence had been noted.

'Rosie,' George said as he and Lily took a step back from each other. 'Come and have a catch-up. I've just got back from showing Dorothy and Angie the flat.' He laughed. 'What a pair, eh?'

'They are indeed,' Rosie said, as they all headed into the kitchen.

'So, how did it go?' she asked as George got a bottle of Rémy out of the armoire and set three glasses on the table.

'Jolly good, jolly good,' George said, sloshing brandy into the crystal tumblers.

'A toast!' he declared. 'To my two new tenants. And jolly nice they are too!'

Rosie took a quick sip.

'I think Angie was a little worried it might be too posh.'

George guffawed.

'I think she still feels that way, but Dorothy wasn't having any of it and pretty much bullied her into it. I've said if they don't like it, or if it doesn't suit, then that's not a problem.'

'You're not going to make them sign some kind of contract?' Lily looked at George.

'Lily,' George sighed. 'Of all people, you should know I'm not the kind of chap to go around getting people to sign contracts and the like.'

'Honestly, George, landlords always have tenancy agreements. Dorothy and Angie aren't exactly what you'd call prim and proper by any stretch of the imagination. They might turn it into a den of iniquity, or damage it, or do a moonlight flit owing you lots of rent.'

'Well, they'll have me to deal with if they do!' Rosie said.

'Exactly – who needs a "tenancy agreement" when you've got a boss like Rosie!' George chuckled and took a swig of his brandy. 'They'll be fine. They might both be as scatty as hell, but you can see they're good girls. I can trust them.'

'Yes,' Rosie agreed. 'George's right, Lily. You *can* trust them. I'll have a word with them as well, just so they know what *is* and what *isn't* acceptable.'

'You're too soft, the pair of you. You'll never make it in business if you keep giving people the benefit of the doubt.'

George almost choked on his drink.

'Well, you're a fine one to talk, Lily! Not only do you not have any kind of contract for the girls working here—'

'That's different,' Lily cut in.

'*But*,' George continued to make his point, 'you have also taken in your fair share of strays. You took Kate in without a second's hesitation.'

'Ah, but I knew Kate was Rosie's old schoolfriend,' Lily defended herself.

'*And* you brought Maisie back from London after you'd only known her five minutes.'

'That was to help with the Gentlemen's Club,' Lily said, getting up again to look for her cigarettes. 'And anyway, she'd been under my employ at La Lumière Bleue.'

'But that doesn't detract from the fact that you took in two young women whom you knew next to nothing about,' George said. 'And if I went back in time, I know for a fact I'd be able to reel off a fair few other examples of you being "soft".'

'We're getting off the subject.' Lily waved her hand, dismissing George's words. 'Rosie and I want to hear how it all went. By the sounds of it the two gadabouts have committed to moving into your bachelor pad.'

'They have indeed,' George said.

'Well, I can't thank you enough,' Rosie said. 'That's one less – actually, two less things to worry about.'

Rosie had confided in Lily and George about the women's secrets and had talked at length about how she and Gloria were trying to work out ways in which they could help their friends, should their secrets ever be exposed.

Lily got up and started raking around in the drawers for her cigarettes.

'I've said it before and I'll say it again. Not only are you too soft, but you're also too protective over that mishmash squad of yours.'

Rosie looked at Lily, who seemed determined to be as fractious as possible this evening.

'Oh, I'm overly protective now, am I?' Rosie asked, suppressing a smile and flashing a quick look at George. 'So, Lily, do tell us. Do you know if Kate's had any more surprise visits from Sister Bernadette – or any of the other nuns from Nazareth House?'

Lily's face immediately flushed.

'No, she hasn't! And they better not put one foot inside that shop. In fact, they better not even look in the window while I'm still drawing breath, otherwise there'll be what for.'

Rosie laughed.

'Eee, Lily, you are funny. And there's *you* telling *me* that *I'm* too protective over my squad ... '

Lily glared at Rosie. 'That's different ... Kate's different. That Sister bleedin' Bernadette has to learn she can't bully our Kate. She's not a child any more. And moreover, she's not on her lonesome now.'

'And how's Maisie?' Rosie quizzed. 'Is she still being hounded by that client of hers from Glen Path?'

'Ha!' Lily said. 'I sent him away with a flea in his ear the last time he came round. Told him straight. If my girls don't want to see a client, that's their choice. No one under my roof does anything they don't want, and if anyone tries to make them, they'll have me to deal with.'

Rosie looked at George, who chuckled.

'I think you can rest your case now, my dear.'

Lily tutted, realising she'd fallen right into Rosie's trap.

'So,' she said, changing the subject. 'When are you off to see Charlotte?'

Rosie exhaled. 'Well, I said I'd try and get to see her in a few weeks' time, and then again before term starts in September.'

'So, you're keeping the poor girl imprisoned in that school for the foreseeable.'

'Hardly "imprisoned"!' Rosie objected. 'Having the best education money can buy, beautiful grounds to run around in, as well as weekly trips into Harrogate, isn't what anyone could call "imprisoned".'

The kitchen door opened and Kate peered in.

'Entrez, ma chérie!' Lily commanded.

'Ah, Kate,' Rosie said, genuinely pleased to see her friend. 'Come and have a cuppa and tell us what you're working on at the moment.'

'Don't think you can change the subject just like that,' Lily scolded Rosie as Kate busied herself with making a pot of tea. '*I* have to fight Charlotte's corner for her, seeing as no one else is!' She shot a look at George, who put both hands up in surrender.

'The girl's practically begged you to come back home and live. She's fourteen years old now and got her own mind. She should be able to choose where she wants to live and where she doesn't.'

George started shifting about uncomfortably. This had become a real bone of contention between the two.

'I know I sound like a broken record,' Lily continued, 'but she's going to have to know about all of this sometime.' She swung her arm around the room. 'The longer you leave it—'

'The harder it'll be,' Rosie finished off Lily's sentence for her. She took another sip of her Rémy. 'I know, I know. But I need to do this gradually. I need to tell her about Peter first of all, which,' she added quickly, seeing that Lily was going to give her another lecture, 'I'm going to do when I see her next.'

'That's great to hear!' George butted in. 'But I think we'll just leave it there and let's hear all about Kate's day.'

Lily opened her mouth and shut it again.

'Well,' Kate said, pouring milk into her tea. 'It's been busy, but it's mainly been alterations. You know, it's all about Make Do and Mending these days.'

Lily tutted.

'What is the world coming to when we're all having to chop up old clothes and make them into something new. I heard this new Utility Clothing Scheme has even gone as far as restricting the number of pleats in a skirt and buttons on a coat. Even the turn-ups on men's trousers are no longer allowed!'

Kate chuckled. 'Just on the ones they're making now.' She looked across at George, who was looking down at his very expensive Savile Row trousers, which had very large turn-ups. 'But it's interesting. It's forcing designers to be different. Inventive. I mean, look at some of Norman Hartnell's creations – and Hardy Amies'.'

'Urgh.' Lily took a sip of her brandy as if to wash away a bad taste in her mouth. 'I've seen them in *Vogue* after that fashion show they had to launch them. Talk about the emperor's new clothing. How were they trying to sell them? That's it: "High-fashion elegance achieved within the strict rationing restrictions." What a load of codswallop. It's just cheap, mass-produced rubbish.' Lily looked at Rosie in her favourite slacks, which Kate had made for her last year. 'And don't even get me started on women wearing trousers.'

'Anyway,' Kate said, seeing that Rosie was about to bite, 'guess who came into the shop today?'

Lily sat up straight. 'Better not have been one of those bleedin' nuns!'

'No, Lily,' Kate said, blushing. She was still embarrassed about her catastrophic fall off the wagon on the day of Sister Bernadette's visit, and the guilt from not having given Rosie her letter from Peter straight away still lingered. 'It was that nice lad from Thompson's.'

Everyone's eyes focused on Kate.

'What? Alfie the timekeeper?' Rosie asked, a smile spreading across her face.

Just at that moment Maisie and Vivian came bustling in, catching the tail end of the conversation.

'Who's "Alfie the timekeeper" when he's at home?' Vivian asked in her best Mae West drawl, arching a well-defined eyebrow.

'Yes. Who *is* Alfie the timekeeper?' Lily's face had reddened even more.

'He's the young lad who clocks us all in and out.' Rosie stared across at Lily, warning her to keep calm. 'He was very helpful when Kate came to the yard that morning with Peter's letter, wasn't he?'

Kate nodded.

'Anyway, he was telling me a little while ago,' Rosie continued, 'that his nana's eyesight's now too bad for her to do any kind of darning or sewing. Poor woman.'

'The boy not got a mother?' Another question from Vivian.

'No mum or dad to speak of,' Rosie said. 'Brought up by his grandparents.'

'And he can't stitch up his own clothes?' Lily was scrutinising Kate, who was clearly perplexed by the interest in Alfie's visit to the Maison Nouvelle. She had only mentioned it in passing.

'What he wanted doing was a bit more complex than that,' Kate explained.

'I'll bet,' Vivian said, but not so loud that Kate could hear.

'His grandmother,' Kate explained, 'gave him an old suit that had once belonged to his granddad. A rather lovely dark grey, woollen suit ... Bit on the big side, though, so I'm taking it in for him.'

'So, you had to measure him up?' Lily asked again.

Kate laughed. 'No, Lily, I just guessed! Of course I took his measurements.'

'Well, I think that's great,' George chipped in, sensing Kate's growing unease. 'But, the most important question, Kate, is ... '

There was an expectant pause.

'Did the trousers have turn-ups?'

Rosie chuckled, Lily pursed her lips, and Maisie and Vivian just looked confused.

'Anyway,' Rosie said, getting up. 'Can't sit around here gassing all evening. There's work to be done.'

'Yes, and I promised to play a game of rummy with the Brigadier,' George said, using his stick to push himself into a standing position.

'And I've got some old wedding magazines I want to go through,' Kate said, looking at Lily. 'You're going to have to give me some idea of the kind of dress you want making.'

'Well, if things keep going the way they are with this bloody war, I'll be doing a Scarlett O'Hara and getting you to make a dress out of those velvet curtains in the front room … Actually, that's not such a bad idea. They're a rather lovely deep red. I can copy Mrs Rosie Miller – ' Lily raised her voice so Rosie could hear ' – and get wed in red!'

As Kate made her way upstairs, she turned and looked down at George.

'I don't suppose you two have set a date yet? I've given up asking Lily. She just keeps saying "All in good time, *ma chérie*!"'

George sighed. 'I know, my dear, I know. Like trying to get blood out of a stone. I'll keep trying.'

'I will too,' Kate said as she continued on her way up to the third floor.

'Good luck with that,' Rosie said, catching their exchange as she crossed the hallway to her office. 'Lily gives new meaning to the word stubborn.'

'Don't I know it, my dear,' George said, sounding more than a little worn out. 'And heaven knows what's got her goat this evening. She seemed to be in a perfectly wonderful mood when I came in.'

'Anyone's guess,' Rosie said. 'She's up and down like a yo-yo these days. I think it's her age. You know, that particular time of a woman's life.'

George looked puzzled.

'Anyway,' he said, his face brightening, 'it's good to see you in such good fettle.'

George and Lily had been massively relieved when Rosie had told them about the envelope of petals she had received in the post. They dreaded Rosie receiving bad news, like poor Polly. The French Resistance might well be doing its utmost, helped by the likes of Peter and other SOE French operatives, but it was still a David and Goliath battle.

'You heard anything from your old chums?' Rosie asked, her voice dropping as one of the new girls and a client passed them on their way up to what Lily liked to call *'les boudoirs'*.

'No, nothing new to report,' he said. George had promised Rosie he'd keep an ear out for any snippets he might hear from his old war buddies. 'The south is still unoccupied, but for how much longer? Who knows ... But don't you worry!'

Rosie nodded.

'Promise?'

'I promise.' Rosie smiled.

'Good.' George opened the door to the back reception room, letting out a stream of smoke and laughter, accompanied by the sound of Vera Lynn's 'White Cliffs of Dover' coming from the gramophone.

'Oh.' Rosie looked up the stairs to make sure no one was about. 'Kate's keeping off the booze, isn't she?'

George nodded gravely. 'We're keeping our eyes on her. We'll tell you if we have any worries. She's still not venturing out much, though.'

'Still a straight line from here to the boutique and back again?' Rosie asked.

Another nod from George. Since Sister Bernadette's visit, Kate seemed to have become averse to going anywhere but the Maison Nouvelle. And they'd all noticed that Kate still jumped out of her skin whenever the little brass bell above the shop door tinkled.

'Well, tell Lily to go easy on Alfie. I think he's been sweet on Kate since the day he met her at the yard. He's a nice lad. Might be good for Kate to go out – even if it's just to a café in town.'

George touched his forehead in a salute, before disappearing into the parlour to join the evening's 'guests'.

'Maisie, can I have a quick word?' Lily said as everyone started to filter out of the kitchen. 'On your own, if you don't mind,' she added.

Vivian threw her friend a curious look and left, shutting the kitchen door behind her.

'So,' Lily offered Maisie one of her Gauloises, 'do you want to tell me what's going on with your Glen Path client?' She lit Maisie's cigarette and then her own. 'Only, he's been round here a few times recently, asking why you're being so evasive.'

Lily blew smoke up to the ceiling.

'If you want me to tell him you're no longer available, then I can. It's not a problem.' She tapped ash into the crystal ashtray. 'But if he's been in any way *unpleasant*, then you *do* need to tell me. I don't want to foist him off on to one of the other girls if you've had to put up with anything that's not acceptable?'

'No, no, Lily, it's nothing like that.' Maisie hesitated for a moment, unsure how much she should tell her boss. 'He's not odd or weird or anything. Just old.' Maisie laughed lightly. 'You'd think he would be past it by now, wouldn't you?'

Lily raised her eyebrows. 'You'd be surprised how old they get before they're past it, believe you me.'

Maisie balanced her half-smoked cigarette in the ashtray and went over to the sink to pour herself a glass of water. She knew Lily had been around the block more than a few times in her life, and was not one to be crossed, but she also knew she was fair – and that she could keep a confidence.

'If I tell you something, will you promise not to tell another soul? Not even George. And definitely not Rosie.'

Lily looked at Maisie and nodded. All her girls harboured secrets and at some stage every one of them had confided in her. Not once had she betrayed their trust.

Maisie took another sip of water.

'For ages now Bel's been going on about finding her father. Apparently Ma had always fobbed her off with some cock and bull story about her dad dying when she was small, but Bel never believed her ... Then I tip up and put the cat among the pigeons, and all of a sudden she's got a sister that she never knew about, and one who then starts wittering on about finding her real dad.'

'The sailor from the West Indies,' Lily said.

'Exactly, but that idea soon died a death. There's no way I'm going to travel halfway round the world to look for someone I'm not even sure is alive – war or no war. God, I wish I'd just kept my mouth shut.'

'Because all your yammering got Bel thinking about *her* old man?' Lily's cockney accent had come to the fore, as it always did when she was having an honest one-to-one.

'Exactly. And it wasn't just *thinking* – she became obsessed with finding out who he was, and when Ma wasn't forthcoming, she decided to go all Miss Marple and find him for herself.' Maisie took her cigarette from the ashtray and inhaled deeply. 'Then one day I was going round to see my Glen Path client and who should I find going door to door, asking if anyone knew of a young girl called Pearl who used to be a scullery maid in one of the houses that overlook Backhouse Park?'

Lily sighed. 'Why do I have an awful feeling I know where this story's going?'

Maisie nodded.

'Bel's theory was that Ma had been going with someone she worked with, but I had an awful feeling it was someone she had worked *for*.'

'Did you talk to Pearl about it?' Lily asked.

'Yes, and you should have seen her face when I told her I'd bumped into Bel along The Cedars. She went as white as a sheet.' Maisie took another sip of water. 'But when she asked me to keep Bel away from Glen Path, it was *me* who went white.' Maisie forced laughter. 'Which is no mean feat.'

Lily looked at Maisie. The girl was stunning. Her caramel-coloured skin had brought many new clients to the bordello.

'You're worried your Glen Path client and Bel's father are one and the same,' Lily surmised.

Maisie nodded. 'Not the nicest of thoughts.'

'Mm ... I can imagine,' Lily said. 'Nor for Bel either, if she ever found out. And from what I've picked up, you two have been getting on pretty well lately?'

'Yes, we have. I don't want to spoil what I've got. I quite like having a sister, even though Bel isn't a bit like me. And I hate to admit it, but I've got a real soft spot for little Lucille. She's just adorable ... Not that I want to be going off and having any children of my own,' Maisie quickly added, worried that Lily might think she was secretly hankering after a husband and family when nothing could be further from the truth. She knew exactly what she wanted: to stop seeing clients and to focus entirely on the Gentlemen's Club. Rosie wasn't the only one who wanted to be a businesswoman; Maisie, though, wasn't going to be held back by any holier-than-thou concerns about being legitimate.

Lily looked at Maisie. She knew for certain she was not destined for a life of domestic bliss. It was the reason she had been so keen to bring Maisie on board.

'Well, Maisie, my advice to you, for what it's worth,' Lily said, 'is that you need to find out either way, and quickly. For your own peace of mind, if nothing else.'

Chapter Eleven

Helen had, as usual, stayed back after the end of the shift and worked late.

Stepping out of her stuffy office and feeling the cool summer breeze on her face, she decided to walk home. Reaching the top of North Sands and turning right into Dame Dorothy Street, she continued along Harbour View, before turning left along the Upper Promenade. Halfway along, Helen stopped. Resting both hands on the stone balustrades, she gazed out to sea. Breathing in the fresh sea air, she forced herself to focus on the thin line where the twinkling North Sea merged with the light milky blue of the early-evening sky.

She purposely ignored the signs that the country was at war – the rolls of barbed wire and the scattering of half-buried landmines on the beaches below – just as she tried to ignore her own physical changes: her breasts had been sore and swollen for some time now, and her stomach looked flat, but was a little rounded and firm to the touch.

It was no good, though. Neither the reality of the surrounding landscape nor the changes in her body could be disregarded.

As Helen dragged her eyes away from the distant horizon and continued her walk home, her mind started to play a flickering newsreel of an alternative reality. One that could have been hers, if it hadn't been for Theo and her mother.

She saw herself looking amazing in a designer dress that showed off her hourglass figure, her thick black hair pulled back into victory rolls, as she stood with the other shipyard bigwigs, overseeing the launch of SS *Brutus*. She was being congratulated by Mr Thompson himself for helping the yard hit an all-time tonnage record. He might even be telling her that she would be looking at a promotion. The first woman to ever hold such a position in any of the shipyards along the north-east coast, probably in the entire country. By her side was her father, looking so proud. Telling those who were shaking his hand that this gorgeous, successful woman standing next to him was *his* daughter.

But the make-believe newsreel suddenly snapped and started clicking round, the screen went white, the lights were switched back on and Helen saw a very different scene. Another future. One where she was lying in some maternity ward, huge as a whale, sweating, in agony, giving birth. There was no one else there, other than the doctor and the midwife. She was alone. And as she gave birth to her fatherless child, SS *Brutus* was being launched, its bulging metal hull slicing into the River Wear. Others taking credit for her hard work. Others celebrating the success of the yard and its new production record.

Glimpsing a preview of the weeks, months and years that followed, Helen forced herself to stop watching.

This was not a film she wanted to see.

'Like mother like daughter!'

Helen opened the front door to hear her grandfather's voice booming out from the front room.

'Well, at least I made sure when I got in the family way that the father wasn't married!'

Her mother's voice was loud and acrimonious.

Helen quietly put her gas mask and handbag down on the hat and umbrella stand in the front porch.

'I just don't understand.'

It was her grandfather again.

'I got rid of the blighter as soon as I found out his marital status – sent the lying toerag back down to Oxford.'

'Well, clearly not soon enough!'

Helen could hear the mother opening up the drinks cabinet.

'A case of shutting the stable door after the horse has bolted!'

Helen put a hand on the oak stand and steadied herself. She had been feeling a little light-headed anyway, but coming back to this had knocked her for six.

So, her grandfather was now aware of her condition.

'Damn him!' Mr Havelock banged the floor with his walking stick in anger. 'Damn, damn, damn! I had such hopes for that girl!'

'Only because she's your only grandchild!' There was the sound of a drink being poured. 'Let's be honest, *Father*, you'd probably be disowning her if you had a *grandson* to fawn over. That is, *if* you'd been able to produce your own son and heir.'

Helen heard her mother slam her glass down.

'A legitimate one anyway!'

Helen expected her grandfather to become apoplectic with outrage that such an accusation even be thought, never mind spoken aloud, but there was nothing. Instead she heard her grandfather's voice growl, 'And you, my dear, would probably have chucked her out onto the streets without a second's thought were you not petrified of the scandal that would undoubtedly ensue.'

There was an angry, silent stand-off for a few moments.

Helen could hear a match being lit, and assumed her grandfather was lighting his cigar, creating clouds of swirling smoke.

Finally, he sighed loudly and impatiently.

'Enough backstabbing. We need to find a solution to this problem. Is there any way we can send her away for a while?' he suggested. 'What is it girls in Helen's circumstances do – go away on some kind of prolonged holiday?'

'It's called *taking the European tour*.' Miriam's voice dripped with condescension. 'It might have escaped your notice, *Father dear*, but we are actually at war. We can't just pack her off to France or Italy – not unless she wants to jump ship and join Hitler and his band of merry madmen.'

Helen forced herself to take a deep breath. Her head was spinning.

'Well, is there nowhere else we can send her?'

Helen could hear the exasperation in her grandfather's voice.

'It's not that easy,' Miriam snapped. 'We can't just get shot of her like you did dear Mama.'

Helen was puzzled. She couldn't remember her grandmother being sent off anywhere, nor think why there would be a reason to 'get shot' of her.

'What about your sister Margaret and that husband of hers, Angus? Couldn't they have her until the time comes? They could even arrange the adoption?'

'Ha!' Miriam let out a loud, mirthless laugh. 'I'm sure my sister and brother-in-law would just love that. They've spent their whole lives trying to have children, year after year of miscarriages and heartbreak – I'm sure they're really going to want to have their pregnant niece living with them, only to then hand her baby over to some stranger.'

'Perhaps,' Mr Havelock's voice rose with hope, '*that's* the solution!'

Helen could hear that her grandfather was walking across the room by the gentle thud of his stick on the carpeted floor.

'Margaret and Angus can pass the baby off as their own!'

'Are you *mad*?!' Now it was Miriam who was sounding at her wits' end. 'The pair of them are old enough to be grandparents! Besides, it wouldn't take a genius to work out that the baby was Helen's. The gossip would spread faster than wildfire.'

There was a moment's quiet.

'But even if Helen did agree to absent herself,' Miriam said, 'and go and live in the back of beyond until she gave birth, I'm not convinced she would be able to then give the baby away. I *know* my daughter. She may seem thick-skinned, but inside she's just like her father – too sentimental for her own good.'

Helen suddenly felt herself well up. What she wouldn't give to have her father here now.

'I do, however, have an idea that Helen might go for,' Miriam said.

Helen swallowed her tears.

'Anything that might prevent dragging the Havelock name through the mire.'

Helen heard her grandfather ask for a drink of whisky.

There was silence and for a moment Helen thought that they knew she was there, earwigging.

'Well, go on,' Mr Havelock suddenly demanded. 'What's this "idea"?'

Another pause.

Finally, Miriam spoke.

'She gets rid of it.'

Helen stood for a moment. There was a weird buzzing sound in her ears and her vision was suddenly filled with tiny, sparkling flecks.

She steadied herself for a moment, before tiptoeing over to the front door, quickly opening it and then slamming it shut.

'I'm home!' she shouted out.

Walking into the hallway, she turned her head in surprise, as though she'd had no idea that her mother and grandfather were in the living room.

'Gosh, you both gave me a surprise there! Hello Grandfather ... Mother.'

Both faces smiled back at Helen, trying hard not to show their shock at her sudden arrival, nor their slight guilt from having been talking about her behind her back.

'I'm absolutely shattered,' Helen said. 'Not stopped all day, so I'm just going to get myself straight to bed.'

Helen made her way up to the top floor – to the sanctuary of her bedroom.

Shutting the door firmly behind her, she leant heavily against it. The words of her mother still hammering in her head.

'She gets rid of it.'

Chapter Twelve

Three days later

Friday 10 July

'Bel!' Maisie shouted out.

She had been on her way to the Holme Café to meet her sister and was surprised to see her coming out of the Labour Exchange in the town centre.

'Maisie,' Bel said, hurrying over.

The pair gave each other a quick hug.

'What on earth were you doing there? You're not thinking of joining up, are you?' Maisie laughed. 'Or getting some kind of wretched war work in some God-awful munitions factory?'

Bel laughed; a little too loudly, Maisie thought.

'I spotted an old friend going in there and went to say hello,' Bel said.

Maisie looked at her sister and knew she was lying.

'Where's Lucille?' Bel asked.

'I took her back to Tatham Street. But don't worry,' Maisie said, seeing the instant look of concern that had appeared on her sister's face, 'there's nothing wrong. Far from it. I bought her a comic and a bag of marbles and she was more than happy to swap sitting with us two in a café getting bored for playing marbles in the backyard with Joe.'

'Why doesn't that surprise me?' Bel said. 'She is such a daddy's girl.'

Maisie noted that Bel was now not only allowing her daughter to call Joe 'Daddy', but also seemed happy to call him that herself.

'Seeing as we don't have little LuLu in tow, I thought we'd be decadent,' Maisie said, taking her sister's arm and turning her in the opposite direction. 'Forget tea and cake – I want to treat us to a drink in the Grand.' She didn't give Bel a chance to agree to the change of plan, but instead pulled her gently in the direction of Bridge Street.

'Are you sure?' Bel said. 'I'm not exactly dressed for somewhere like the Grand.'

Maisie looked at her sister, who had her best summer dress on and a perfectly made-up face, while her blonde hair looked like it had just been washed and set.

'Actually, I'd disagree. I do believe that you've made quite an effort today.' Maisie gave her sister a quizzical look.

'Well, I thought I'd smarten myself up for a change,' Bel said.

Another lie, Maisie thought.

'Any reason for your sudden urge to be "decadent"?' Bel asked, changing the subject.

'Does one have to have a reason?' Maisie laughed.

This time it was Maisie who was lying.

'I'll have a gin and tonic, please,' Maisie told the waitress once they were settled in their plush cushioned armchairs in the reception lounge of the Grand.

Bel thought that the young girl taking their order had done a good job at masking her surprise at seeing someone of mixed race in the town's most exclusive hotel.

'Yes, I'll have the same, please,' Bel said, looking at the waitress. Sometimes Bel felt the urge to shock people and refer to Maisie as her sister, just to see the look on their curious faces.

'So,' Maisie said, as the waitress hurried off, 'are we to be hearing the pitter-patter of little feet any time soon?'

'No. I'm afraid not,' Bel said simply. Her sister was the only one who ever asked her outright if she had managed to fall.

'It'll happen, you'll see,' Maisie said, squeezing her sister's hand. 'Anyway, how's that mother of ours? Is she behaving herself?'

'Amazingly so,' Bel said. 'Actually, I've not seen that much of her really. She spends just about all her time at the Tatham. She's more or less running the place with Bill.'

They both thanked the waitress as she put their drinks down on the table.

'Do you think Ma's sussed out that Bill wants them to have more than a working relationship yet?' Maisie asked.

'Still no idea,' Bel said.

'You'd think someone who's had her fair share of men,' Maisie lowered her voice, 'would know when a bloke has the hots for her.'

'I know,' Bel agreed. 'But I think Ronald – you know, the one who Ma's always scabbing fags and whisky from?'

'The one lives out the back?'

Bel nodded. 'Well, he seems pretty determined to win Ma over, and to be honest I think he's more her type.'

Maisie pulled a face. 'Honestly, I don't understand that woman. Bill's much nicer. He might have a bit of a paunch on him and is lacking in the hair department, but he seems like a really decent bloke.'

'Perhaps that's the problem,' Bel mused. 'Ma's always gone for the Ronalds of this world.'

'Shame,' Maisie said, taking a sip of her drink and spotting two rich, middle-aged women, both done up to the nines, swagger into the hotel as if they owned the place.

'So,' Maisie took another sip of her drink, 'we've not really had a chance to talk about your "walk" with Ma. I think this is the first time we've actually managed to have a chat, just the two of us.'

'I know,' Bel agreed, a little distractedly. She had also just noticed the two women, who were now being greeted by a couple of Admiralty officers.

'I wanted to apologise,' Maisie said, as her sister continued to eyeball the women.

'What for?' Bel asked.

'For saying I had checked out everyone living along Glen Path.' Maisie dropped her voice.

Bel brought her attention back to Maisie. 'Don't worry. Ma said she'd asked you not to ... that she wanted to tell me herself ... you know ... rather than me guessing or finding out from anyone else.'

Relieved that her sister wasn't harbouring any resentment, Maisie knew the time was right to find out what she really needed to know.

'So,' Maisie said, looking at her sister, 'I'm guessing Ma finally told you?'

'Told me what?' Bel's attention had wandered back over to the two rich women who were now sitting at the bar with the high-ranking naval officers in their white uniforms.

Maisie leant towards her sister, trying to bring her attention back to their conversation.

'*About who your father is,*' Maisie whispered into Bel's ear.

'Yes, yes, she did,' Bel said, distractedly.

'So?' Maisie's heart was pounding. Finally, the moment of truth was here. *Was her Glen Path client Bel's father, or not?*

'What do you mean, *"So"*?' Bel asked, perplexed.

'So, who *is* he?' Maisie asked, exasperated.

Bel looked at her sister.

'It's a bit complicated.'

'What do you mean, *"it's a bit complicated"*? Did Ma actually tell you who he is?'

Bel nodded.

'And?'

'And,' Bel's attention had been pulled back to the two women, 'I'm not sure if Ma would want me to go broadcasting it.'

Maisie expelled air.

'I'm hardly going to announce it on the bloomin' BBC Home News, am I?' Maisie tried hard to keep calm. How difficult could this be? She just needed a name. She was resolute: she was not leaving until she had her answer. She signalled over to the waitress that they wanted the same again.

'Bel, you seem distracted. What's caught your interest? I hope it's not some man in uniform?' she joked.

'No, it's that woman over there. Don't stare.'

Maisie pretended to be looking for the waitress, whilst clocking the two women.

'Do you know them?' She nodded over in their direction.

'One of them,' Bel said, conspiratorially. 'The loud, blonde one.'

'So, who is she?' Maisie asked.

Bel looked at her sister.

'You're not going to believe me.'

Bel paused.

'Go on. Don't keep me in suspense,' Maisie cajoled.

'Well,' Bel said. *'That's my sister.'*

'God, you could have knocked me down with a feather,' Maisie said to Vivian.

It was late and all the clients had gone. The two friends were on their own in the kitchen, drinking tea.

'So, Bel's father is Mr Havelock?' Vivian couldn't keep the astonishment out of her voice. 'But, he's like royalty in these parts.'

'I know, Viv. I do read the papers as well.' Maisie shifted about uncomfortably in her chair. 'All the more reason why you can never, *ever* utter a word about this to anyone.'

'Maisie, if you can't trust me, who can you trust?'

'I mean, you couldn't have made it up.' Maisie took a sip of her tea. 'There's me plotting and planning to get Bel on her own so that I could finally find out who her father is and hopefully put myself out of my misery – and then in struts Bel's sister.'

'Half-sister,' Vivian said. 'Same father, different mother.'

'Well, I don't see Bel as my half-sister,' Maisie said, a little defensively. 'To me she's my sister.'

'Yes, but that's different,' Vivian said in all seriousness. 'You two share the same mother.'

Maisie looked at Vivian and decided not to argue the point. She had learnt that her best friend's logic could often be more than a little questionable.

'Well, they certainly don't look like *half*-sisters,' Maisie said. 'If there wasn't such a big age gap, you'd just *presume* they were sisters.'

'I'm guessing she didn't go over and introduce herself?'

'God no, but we stayed there for a good while and watched her.'

'And what was she like?'

'Attractive. Especially for her age. Very classy-looking. Old-money attitude. You know the type. Arrogant. High and mighty. Really flirty with the uniform she was with, teasing almost, but I'd doubt she goes any further.'

'Yep, I know the type,' Vivian said.

'What a turn-up for the books, eh?' Vivian raised her cup to her lips and drank her tea. 'But at least,' she said, 'you now know you've not been doing the business with your sister's dad, eh?'

Maisie nodded.

'Yes, thank God. There is that.'

She had to admit that Bel's revelation had put her own worries into perspective.

If *she* had suffered sleepless nights over 'doing the business', as Vivian put it, with her sister's father, then she was sure that both Bel and their ma had had more than their fair share of tossing and turning.

She would not like to be in either of their shoes, that was for sure.

Chapter Thirteen

The South Docks, Sunderland

Saturday 11 July

'How's young Tommy doing?' the fisherwoman asked as she wrapped up two good-sized pollack in some old newspaper and handed them over to Arthur.

Polly looked at the old man, glad that the question had been directed at him and not her. Whenever anyone asked her about Tommy she tended to freeze.

'Well, Mrs Davis,' Arthur said, taking the fish and trying to hand her some money, which was refused with a resolute shake of the head. 'It's not good. He's been declared "missing", so we're not sure how the lad is, I'm sorry to tell yer.'

The sparkle left the old woman's eyes and she looked at Arthur and then at Polly.

'Ah, I'm sorry to hear that.' She wiped her hands on her pinny, leant over the square wooden chopping block she was standing behind, and gently squeezed Arthur's arm.

'I'll make sure the priest includes him in the prayers this Sunday,' she said quietly, looking at Polly with sad eyes.

'Thank you, Mrs Davis,' Arthur said, moving away from the fish stall to allow another customer to be served.

'And thank you for the pollack,' he added, raising the parcelled-up fish in the air.

As he and Polly continued walking along the docks, they were quiet, both content to let the chatter of the fishwives and the general hustle and bustle of the quayside fill their silence.

When they walked past the Divers' House, where Arthur had lived for many years with Flo and Tommy, the old man stared at the slightly dilapidated frontage. The wooden door and window frames were cracked and worn from years of being battered by the harsh winds and rain, and from being doused with salt spray from the North Sea.

'Aye, we had some happy times in that there house,' Arthur said, as though continuing aloud a conversation he had been having in his own head.

Polly looked at Arthur and at the tired-looking home that also held so many memories for her – albeit more recent ones. It was there a year and a half ago that Tommy had proposed to her. It had been a night of mixed emotions. Elation and love, but also sadness and worry, knowing that the man she loved – whom she had just agreed to marry – was soon to leave for war.

'Not that Flo could ever keep our Tom in the house for long.' Arthur let out a slightly melancholy chuckle. 'From the moment he could walk, he *hated* being indoors ... Was always out. The only time Flo could keep him in was when there was food to be had, or it was time for bed.'

Polly looked at the old man whose mind was no longer in the here and now, but in the distant, much happier past.

'Tommy told me once that he felt trapped when he was indoors. Even when he was older,' Arthur said, 'when we'd go for a pint after work, he'd always insist we went to one of the inns by the quayside so we could sup our ale outside 'n look out across the river.'

Polly listened, imagining Tommy as a boy and then as a young man.

For the first time it occurred to her that most of their courtship had actually been conducted outdoors: they'd met each other out in the yard at Thompson's, would eat their lunch together outside, providing the weather wasn't too bad, and would go for rides on his motorbike along the coast and for long walks that more often than not ended up with them kissing their goodnights under the canopy of one of the large oak trees in the Winter Gardens.

'How strange,' Polly mused as they stopped to stare out to sea, 'that Tommy would choose to spend so much of his life encased in a copper helmet and canvas suit, weighed down by lead boots and submerged underwater.'

Arthur smiled. 'Aye, I guess when you put it like that, it is.'

He looked at Polly, before pulling out a handkerchief and blowing his nose.

'It was like he couldn't keep out of the water. Used to worry Flo sick. Any chance he got, he'd be swimming in the sea or jumping into the river. I remember saying to Flo that for Tommy it was as though water and air were one and the same. He needed both to *live*.'

Polly felt her heart contract on hearing the word 'live'. She looked at Arthur and saw a reflection of her pain in the old man's face.

'Eee, Arthur,' Polly said, her voice suddenly thick with the beginnings of tears, 'I don't know what I'll do if Tommy doesn't come back.'

She bit her lip and tried to stop herself from saying the words that were lying heavy in her heart, but which needed to be spoken aloud.

'I just don't know how I'll live if he doesn't come back.'

Arthur turned and looked at Polly.

'Come on,' he said, moving away from the edge of the quayside. 'Let's go and give this fish here to yer ma.'

As they started walking back towards the east end, Arthur looked at the young woman who had made his grandson so happy, and whom his grandson loved so much – a young woman whom he himself now loved as though she were his own flesh and blood. He wanted to talk to her about the nature of grief and how she *would* live if Tommy did not return, but this was not the time.

Later on that evening, when Polly was lying in her bed, her mind kept flitting back to the walk along the south docks with Arthur. If Tommy was still in Gibraltar, she would be writing to him, telling him all about it. She would probably enjoy ribbing him about his childhood – about his wilfulness as a young boy and the worry he'd caused his grandmother.

All of a sudden a thought occurred to Polly and she sat up.

So what if she couldn't actually send any letters to Tommy. She could still write to him, couldn't she? If he came back – no, *when* he came back – she would give them to him. He would know exactly what had been happening while he had been missing.

Polly swung her legs out of bed, tiptoed over to her dressing table and opened up the top drawer. She pulled out a pen and notebook and padded back to her bed. Fluffing up her pillow, she sat up.

Resting the pad on her knees, she started writing.

Dear Tommy …

Chapter Fourteen

The following week

Tuesday 14 July

'Eee, Ma, you gave me the shock of my life! I didn't think there was anyone in. You're sat there, quiet as a mouse!' Bel looked at her ma, who was sitting at the kitchen table drinking a cup of tea. She had a fag between her fingers ready to have her first smoke of the day.

'And yer like a bleedin' whirlwind.' Pearl looked at her daughter. 'Where yer off to all done up like that? Yer've not got a fancy man, have ya?'

'We're not all like you, Ma,' Bel said, grabbing her handbag from the sideboard.

Pearl let out a laugh that morphed into a cough. 'I wish I had the time fer a fancy man, it's all work 'n nee play fer yer poor ma here.'

'Well, you're not short of offers.' Bel hurried into the scullery, turned on the tap and had a quick handful of water.

'Wot do yer mean by that?' Pearl looked genuinely puzzled.

'Nothing, Ma. Go and have your fag. You sound like you need one.'

'Where's everyone, anyway?' Pearl asked.

'Joe's out with the Home Guard, Arthur's at the allotment, and Agnes is next door with LuLu and Hope.'

'Not very often yer let anyone have the bab,' Pearl said. She hadn't been the only one to notice Bel's growing attachment to Gloria's little girl.

Bel ignored her mother's comments.

'Right, I'm off. See you later!'

Pearl was just about to say something when she heard the front door slam shut.

As Bel hurried down Tatham Street she decided to get the bus over to Thompson's. If she took the ferry, her hair would be all over the shop by the time she got there and she wanted to look her best, give a good impression.

Bel had a stab of guilt that she hadn't told anyone where she was going – not even Joe. She hadn't wanted everyone quizzing her. Anyway, the chances were that she wouldn't get the job – couldn't believe she'd actually got an interview at all. When she'd gone to the Labour Exchange on Friday they hadn't seemed at all perturbed that she didn't have any secretarial skills. Then again, the woman before her in the queue didn't have any experience doing something called 'splicing', and they'd given her a job on the spot. Perhaps it was a case of any port in a storm these days.

Jumping on the bus over to the north side, Bel thought about her ma. They'd not mentioned the walk they'd had, or, rather, what her ma had told her that day – nor what she *hadn't* told her. But, all the same, Bel knew it was playing on her ma's mind. Just as her ma knew it was playing on her daughter's mind. The pair of them had kept up their usual verbal sparring, but they'd just been going through the motions. Their hearts weren't really in it. They were simply keeping up appearances.

As the double-decker trundled slowly over the Wearmouth Bridge, Bel looked down at Thompson's and at the river itself, its waters barely visible due to the vast array of tugs and trawlers, cargo carriers and colliers. Getting off halfway along Dame Dorothy Street and making her way down to Thompson's, she felt the nerves she'd had since getting up this morning notch up a gear.

'Admin?'

Bel looked up at the young lad in the timekeeper's cabin. Because of the noise, she simply nodded.

Alfie pointed to a building on the left.

Taking a deep breath, Bel headed over to it. When she reached the main entrance and started up the stairs she passed another young woman, who, Bel guessed, had just had her interview and was on her way out.

On entering the main office, Bel looked around at the workers, most of whom were either typing or punching numbers into little green machines.

'Mrs Elliot?'

Bel was greeted by a young woman with ginger hair, lots of freckles, and a clipboard in her hand.

'Yes, that's me,' Bel said, putting her hand out. 'But, please, just call me Bel.' Judging by her looks and hearing a slight hint of an accent, Bel guessed Marie-Anne was of Irish descent.

'Marie-Anne.' The woman smiled, shook Bel's hand and showed her into a small, windowless office.

'The boss is out for a few hours, so I'm doing all the interviews in here. Away from prying eyes.' She smiled again at Bel. This was her last interviewee of the day. Hopefully it would be a case of saving the best until last.

'So, Bel. What makes you want to work here at Thompson's?' Marie-Anne looked at the pretty blonde opposite her and wondered why she wasn't going for a position with one of the more upmarket department stores in town.

'Well, I've always wanted to work in an office, and the shipyards are doing such vital war work, I guess I wanted to feel as though I was a part of it – doing my bit.' Bel gave her well-rehearsed response, knowing this would be one question she would most definitely be asked.

Marie-Anne looked at Bel and thought she certainly looked the part – very smart and presentable, and what was particularly encouraging was that she had quite a lovely manner of speaking. Soft and gentle, but still clear and articulate, with just the hint of an accent. She'd be good on the phones, taking orders and dealing with management.

Marie-Anne scanned the handwritten card she had been given by the Labour Exchange, on which there were the usual details of name, age and previous employment.

'I can see here that you used to work on the buses.' Marie-Anne looked back up at Bel. 'Can I ask why you stopped working there?'

She looked back down at the card to find the date Bel had ended her time with the Corporation. A slightly puzzled look appeared on her face.

'I'm not sure if they've made a mistake here, but it looks like you took six weeks off, went back, but left after just a day?'

Bel felt herself stiffen. She still felt mortified by her awful behaviour that day. How rude she had been to the passengers, and how her kindly boss Howard had told her as nicely as possible that he didn't think she was ready to come back to work.

'Well ... mmm ... ' Bel stuttered, not sure what to say. She could feel herself blush.

Marie-Anne's heart was starting to sink. There was always something.

'Actually,' Bel took a deep breath and looked Marie-Anne in the eye, 'I'd not long been told that my husband had been killed in action. In North Africa.' Bel took another breath. 'I wasn't really myself. With hindsight, I shouldn't have gone back so soon.' She still battled to keep the tears at bay whenever she talked openly about Teddy.

'Oh, I'm so sorry.' Marie-Anne could feel the tears forming in her own eyes. 'I'm so sorry I asked.'

Bel blinked hard and gave Marie-Anne a sad smile.

'No, it's all right. Honestly. You weren't to know. Besides, I'm not exactly the only woman to lose her husband these days. Far from it.'

Marie-Anne nodded, taking a handkerchief from her handbag and offering it to Bel, who politely waved it away.

'Actually,' Marie-Anne said, using the hanky to dab her own eyes, 'we've got an Elliot here, working in the yard. I'm sure I heard that her brother was killed a while back. Also in North Africa ... '

'Yes, Polly,' Bel said, brightening up. 'Polly Elliot. She's my sister-in-law. We live together.'

'Ah, now I know why you want to work here,' Marie-Anne said. 'You two are close, I take it?'

Bel nodded. 'Very. We've known each other since we were small.' She didn't add, though, that her wanting to start at Thompson's didn't have anything to do with Polly working there.

'Well then,' Marie-Anne declared, stuffing her hanky back into her bag, 'Polly will have told you all about Thompson's. What it's like here ... How it all works ... '

Bel chuckled.

'I think I know all about welding. And, of course, I know all Polly's workmates. But that's about it. I have to admit I really don't know much at all about working in an office.'

Marie-Anne shook her head. Her mind was made up.

'That's not a concern,' she said, clearly relaxing now. 'You'll pick it up in no time.'

'But don't I have to know how to type?' Bel was starting to panic a little. She needed Marie-Anne to know that she really did not have *any* kind of clerical skills – whatsoever.

'Ah,' Marie-Anne smiled, 'you'll learn that in no time. I'll teach you myself. The more you type, the easier it is, and the faster you become. You'll be doing thirty words a minute in no time at all.'

Marie-Anne stood up and looked out at the dozen or so admin staff beavering away in the open-plan office. Bel followed Marie-Anne's lead and stood up to stare out at a row of typists who looked as though they were doing more like a hundred words a minute, never mind a mere thirty, the palms of their hands slapping the steel arms of their typewriters with rhythmic regularity. Everyone looked so proficient. So confident.

Marie-Anne turned to Bel.

'Well, I think you'd be a perfect fit, don't you?'

Bel lied and mumbled that she would.

'Congratulations, then. The job's yours.' Marie-Anne gave Bel a genuine smile and extended her hand. 'Welcome aboard!'

'Thank you!' Bel shook Marie-Anne's hand. 'Gosh, I didn't think I'd get to know so quickly.'

'No time like the present,' Marie-Anne said, good-naturedly. 'Besides, there's no messing around these days. It's full steam ahead at the moment. Actually, I lie – *all the time*. It really is one deadline after another.'

She paused for a moment.

'So, we'll see you in the morning?' She knew she was pushing it. 'Nine o'clock sharp?'

'Oh my goodness,' Bel said, surprised. 'You want me to start tomorrow?'

'Yes, unless that's going to be a problem?' Marie-Anne smiled, secretly crossing her fingers. If she managed to get the new girl to start tomorrow, she would also earn herself some much-needed brownie points with Helen.

'Oh, sorry, I forgot to ask.' Marie-Anne had a sudden thought. 'Have you got children?'

'Yes, I've got a daughter, Lucille, but there's no worries there,' Bel said. 'My mother-in-law runs a sort of makeshift nursery from our neighbour's house. And, of course, there's other family members who can look after her.'

Marie-Anne kept a straight face, even though inwardly she was doing a little jig.

'Great! So, I shall see you tomorrow at nine.'

'Yes, yes, nine o'clock,' Bel repeated. She still couldn't quite believe she'd got the job.

She turned to leave.

'Oh, do I need to bring anything with me? A pad or pencil?'

Bel immediately felt foolish for asking.

'Just yourself!' Marie-Anne reassured.

As Bel turned to open the office door a huge horn sounded out, making her jump.

'You'll get used to it!' Marie-Anne laughed. 'See you tomorrow!'

As soon as Bel stepped outside she saw that the whole yard had come to a virtual standstill.

A huge hook dangling from a nearby crane was still swinging, but the crane's operator, a young boy who looked barely out of short trousers, was jumping out of the metal cabin and shouting over to a group of other young lads milling around a brazier, rolling cigarettes and joking around.

Spotting Polly and the rest of the women welders making their way over to a spot by the quayside, Bel hurried across the yard to join them. As she did so she saw a group of blacksmiths, their faces red and sweaty, blinking in the light as they emerged from the darkness of the forge.

Bel felt as though she had been transported into a different world.

As she reached the women, Dorothy was the first to spot her.

'Pol's not forgotten her bait again, has she?'

'No,' Bel laughed.

'Everything all right?' Polly asked, although she could tell by Bel's demeanour that, thankfully, her sister-in-law was not the harbinger of any more bad news.

'Yes, more than all right!' Bel said as they all crowded around.

'Go on then, don't keep us all in suspense,' Polly demanded. 'What's up?'

Bel looked at the women welders.

'I've just got a job!'

Six dirty faces broke out into smiles.

'Eee, that's brilliant!' Martha said. 'Where?'

'Here!' Bel chuckled. 'I've got Sylvia's old job.'

'Well, congratulations!' Rosie said, although she too, like Marie-Anne, was surprised Bel would *want* to work in a shipyard.

'Oh. My. God!' Dorothy grabbed Angie's arm in mock horror. 'That means you're going to be working within spitting distance of *the Witch*.'

Bel looked at Dorothy and Angie for an explanation.

'Helen!' they said in unison.

'Why didn't you tell me?' Polly sounded put out. 'I didn't think you were looking for a job – especially one here.'

'Bit spur of the moment, really,' Bel confessed.

'Have you told our Joe?' Polly asked.

Bel couldn't keep the guilt from showing on her face – for not having told Joe, but also Polly.

'No, I didn't think I'd get it, to be honest. But Marie-Anne was really nice – said it didn't matter I couldn't type, and that she thought I'd be perfect for the job.'

'Well, I'm sure Joe won't mind,' Polly said, although she did wonder whether he might feel that it should be him working in the yard, instead of the two women in the family.

'When do you start?' Martha asked.

'Tomorrow!' Bel's eyes widened.

'Blimey,' Martha said.

'Well, I think that's a good thing,' Gloria said. 'No time to get nervous or anything.'

'Oh, Gloria, I'm so sorry. I should have really asked you first. You're not worried about me abandoning Hope, are you?' Bel asked, guiltily.

'Yer dafty, yer don't have to check with me first. I'm just lucky I've had yer looking after Hope fer so long – 'n it's not as if there won't be anyone else to look after her.'

In fact, Gloria felt strangely relieved.

Like the fastest runner had just dropped out of the race, giving her the chance to reclaim the lead position.

Chapter Fifteen

'Any more for any more?' The ticket collector made his way down the carriage, looking from left to right, stopping occasionally to take someone's fare.

Sitting on the eleven o'clock train to Ryhope, a village three miles south of the town, Helen looked out the window at the passing farmland. The local service, which went as far as Seaham further down the coast, was slow, but Helen didn't mind. She had given herself most of the day off, glad to leave the interviewing for the new admin assistant's job to Marie-Anne.

Opening her handbag and pulling out her compact, Helen checked her reflection. She was reassured to see that the attractive, made-up face that stared back at her showed no signs of what was really going on in her head.

When the train pulled into Ryhope station, Helen carefully stepped down onto the platform, making a point of closing the carriage door firmly behind her.

Soon, she thought, she would be closing the door on a part of her life that she never again wanted to revisit. When all of this was over and done with, she would happily wipe the past seven months from her memory for ever.

Thank God she had realised that there was a way she could erase from her life for good the debacle of her relationship with Theodore and start afresh.

Although, why she hadn't thought of it beforehand, she had no idea.

It was the one thing, Helen thought bitterly, for which she had her mother to thank.

Overhearing her words last week, it was as though a light had suddenly been switched on – a light that had finally enabled her to see her way through the darkness.

'Helen! It's lovely to see you!'

Dr Parker put his hand out to greet Helen as she walked down the main pathway to the entrance of the Ryhope Emergency Hospital, originally built to cope with the hundreds of injured soldiers shipped back from Dunkirk. He had recently asked to be transferred here from the town's main hospital, which was where he'd originally got to know Helen when her father was ill.

'Dr Parker!' Helen put out her hand.

When she had come to the Ryhope to tell Theo she was pregnant, and had instead found out he was married and had gone back to Oxford to be with his wife and children, Dr Parker had told her to call on him if she ever needed to. They were words that had come back to her this past week, and which had propelled her to ask him to meet her today.

'Please call me John,' Dr Parker insisted with a smile. 'Otherwise I'm going to start calling you *Miss Crawford*.'

'All right ... John.' Helen forced a smile; she was feeling more nervous than she'd anticipated.

'Are you happy to walk around the grounds while we chat? Only, it's such a beautiful day. I can't remember the last time I felt the sun.' Dr Parker lifted his face slightly to the skies, revelling in the feel of the sun's warm rays on his skin.

'Of course,' Helen said, glad to be outdoors herself.

'Not that I'm complaining.' Dr Parker drew his attention back to Helen as they started to walk. 'Not when I see the states some of our boys are coming back in.'

His face clouded over and Helen saw that her father's former doctor had dark circles under his eyes, and his pallor was indeed that of someone who rarely went outdoors.

'But,' Helen said sadly, thinking of Tommy, 'at least they have made it back.'

Dr Parker looked at Helen.

'Have you lost someone?' he asked, concerned. These days it seemed unusual to meet someone who hadn't.

'A friend,' Helen said. 'He's been classed as "missing", but I think we all know what that means.'

Dr Parker nodded. 'Army?'

'Navy,' Helen said, her eyes stinging with the beginnings of tears. 'A diver. A naval clearance diver.' She paused for a moment. 'I knew him from when I was small. He worked the docks for the Wear Commissioner.'

Helen paused for a moment.

'I loved him,' she said, simply. Her vision blurred with tears as they both walked in silence for a short while.

'Come, let's have a sit-down,' Dr Parker said, taking her gently by the arm and guiding her to one of the wooden benches that had been placed around the hospital grounds.

They both sat quietly for a moment.

Helen dabbed her eyes with a handkerchief.

'Sorry,' she said, taking a deep breath. 'I keep feeling tearful and I don't seem to have any control over it.'

'Perhaps that's not such a bad thing,' Dr Parker said. 'Better than keeping it all in. That doesn't do anyone any good.'

Helen let out a little laugh as she rummaged again in her handbag for her compact and checked that her mascara hadn't run. 'It's no good for your make-up, though.'

Dr Parker turned a little to face Helen. He had felt terribly sorry for her when he had seen her last and he'd had to give her the news that Theodore had gone back down south. He had guessed that Helen was Theo's latest squeeze but had been unsure whether she knew he was married. Seeing the shock on her face that afternoon had given him his answer.

'How have you been since I saw you last?' he asked as gently as possible.

'I'll be honest, John, I've not been all that marvellous.' Helen looked at Dr Parker and prayed she could trust him. Prayed he would not be affronted, or angered even, by what she was about to ask him.

'I don't know how to say this.' Helen looked around to make sure no one else was near and could overhear them.

Dr Parker looked at Helen.

'Well ... ' Helen hesitated. 'The thing is ... '

Another pause.

'The thing is ... Dear me, this is difficult.'

'Go on,' Dr Parker urged.

'The thing is ... '

Helen finally spat the words out.

'I'm bloody well pregnant.'

Dr Parker felt his heart sink. He liked Helen a lot. An awful lot. And even though they'd only really spent time discussing her father's health, he felt as though he knew her.

'Would I be right in guessing that the father is Theodore?'

Helen nodded.

'Have you told him?'

Helen shook her head.

'Is that why you came to the hospital a few weeks ago? To tell him?'

Helen nodded again.

'And the reason you're here again today is because ... ?' Dr Parker let the question hang in the air.

'Because I wanted to ask if you could help me.' Helen took a breath. When she had first heard her mother's words, she had immediately been struck by images conjured up from awful stories of backstreet abortionists, but they had been followed fairly immediately by an image of Dr Parker.

'When I was here last you said to come and see you if I wanted to chat – or needed anything.'

'And I meant it,' Dr Parker said in earnest. 'Have you thought about what you're going to do?'

'I have,' Helen said, 'but I don't know how to go about doing what I want to do, which is why I have come to you.'

Dr Parker was quiet.

'I don't want to keep it,' she said, almost in a whisper. 'And I thought you might know of someone who can do what they've got to do.'

Dr Parker took Helen's hands in his and forced her to look him in the eye.

'Have you *really* thought about this, Helen? I mean *really* thought about it?'

'I have,' Helen said, feeling strangely comforted by his hands on hers.

Dr Parker leant forwards a little. 'You do understand that such procedures are against the law? And that they are not always straightforward?'

'Yes,' Helen said. Her throat felt dry. 'But not anywhere near as risky as if I were to go elsewhere.'

This time it was Dr Parker who nodded. He had done a short stint on the gynaecological ward at the Royal in town and had seen a few examples of what happened to a woman after being butchered by some backstreet abortionist.

'Have you talked to anyone else about this?' Dr Parker asked.

'No,' Helen said, sharply. 'It's not anyone else's business.'

'What about your mother?' Dr Parker had met Mrs Crawford. She was a carbon copy of his own mother – completely self-obsessed, totally lacking in any kind of empathy, and without a single maternal bone in her body.

'No.' Helen's reply was curt.

'Your father?'

'He's in Glasgow for the foreseeable. He knows nothing about any of this. Nor will he. Ever,' Helen stressed.

'Any friends?' Dr Parker asked. 'It would be good for you to talk this through with someone.'

Helen thought about Gloria. She had gone to see her and Hope last night, had nearly told her what she was planning, but had thought better of it. Gloria, she was sure, would try and talk her out of it.

'I don't *need* to talk this through with anyone. I've made my mind up.'

Dr Parker looked at Helen.

'All right, but *we're* going to have to talk it all through. It's not as easy or as straightforward as it might seem,' he explained. He felt the heavy weight of responsibility press down on him as he realised that he was the only person Helen had spoken to. How he dealt with this situation could and would have repercussions. Whether he helped her or not. If he refused to be a part of what Helen planned to do, she might well seek help elsewhere, and he dreaded to think of where that could lead.

'First of all,' Dr Parker said, 'I have to ask you, is there no way you would consider actually *having* the child, either bringing it up yourself or having it adopted?'

'No. And no,' Helen said. Her face was set. Determined.

'Have you considered talking to Theo about the situation?' Dr Parker knew he was treading on potentially explosive territory, but it was something he had to ask.

'Absolutely not. No way!' Helen could feel her face flush. She still felt a huge well of anger whenever she thought of Theo.

'Ethically,' Dr Parker continued, 'I have to say to you that it is his child as well, and as such some may argue that he should also be involved in the decision.'

'Well, some people can argue until they are blue in the face, but this is my decision and my decision alone,' Helen snapped. 'That man ... That lying, cheating coward of a con man has no right to anything. Anything at all.'

Helen could feel her heart thumping in her chest.

'That's all right.' Dr Parker was still holding Helen's hand. 'And finally, we have to consider the role of those who can help you in all of this – after all, what you want to do is against the law.'

'I know,' Helen said, 'although why it's illegal is beyond me.' She'd never thought about it until now. Why would she? She'd never have guessed in a million years she would find herself in such a nightmarish scenario.

'I have thought about this,' she said, 'and I would, of course, be able to pay a considerable sum, knowing how big a risk it would be.' Helen let go of Dr Parker's hand and reached down into her handbag to get her cigarettes. Dr Parker pressed the palms of his hands together as though in prayer. He could still feel the warmth of her hand on his own.

'I have done some research,' Helen said, taking a cigarette from the packet of Pall Malls and lighting it. 'From what I can gather, there have been lots of women's groups and even male MPs who have been arguing the case for a change in the law for years now.'

Dr Parker nodded, knowing that there would be plenty of doctors like himself who would add their voice to such a campaign.

'And it would seem that there is also a loophole in the law ... ' Helen blew out smoke ' ... which stipulates that if a woman is deemed to be in danger of losing her life by going ahead with a pregnancy, then the termination of that pregnancy is legal.'

On hearing her words Dr Parker realised just how determined Helen was. This was not some spur-of-the-moment decision. She had done her homework.

'I believe,' she continued, 'it is called a "medically sanctioned" abortion.'

There was a short silence while Dr Parker thought for a moment. He knew from his time working at the Royal of a doctor there who could help – a gynaecologist who, for a decent wad of cash, had 'helped' other women of Helen's social standing.

'Yes, you're right, Helen. The only problem is that your present condition is not putting your life in danger as such.'

'I know,' Helen said, taking another drag of her cigarette, 'but from what I have gleaned it is not uncommon for those in the know – and, of course, with enough cash – to be able to find a doctor who might be able to embellish the truth a little ... And that such embellishing can be done discreetly? I can, of course,' Helen said quietly, 'make sure that you too are given a generous sum for helping me out.'

Dr Parker's head snapped round to look at Helen.

'If I do this for you, Helen, it is as a friend. As a person who cares.'

Helen sat up with a jolt. Dr Parker's eyes burrowed into her own and it was only then that she noticed their colour – a dark brown – and a seriousness she had never seen before.

'Sorry, John, I didn't mean to offend you. I just wanted you to know that I wasn't expecting you to do this for nothing.' Helen hesitated.

Dr Parker watched as Helen tossed her half-smoked cigarette to the ground and sat quietly for a moment.

'How far along are you?' Dr Parker asked.

'About ten ... eleven weeks,' Helen said.

This time it was Dr Parker who was quiet while he considered the options.

He knew that for the right price this particular doctor at the Royal would do what Helen wanted, and that with the world at war, any concerns about the legality of what she wanted done would probably be overlooked.

'Give me a call on Saturday,' Dr Parker said. 'I'll see what I can do.'

Helen stood up.

'Thank you, John. Thank you so much.'

Dr Parker followed suit and got to his feet. He was surprised when Helen took his arm as they walked back to the hospital entrance. What a fool she had been to give herself to someone like Theodore. He knew that if Helen had a baby out of wedlock, and with a man who was already married, her life would, to all intents and purposes, be ruined. This was Helen's way of getting her life back.

As Helen turned to leave, Dr Parker took her hand.

'I want you to really think about this,' he said, looking at her. Her emerald green eyes never failed to take his breath away. 'To be one hundred per cent certain this is what you want.'

Helen held Dr Parker's gaze. She knew he meant well.

'It's important you have no regrets,' he added. 'Whatsoever.'

Helen nodded.

'And if you change your mind, I'll still help you in any way I can. That goes without saying. All right?'

Helen nodded again, although she was quite sure there was no way she was going to have a change of heart.

No way.

Chapter Sixteen

'Daddeeee!'

Joe had just stepped off the bus at the main depot in Park Lane and had been greeted by Lucille pelting full force towards him.

'Well now, to what do I owe this pleasure?' He quickly put his walking stick under his arm, grabbed Lucille and raised her squealing into the air.

Watching them both, Bel had a sudden flashback of going to meet Joe off the train after returning from North Africa, and how Lucille had run to him as fast as her little legs would take her. Bel had been furious that her daughter had thought Joe was Teddy. How ironic that she had ended up falling for the man she had been determined to hate.

'What a lovely surprise,' Joe said, putting Lucille down and hobbling towards Bel.

The pair stood for a moment, kissing.

'Daddy!' Lucille started tugging at the arm of Joe's khaki uniform, wanting his attention.

'So then, what's the special occasion? This isn't anyone's birthday, is it?' Joe looked down at Lucille, who shook her head with a stubborn expression on her face. Her fourth birthday was just over a fortnight away and she was counting down the days.

'I thought it would be nice for us to come and meet you off the bus for a change,' Bel said. 'Go for a little walk through the park.'

Joe eyed his wife with suspicion.

'Sounds good to me,' he said, as Lucille positioned herself between her mammy and daddy, holding both their hands and demanding they swing her.

When they reached the park gates, Lucille broke free and ran to the top of the small grassy embankment.

'So, come on then,' Joe said, taking hold of Bel's hand. 'Spill the beans.'

'Well,' Bel said, knowing she had limited time as the thrill of being in the park would only hold Lucille's attention for so long. 'It's good news. Well, *I* think it's good news. I just hope *you* think it's good news too.'

'Go on then, spit it out,' Joe said, quickly checking that Lucille had not wandered out of sight.

'Well,' Bel said, straightening her back, 'I've got a job!'

Joe stopped walking and looked at her.

'Now, that is a surprise,' he said. 'A bit of a bolt out of the blue. What job? And where?'

His face didn't give away whether he was pleased or not.

'And why didn't you tell me you wanted a job? I thought you were happy at home ... '

'I know, I'm sorry, Joe. I know I should have told you. To be honest, I didn't think I'd get it. It was a moment of madness really.'

'So, tell me more,' Joe said, curiously. 'You're not going back on the buses, are you?'

Bel shook her head. 'I don't think they'd have me back even if I wanted to.'

'So, where's the job? Or rather, *what* is the job?'

'It's a clerical job,' Bel said.

Joe's eyes widened.

'I know,' Bel said. 'I can't even type. But they reckon I'll pick it up quickly.'

'I've no doubt that you will be the best and the quickest,' Joe said. 'You're as bright as a button. Always were. Even as a bairn. Just like this one.' He looked over to Lucille, who was walking back towards them, dangling a daisy chain in the air.

'So, come on, don't keep me in suspense,' Joe said, squeezing his wife's hand. 'Who's going to have the good fortune to have you working for them?'

Bel decided it was best to just come out and say it.

'Thompson's.'

'What, J.L. Thompson's? A job at the yard?' Joe was taken aback.

Bel nodded, scrutinising her husband's face.

'That's the last place I thought you'd want to work.'

'You don't mind, do you?'

Joe looked at Bel quizzically. 'Of course I don't mind. Although I can't say I won't be a little worried with all the air raids we've been getting.'

'But rarely during daylight hours,' Bel said.

'Mm,' Joe was forced to agree.

'So, you don't mind?' Bel implored.

'No, of course I don't mind. Why would I?' Joe asked, genuinely perplexed.

Bel let out a sigh of relief.

'Oh, it's just me being silly. I thought you might feel … I dunno … perhaps a bit resentful. I know how much you miss working in the shipyards.'

'Oh, yer dafty, of course I'm not resentful. I'd be lying if I said I didn't miss it. But I'm lucky to still have my own two legs, even if one of them is gammy. And more than anything I just count my blessings Major Black was able to make use of me.' Joe paused. 'I guess I'm just surprised you would want to work somewhere like that. I wouldn't have thought it would have been most women's first choice of a job.'

'It was Polly's,' Bel countered.

'Aye, but Polly was always obsessed with the yards from very young. Mind you, she's going to be over the moon when she finds out.'

'She *is*! Although I think she was a little hurt I hadn't told her beforehand.' The words were out before Bel had time to think.

'Ah, I see,' Joe said in mock earnestness. 'So, I'm the last to know, am I?'

'No,' Bel said, waving at Lucille to come and join them. 'Polly's the only one to know. Apart from Gloria, of course, and the other women welders.'

Joe laughed again.

'Yer know how to make a man feel important.'

He put his arm around Bel as they made their way over to Lucille, who was concentrating on making more daisy chains.

'I'm pleased for you,' he said, kissing his wife's forehead.

As they made their way home to break the news to the rest of the household, Joe thought about the Havelocks and their long association with Thompson's. Mr Havelock's son-in-law, Jack, had been there all of his life until just recently; his granddaughter, Helen, was rapidly making her way up the managerial ladder; and it was known that Miriam occasionally showed her face there.

If Bel wanted to put the recent revelations about her paternity behind her, then this was not the way to go about it.

'I don't believe it!' Agnes was standing in the doorway of the scullery with her hands on her hips. 'So, now I've got double the worry. My daughter *and* my daughter-in-law both working in that bloody shipyard!'

Agnes was trying her hardest to keep her voice down as Joe had just taken Lucille upstairs to bed, having promised to read her a bedtime story; she didn't want her granddaughter hearing her nana spitting nails.

'Ma, she's going to be doing an office job. The worst she can expect is a paper cut!' Polly looked across at Bel, who was trying but failing to keep a straight face.

'Ah, so all this is a laughing matter, is it?' Agnes stomped across to the kitchen table, picked up the plates and cutlery and stomped back into the scullery, letting the dirty dishes clatter into the porcelain sink.

'I'll tell yer what,' Agnes said, 'I'll go and get meeself a job down the yards as well, why don't I?' The Irish in Agnes was now well and truly fired up. 'I'll go down there in the mornin' and get meeself a job working right out there in the middle o' the yard – or better still, up on one o' the top decks, so I can wave at them German bombers when they come flying over. What do yer reckon, eh?

'Oh,' Agnes made a pantomime expression of having just had a great idea, 'and better still, I'll get me little granddaughter there as well, helping the little tea boy scurry around the workers. Mm? Then we can all stand and wave at the bloody bombers! We can all jump up and down with excitement that every one of us Elliots have worked in the blasted shipyards.'

'I'll leave yer all to it, then.' Arthur pushed himself out of the armchair next to the range and gave Tramp and Pup each a pat on the head.

He was just leaving the kitchen when Pearl came clomping down the hallway.

'Y'all right there, Arthur?' she asked.

Arthur gave Pearl a nod, before making a beeline for his bedroom.

'Eee, yer could cut the atmosphere with a knife,' Pearl said, walking into the kitchen and taking one look at Agnes, Polly and Bel. She glanced down at the two dogs. 'Even the mutts look like they wanna fade into the background. Who's in the doghouse then?' She hooted with laughter at her own joke.

Agnes cast an angry look over to Bel.

'Yer daughter here has got herself a job at Thompson's.'

The shock on Pearl's face was obvious for all to see.

'Why dee yer wanna work there?' Pearl asked, all joviality now gone. 'And what about the bab? And LuLu? And the neighbour's bairns 'n all the laundry yer take in?'

Bel looked at Agnes and back to her ma. 'Beryl has all the children round hers now.' Her tone was placatory. 'And Lucille's always round there anyway. There's loads of people that can look after Hope – Agnes, Beryl ... there's even Joe and Arthur if need be.'

The room was quiet.

'And if there's any laundry to be done, I can do it when I get back from work. And don't forget, there's going to be an extra wage – it'll help out no end.'

Agnes and Pearl looked at each other.

Neither was convinced by Bel's argument.

For once, the pair were in agreement, although the reasons why they were against Bel working at Thompson's could not have been more different.

After Pearl had gone back to the pub, and Bel had made her escape upstairs using the excuse of getting her clothes ready for tomorrow, Polly made Agnes a cup of tea and suggested they both take two chairs out in the backyard and sit for a little while before hitting the sack themselves.

'You know, Ma,' Polly said, turning her teacup around on the saucer so as not to drink from the side with the chip, 'this job of Bel's might be just what she needs.'

'How do you work that one out?' Agnes was still far from happy about Bel's new job, but her anger was waning.

'Well, she won't admit it, but I can tell she's really upset 'cos she's not fallen yet. It's been eight months now since the wedding.'

'I know, and she fell straight away with Lucille,' Agnes mused.

'And all Bel's ever wanted, even from being a child, is to be a wife and mother and have loads of children.'

'I know,' Agnes agreed, pouring the tea from her cup into the saucer to cool it down and taking a slurp.

'And, if you think about it, she's spending her days looking after other women's little 'uns when all she wants is to have her own.'

'Yer right, Pol,' Agnes sighed. 'And there's a couple round the doors who are in the family way. Suppose it can't be easy.'

'And she's become so close to Hope. A bit too close, in my opinion,' Polly said quietly.

'Mmm,' Agnes murmured. 'Anyone who doesn't know her always presumes Hope's hers. Sometimes she's not put them right. I keep trying to take Hope off her hands, but she won't be having any of it.' Agnes looked at Polly. 'And I'm sure Hope called Bel "Mama" the other day. The little mite clearly thinks she's got two mammies.'

They both sat quietly for a little while.

'I just worry,' Agnes said. 'I worry about yer working in that yard, especially after that poor chap got his leg crushed last year. I can't help it. And I know I sound like a broken record, but the yards are that madman's prime target. I couldn't bear for anything else to happen to any of yer.'

Polly looked at her ma and thought that she looked older. Tired.

'I know, Ma, but you can't keep us all nicely tucked up at home,' she sighed, 'and besides, it's not as if being at home is all that safe either. Jerry has hit more homes than anything else. And not exactly a million miles from here.'

Polly exhaled. 'Don't worry about me or Bel, Ma. We'll be all right. And besides, with the extra wage things won't be so tight, and it'll mean you don't have to take in so much laundry.'

Agnes slurped down another mouthful of tea.

'I'd take in a mountain of laundry if I could just keep yer all safe 'n sound.'

Agnes looked at her daughter. It wasn't often it was just the two of them. Polly spent a lot of time with Arthur when she came back from work, either meeting up with him down the docks, or sometimes going to the allotment he kept with his friend Albert. Agnes didn't mind. She was pleased. She knew it was her daughter's only connection with Tommy and that it brought her comfort.

'Anyway, how are *you* feeling about everything?' Agnes asked. The change in her tone made it clear to Polly that her ma meant Tommy.

Polly was quiet for a moment.

'To be honest, Ma, I'm not sure.' Polly looked down at her tea as though she might find the answer there. She could feel the tears that she normally kept at bay until she was on her own rising to the surface.

Agnes reached out and took hold of her daughter's free hand.

'I keep trying to convince myself that everything's going to be all right.' Polly's voice was shaking with emotion.

'That Tommy's fine. That he's somewhere, we just don't know where, and for a while I can trundle along in my head actually believing that – and then suddenly it'll hit me like a brick. That everything isn't fine. That everything's far from fine. That I'm just kidding myself thinking there's a chance he's going to come back. That I'm living in cloud cuckoo land ... When people ask me about Tommy and I tell them he's been reported missing, I can see it in their faces. Their reaction's the same as if I'd said he was dead. And then all of a sudden I'm thinking what they're thinking.'

She looked at her ma.

'That he's dead.'

Polly tried to restrain the tears but failed.

Agnes put her cup and saucer down on the ground and moved her chair so that it was right next to Polly's.

'Come here,' she said, putting her arm around her daughter's shoulders and pulling her close. Polly put her arms around her ma's waist, buried her head into her chest and sobbed her heart out.

Agnes was old enough and wise enough to know that sometimes words had the ability to heal, other times they were totally futile. This was one such occasion, and so she just held her daughter tight, like she had done when she was a child.

Brushing a loose strand of thick brown hair away, Agnes bent her head and kissed Polly's furrowed brow.

How she wished she could take the pain away and suffer it herself, but she couldn't. This was Polly's journey in life, and she had to endure the lows, just as she had enjoyed the highs.

She just prayed to God that the low her daughter was presently dragging herself through would not last so long that it became the norm.

When Agnes went to bed she pulled out the top drawer of her bedside table and took out Harry's war medal – the Military Medal for 'acts of gallantry and devotion to duty under fire' – along with the telegram that she had received twenty-five years ago informing her that her husband was missing. Unlike Polly's letter, though, the word 'missing' had been followed by 'presumed dead'.

For months after receiving her letter, Agnes had lain awake, begging the good Lord to bring her Harry home, just like she was sure Polly was doing every night.

Of course, the good Lord hadn't done what she'd pleaded for him to do and in the end she'd had to finally accept that, along with thousands of other women the length and breadth of the country, she would never get to see the man she loved ever again. Nor would she get to give him a decent burial, and in doing so be given the minor consolation of being able to visit his grave.

Agnes had been about the same age as Polly when she had lost the man she loved.

She knew only too well what her daughter was feeling.

She might have lost her husband a long time ago, but she could still remember how it felt as though it were yesterday.

Why was it that history often had a way of repeating itself – and not in a good way either?

Agnes hoped, for her daughter's sake, that she did not have to go through the pain of not knowing for long, and that soon she would know whether the man she loved was coming back to her – or not.

Downstairs, Polly sat in bed, holding Tommy's last letter in her hands. When she had originally received it, her heart had filled with joy as she read the words of the man she loved telling her how proud he was that she was building ships and doing her bit to help win the war. But as time had gone on, and there had been no other letters arriving from Gibraltar, she had read and reread Tommy's words and had seen them in a different light.

It was as though Tommy had known that this might well be his last letter to her, and because of that he had wanted to tell her just how much he loved her – and how proud he was of her. She had told Bel she wondered whether Tommy had had some kind of a forewarning, and had anticipated her grief and known that the best way for her to deal with it would be to carry on working, to keep doing the job she had always dreamed of doing.

Bel had told her that she had thought the same about Teddy's last letter, but that now, with hindsight, she believed that he, like Tommy, had not had any kind of premonition of his own impending death, but rather he'd had the sense to know that they could die at any time. Teddy had written his letter just before a large-scale military operation, while it was Tommy's job to remove limpet mines from the hulls of Allied ships. Their odds were not good.

As Polly carefully folded her letter and placed it back in its box, along with all the others Tommy had sent her this past year and a half, tears started to trickle down her face.

Switching off her bedside light, she allowed her sorrow and heartache a free rein.

Next door, Arthur could hear Polly's muffled cries, as he did most nights, and as he listened the ache in his own heart became even more unbearable.

Salty tears ran down the old man's folds of weather-worn skin.

If he could only swap his own life for Tommy's.

If only.

Chapter Seventeen

Wednesday 15 July

'Good luck! You'll be brilliant!' Joe shouted out to Bel as she started to walk towards the large metal-gated entrance to Thompson's.

'Bye, Mammy!' Lucille waved from the lofty heights of her daddy's shoulders.

Bel threw them both a kiss. It was a quarter to nine and Bel was glad Joe and Lucille had accompanied her across to North Sands. On the way here, Joe had made her chuckle with his usual banter and carry-on, knowing it would keep his wife's nerves at bay.

'See you both later!' She turned and walked to the time-keeper's cabin.

After collecting her white board from Alfie, Bel headed towards the admin building. Reaching the main double doors, she stopped for a moment, her attention drawn to what looked like two huge mechanical lobster claws. A team of men were placing a metal plate between its nippers, while another gang of workers threw red-hot rivets onto the plate, just as the claws closed and pressed them into their designated holes.

'After you, pet?'

Her attention was broken by an older man, wearing a dark grey suit and a bowler hat, who was holding the door open for her.

She smiled and thanked him and hurried up the stairs to the first floor.

'Morning, Bel,' Marie-Anne chirped when she saw the new girl walk into the office. 'Let me take you to your workstation and show you the ropes.'

Bel felt a rush of nerves as they arrived at her designated 'workstation' – a solid wooden desk to the right of Marie-Anne's, which was twice the size and piled high with files and what looked like very important paperwork.

'I thought I'd put you here so that I can show you how things are done, but also because I want you to answer my phone if I'm not about.'

Bel looked at the black Bakelite phone – the only one in the entire office.

'If you listen to me when I take calls, you'll soon know what to do and what to say,' Marie-Anne added. 'But first off, have you any questions?'

Bel looked around her at the dozen women, all of whom looked about the same age as herself. Every one of them looked very serious and completely focused on whatever it was they were doing.

'I *am* curious as to what the green machines are for.' Bel looked over to the far side of the office where there were six women all using what looked like miniature tills. Every now and again they would stop and scribble something down.

'Ah, the wonders of modern technology,' Marie-Anne said. 'They are comptometers – machines used to calculate numbers, to add and subtract, that kind of thing. That section you're looking at is the finance department. How are you with numbers?'

Bel chuckled. 'Not exactly a natural,' she confessed, 'although I had to do basic arithmetic when I was taking fares on the buses.'

Seeing the slightly apprehensive look on Bel's face, Marie-Anne reassured her. 'Don't worry, you won't be required to use one, unless you've a burning desire to become a comptometrist.'

Bel chuckled. 'I don't think I could even pronounce it, never mind be one.'

Marie-Anne laughed.

'You do, however, have to be able to use a typewriter,' she added, 'which the comptometrists might well argue is actually harder to use than their mechanical calculators – that is, if you type properly and don't just stab away with one finger.'

Marie-Anne sat down in her chair and placed her hands on the round, ivory-coloured keys of the Imperial typewriter.

'Stand behind me and watch.'

Bel did as she was told.

'So, this is where your left hand goes,' she demonstrated. 'See how the little finger is resting lightly on the A key and the index finger on the F . . . '

The women all looked at Bel as she hurried over to meet them outside the canteen at the start of the lunch break.

'Gosh, it's quite nice being out here,' she said. 'At least there's a bit of a breeze.'

Bel looked around at the huge, cathedral-like platers' shed, the towering cranes and overhead gantries; there was a steel-grey destroyer in the dry dock, and, of course, everywhere there were scores of men, mostly in groups, laughing, chatting, smoking.

'So?' Dorothy couldn't hold back. 'How was it?'

'Honestly,' Rosie butted in, 'let the poor woman get her breath.'

'Come on,' Polly said, opening the door of the canteen, 'let's get some lunch and then we can hear all about it over a big pot of tea.'

'I think I'm more in need of a bucket of cold water,' Martha said. 'I've been sweating like a pig all morning.'

'You 'n me both,' Angie agreed, taking off her headscarf and using it to wipe her forehead and neck.

'It's being stuck in that metal box for the past two hours,' Gloria said. She also looked flushed.

As most of the shipyard workers had opted to eat their packed lunches outdoors, the women were able to go straight to the food counter.

'So, this is the new girl, is it?' Muriel elbowed aside one of the younger girls who was just about to serve the women.

'It *is*, Muriel,' Gloria said, before turning to the women and nodding over to their usual table at the side of the canteen.

'I'll get this,' she told them.

'I think we're all gonna have a big pot of tea, please, Muriel – and a round of sandwiches to share. Too hot for anything else. Bet your lot have been cooking in all ways in here today?'

'Aye, we have,' Muriel said, her eyes not once leaving Bel.

Rosie grabbed the tea tray while Gloria paid and took the sandwiches.

'Well done,' Rosie whispered under her breath to Gloria, as they made their way across to the women.

As Martha poured the tea, Bel looked about her. 'I didn't know they played music here.'

'It's the radio,' Angie said. 'Yer can't normally hear it, 'cos of all the men gobbing off. It's not usually this quiet.'

'Here they are!' Martha said as Hannah and Olly hurried over to them.

'How was it, Bel?' Hannah asked, pulling up a chair.

'Dinnit speak too loudly,' Angie warned, before Bel had a chance to answer. 'That Muriel's got flapper lugs on her.'

'Yeh, and the next thing you know every word you've said is winging its way around the yard,' Gloria chipped in.

They all chuckled.

'So,' Polly said, 'how did it go?'

'What's it like working for *the witch*?' Dorothy couldn't hold back any longer.

Bel spluttered a little on her tea.

'Well, to be honest, I didn't really see her. Sorry to disappoint,' Bel said, looking around the table at the expectant faces. 'She only really seems to talk to Marie-Anne. She doesn't even come out of her office all that much. From the little that I could make out from my desk, people go to see Helen, not the other way round.'

'Sounds about right,' Polly said.

'But I've been warned more than once by a few of the other girls to keep my distance. If Helen takes a disliking to you she's been known to make your life hell.'

'Remember, people love to exaggerate,' Gloria butted in. 'I always think it's best to make your own mind up about people.'

Dorothy looked at Bel and dramatically raised her eyes to the ceiling. 'You'll get used to Glor here defending Helen to the hilt. She won't hear a bad word said against her.' She dropped her voice to a hissed whisper. 'Even though Helen's been a total cow to us all since we started here.'

There were a few mutterings of agreement.

Bel looked at Gloria, who appeared to be about to say something then thought better of it.

'Well,' Dorothy said, 'as long as she doesn't pick on you because your Polly's sister-in-law. If she doesn't know already, she will soon enough.'

'She better not,' Polly said, her face stony, 'otherwise she'll have me to deal with.'

'I'm sure she won't,' Rosie said, with a placatory smile. 'She seems pretty preoccupied at the moment.'

'Why's that?' Bel asked.

'We're looking towards hitting a thirty-six-year production record this year. Helen's all out to make sure that happens,' Rosie said.

'Anyway, enough about Helen,' Polly said, feeling herself getting angry again. 'Did it go all right?'

'And did you manage to type?' Olly asked.

'Well, I don't know if you could call it typing,' Bel grimaced, 'but I managed to do a short letter. And Marie-Anne's really nice.'

Another murmur showing they all agreed.

'She's teaching me how to "touch-type". That's when you use all your fingers,' she explained quickly. 'She says if I learn how to type properly from the off it'll be much easier. And she says once I get the hang of that she's going to see how I get on with learning shorthand.'

'Blimey, you'll be a proper secretary then,' Angie said, taking a bite of her sandwich.

'I think there might be a way to go yet,' Bel laughed. 'But enough about me – what have you lot been doing?'

This time there was a communal groan as they told Bel how they had been doing vertical and flat welds all morning inside one of the ship's holds – how boring it was, and how hot it was, especially with their helmets on and their thick denim overalls.

'Well, you either roast or you get burnt and are up all night with "arc eye", so don't think for one moment about doing even a few seconds of welding without your masks on,' Rosie nagged them.

Bel looked at the splattering of burn marks on Rosie's face and thought that if the women welders ever needed a warning, they had it right there in front of them. She would never forget how Agnes had nursed Rosie that night after her uncle had forced her head over a live weld – nor her screams of agony, which had resonated throughout the house.

'So, when are you off to see Charlotte?' Polly asked Rosie as they all polished off the sandwiches and drained the pot of tea.

'A few weeks' time,' Rosie said.

'When are you going to bring her here?' Dorothy said. 'We all can't wait to meet her.'

'Yeh, when we gonna get to see her, miss?' Angie chipped in.

Rosie's face dropped.

'Don't you lot start. I get enough hassle from Lily.' Rosie looked over at Bel. 'As well as that sister of yours. She's been joining ranks with Lily, telling me I should bring Charlotte back.'

Bel had heard about Rosie's dilemma, and could understand why Rosie was reticent.

'I don't want Charlotte thinking life here is a bed of roses. It's not as if we'll be living where we were brought up, in some cosy little cottage in Whitburn, spending our days walking on the beach and picking whelks off the rocks.'

No one said anything. They all knew that the only person Rosie was really fighting against when it came to Charlotte coming back home was herself.

'Get her a job with the red-leaders,' Angie said. 'That'll have her running back to that posh school she gans to faster than the speed o' light.'

'What's a red-leader?' Bel asked.

'Only *the* most boring job in the yard,' Dorothy said.

'Bar being a sweeper-upper,' Martha said.

'Red-leaders,' Rosie explained, 'put an anti-corrosive paint onto the ship's hull to protect against rust.'

'Yeh, the stuff's red 'n it's got lead in it – 'n it stinks to high Jesus,' Angie said.

'It's certainly not the nicest smell,' Rosie agreed, 'and you have to have a good head for heights.'

Bel nodded. She had seen the women she now knew to be red-leaders working from scaffolding that must have been a good thirty feet high.

'So, Glor, are we ever going to see Jack again?' Dorothy asked. 'Or is he going to defect for good and run off into the Highlands in just a kilt and live off haggis, neeps and tatties for the rest of his life?'

Everyone laughed.

'There's more to Scotland than kilts 'n haggis, yer know,' Gloria said, stalling.

'Sorry, Glor, I forgot ... There's also bagpipes and the Loch Ness Monster,' Dorothy said, straight-faced.

'Seriously, though,' Polly butted in, 'do you think he's going to be back any time soon?'

When Jack had initially been forced to leave town, Gloria had told the women that he was needed at Lithgows shipyard on the Clyde because of his knowledge of the new Liberty ships. The women had accepted that at first, but it was now over six months since he'd gone and Gloria worried that they might realise she wasn't being entirely truthful with them.

Gloria took a slurp of her tea.

'Actually,' she said, looking at all the women, 'he's just been told he has to stay up there.'

'Oh, no, Glor, that's awful.' Dorothy looked crestfallen.

'Why?' Martha asked.

'It's not like the yards here don't need him,' Polly said.

'I couldn't agree more, Pol,' Gloria said. 'But it's them high up who think they know what's best and what's not, and they reckon they can't do without Jack now 'n he has to stay there for a good while yet. Maybes even till the end of the war.'

The women all voiced their outrage.

'I'm sorry to hear that, Gloria,' Bel said. 'He must be dying to see Hope.' She kept her voice down, having noticed Muriel loitering around the counter moving dishes about, but not actually doing anything.

'Can't he come back for a weekend?' Dorothy asked; her face showed genuine concern.

'Yeh, they've got to give him some time off,' Angie agreed.

'At the moment, they're like us, working six, seven days a week.'

'Well,' Hannah said, 'I think the solution is for you and Hope to go up there for a short break. You must be due some time off?'

Everyone looked at Rosie.

'Well, yes, without a doubt. But it's not me that makes those decisions. I can certainly ask, though, eh, Glor?'

Gloria nodded.

'I'm sure we'll work something out ... Anyway,' Gloria looked at the squad's 'terrible two', 'when are you two moving into your new pad?'

Dor looked up to the ceiling. 'When this one here breaks the news to her mam and dad.'

'Which I'm ganna dee this weekend,' Angie said, sullenly. 'When they're both together. If I tell ma dad first, then ma mam'll be like *I'm the last to know* and if I tell ma mam first ma dad'll go off on one about him being the man of the house 'n *he* should've been told first.'

Gloria relaxed as the chatter turned to moving house, and what they would need and not need, and if they were going to have a 'moving-in' party, which Dorothy said they would be having, without a doubt.

As they all ate and chattered and drank tea, Bel admitted to the women that she had been knocked sideways by the noise and hadn't realised it would be quite so loud and unrelenting. They all laughed and said she would get used to it, which was exactly what Marie-Anne had said.

When Polly nipped off to use the washroom, Rosie quietly asked Bel how she thought Polly was coping, and Bel admitted that her sister-in-law was crying herself to sleep most nights, but working at Thompson's seemed to be helping – or at least giving her some respite.

They quickly changed the subject when Polly returned.

Dorothy and Angie told Bel to be wary of any pranks the men might try and play on her. So far they had all, at some point during their time working in the yard, had had a dead rat with a piece of string attached to it yanked across their path. It had caught them all out, even Martha, who claimed not to mind rats. Bel visibly blanched and they all laughed, giving her some comfort by telling her she might escape such stunts because she was an office worker.

Angie told Bel which workers – both in the yard and in the offices – were known Lotharios, and Polly said she would be spreading the word that her pretty blonde sister-in-law was very much taken, and that her husband was more than capable of sorting out anyone who might think about trying their luck. Bel pointed out that she was wearing a wedding ring, but the women just laughed and said that didn't mean much these days.

'Eee, well, I'd better get back,' Bel said, looking up at the canteen clock. Her head felt like it was overloaded and she had yet to get through the afternoon. 'I better get to my desk before that horn goes off. Give a good impression on my first day.'

'See you back home later,' Polly said as Bel stood up and straightened her dress, which was not only her best summer dress, but her only one.

'Yeh, good luck,' Dorothy and Angie chorused.

'And don't forget,' Hannah said, 'I'm just next door if you need anything.'

'And if you can't see Hannah, just get me. I'm usually on the benches by the front door,' Olly added.

Bel thanked them all and hurried off out of the canteen.

'That was a bit awkward, wasn't it?' Rosie said to Gloria as they made their way over to *Brutus*.

'About Jack?' Gloria said.

Rosie nodded.

'I know. I'm surprised none of them have sussed out something's up.'

'You know,' Rosie said, 'it mightn't be too long before we can get him back here. Miriam's hold over you both is starting to slacken.' She moved to the side to let Mickey the tea boy pass with his swinging pole of tin cups. 'I mean, now that Rina's got her job at Vera's there's no worry about her and Hannah keeping a roof over their heads, and anyway, I really don't think Miriam would be able to get our little bird sacked. She's become Basil's protégée. I know he'd fight tooth and nail to keep her.

'And,' Rosie continued, 'it's not as if Miriam can cause any problems for poor Polly and Tommy – she can make up whatever rumours she wants now, it doesn't matter. And Dorothy and Angie are getting their own place, which means there's only really Martha that she could hurt.'

'I guess so,' Gloria said. 'But that's one problem I can't see us ever being able to solve. Martha can never know about her real mother.'

'I know,' Rosie agreed. 'I just hate to think of Miriam having such control over you.'

'I think,' Gloria said, 'I've just accepted that this is the way it's going to be for the time being ... Jack and I'll be all right. Things'll sort themselves out in time.'

Rosie looked at Gloria. Something told her that there might well be some other reason her friend seemed so resigned to the fact that Jack was not able to return home.

Chapter Eighteen

Tuesday 21 July

'Ohh, Helen, are yer sure? There's so many things to consider.'

Gloria was finding it hard to keep her voice level. She wanted to scream, plead and beg – do anything that might make Helen change her mind.

'I know this is what you feel like you want to do at this very moment in time,' Gloria desperately tried to keep her voice calm as she fed Hope, 'but you might feel different in a week or so. Perhaps you can hold off for a little while. Give yourself more time to think things through.'

Gloria looked at Helen, who was sitting on the bottom step that led from her basement flat up to the street. It had been a hot day and the evening was warm and muggy, making the flat feel airless. Sitting by the front door gave them a reprieve from the stuffiness, as well as providing some privacy as no one could see them unless they hung over the metal railings at the top.

'Gloria, I can't leave it any longer,' Helen said, fanning herself with her father's most recent letter. 'I'll be showing soon. Besides, the doctor said the sooner the better.'

Gloria shot a look at Helen.

'What doctor? What, you've seen someone already?' Gloria tried to keep calm but it was becoming increasingly difficult.

'Yes, up at the Royal. He's going to do it next week.'

'But I don't understand. I didn't think it was ... allowed. Legal?' Gloria wiped Hope's mouth and sat down on a chair that she had used to wedge open her front door.

'Well,' Helen said, 'like all things, it would seem that there are ways in which the laws of the land can be circumvented, especially if you've got money.'

Helen looked through into the living area to see Hope sitting up in her high chair, her bib covered in orange goo from the pureed carrots Gloria had just been feeding her.

'Well, I still don't like the sound of this one bit. Please let me talk to yer dad about all this?'

God, how she wished she could tell Jack. She was sure he would be able to talk some sense into her.

Helen shook her head.

'No. No way, Gloria. Remember, you promised me.'

'There are reasons these practices are against the law.' Gloria didn't particularly believe what she was saying, but she was clutching at straws. 'There are other ways around all of this,' she added.

'I'm sorry, Gloria. I know this wouldn't be what *you* would do, but this really is the only way for me,' Helen said, opening up her handbag and pulling out her cigarettes.

'If you don't want to keep the baby, how about having it adopted out?' Gloria suggested.

'I'm not going to disappear somewhere for the next six months,' Helen said, 'have a baby and then just hand it over to some stranger. I just couldn't do it. I know I couldn't.'

Suddenly Gloria was struck by an idea. Her face lit up.

'What about if I took the baby? Pretended it was mine. Then you wouldn't be handing your baby over to some stranger. You could come and see your baby as much as you wanted. She would be Hope's little sister.'

Hearing her name, Hope shouted out 'Mama.'

'Oh, Gloria.' Helen let out a sad laugh. 'You're even nuttier than I thought you were.' She shook her head, all the while her eyes fixed on her little sister.

'Why is that such a mad idea?' Gloria said, hoping upon hope that there must be some way to convince Helen to keep her baby.

'There's so many reasons,' Helen said, lighting her cigarette and blowing smoke up into the sky. 'I'd be here all night going through them all. Besides, I've made my decision. It's all arranged.'

Gloria disappeared into the kitchen, reappearing a few minutes later with two cups of tea. She handed one to Helen and perched herself back on the chair.

'All right, I'm not gonna keep harping on at ya, but I have to ask, have yer talked this through with yer mam?'

Helen let out a bitter laugh.

'God, she would be champing at the bit if she knew what I was going to do. In a roundabout way it was my dear mama that put the idea in my head in the first place.'

'What do you mean?' Gloria could feel her hackles rise.

'I overheard her and Granddad chatting about me – about my dire situation – and Mum said that the only real solution would be for me to "get rid of it".'

Gloria was aghast.

'But I'm sure she didn't really mean it.'

Helen let out another mirthless laugh.

'Oh, Gloria, she meant it. Believe you me, she meant it. She'd be over the moon if she was listening in to our conversation now. She'd be rushing faster than normal to the Grand to celebrate with that Amelia woman.'

Gloria was quiet. She knew there was truth in what Helen was saying.

'Which is exactly the reason why I'm not going to tell her. I'm going to make her suffer for as long as I can. Have her worry herself silly that she's going to be the talk of the town. That the family are going to be scandalised. And that she is going to suffer public humiliation. God knows what she'd do to try and keep it under wraps that the baby's father is a married man ... Now, that *would* have been interesting.'

Gloria sighed. Helen's anger towards her mother was seething out of every pore. And understandably so. She would feel exactly the same had she had a mother like Miriam.

'The funny thing is, if my love affair with Theo had been real and not a sham, I might have considered keeping the baby. I think I could have coped with the stigma if I had got pregnant outside of wedlock and the baby's father was someone I loved and who loved me back, or he'd had to go off to war, or died before we'd managed to get married, but I cannot have a baby by a man who doesn't love me, who's married to someone else, who's already got two children and has just had a third – a man who quite simply just used me and then tossed me away ... I cannot have a baby with someone like that.'

Gloria was quiet, trying desperately to think of the best thing to say.

'You know, Helen,' she said gently, 'it's not just *his* baby. It's *yours* as well. It would be tough, but you've just said yourself that you could deal with it. And you must know that your dad would be there to support you – and obviously it goes without saying that I'd be here too.'

'I think you're wrong about Dad,' Helen said sadly. 'He's more old-fashioned than you think. And I *am* his little girl, after all.'

'Helen, he's not going to judge you when he's had a child with a woman who's not his wife!'

Gloria wanted to shake Helen. She really did idolise her father – was terrified of being seen as anything less than perfect in his eyes.

'But that's different,' Helen said. 'It's different for men for starters, and I'm his *daughter*. Daughters don't go and get pregnant by married men who want nothing more to do with them.'

'Perhaps not,' Gloria agreed, 'but that doesn't mean yer dad 'n I won't be here to help you 'n yer baby. Yer won't be alone!'

Helen got up from the steps and walked back into the flat. She put her cup and saucer on the side and went over and picked up Hope, whose face had started to crease as though she was about to cry.

'What happens if something goes wrong?' Gloria said. She'd heard of the terrible after-effects that often befell women who had decided to end a pregnancy.

'Gloria, I've got one of the top gynaecologists in the whole of the north-east, who is also being paid an awful lot of money to do the job properly – as well as to keep his mouth shut. Believe you me, nothing'll go wrong,' Helen said simply.

'Well, you can never be sure with these things – top-notch doctor or not,' Gloria warned.

Helen didn't say anything. She'd had a good talk with the elderly Dr Billingham and it was clear he had been doing these sorts of operations for a good while. Besides, he had reassured her that she had been wise in acting so quickly and coming to him so early in the pregnancy.

'I know yer don't want to hear this,' Gloria said, watching Helen fuss over Hope, 'but you really would make a great mam. You're a natural with Hope.' She paused. 'I think you're making a huge mistake. I wish I could change yer mind. I really do.'

As Helen gave Hope a kiss and put her back in her high chair, she turned to Gloria. There were tears in her eyes and she did something that shocked Gloria – she gave her a hug.

'Well, I think *you're* a great mam.' Helen's words were spoken quietly and with a deep warmth.

'I just don't want you to do anything you might regret,' Gloria said.

'I won't,' Helen said. 'Believe you me, I won't.'

When Helen had gone, Gloria managed to get Hope down for the night without too much bother. She herself, though, felt restless and troubled. Not being able to chat to Jack about Helen and the difficulty his daughter had found herself in felt like trying to box with your hands behind your back. If Helen had been *her* daughter she was sure she would have been able to convince her to keep the baby.

But Helen wasn't her daughter.

She was Miriam's daughter.

And from what she had just been told, there was no way that Miriam would even try to get Helen to change her mind. Quite the reverse. She wouldn't *want* Helen to change her mind.

God, what hope did the poor girl have?

Chapter Nineteen

The GPO, Norfolk Street, Sunderland

Saturday 25 July

'I got another letter from Helen today!'

There was no disguising the happiness in Jack's voice.

'She spent most of the letter telling me about Hope. She really does love her little sister, doesn't she?'

'She does,' Gloria agreed. 'She's a real natural with her as well.'

All the more reason she shouldn't do what she's planning on doing! a voice in her head screamed.

'And,' Jack said, 'she's really keen to come up to the Clyde 'n visit sometime soon. She reckons she'll be able to get some time off work in a few weeks.'

Gloria had to bite her tongue. She knew the only reason Helen had made such a promise was because by that time she would no longer be with child.

'Yer know, Gloria, I really feel like things are on the up. You've got yer divorce, 'n I've got my daughter back. And my memory. And you've just had word from yer boys. I have a good feeling that everything's gonna turn out all right.'

Gloria had her ear pressed to the receiver, silently thanking the Lord that Jack could not see her face at this moment, otherwise he'd know straight away that something was wrong – that everything was far from turning out all right.

'Ah, that's great to hear, Jack. I'm sure it will ... So, how's work going?' Gloria asked, changing the subject. She didn't trust herself talking about Helen.

'Full pelt as usual,' Jack said. 'Ya know, it's like that terrible bombing last year has made the people here even more dogged. More defiant. Mind you, that's the Scots fer ya. They're a hardy lot. And bloody obstinate.'

As Jack chatted on, normally Gloria would have listened intently to every word he said, especially as the time they managed to speak to each other was precious, but today her mind was elsewhere. All she could think about was Helen – and, moreover, the urgency of her situation.

Just tell him! she berated herself.

If Gloria told Jack, there might be a good chance that he would be able to talk Helen around. That Helen would realise she was making a massive mistake and that they would support her.

But you made a promise! another voice screamed. Helen had made her swear that she would not tell her father, and Gloria had told Helen that she was a 'woman of my word'.

'You all right there, Glor?' Jack suddenly asked.

The two internal voices were silenced.

'Yes, yes, I'm fine, Jack. Sorry, I just got distracted there. Someone's trying to get me off the phone.'

'Well, tell them to bugger off!' Jack's voice was jocular. 'No, I'm only joking,' he added. 'Get yourself off. This must be costing yer a small fortune. Try 'n call me the same time next week. And don't forget to give Hope a big cuddle from me. I *do* miss her, yer know.'

'I know yer do, Jack.'

'All right, then, you put the phone down. But before you do, remember, *I love yer to pieces*.'

Gloria was quiet for a moment.

'Jack?'

'Yes, Glor?'

It was now or never.

'I just ... '

Another pause.

'I just wanted to tell you something ... '

'Go on, Glor – what is it?'

'I just wanted to say ... ' Gloria breathed heavily into the phone. 'I just wanted to say ... '

It was no good. She couldn't do it.

'I just wanted to say how much I love ya, Jack.'

Gloria felt her whole body deflate. She was in an impossible position. She couldn't betray Helen's trust. No matter how much she wanted to.

'Aye, I know yer do, Glor,' Jack said. 'Yer sound tired. Get yourself home 'n get some rest. I'll write to yer tomorrow.'

As Gloria pushed Hope home in the pram she felt completely alone.

Her head was stuffed so full of secrets she was now almost frightened to speak.

She couldn't tell her workmates the real reason Jack was not able to come home.

Nor could she tell them about Helen, and show them that she was not the 'witch' they all thought she was.

But worst of all, she wasn't able to tell Jack the truth about his own daughter, and thereby stop Helen doing something Gloria was sure she was going to regret.

Chapter Twenty

Monday 27 July

Helen stood at the open window of the office. She had a cigarette loosely scissored between her fingers, but she was not smoking it. Her pregnancy had affected her in ways she wouldn't have guessed. Her sense of smell seemed to be more acute, and although she had started to crave certain kinds of foods, some things tasted different. She had occasionally enjoyed a cup of coffee, but now she couldn't abide the taste. The same with smoking. She only took a few drags before either stubbing it out, or letting it burn to the butt.

She still made a show of smoking, though, as it gave her an excuse to just sit and think, or, like now, stand and look out at the yard.

'Sorry to bother you, Miss Crawford.' Marie-Anne broke through Helen's thoughts. 'But there's a gentleman here to see you. He says his name's Mr Parker. Mr John Parker.'

Helen looked over Marie-Anne's shoulder to see John standing in her office, looking uncomfortable.

'Well, if he *says* his name's Mr Parker, it probably *is*, Marie-Anne.' And with that Helen tossed her cigarette out the window and marched over to her office.

'John,' she said, closing the door behind her. 'Is everything all right?' She kept her voice low. 'Is everything still on for tomorrow?' Her voice was now almost a whisper.

'Yes, yes, no problems there,' Dr Parker said.

'Come, sit down.' Helen waved her arm at the chair. 'Thanks for not using your title.'

John put up his hand as if to stop her gratitude.

'I actually prefer *Mister*. As soon as people know you're a doctor, that's it, you're stuck listening to a list of their lifelong ailments and being asked for an immediate cure ... Do you mind if I take off my jacket?' he asked as he pulled the chair out. 'I can't believe how hot it is today.'

'It's been like this for weeks now,' Helen laughed. 'When was the last time you were out during the day?'

'I know. I think I'm going to turn into some kind of vampire, only leaving the sanctuary of the hospital when it's dark.' Dr Parker chuckled, slinging his dark grey jacket on the back of the chair.

'Can I get you anything?' Helen asked. 'A drink of anything? I can get one of the girls to go and get you a tray of tea and sandwiches if you like?'

Dr Parker shook his head. 'No, no, thank you anyway, Helen. I just really wanted to have a quick chat to you about tomorrow.'

Helen automatically went for her packet of cigarettes. She pulled one out but didn't light it.

'All right, fire ahead,' she said, suddenly hit by a flurry of nerves. She was fine whenever she was thinking – or, rather, daydreaming – about life after her pregnancy, but whenever she thought about the actual ending of the pregnancy itself, and the reality of what she was going to have done, she felt anything but fine.

'First of all,' Dr Parker said, 'are you happy for me to chat to you about it here? We can go somewhere else if you want? I've got the time. I don't have to be back at the hospital until two.'

'No, no, you're all right. It's pretty soundproof in here. Even if someone had their ear to the door they'd struggle to hear anything with the noise out in the yard.'

'Yes, it is pretty overwhelming, isn't it? I'm surprised everyone here's not partially deaf.'

'Pardon?' Helen said, deadpan.

John gave a bark of laughter, and Helen smiled. She wished more than anything that they could just sit and chat like two ordinary people, instead of talking about something so dreadfully serious.

Dr Parker leant forward and put his elbows on his legs and clasped his hands, his face now masked with a professional veneer.

'I know we've talked through all the ins and outs of what's going to happen.'

Helen nodded.

'But I just wanted to go over everything with you one more time.' Dr Parker looked into Helen's amazing eyes and realised with a jolt that what he saw was fear. His heart went out to her.

Personally, he was far from convinced that what she was doing was the right thing, but what did he know? For starters he was a man. And secondly, he had no idea how it must feel to be in Helen's shoes. This was her decision. And hers alone. He had a responsibility to help her, as he had promised he would. It was not his job to persuade her to do what *he* thought she should do, or what anyone else thought she should do, for that matter.

'So, first of all, you know where you're going and at what time, and who you should ask for?'

Helen nodded.

'And I know you've heard this all before, but I need to recap everything we have talked about thus far.'

This time he saw an incredible sadness in Helen's eyes.

He kept eye contact with Helen as he spoke softly but clearly and slowly.

He saw the change of emotions as he talked about the procedure, what would happen during it, and what would happen afterwards – as well as the possible side effects, and what might feasibly go wrong.

By the time he finished talking, he could see Helen's eyes were glistening with the beginnings of tears.

'Are you absolutely sure this is what you want to do, Helen?'

Helen nodded, not trusting herself to speak.

'Well, just remember, you can change your mind at any time.'

Helen tried to force a smile.

'I know,' she said, her voice croaky.

Dr Parker stood up.

'And remember,' he said, sliding his jacket off the back of the metal chair and hooking it over his arm, 'that once it's done, it's done, there's no changing your mind then.'

He was going to stop there, but something propelled him on and he said something that he hadn't intended to say:

'This is an important decision, Helen. It's one that you will have to live with for the rest of your life.'

When Dr Parker had gone, Helen shut her office door and went back to her desk to light her cigarette. It tasted awful, even made her feel a little queasy, but she forced herself to smoke, to push back the feelings that had come rushing to the surface.

Just do it! she told herself, as she pretended to rifle through a mound of invoices.

Just get it done and then forget it! she silently ordered herself as she took another long drag on her cigarette.

Chapter Twenty-One

Park Avenue, Roker

'So it's definitely happening tomorrow?'

Miriam was standing at the bay window that looked out onto the perfectly landscaped Roker Park, but she was not admiring the view. She was checking that her daughter was nowhere to be seen.

'Yes, that's what my sources say,' Mr Havelock said. He was sitting on the sofa, a large tumbler of whisky in one hand, his cigar in the other.

Miriam looked at her father. She had to hand it to him, he still carried weight – certainly in the town's hospitals. At least all that money he made a great show of donating was paying dividends.

'And the doctor – this Dr Billingham who's doing it – he's up to the mark?' Miriam asked.

'Of course. You don't think I'd have some butcher operating on my granddaughter, do you?' Mr Havelock groused. He'd known Billingham for a good number of years – decades, in fact – and he knew from experience that he was up to the job.

'And she definitely has no idea that we know?' Miriam asked, taking another drink, all the while keeping her eyes trained on the street.

'Of course not.' Mr Havelock's feathers were now getting ruffled by the barrage of questions. 'Billingham knows what side his bread's buttered. On top of which he's getting handsomely paid for both his expertise and his silence.' He took a drink. 'And, of course, the packet he got from coming to me in the first place.'

'Well, I have to say, I think we both deserve a huge pat on the back.' Miriam took another drink.

Mr Havelock huffed his agreement. 'Thank God the family name is saved from scandal.'

'Not for the first time,' Miriam said under her breath.

'What's that?' Mr Havelock put his hand to his ear.

'I was just saying, "In the nick of time,"' Miriam said.

'I'm just glad lady luck was on our side,' Mr Havelock picked up his cigar from the ashtray, 'and that the young doctor she's friendly with knew who to send her to.'

'I don't think we have lady luck to thank, dear Papa. Don't forget it was me who put the idea in Helen's head in the first place.'

'Well, I think we have her eavesdropping to thank for that,' Mr Havelock said. 'Although I personally think she would have come to the same decision even if she hadn't heard us talking that night.'

'Well … ' Miriam said. Getting a compliment out of her father was like getting blood out of a stone. 'Let's just thank our lucky stars she's getting rid of it. I don't even want to think about life if she'd decided to keep it … God, the humiliation. I'd never be able to show my face in public ever again.

'And not wanting to blow my own trumpet – but it's also thanks to me that she's not in communication with her father. I actually think she hates him now. And he's even stopped writing to her.'

'Really? That surprises me.' Mr Havelock thought for a moment. 'If they had been getting on, do you reckon Jack would have tried to stop her? Do you think he would have *wanted* her to have the bastard?' Mr Havelock took a puff on his cigar.

'Without a doubt,' Miriam said, coming away from the window. She stared at her father, who looked like he was getting settled for the evening.

'Well,' Miriam made a show of looking at her watch, 'I don't want to seem like I'm kicking you out, but I think it might be a good idea if you're not here when Helen gets back. She'll be in any minute now and we don't want her thinking we're here conspiring against her again.'

In truth, Miriam thought it unlikely that Helen would be back for a good while. Ever since the fiasco with Theodore, she'd been working late most nights. But time was getting on and she didn't want to keep Amelia – or their two naval officers – waiting, did she?

Chapter Twenty-Two

Tuesday 28 July

After Helen had zipped up her vanity case, she sat back down on her bed.

It had just gone six o'clock. She still had another two hours before she had to be at the hospital. She'd given up on sleep at five and had slowly got ready – not that she had much to do as she'd been instructed not to put on any make-up and to wear loose, comfortable clothing.

Dr Parker had offered to meet her there, but she'd declined. And Gloria had also offered to go with her, but even if Helen had wanted her there, it simply wasn't an option.

Picking up her little cream leather case, Helen quietly tiptoed downstairs, not wanting to wake her mother. The last thing she needed was for her to start quizzing her about where she was going in a floral cotton dress with not a scrap of make-up on.

As the sun was already up and she had plenty of time, Helen decided to walk part of the way. It was certainly early enough for her to do so without the worry of bumping into anyone she knew.

As she strolled along the coast road, her mind started to wander and a picture of Hope came to the fore. Helen had taken her a lovely little green and blue dress the other day and Gloria had commented that it perfectly matched Hope's eyes. Helen had agreed; it was why she had chosen it.

Hope really was such an adorable little girl, and it never ceased to amaze her how similar she and her little sister were in looks. She had clearly inherited the Crawford dark locks and her own startling emerald eyes.

Walking past the Bungalow Café and following the road around onto Harbour View, Helen started to wonder:

What would my child have looked like?

Would she have looked like Hope?

Helen suddenly stopped walking.

Stop it! she silently screamed at herself. She felt like slapping herself on the head, knocking such stupid thoughts out of her thick skull.

Why are you thinking this now?

Helen started walking again, faster, as if by doing so she might leave her thoughts behind.

She strode along Dame Dorothy Street, looking down at Crown's shipyard and then at Thompson's. Looking up, she saw the granite grey barrage balloon, like a lost thundercloud that had drifted into a perfectly clear blue sky.

'Look to your future.' Helen said the words out loud, determined to override thoughts of the child that would never be, forcing herself to replay the scene in her head of the launch of SS *Brutus*, her father by her side, looking as proud as punch.

Having reached the Wearmouth Bridge, but still not wanting to stand still and wait for a tram to take her over to the other side, Helen kept on walking.

When she reached Park Lane, however, she started to tire, and was glad to climb on board a single-decker bus headed for New Durham Road.

By the time it pulled up at the Royal, Helen had successfully put her thoughts back on track. She focused on the future – when she would be free of this burden in her belly and be at liberty to do as she wished, to enjoy the success that awaited her, but that would only be hers without the encumbrance of a child.

Walking along to the hospital, Helen looked at her watch. She was early. She looked over at the entrance to Burn Park and decided to go and sit on one of the benches and continue to focus her thoughts on what was to be.

Just like the array of colourful flower beds that had been carefully nurtured in this little floral haven, her future looked rosy.

Didn't it?

'You ready, Parker?' The surgeon looked across the tray of glinting stainless-steel surgical instruments. He hoped they would do more good than harm in extracting the shrapnel from the deep wound in the young soldier's leg.

'Get with it, Parker! You look miles away there. I need you focused on the job in hand.'

'Yes, sir, all ready. Fully focused, sir,' Dr Parker reassured, looking over at his superior.

The head surgeon he had been assigned to today had read him well. He *had* been miles away – approximately five miles away at the Royal.

He had been arguing with himself all night whether to ring this morning and say he had been called away on a family emergency so that he could go and meet Helen. He had wanted to be there to talk to her one last time, to make sure she really was certain that this was what she wanted. When he had seen her at Thompson's yesterday, he'd picked up a hint of uncertainty – seen a mix of emotions flit across the surface of those incredible eyes of hers.

'Scalpel,' the surgeon demanded from the theatre nurse.

Dr Parker's heart went out to Helen. She tried to make out she was incredibly self-assured and a woman of the world, but she was anything but. If she *had* been, she wouldn't presently be waiting to go into surgery herself.

No, there was absolutely no doubt in his mind whose fault this all was.

Theodore bloody Harvey-Smith.

He had used Helen's naïvety to get what he wanted, but it was Helen who was paying the price.

As Dr Parker watched the surgeon prepare to begin the operation, he wished more than anything that it was Theodore laid out unconscious in front of him – and that it was his own hand that was about to make the first incision.

'Pol, will you tell Rosie that something's come up?' Gloria was staring at her workmate and praying she wouldn't ask too many questions.

'Yes, course I will.' Polly looked at Gloria, puzzled. She'd seemed distracted from the moment she had arrived to drop off Hope.

'Is everything all right?' she asked.

'Nothing serious,' Gloria said, starting to turn and make her way back up the embankment onto High Street East.

'It's just something I've got to do,' she said, raising her voice as she moved against the swell of bodies heading towards the ferry.

'How long will you be?' Polly shouted as she herself was pushed forward by the incoming tide of flat caps.

'Couple of hours. Tops!' Gloria's voice could be heard, but she was no longer visible.

When Gloria reached the main road, she looked to see if there was either a bus or a tram coming, but there wasn't.

'Typical!' she said aloud as she started to break into a jog.

By the time she reached the centre of town she was dripping with sweat. Running in heavy leather boots on a hot summer's morning was bloomin' hard work. Gloria looked at the clock hanging above the main office of the bus depot. She wouldn't make it if she ran, but she would have a chance if a bus came in the next few minutes.

As luck would have it, a bus pulled up. Gloria paid her fare and thanked the gods above when the driver immediately revved the engine and drove out of the station.

Helen looked at her watch. It was a quarter to eight. Time to go. As she walked across to the Royal, she couldn't help but think that it was the most beautiful yet the most awful day ever.

As she stepped through the swing doors and followed the signs to the gynaecology ward, she tried to keep her mind on the future. On tomorrow. When all of this would be over with and she could begin her new life.

So why couldn't she get John's blasted last words to her out of her mind?

'This is an important decision, Helen. It's one that you will have to live with for the rest of your life.'

When Gloria reached the hospital it was gone eight.

'Still time,' she muttered as she stepped into the cool of the hospital reception area, walked straight ahead, then turned right down a long corridor. She knew where she was going. She'd had both boys in this hospital and would have had Hope here as well had her impatient little girl not decided to make an early appearance.

Reaching the thick swing doors of the gynaecology ward, Gloria peered through the small glass panels in the top, but was unable to see Helen.

Pushing the doors open, she saw the ward nurse sitting behind a table to the right. Gloria was suddenly conscious of how she must look. A red-faced, middle-aged woman in dirty overalls and hobnailed boots. Still, she didn't care. She had to see Helen. Sod the consequences.

'Sorry to bother yer,' Gloria put on her friendly face and tried to appear calm and normal, 'but I'm looking fer a friend of my daughter. She will have just been admitted. She's probably just come in, actually.'

'Oh, yes.' The young nurse looked down her admissions list, which was attached to a clipboard lying on her desk. 'Helen Dodds.'

For a moment Gloria was puzzled, before realising that Helen was obviously not going to be there under her real name.

'That's her. Helen Dodds,' Gloria repeated.

The young nurse looked back down at her list and then fumbled around for another sheet of paper before looking up again.

'Oh, looks like she was first on this morning's rota.' She smiled up at Gloria. 'Always good to be first to go down. No hanging about.' The nurse smiled again.

Gloria stared at her.

'What? So she's gone down to surgery already?'

The pretty blonde nurse nodded again.

'Yes, the porters wheeled her down a few minutes ago.'

Gloria felt her heart sink to the bottom of her boots.

'Did you want me to give her a message when she comes back up?' the nurse asked.

Gloria shook her head.

'No, no … Thanks anyway.'

And with that Gloria turned and made her way out of the hospital and back to work.

Chapter Twenty-Three

A week later

Tuesday 4 August

'"Victory. Victory at all costs. Victory in spite of all terror. Victory, however long and hard the road may be, for without victory there is no survival."'

Dorothy stood on a crate, the end of a welding rod in her hand, pinching it between two fingers as if it were a real cigar.

Angie, Martha, Hannah and Olly were chuckling away at Dorothy's midday performance. A group of caulkers sitting eating their lunch by the quayside were also laughing at Dorothy's very convincing imitation of the country's leader.

Rosie, Gloria and Polly looked at each other and shook their heads in mock disapproval.

'And may I introduce to you my lovely wife, Clementine.' Dorothy threw her arm out in Angie's direction.

'Give over, Dor.' Angie shuffled back on the bench she was sitting on. As she did so she caught sight of Bel walking across the yard.

'Here's Bel! She can be your Clementine,' Angie declared.

'No, she can't!' Bel shouted back. She had been watching Dorothy's impression as she had walked across the yard. 'I've come here for a bit of peace and quiet.'

Everyone laughed.

'Well, I don't think you'll ever get that here, certainly not when we have our very own female Laurel and Hardy as part of the squad.'

Angie tutted at the comparison. 'Why do I think I'd be the skinny one that's always scratching his head 'n being bullied by the fat one?'

Dorothy jumped down off the crate and pulled out an old jumper she'd found in the shed and used to create Churchill's substantial girth.

'I don't bully you, Ange. Do I?' She looked around the women for support and was met with a silent show of solidarity for Angie.

'Talking of which,' Rosie looked at Angie, who was taking off her headscarf and tucking her blonde hair behind her ears, 'has Dorothy managed to coerce you into moving yet?'

Angie opened her mouth to speak, but Dorothy beat her to it.

'I wish! I've never known anyone to procrastinate so much in my entire life.'

'Speak English, Dor!' Angie demanded.

'Put off … dither!' Dorothy sounded genuinely exasperated.

'But I thought you were going to tell yer mam and dad over the weekend, Angie?' Gloria asked as she took a seat on what had been Dorothy's soapbox.

'I was, but Mam had to do more overtime, so I still haven't managed to get them together.'

'Why don't you tell your mam first,' Gloria suggested. 'But tell her not to let on she knows – then you tell your da. That way your dad still thinks he's the big man and head of the house, but your mam is happy because you've actually told her first.'

'Bloomin' good idea, Glor!' Angie said.

'Yes,' Dorothy was nodding enthusiastically, 'and that way everyone's happy and you manage to keep the peace – and then we can finally move in!'

'Eee, I could learn a lot from you lot!' Bel said. She and Polly were now sitting on top of a pile of wooden pallets.

Rosie laughed. 'Yes, the wily woman's art of manipulation.'

'You better get a move on, Angie,' Gloria piped up, 'otherwise George might rent his flat out to someone else.'

A look of panic shot across Dorothy's face and she looked to Rosie, who gave her the reassurance she was looking for with a quick shake of her head.

'So,' Hannah said, looking over at Bel, who was drinking her tea and nibbling on a corned-beef sandwich. 'How's life in administration?'

'Yes, all good, thanks, Hannah. I can now type using all my fingers, but I'm still pretty slow.'

'And what about Helen?' Martha asked. 'She giving you any hassle?'

'No, no hassle,' Bel chuckled, although she didn't think she would tell them if she was being picked on as she seriously believed they would lynch Helen if she was anything but nice to her. The sunny weather might be making everyone feel a bit chirpier but none of the women had warmed at all towards their nemesis. Apart from Gloria, of course, who had told Bel when they had been on their own that she really didn't think Helen was as bad as everyone made out.

'To be honest,' Bel added, 'I've not really seen her giving anyone any hassle. I mean, she's not exactly the friendliest boss you could ask for. She's ever so curt when she's speaking to Marie-Anne, but I've not heard her really sound off at anyone.'

Bel had, in fact, been keeping a sharp eye out whenever Helen came out of her office. She was intrigued by her, which, she realised, wasn't so surprising. The two of them were, after all, related. Not that anyone would ever have guessed. Although having seen Miriam, it would not take such a great leap of faith to believe that Bel was related to Helen's ma. When she had seen her that afternoon in the Grand it had been like looking at an older version of herself, twenty years from now.

'Helen's probably all taken up with that toffee-nosed fella we've seen her with,' Angie said, biting into a slightly bruised apple.

'Oh, I don't reckon she's still with him.' The words were out before Gloria had time to swallow them.

'What makes you say that?' Polly asked. She still wanted to know everything about Helen, even though just talking about her made her angry.

'I'm just guessing,' Gloria said, quickly trying to cover her tracks, 'as our two eagle-eyed socialites here haven't seen her on the town for months now.'

'Miss Not-so-prim-and-proper and her Prince Charming have probably just had their fill of slumming it,' Dorothy said.

'Yeh, they probably go to the Palatine or the Empress or somewhere like that now.'

'Anyway, talking of going out,' Bel said, 'I actually came over for a reason.'

Everyone looked at Bel in her colourful dress. She stood out like a sore thumb amongst the dirt-smeared grey and blue denim.

'It's Lucille's fourth birthday a week on Saturday, so she's going to have a little tea party with a few of her friends from around the doors and I wondered if you wanted to come along near the end and we could all go for a drink in the Tatham?' Bel looked at Gloria. 'And I do believe there's a very special little girl going to be one year old on the

Thursday before, so I wondered if we should perhaps have a joint celebration?'

'That sounds like a marvellous idea,' Gloria said. 'Are you sure Lucille won't mind sharing her special day?'

'No, I've checked with Her Highness,' Bel laughed, 'and she said in that very grown-up way of hers that she wouldn't mind at all.'

'Ah, I'm afraid I won't be able to make it, Bel. I'm going to see Charlotte in Harrogate that weekend,' Rosie said. She grimaced slightly. 'God help me.'

'That bad?' Bel asked.

Rosie nodded. 'Honestly, she'd try the patience of a saint at the moment.'

Dorothy opened her mouth to speak.

'Don't, Dorothy, don't say it. If another person tells me to just "let her come home" one more time, I might just scream.'

Bel stood up and dusted her dress of crumbs. 'Hannah, can you tell your aunty Rina that I'll be popping by sometime over the weekend to see if she and Vera can sort out a birthday cake, but please tell her there's to be no special discount ... Anyway, I best be getting back. Don't want to be seen as a slacker.' She picked up her flask and lunch box. 'See you all later.'

As Gloria watched Bel head back to the administration offices, she saw Helen looking out the window. Her face looked stony-serious, or was that just her imagination?

It had been a week now since she had gone to try and stop Helen from ending her pregnancy. She had no idea how she was. Helen hadn't come round to the flat, which, she guessed, was because she was tired and recovering. Still, there hadn't been a day gone by this past week that Gloria hadn't cursed herself for not getting to the hospital just a few minutes earlier. If she had, she might have been able to stop her. But now she'd never know.

Those few minutes, Gloria knew, would always plague her.

'You all right?'

Gloria's thoughts were broken by Rosie, who had been watching her workmate looking over at the main admin building.

'Yes, yes,' Gloria said. 'Just in a daze. It's this weather. Makes you feel half asleep sometimes.'

'You don't mind taking over the reins while I'm off seeing Charlotte, do you?' Rosie asked.

'Course not,' Gloria said. 'You gonna finally tell her you've got married?'

Rosie nodded. 'I wish I hadn't put it off. Wish I'd just bitten the bullet and told her when I saw her last. Or even just written to her right afterwards.'

Gloria looked at Rosie's worried face.

'She's gonna give you hell, you know?'

'I know,' Rosie said.

'And she'll use it as leverage to come back here,' Gloria added.

'I know,' Rosie said for the second time.

When the klaxon sounded out and they all made their way back over to *Brutus*, Dorothy caught up with Gloria and nudged her gently.

'Thanks, Glor.'

'What for?'

'For your suggestion.'

'About Angie telling her mam first and then her dad?'

Dorothy nodded.

'I'm guessing this is a big move for Angie. What's that word you used?'

'Procrastinate?'

'That's the one. Delaying tactics. You do think she wants to move, don't you?'

Dorothy was quiet for a moment.

'Yes, I'm pretty sure she's up for it. I honestly think she's just worried about upsetting her mam and dad. Angie might seem like a right toughie, but when it comes to her family, she's really soft. And it's not helped by Liz running off to join the lumberjills.'

Gloria laughed. 'You make it sound like she eloped.'

'Might as well have,' Dorothy said in all seriousness. 'It's had the same effect. Left Angie with all the responsibility. I could strangle that mother of hers. She just flits about doing exactly what she wants – and Angie has to cover for her.'

'What do you mean, *cover for her*?' Gloria asked.

Dorothy didn't say anything, but raised her eyebrows.

'Well, let's put it this way,' she dropped her voice. 'I don't think her mam's always doing the overtime she claims to be doing.'

Gloria's eyes widened.

So, Angie did know about her mam's affair.

'But, for goodness' sake, Glor, don't breathe a word,' Dorothy begged.

'Course, I won't,' Gloria said.

'Not a whisper?' Dorothy said.

'Not a dicky bird,' Gloria reassured. 'I'm a woman of my word.'

Gloria sighed inwardly.

Sometimes, life would be easier if she wasn't.

Chapter Twenty-Four

Four days later

Saturday 8 August

'I did it!' Angie was walking down the top of Foyle Street with a heavy overnight bag banging against her legs. She was still in her work overalls, but her shoulder-length blonde hair had been freed from its headscarf.

Dorothy was waving, but took a step back so that Angie could see that George was also with her outside the flat.

George held out his hand to Angie. 'Well, whatever you did, it sounds like it was a good thing!'

'Aye, it was, sir. A very good thing.' Angie shook hands with George.

'No need for the *sir*, "George" is just fine by me ... Right, well, you've seen the flat before, so there's no need for me to come in and show you around.' He fumbled in his pocket. 'So, here's two sets of keys. One for you, Dorothy. And one for you, Angela. The smaller of the two is for the main entrance.' George looked up at the black front door framed by two narrow stone pillars. 'And the large one is for the actual door to the flat.'

'Thank you, sir,' Angie said. Her face was flushed from having hauled her heavy bag across town.

'Thank you, George.' Dorothy paused. 'Are you sure you don't want any rent now? Upfront. In advance.'

'No, I shall pop around at six o'clock next Friday for the rent and will do so every week thereafter. If you're working overtime, just tell Rosie and I'll come later, or on Saturday at a time that suits.'

'Thank you, sir,' Angie said.

George suppressed a chuckle. Rosie had told him about the youngest of her crew and how she insisted on calling her 'miss', no matter how many times she'd told her it wasn't necessary.

'And if for whatever reason it does not suit you both and you decide to vacate the property, just tell me.'

'No, I'm sure we're going to be more than happy here,' Dorothy said, nudging Angie.

'Oh, definitely. More than happy,' Angie said, copying Dorothy.

'Righty-ho then, I'll get myself off. Got an old friend round on John Street I'm off to see.' He shook both Dorothy's and Angie's hands again, tipped his fedora and hobbled off down the street, leaning heavily on his walking stick, but still managing to make haste.

'Oh, Angie. This is *so* exciting!' Dorothy had to stop herself grabbing her friend and twirling her around on the street.

'I know,' Angie said. 'Eee, I've got loads to tell ya.'

Dorothy raised her keys in the air. 'Let's get a brew on then, shall we!'

Letting themselves into the property, which had been split up into three decent-sized flats, they trudged up two flights of stairs, before dumping their bags outside their new front door.

'I'm glad we've got the top flat,' Dorothy said. 'Means we won't have anyone stomping around above us.' She opened the door and they walked in.

The place was spotlessly clean.

'Cor.' Angie's eyes were agog. 'I still can't believe we've got our own bedrooms. I've never had my own room. And look, there's sheets and blankets on the bed!'

Dorothy, meanwhile, was looking in the small bathroom. 'He's even left us a new bar of soap and some towels.'

Angie came in and touched the towels. 'Blimey, feel how soft they are!'

'Come on, let's have that brew,' Dorothy said. 'Then I reckon we get ourselves cleaned up and go and see Gloria and Hope.'

'Eee,' Angie said, 'you might have to drag me out of that bath. Out of this flat, actually.'

'Come on, let's get the tea made. I want to hear what happened with your mam and dad.'

'Well, I couldn't believe how well it all went.' Angie was sitting at the little dining-room table with her china cup held like she was drinking tea with the King, her little finger sticking out to the side.

'I did just like Gloria said. I went to see my mam first. Caught her coming out of work.' She paused. 'Before she nicked off to see that bloke of hers.'

'What did she say?' Dorothy asked, pulling out a packet of biscuits from her own bulging holdall she'd dumped on the kitchen floor.

'She was all right about it. I mean she had a moan about me 'n Liz leaving her with all the bairns, and she groaned that she "didn't know how she was gonna manage".'

Dorothy huffed. 'Well, they are *her* "bairns"!'

'Aye, exactly.' Angie took another dainty sip of her tea. 'I said to her if she wasn't sloping off with that bit of stuff from Howick Street every spare minute, she might be able to manage better.'

'Really!' Dorothy's eyes were wide. 'What did she say when you said that?'

'She gave me a look like the summons,' Angie said, opening up the packet of biscuits. 'I thought she was gonna give us a slap, but she just said that I was obviously a big girl now with an even bigger gob 'n I could do what I wanted.'

'So what did you do then?' Dorothy said as she watched Angie retrieve a plate from the cupboard and lay the biscuits out. Normally she'd just scoff them straight from the packet.

'So, then I went to see my dad. Caught him just as he was about to leave for the night shift. The neighbours had the bairns so it was nice 'n quiet for a change 'n I just told him that I'd got this great flat with you, 'n I was moving out.'

'What did he say?' Dorothy was entranced.

'He said the same as Mam – mithered on about how would they manage, especially now Liz was gone. I told him it was the same as if me 'n Liz had both got married. We wouldn't be there then. He thought for a while, which is hard work fer ma dad.' Angie chuckled as she picked up a biscuit, holding her hand underneath so as not to drop any crumbs. Again it was something Dorothy had never seen her do. 'And then he just said, "Aye, yer reet there, Angela. Well, if yer mam gives yer the thumbs up, then get yerself off!"'

Dorothy clapped her hands in excitement.

'As soon as he was out the door, I crammed as much into my bag as possible, and I tore out the house. I was so excited! I jumped on a tram 'n practically sprinted from Fawcett Street to here.' Angie looked round the flat with a big smile on her face. 'Eee, I can't believe this is our new home?'

'I know, me neither,' Dorothy agreed, with an equally big grin on her face.

'Go on then, let's get ourselves ready and go and see Gloria. Tell her the good news,' Dorothy said, as Angie popped the rest of the biscuit into her mouth and headed for the bathroom.

'So, what did *your* mam 'n dad say?' Angie shouted through the bathroom door as she gave herself a wash-down. 'Or rather *yer mam*,' Angie corrected herself, knowing that Dorothy would not even have considered asking her stepfather's permission.

'God, you know my mother,' Dorothy said. 'Hardly batted an eyelid. The girls were running riot and little Christie was demanding her attention, as always. All she said was to make sure I left her the address so she knew where I was, and was it "normal for two girls to be living together?"'

'What did she mean by that?' Angie said.

'She thinks I should be married now and settled down. She hates it when I tell her I'm never getting married.'

'Do yer really never want to get married, Dor?' Angie's head popped round the door. She was drying her face on the fluffy white towel, which Dorothy noticed had *G.R.M.* embroidered in gold thread in the bottom corner.

'Nah, I just say it to wind her up.'

'Well, Dor, I reckon I'm gonna marry someone really rich so I can afford to buy towels like this one.' Angie put the towel against her cheek and closed her eyes in bliss.

'Well, I'll have to give you intensive elocution lessons if that really is your aim.'

'Ah, Dor, I wish you would use words I understood.' Angie reappeared from the bathroom, her face glowing clean, wearing a slightly crumpled cotton dress.

'Go on, your turn!' she declared, holding the bathroom door open for her friend.

While Dorothy washed her face, Angie did another tour of the flat. Walking into one of the bedrooms, she noticed that there was a loft. Taking a chair from the kitchen, she reached up and opened the little hatch. Poking her head through, she looked around, and as her eyes adjusted to the dark, she spotted a small paper bag and what looked like a pile of rags. She reached out and pulled them towards her. A small cloud of dust and dirt made her sneeze.

'I've found summat in the loft!' she shouted down to Dorothy, who was doing a rather good Judy Garland impression of 'Over the Rainbow' in the bathroom.

Angie tossed the paper bag onto the bed. It made a clinking sound as it landed. She pulled the rags, which seemed to be made from some kind of heavy green material, and let them fall freely to the ground. Jumping off the chair, she looked down at what she could now see was an old uniform. She sneezed again as she shook it out, producing another cloud of dust. She laid the khaki green uniform on the bed and picked up a peaked cap. She then opened up the paper bag and emptied the contents onto the bed.

She gasped as a cluster of medals and ribbons were revealed.

'Dor! Come and see what I found!'

Dorothy hurried through to the bedroom. She too was now wearing a summer dress, not unlike the one Angie had on.

'Blimey, Ange, where did that come from?'

Angie raised her eyes to the ceiling.

'The loft? You've been in the loft?'

'I just thought I'd have a neb 'n I found all this ... '

They both stared at the creased-up officer's uniform, the cap that was covered in cobwebs, and the mound of medals that were in need of a good polish.

'I'm guessing it belongs to George,' Angie said.

'Gosh.' Dorothy was looking closely at the medals. 'These are really impressive medals.'

'What do you mean?'

'I mean, they're pretty rare, which means George must have done something pretty spectacularly brave to get them.'

Angie stood and stared.

'Eee, you'd never think it, looking at him, would ya? I mean ... he's skinny as a rake ... *and* posh ... *and* old.'

'Well, he wouldn't have been old in the First War,' Dorothy mused, 'and being posh or skinny doesn't mean you can't be brave.'

'What shall we do with it all?'

They were both quiet.

'Shall we stick it back in the loft? We don't want him thinking we've been nosing around.'

'No, it doesn't seem right shoving it all back up there.' Dorothy looked around the room. 'Let's hang the uniform in the wardrobe for the time being.'

'And leave the medals out on the side. We can shine them up later.' Dorothy spread the medals out on top of the chest of drawers.

'Come on then, let's go and see Gloria and Hope,' Dorothy said as they both left the bedroom and made their way along the short hallway. After they shut their front door and began to make their way down the two flights of stairs, Angie leant into Dorothy and whispered, 'Do yer know anything about the others who live here?'

When they got to the bottom, Dorothy whispered back, 'Just that the basement flat is owned by some bloke who works for local government. And that his name's Quentin.'

'Quentin? He sounds posh,' Angie said, as they stepped out the front door and walked down half a dozen stone steps that led to the pavement.

'I think you can safely say he will *most definitely* be posh with a name like that, Ange.'

When they stood on the pavement they looked up at their new home and linked arms.

'Eee, I'm dead chuffed, Dor.' Angie looked at her friend.

'Me too, Ange, *dead chuffed*.'

They both stood for a moment before they turned to continue on their way. They let an old man and his wife past, but when they saw who was walking behind the elderly couple, they remained rooted to the spot.

'Oh!' Dorothy couldn't keep the shock out of her voice. 'Helen! What a coincidence to see you here.'

Helen looked equally taken aback.

'Likewise!' Her reply was curt, but she couldn't keep the surprise out of her voice either.

The three women stood looking at each other, no one knowing what to say.

'You two visiting friends?' Helen asked eventually, knowing she had to say something.

'Actually, Angie and I have just moved into a flat here.' Dorothy looked up at the house. Angie was standing ever so slightly behind Dorothy, but had followed her friend's gaze and was now proudly looking up at their new abode.

'Oh, that's nice.' Helen was the epitome of politeness as she gave them a tight smile. 'Well, nice to see you both. Have a good evening.'

And with that Helen went on her way.

Dorothy and Angie walked at a distance behind her as they were all clearly heading in the same direction. They noticed Helen was carrying a neatly wrapped present with a pretty pink bow on it. When she reached the end of the street she turned right, as did Dorothy and Angie. Helen walked along Borough Road. As she passed Gloria's basement, she turned her head slightly but carried on walking.

Angie nudged Dorothy.

'Eee, for a moment there I thought she was gannin to Gloria's!'

'Cooeee! Glor, it's us! Your two favourite people! Dor and Ange!'

Gloria came hurrying to her front door. She had heard the knock and had been convinced it was Helen before she heard the terrible two's distinctive voices.

'Come in, come in!' Gloria ushered them both into the flat.

'Oh, my God, Glor! We've got loads to tell you.' Dorothy bustled in, followed by an excited-looking Angie.

'We've just moved into the flat and Ange's told her mam and dad!'

'Eee, Glor, it's lovely. Nippin' clean, we've got a bedroom each, and an indoor bathroom – and there's even towels!' Angie said, her eyes wide as if to stress the point.

'*And* we found an old officer's uniform and some pretty impressive medals,' Dorothy said.

'In the loft,' Angie added.

'But,' Dorothy said dramatically, 'wait until you hear who we just bumped into?'

Gloria felt as though she had just been caught in a whirlwind. Despite her workmates' verbal bombardment, though, she knew instinctively who it was that they'd 'just bumped into'.

She feigned innocence. 'No, who?'

'Helen!' Dorothy and Angie spoke in unison.

'Never!' Gloria hoped she sounded suitably shocked.

'Yeh, 'n she looked like she was off to a party or summat, 'cos she was carrying a present with a geet big pink bow on it.'

As she made them all cups of tea and Dorothy and Angie chatted on whilst fussing over Hope, Gloria's mind kept wandering to Helen. She had clearly been on her way round to see her. Gloria had tried not to worry about Helen these past ten days, but hadn't succeeded. Her mind would only be put to rest when she managed to see her and find out how everything had gone – and, most importantly, ask her how she was feeling.

And as much as Gloria thought the world of the two young girls presently buzzing about her flat, chatting away and laughing, she wished their new digs hadn't been quite so near to her own.

Chapter Twenty-Five

'Bloody, bloody typical!' Helen murmured under her breath as she carried on walking along Borough Road. 'Out of all the places in town those two could have rented, they had to get somewhere right next to Gloria.'

Helen turned right up Fawcett Street and jumped on a tram. She might as well go straight home.

This was so frustrating.

She'd tried to see Gloria and Hope the other day, but they'd not been in. She'd been really looking forward to seeing them this evening – had even nipped into town and bought a really cute sun hat for Hope at Risdon's. It was to be an early birthday present, as she'd heard Bel chatting to some of the workers the other day, telling them about her daughter, Lucille, and how she was having a joint birthday party with her friend's little girl, who was just about to turn one. When Helen had realised it was Hope she was talking about, she'd stupidly felt hurt that she hadn't been invited.

So what if Hope was her sister? Even if it did become common knowledge, she was in no doubt that she would be the last person Polly's sister-in-law, or any of the other women welders, would want to invite to any kind of a social do.

Helen looked down at the perfectly wrapped present in her lap.

Well, it looked like she'd just have to wait to give it to Hope.

*

When Helen walked through her front door, she sensed that, for once, she was not coming into an empty house. When she stepped into the hallway her instinct was proven right.

'Helen, is that you?'

'Who else is it going to be, Mother?' Helen said, wearily. She had actually got used to coming home to an empty house. Quite enjoyed it now. The only person she was ever really pleased to see when she got home was Mrs Westley the cook, but she was usually gone by the time Helen got back from work.

'I'm in the sitting room!' It was an order as opposed to a statement.

Helen deliberately walked past the open door of the front reception room and carried on through the breakfast room and into the kitchen. Her spirits lifted when she saw that Mrs Westley had left one of her scrumptious homemade steak and kidney pies on top of the Aga.

Miriam tried to curtail her anger at being so blatantly ignored.

'Are you deaf?' Miriam's sing-song, but slightly shrill voice resounded through the house as she went to find her daughter.

'No, Mother,' Helen said, cutting herself a piece of pie. 'My hearing's fine, thanks for asking.'

'I was actually hoping,' Miriam softened her tone, 'that you and I might have a little chat.'

Helen looked at her mother's face.

The pair now barely spoke to each other.

'Mother, why don't you just tell me what it is you want. It always unnerves me when you try to be nice.'

Miriam let out a tinkle of laughter.

'Oh, Helen, I'm *always* nice.'

Helen gave her mother a look of disbelief, sat down at the kitchen table and forked a large piece of pie into her mouth.

'Mm, Mum,' she said through a mouthful of food, 'you really want to try this pie. Mrs Westley has surpassed herself.'

Miriam took a deep breath, forcing herself to keep calm. She was determined this conversation they were about to have would build a bridge across their fractured relationship. Now that her daughter had done what she was supposed to, she wanted her back as an ally. Or at least, for life to be back to the way it had been before this Theodore debacle.

'I'll give the pie a miss this evening, darling. But I will be sure to tell Mrs Westley how much you relished it,' Miriam said, all the while thinking she would, in fact, be lambasting the cook for defying her orders yet again. Helen would look like the back end of a bus if Mrs Westley had her way. At least, she thought, she no longer had to worry about Helen gaining excess weight for any other reason.

'So, Mother, what is it you wanted to chat to me about?' Helen put another forkful of food into her mouth.

Miriam had to bite her tongue. 'Darling, why don't you stop eating for a moment? There's nothing more uncouth than talking with your mouth full.'

Helen could feel her hackles starting to rise. Putting her knife and fork down, she glowered at her mother.

'All right, Mother. Go on, spit it out. Tell me whatever it is you want to tell me – or ask – and then you can get back to the Grand, and I can continue to enjoy Mrs Westley's pie.'

'Well ... ' Miriam sat down on the kitchen bench opposite her daughter and reached out to take her hand. 'I just wanted to say to you, darling, that I'm so pleased you saw sense.'

Helen looked at her mother for a moment, confused. A myriad thoughts flashed across her mind.

'Sorry, Mum, I'm not sure what you mean?'

Miriam stretched her other arm across the table and took hold of Helen's other hand.

'I mean, what you did the other week … Or rather … ' she paused ' … what you *had done* the other week.'

Helen stared at her mother. She pulled her hands away.

'What did I "have done"?' She could feel her heart pounding. *Did her mother know?*

'Darling.' Miriam tried to take hold of Helen's hand again, but Helen pulled it out of reach. 'You know? The solution to your little problem?'

Helen could feel the anger rising inside her.

'How did you know?' Helen paused. 'How did you know about the solution to what you call my *little* problem?'

'Your grandfather – who else?' Miriam fought down the irritation welling up inside her. This was proving harder work than anticipated.

'And how did Grandfather know about it?' Helen demanded.

'Oh, Helen, my dear, you should know by now that nothing in this town – and especially anything out of the ordinary that might take place in any of our hospitals – gets past his notice. You don't plough the amount of money he does into these places without having just about everyone in your pocket.'

'Dr Billingham,' Helen said, angrily. She'd paid him a fortune to keep his trap shut. Clearly her grandfather had paid him more.

'So, what *did* Dr Billingham tell Grandfather?' Helen's eyes narrowed.

'That a young doctor you knew had come to him and asked if he would be prepared to help you sort out … ' Miriam stopped, trying to think of the right words.

'What? Sort out a *little* problem I had?' Helen could feel herself starting to shake with fury.

Miriam nodded.

'Oh, darling,' she gushed. 'You can't imagine what a relief it was. For me and for your grandfather. I was beside myself with worry about what we were going to do. I mean, can you imagine? The scandal would have been totally disastrous – not just for the family and the Havelock name, but for you too.' Miriam took a deep breath, relieved they had now got to the reason she was sitting here, in this kitchen that stunk of kidneys and gravy, instead of at the Grand, where she should have been, sipping gin and nibbling on some salmon hors d'oeuvres.

'So,' Miriam continued, with a thin smile, 'we can get back to normal now, can't we? I thought you might even want to come out and celebrate with me this evening. Or perhaps tomorrow? Make a night of it. Or if we went out on Monday we could also go and see that seamstress on Holmeside and get you fitted up with a new dress.'

Suddenly Helen burst out laughing.

Miriam thought her daughter seemed a tad unhinged. This was not quite the reaction she had expected, but who cared? The catastrophe that had threatened to ruin her life was over. That was the main thing.

'Oh, Mother, dear ...' Helen was still laughing; tears had now come into her eyes. She got up and disappeared into the scullery for a few moments, reappearing with a bottle of brandy. She collected two tumblers from the sideboard and put them both down on the kitchen table, sloshing a good amount into each glass.

'Oh, Mum, I do believe you are going to have to get me a new outfit. Most definitely. And we can certainly go out for a little celebration afterwards, if you fancy? But I think it may be a case of you drowning your sorrows, for I'm afraid my *little* problem, as you like to refer to it, is, in fact, going to become quite a big problem.'

Helen took a sip of brandy.

'A very big problem – in all ways.'

Helen raised her glass.

'But, Mum, come on, let's put our differences aside and make a toast.'

Miriam looked totally confused as she raised her glass in the air.

'Here's to you, Mother,' Helen said.

She paused and smiled.

'To becoming a grandmother for the first time!'

Helen took another small sip.

'Congratulations!'

Helen thought her mother looked as though she had been turned to stone.

'And only another five months to wait! How exciting is that?' she added.

Miriam's mouth opened and shut again.

'You mean to say you haven't had it done?' she asked.

'What?' Helen asked, all laughter now gone. 'You mean, have I not *got rid of it*?'

Miriam nodded. There was a part of her that was hanging on to the last vestiges of hope that her daughter might be playing some cruel trick on her.

'No, I haven't,' Helen said simply.

'But you were scheduled to have it done last week. On Tuesday?' Miriam still couldn't believe what she was hearing.

'That's right, Mother.' Helen's face was impassive. 'You were correctly informed by Dr Billingham that this was indeed the date I was due to go to the Royal to sort out my *little problem* ... And I did go to the hospital on the arranged date – at the time stipulated. And my goodness, it really was the most beautiful summer's morning … But, anyway, I digress.

'So … yes … I did go there – to the Royal … I was even admitted to the ward. Lovely young nurse in charge … And I was given the number-one slot. First to go down … And two very nice elderly porters even took me to what I believe they call the "prep room", which is where you go before they wheel you into theatre.'

Helen sat back and took another small sip of her drink.

'But what Dr Billingham obviously failed to tell Grandfather was that this was as far as I got. I never made it into the operating room. I got up off the stretcher, had a quick word with Dr Billingham, reassuring him that, of course, he would still be paid in full, and walked back up to the ward, got dressed, said goodbye to the nice young nurse, and walked out of the hospital – along with my *little* problem.'

Miriam looked as though she was going to self-combust.

'You stupid, stupid girl!' Miriam's stare was venomous.

'I think you've already told me that on a number of occasions of late, Mother. I think we've ascertained that you are of the firm belief that your daughter is "stupid".'

Miriam gulped back the entire contents of her glass of cognac in one go.

She looked at Helen with slightly deranged eyes.

'The shame. The shame of it all. My daughter. Having a bastard by a married man! You've ruined the Havelock name. You do realise that, don't you? Your grandfather will probably disinherit you. You're ruined. Your future is ruined. You'll never get married. Never even get another bloke. You'll be known as a harlot. A whore. You and your bloody father have decimated my life!'

'Actually,' Helen said, as though they were talking about something as mundane as the weather, 'just so you know, I want to be the one to tell Dad that he's going to be a grandparent. If you tell him, rest assured he will know all about your ruse with his letters, and the real reason you had a postbox put at the front door.'

Miriam looked gobsmacked.

'Yes, Mother, I know all about it.'

Helen stood up.

'Well, I don't know about you, but I've somewhere I've got to be this evening.'

Helen walked to the kitchen door and turned around.

'Honestly, Mum, I'd try some of that pie if I were you. It *really* is rather delicious.'

Chapter Twenty-Six

The Tatham Arms

Saturday 15 August

'Happy Birthday!' Dorothy raised her glass of port and lemonade up to the yellow, tar-stained ceiling of the Tatham. 'To two very special girls – my gorgeous goddaughter, Hope, and to Bel's equally gorgeous daughter, Lucille.'

'Hear, hear!' There was a general rumpus of agreement, and everyone took a sip of their drink.

'Thanks, everyone,' Bel said, looking around at Polly, Martha, Hannah, Dorothy and Angie, all standing at the end of the bar. They hadn't been able to get a table as it was Saturday night and the pub was heaving.

'Where's Joe?' Martha asked.

'He kindly offered to stay behind and clear up the debris,' Bel said.

'Eee, that's nice,' Angie said. 'Not many men would dee that.'

Bel chuckled. 'I think it might have been more a case of him not wanting to come out for a drink with a gaggle of gossiping women.'

'It's a shame Gloria couldn't come to the pub with us, though,' Dorothy said.

'I know,' Bel agreed. 'But I think she was glad of the excuse to get Hope home. I don't know who looked more tired.'

They had all done a half shift at the yard, with Gloria at the helm, before hurrying back home, getting changed and going round to help out at Lucille's and Hope's joint celebration.

'Gloria's always shattered whenever she has to cover for Rosie,' Polly said. 'I think it takes it out of her more than she lets on.'

'I'd hate to be in charge, even for just a day,' Angie declared.

'I think I'd love it,' Dorothy countered. 'It'd be great being able to boss everyone around.'

Martha guffawed. 'You do that anyway.'

Hannah chuckled. 'Martha's right, Dorothy, you are ... what's that expression?' She thought for a moment. 'That's it, you're a "reet auld bossyboots".'

Everyone laughed, apart from Dorothy, who had adopted an expression of deep hurt, even though she was really loving being the centre of attention.

'I don't know how you manage to live with her.' Polly looked at Angie.

'Me neither!' Angie let out a loud laugh.

There was a moment's quiet.

'Did Maisie not pop in today?' Polly asked Bel.

'No way. She may love Lucille, but she's not a great fan of children in general. Not exactly maternal, our Maisie. She's going to treat Lucille to a trip to the pictures to see this new Walt Disney film called *Bambi* tomorrow.'

'That's nice,' Hannah said.

Bel chuckled.

'I don't think she realises that the cinema is going to be filled with a load of screaming, bawling, excited children and their overworked mams. I thought I'd let her find out for herself, but I'll bet my week's wages she doesn't offer to take LuLu to the midday matinee ever again.'

Everyone laughed, knowing that Maisie was in for a shock.

'All right, my round,' Bel said. 'My way of saying thank you for helping out today, especially Angie here, who seems to have a natural ability to keep a roomful of children under control – and entertained.'

'I'm used to it,' she blushed. 'Being brought up with my lot.'

'You know what,' Polly said, 'it occurred to me during a rather raucous game of pass the parcel – ' everyone groaned as there had been a small altercation between two of the partygoers as to who had been holding the parcel when the music stopped ' – that it's now two years since we all started at the yard.'

'God, I can't believe it's been that long,' Dorothy said. 'Mind you, sometimes it feels more like twenty than two.'

'So much has happened in that time, hasn't it?' Martha said.

As Bel handed out everyone's drinks, they chatted away, reminiscing about the past couple of years. They all ribbed Martha about how she never used to speak, and how Hannah had only been able to speak pidgin English, but now could speak like an honorary north-easterner if she wanted to. How Dorothy had been the trainee welder that Rosie had thought wouldn't last the course, but who had ended up being the best and the fastest in their squad; and how it was due to Polly's love affair with Tommy that they had all suffered the wrath of Helen, who had then tried to split up their squad.

At the mention of Tommy, they all looked at Polly, but it was Hannah who plucked up the courage to say what they were all thinking.

'You know we're still keeping our fingers crossed for Tommy, don't you, Polly?'

Polly nodded, not trusting herself to speak.

'You don't mind us mentioning him, do you?' Martha said.

Everyone looked at Polly, who was shaking her head vehemently.

'No, not at all, far from it,' she said. Her voice was shaking a little. 'It's nice. I like it. I like talking about him.'

Bel looked at her sister-in-law and knew this to be true. She had often come into the kitchen to hear Arthur and Polly chatting about the man they both loved. Sometimes she caught little snippets the old man was telling Polly about Tommy when he was young; other times Polly would be telling the old man something that Tommy had done at work, or had said in one of his old letters to her.

'I still have hope,' Hannah said, giving Polly a hug.

Polly returned her embrace, forcing back tears.

They were all quiet for a moment, before Polly took a deep breath, forcing herself to perk up and break the sombre mood.

'So, without wanting to sound like Dorothy's double, *have you all heard the latest about Alfie?*'

Everyone let out whoops of excitement and demanded more information.

'Well,' Polly said, looking round at her workmates, 'it looks like he's really sweet on Kate.'

'Really!' the women all exclaimed in unison.

Dorothy gasped dramatically in disbelief.

Polly looked at Bel for permission to repeat what she'd told her. She nodded, quietly over the moon to see Polly being frivolous. Even if she knew it was a bit of an act.

'Well, from what Maisie's said, it looks like love-struck Alfie is probably ripping his clothes on purpose, just to have something for Kate to fix. And, of course, Kate being

Kate, she's clueless as to the real reason Alfie has suddenly become her most regular customer.'

There were lots of questions, and laughter, and light-hearted banter.

When they had all exhausted the topic, Polly dropped her voice and said to Bel, 'It's a bit like your ma.' She cocked her head in the direction of the bar. Everyone looked over to see Bill, who was standing next to Pearl helping her with a particularly large round of drinks, and Ronald, on the other side of the bar, clearly vying for her attention.

'You've noticed too then?' Bel asked quietly.

Dorothy couldn't contain herself. 'You'd have to be daft or blind not to notice.'

Bel chuckled.

'Well, my ma isn't blind, she never misses a trick, but I think she is a bit daft when it comes to them two Romeos.'

The women chortled.

'And talking about Romeos,' Dorothy looked at Hannah, 'how are you and young Olly getting along?'

They all looked at their 'little bird', who was taking a nervous sip of her orange juice.

'Well, actually, Olly's asked me if I would stop calling him my *friend boy* and instead refer to him as my *boyfriend*.'

The women all let out loud exclamations of shock and excitement.

'So, yer now like a proper courting couple?' Angie asked.

'Yes.' Hannah had gone bright red. 'I guess that's what you could say ... that we are now *courting*.'

'Will we all be needing to gan out 'n buy ourselves hats soon?' Angie nudged Hannah, who rolled her big brown eyes to the ceiling.

'Nooo. We're just courting. That's all.'

*

'Yer can come out now, Arthur, the coast is clear.' Joe was standing in the doorway of the kitchen, leaning heavily on his stick. His gammy leg was giving him gyp, which was nothing new.

As Joe turned back, he heard Arthur's bedroom door creak open, and the sound of the old man shuffling down the hallway in his slippers. Arthur raised a bottle of Scotch in the air as he came into the kitchen, spying Joe.

'I think we deserve a bit o' this after today,' he chuckled.

'Too right,' Joe agreed, abandoning the kettle he was filling and getting two tumblers instead.

The two men sat down and Arthur poured a good measure into each glass.

'To Lucille and Hope. May they grow up in a land that is free,' Arthur said, raising his glass.

'I'll toast to that,' Joe agreed, his face suddenly serious, as they both savoured their drinks as well as the quietness that had finally descended on the house.

'How's Major Black 'n yer unit?' Arthur asked. He didn't often get the chance to chat to Joe on his own, especially about the war and what Joe was doing with the Home Guard.

'They're both good. We're all doing the best we can, all things considered.' Joe's hand automatically went to his bad leg. 'Reckon we'd put up a good fight if need be.' Joe smiled, but Arthur knew he'd have given anything to be back on the front line, risking life and his other limbs for his country.

'What's been in the news today?' Joe asked, taking another nip of whisky and stretching his leg out under the table. 'I haven't had a chance to even glance at a paper today, never mind listen to the radio.' He smiled. 'Bel forbade any kind of war talk. Said today had to be one of celebration.'

'I can understand her for saying that. Yer don't think she minded me just sneaking off there, do yer?'

Joe laughed out loud. 'Course not!'

Arthur pushed himself out of the chair. 'Let me get the *Echo*.'

Two minutes later he had reappeared with a copy of the town's local newspaper. He settled back down. Licking his finger and thumb, he brushed through the first couple of pages.

'More on the Japs and the Yanks ... Looks like the Japs have now got Burma totally under their control.' Arthur knew Joe's primary interest was North Africa and any news about the Eighth Army, in which he had served along with his twin brother, Teddy.

'There's lots of talk about this new general ... General Bernard Montgomery ... I think Churchill wants to see more offensive action out there,' Arthur said, his eyes scanning down the article.

'And I agree with him.' Joe had been devastated when Tobruk, a port city in Libya, had been captured by Rommel's Panzer Army Africa.

'I miss Teddy,' Joe said suddenly.

Arthur nodded, but didn't say anything. He knew from what Agnes had told him that Joe and Teddy had been very close, which wasn't surprising as they were twins after all.

'Sometimes Lucille will just pull an expression or say something and I see Teddy – as clear as day ... I still get so angry,' Joe said, rotating the tumbler of whisky on the kitchen table. 'So angry that all this death and destruction is because of one man.'

'And those that support him,' Arthur added.

'Aye,' Joe conceded. 'I just need us to hold North Africa.'

'Because it'll feel like Teddy's death wasn't in vain?' Arthur surmised.

'Exactly,' Joe said, glad of the understanding.

'Well,' Arthur said, 'I reckon you may well get yer wish.'

'Do yer reckon? It's not been looking good so far.'

'Aye, but I think it'll turn. I think this Montgomery bloke will help our boys take back El Alamein. I think they might well beat Rommel.'

'I hope yer right, I really do.'

The two men were quiet once more, both lost in their own thoughts.

'I thought our Pol might have heard something about Tommy by now,' Joe said.

'Aye.' Arthur's voice was sad. 'I did too. I think if he was POW we'd know by now. Same as if he'd been injured.'

'You never know,' Joe said, trying to sound optimistic.

Arthur nodded, even though he knew that Joe, like himself, did not hold any real hope of Tommy's return.

'I heard Bel chatting in the office about Lucille's and Hope's birthday party,' Helen said as she bustled into Gloria's flat, dumping her gas mask and handbag on the floor. 'And how they were all planning on going for a drink afterwards. I guessed you wouldn't be going because of Hope.'

'Well, I'm so glad yer came.' Gloria gave Helen a quick hug. 'Come on, sit down, 'n I'll make us a brew.'

Helen lifted up Hope's present for Gloria to see. 'Can I give this to Hope? I won't disturb her if she's asleep.'

'Course yer can,' Gloria said, bustling into the kitchen to make the tea.

A few minutes later Helen appeared at the kitchen doorway with Hope on her hip wearing her new pink sun hat.

'Oh, that's adorable, Helen!' Gloria looked at her daughter, who was smiling up at her big sister. 'Eee, she's been thoroughly spoilt today,' she said, putting the teapot, cups and saucers on the tray.

Helen moved to let her through to the living room.

'Isn't it strange? I remember this time last year hearing that you'd given birth in the middle of the shipyard.'

'And in the middle of an air raid!' Gloria laughed.

'God,' Helen looked at Hope, 'what a way to come into the world.' She paused. 'I didn't really think much about it at the time, but that must have been terrifying for you.'

'It was,' Gloria conceded, 'but it's funny, I didn't feel that scared. For starters it all happened so quickly, much quicker than when I had the boys, but also I had everyone there – Rosie, Polly, Martha, Hannah, Dorothy and Angie.' Gloria smiled to herself at the memory. 'They were running around like nutters. I still can't believe it was Dorothy who actually delivered Hope.'

Gloria put the tray down on the coffee table and started pouring the tea. Helen sat down in the armchair with Hope on her lap making sing-song noises and playing happily with Helen's hair.

'It must be nice,' Helen said, a sadness creeping into her voice, 'to have such good friends. I mean, they could have just run off and left you when the sirens went off. But they actually risked their own lives to save you and Hope.'

'Yes, they're a good bunch. Very loyal.' Gloria looked at Helen and for the first time realised just how lonely she was. 'But, enough about me and Hope,' she said, her voice becoming serious. 'I want to hear about you. I have to admit, I've been a bit worried.'

'I know,' Helen said. 'Or rather, I should say that I thought you might be. I've called round a couple of times but you either weren't in or already had guests.'

'Dorothy and Angie,' Gloria said, taking a sip of her tea. 'They mentioned they had seen you. Angie even joked that for a mad moment she thought you were coming here … But anyway, how are you feeling?

Gloria looked at Helen and thought she looked surprisingly well. Much better than she had anticipated.

'I'm feeling good,' Helen said, the beginnings of a smile on her face. 'Really well, actually.'

'So,' Gloria asked, a slight frown appearing on her brow, 'how did it all go?'

Helen paused and adjusted Hope's hat, before looking back at Gloria.

'Well, I can't answer that really – because ... Actually ... I didn't go ahead with it!'

Gloria stared at Helen.

'What?'

'I didn't get it done! I was all ready and waiting, literally just about to go into theatre, and I realised I couldn't go through with it.'

'Oh my goodness!' Gloria said. 'That's wonderful news. Really, *really* wonderful!'

'So,' Helen said, glancing down at Hope, who was gurgling away, looking at her mammy one moment and her sister the next, 'looks like this one here is going to have a new playmate.'

Gloria couldn't restrain herself any longer. She got up from the sofa and clasped her hands around Helen's very beautiful face, and kissed her on the forehead.

'I'm over the moon. Congratulations!'

Tears came into Helen's eyes, which she fought to stop.

She wanted to tell Gloria that she was the first person to congratulate her, but she didn't trust herself not to start sobbing.

Later that night, when Helen was lying awake in bed, her mind drifted back to the first time she had gone to see Gloria the day she had found out she was pregnant. Gloria had spoken words to her that she'd hoped to have heard from her own mother – not someone she barely knew – reassuring her that everything would be all right, that sometimes life takes an unexpected turn, but she'd deal with it.

'You're strong and you're brave,' Gloria had told her, reminding Helen of how she had saved Gloria from Vinnie – whacking him over the head with a shovel. 'You'll manage.'

Helen had replayed Gloria's words more than once, telling herself that it was true – she *would* manage, and that the time had come for her to be brave again, only this time in a very different way.

Having written her letter to Tommy, something she was now in the habit of doing every night, Polly thought about her workmates' excited chatter from earlier on in the evening. Their energy and life were like a breath of fresh air. She wondered how she'd cope without them. Hearing about the blossoming romance between Hannah and Olly – and perhaps also between Alfie and Kate – had taken Polly back to the beginnings of her own love affair with Tommy, how exciting it had been, how passionate their feelings were for each other . . .

But as much as a part of her enjoyed reminiscing about her and Tommy's own courtship, another part of her felt desperately sad.

Would it always be just that?

A memory?

Chapter Twenty-Seven

Thursday 20 August

Helen heard a quick rat-a-tat-tat on her office door, which had been left open because of the humid weather. She looked up to see Dr Parker standing there. He had his jacket draped over his forearm and his shirtsleeves rolled up. He looked hot and a little sweaty.

'Right,' he commanded, 'get your nose out of that ledger – we're going for a quick bite to eat.'

'Oh, John,' Helen started to argue, 'I'm really not that hungry.'

'That's not a problem.' He stepped into the office, picked up Helen's gas mask and handbag and put out his elbow. 'You can watch me eat. I'm starving. Now come on, chop, chop!'

Helen smiled and stood up. Walking over to him, she batted away his elbow and took her handbag and boxed-up gas mask off him. 'As long as I'm back in time for the afternoon shift,' she said. 'So, where are you taking me, *Dr Parker*?'

'Well, you know me, nothing but the best,' he laughed as they made their way down the stairs and out into the yard. 'There's a smashing little place just up the road. Wonderful views.'

'Let me guess. The Bungalow Café?' Helen said.

'Beats the Grand any day,' Dr Parker joked.

'Well, I think I'd agree with you there,' Helen said, her voice serious. 'At least we don't have to worry about seeing my dear mama.'

Dr Parker didn't say anything. He, too, was glad they wouldn't risk bumping into Miriam. Helen had told him what her mother had said when she'd learnt that Helen had not gone through with the termination.

Dr Parker looked at Helen as they walked out of the yard and along the road that led on to Harbour View. They chatted for a short while about the failed attempt to seize the German-occupied French port of Dieppe, and how, because of the huge number of casualties, the Allies had been forced to retreat.

After a little while the conversation steered back to events closer to home – and in particular, closer to Helen's home.

'Have you thought any more about when you're going to tell your father?' Dr Parker asked tentatively. Helen had rearranged her trip to see her father after she'd decided not to go ahead with the termination.

'I'm going to go up to the Clyde next month,' Helen said. 'I want to tell him face-to-face.'

Dr Parker looked at Helen and thought she couldn't leave it much longer than that as she'd be showing soon. As soon as people started to guess that she wasn't simply putting on weight, the whispers would quickly find their way across the Scottish border.

'I know you're worried about telling your father, but I really believe he'll be all right. Obviously, he'll get a shock, but he'll support you. I honestly do believe that.'

Dr Parker knew Jack thought the world of his daughter, and, more importantly, that the love he had for Helen was unconditional.

'I know you do,' Helen said, 'and Gloria keeps saying exactly the same thing, but I'm still not so sure ... We'll see anyway, when the time comes.'

They walked for a few more minutes, both looking out at the harbour and enjoying the cool sea breeze on their faces.

When they reached the café, they walked in just as another couple were getting up to leave.

'Perfect timing,' Dr Parker said. 'Go and grab their table. I'll get the scram.'

A few minutes later the pair were sitting opposite each other at a little table next to a window that, despite the brown anti-blast tape, had the most wonderful view out to the North Sea.

'So,' Dr Parker said, 'how've you been feeling since I saw you last?'

'All right,' Helen said, pouring their tea and adding milk, 'still a little nauseous, but otherwise no different really.' Helen looked at Dr Parker and leant forward slightly to ensure no one could overhear their conversation. 'You know, you don't have to keep checking up on me and popping in to see me. I know how busy you are up at the hospital.'

It was just over three weeks since Dr Parker had gone to visit Helen at the Royal, only to find that she wasn't there – that she'd had a sudden and quite dramatic change of mind. He'd immediately jumped on a bus and gone to see her. She had cried a lot and he'd silently resolved to see her as much as he could.

'I do appreciate it.' Helen paused. 'But I don't want you to feel like you're obliged in any way to ... you know ... well ... to *look after me*.'

Their faces were so near Dr Parker could smell the perfume she was wearing.

'Helen,' he said, 'I by no means feel in any way *obliged* to look after you. I think you are more than capable of looking after yourself. I certainly don't feel like I have to check up on you.' He was lying, of course. He *was* concerned about her, especially as there didn't appear to be anyone else who was – apart from Gloria, of course.

'I like you, Helen,' he said simply. 'And because I like you, I can't help but also care about you.' He sighed as if struggling to get the right words out. 'And more than anything, I enjoy being in your company.'

Helen leant back in her seat.

'That's nice, John. Thanks. I feel like you and Gloria are the only two people I can really be myself with. It sounds a bit childish, but I feel as though you two are my friends. My *only* friends.'

Dr Parker looked into Helen's emerald eyes and smiled.

'Well, as your friend, will you please help me eat these sandwiches?' he said.

'If I must,' Helen sighed, although she was now quite hungry and happy to oblige.

They were both quiet as they ate and looked out at what really was a magnificent view.

'I don't suppose you've thought any more about the Theo problem?' Dr Parker asked, as he poured them another cup of tea.

'I have ... ' Helen wiped her mouth with the paper serviette ' ... and I've actually come to a decision.'

'Really?' Dr Parker was intrigued.

'I've decided I'm going to go and see him.'

Dr Parker looked surprised, but didn't say anything. He still felt a rush of anger whenever he thought about Theo.

'I'm going to tell him,' Helen dropped her voice to barely a whisper, 'that come the New Year he's going to be a father for the fourth time.' She paused. 'Two babies in seven months. That's no mean feat.'

Dr Parker leant forward.

'Are you going to go there on your own?'

Helen let out a light laugh.

'Who else would I take?'

'I could take time off?' Dr Parker suggested.

'No, John.' Helen's face was serious. 'This is something I've got to do on my own.'

Dr Parker nodded his understanding, before checking his watch.

Seeing that time was getting on, they left the café, which was now heaving, and walked back to Thompson's, both chatting about their respective places of work.

After they said their farewells at the shipyard gates, it occurred to Helen that she had never really talked about work to anyone – other than her father. It felt good, and it certainly helped take her mind off her present situation – although, she had to admit, her trip to Oxford was something she didn't mind thinking about.

Her carefully planned revenge was going to be sweet.

Very sweet, indeed.

'Guess who's just been seen swanning off with some blond-haired bloke?' Dorothy said as she arrived back from the canteen with a cold meat pie.

'Let me guess,' Gloria said. 'Your favourite person, Helen?'

'*Your* favourite person,' Dorothy jabbed back.

'Who do you reckon this blond fella was?' Polly asked, trying to keep the animosity out of her voice. It was hard. As the weeks had worn on and she'd continued to live in a hellish limbo, not knowing if Tommy was alive or dead, her grief and anger seemed to have latched themselves firmly on to Helen.

'I reckon it's her new bloke,' Angie chipped in.

'Could it not simply be a friend?' Gloria asked. From what Helen had told her, this Dr Parker seemed like a decent chap, but there was clearly nothing between the pair.

'Pah!' Dorothy said. 'Helen doesn't have friends.'

She turned her attention to Bel.

'What do you think? Friends or lovers?'

'He's popped round quite a few times lately,' Bel mused, 'but they didn't look like they were courting to me. More like mates.'

Having noticed Polly's face cloud over at the mere mention of Helen, Bel changed the subject.

'So, Rosie, I haven't had a chance to ask you – how did it go with Charlotte? It feels like you've been away for ages.'

Rosie let out a weary sigh.

'Well, five days did feel like an age, if I'm honest. I really don't know what I'm going to do with her.'

'She sounds like she's been a reet little madam,' Angie said, slurping her tea back, then spilling some of it after receiving a nudge from Dorothy.

'I think what Angie means,' Dorothy said, 'is that Charlotte is just at an awkward age and not really wanting to do what others tell her – particularly her older sister.'

Rosie nodded. 'Well, I think you're both right. She *is* being a bit of a madam. And she's certainly not wanting to do what I tell her, that's for sure.'

Angie gave Dorothy a triumphant smile.

'So, she's still wanting to come back here, I take it?' Bel asked.

'Oh, yes,' Rosie said wearily.

'And did you tell her *your* news?' Bel asked gingerly.

'Oh, yes,' Rosie repeated. 'I told her that I'd got married, and that was why I'd moved house, but that Peter was away at war so unfortunately she wouldn't get to meet him any time soon.'

'And what was her reaction?' Bel was intrigued.

'Exactly what I thought it would be,' Rosie said. 'Her first reaction was surprise. Then I could almost see the cogs whirring around in her head as she sussed out how this latest turn of events could actually work in her favour.'

Everyone chuckled. They had quizzed Rosie about Charlotte yesterday on her return from Harrogate and had all agreed that Rosie was fighting a losing battle.

'And?' Bel asked.

'Oh, well, that was it!' Rosie said. 'That just cemented her argument that she *had* to come back here to live. That it was imperative she be included and not be *left out in the cold, banished to her boring boarding school in the outback* – her words exactly.'

Bel hooted with laughter.

'Talk about making you feel guilty!'

'I know!'

'So, how did you leave it?'

'I told her that I would never leave her out in the cold, and that as soon as Peter came back we'd look at the situation again.'

'Clever move,' Bel said.

'I thought so too, but I think it's only won me a temporary reprieve.'

As they all made their way back to the dry basin, where they were to spend the rest of the day patching up a cargo vessel that had taken a blast from a floating landmine, Rosie found herself being ambushed.

'Here, miss!'

Rosie jumped as Dorothy and Angie suddenly appeared on either side of her.

Dorothy pulled out a large handkerchief in which she had wrapped George's medals.

'We've polished them up as best we could,' Angie said, keeping her voice low, as though they were handing over state secrets.

Rosie took the medals and slipped them into the side pocket of her haversack.

'Thanks, you two. I really do appreciate this.'

'What about the uniform?' Dorothy asked.

The three women walked on.

'Would you mind awfully getting it dry-cleaned?' Rosie said. 'I'll give you the money, of course. But can you just keep it at the flat for the time being?'

'Aye, course we will, miss. Mum's the word,' Angie said.

Rosie smiled.

'You two still happy in your new pad?'

Her question was met by two beaming faces.

'Love it!' they both said.

'Not too posh then?' Rosie raised an eyebrow at Angie.

'Oh, aye, miss, *far too posh*, but I think I could get used to it.' Angie let out a howl of laughter, causing a look of total despair to cross Dorothy's face.

A look that Rosie couldn't quite decide was meant to be comic – or not.

Chapter Twenty-Eight

Tuesday 25 August

When Helen woke up she had to think for a moment where she was.

Oxford.

The Randolph Hotel.

It had been a long journey down, made all the more arduous by having to change at Newcastle and then Birmingham. She had travelled first class, which took the edge off, and had only had to lug around a relatively light vanity case, so all in all it hadn't been too bad. The train had been packed, full of soldiers, sailors and air force personnel, as well as your everyday common or garden travellers. Thankfully, though, the majority had been herded into the second- and third-class compartments.

She'd arrived in Oxford late and had taken a cab the short distance from the train station to the hotel, which was located right in the city centre. It was a magnificent Victorian Gothic-style building, the interior of which was equally impressive – full of huge oil paintings, plush velvet ceiling-to-floor curtains, polished parquet flooring, and oak-carved four-poster beds.

Helen should really have been in seventh heaven, revelling in the decadence of staying in a place that just about managed to blot out all reminders that the country was at war. Helen, though, had no interest in enjoying such a respite. She was staying at one of the most exclusive hotels in the country – in a city that had so far not been blighted by a single bomb blast – for revenge, nothing more.

Helen was here to detonate her own explosion – one that would wreak havoc and give her the retribution she had been craving.

It had surprised Helen that she had slept so solidly, as her mind had been working overtime on the journey down, not just going over and over her plan of action, but also in contemplation of the year's events.

She still rued the evening she had met Theodore outside the Burton House hotel and deigned to give him the time of day. She had lost count of the times that she had berated herself for allowing him to wheedle his way into her life. She had to hand it to him, though, he had been good at getting what he wanted, especially as she hadn't even been that attracted to him. Nor was he even that interesting. It hadn't taken long for their conversations to end up focusing on his own good self.

But Helen had to concede that she was also responsible for what had happened, for she had so wanted – *needed* – him to be her knight in shining armour. Because of that desperation she had fooled herself – just as much as he had fooled her.

Helen sat up and looked at her bedside clock. It was seven o'clock – time to put her plan into practice. She reached over and dialled room service to tell them she would have breakfast in her room. She then got out of bed and drew herself a bath.

'Theodore Harvey-Smith,' Helen spoke the words aloud to the tiled bathroom walls, 'I'm going to make sure that *you* are also going to suffer the consequences of your actions – and most of all, I'm going to make damn sure you continue to suffer those consequences for the rest of your miserable life.'

*

As Helen walked up the wide tree-lined street known as St Giles', she marvelled at the incredible architecture and the palatial family homes, many of which were adorned with the most gorgeous *Romeo and Juliet* wrought-iron balconies. Looking across the busy road she saw the entrance to St John's College, and as she walked on, she came to a little pub called the Eagle and Child, which, Theodore had told her, had once been the watering hole for such literary greats as C.S. Lewis and J.R.R. Tolkien.

Just before she reached the entrance of the Royal Infirmary, she crossed over the road and walked through the cemetery of St Giles' Church before turning left to continue up the Banbury Road.

Helen looked at her watch. It was ten minutes to nine. Carrying on for another hundred yards or so, she slowed her pace until she reached the very grandiose residence she knew to be the family home of the Harvey-Smiths. She had done her research, and providing there had been no upsets to the family's usual weekday routine, Helen would soon be seeing Theodore's wife for the first – and, after today, undoubtedly the last – time.

Crossing the road so she could watch the large Georgian house without arousing suspicion, Helen positioned herself next to a thick trunked oak tree beside a bus stop. Helen glanced at her watch again. Five minutes to nine. For the first time she felt a fluttering of nerves and she subconsciously ran her hand across her stomach. To a casual observer, Helen's figure would appear perfectly normal, if not a little voluptuous; they would not guess that she was expecting. However, if someone were to *really* inspect her from all angles, they would see a distinct bump. A small bump, but a bump all the same.

Two students on bicycles passed, followed by a single-decker bus; its brakes squealed as it slowed to a halt, letting off a grey-haired old man dressed in a tweed three-piece suit and smoking a pipe, and a young, harried-looking mother with twin boys, who looked about the same age as Hope.

As she took a step back to show she didn't want to board, the bus accelerated away, just in time for Helen to see the black front door of the Harvey-Smith household swing open.

The flutter of nerves she had felt just a few minutes previously returned. Her heart started hammering and she felt short of breath, something she hadn't experienced for a while.

So this was Franny.

This was Theo's wife.

Helen squinted against the morning sun. She looked unremarkable, surprisingly slim considering she had given birth just a few months previously, and her light brown hair was scraped back into a bun, showing a slightly pinched, plain-Jane face.

Helen felt herself stiffen as two young children came bursting out the front door and started to run around on the gravelled driveway.

Tamara and Stanley!

It was clear from the way Theo had described the boy and girl that he loved them very much. But he had described them as his younger siblings, not as his *son and daughter*. Helen couldn't tear her eyes from them. They looked so happy, so full of life. They were playing a game of tag and circling their mother, who was laughing and trying to tag them back, albeit unsuccessfully. Helen found herself staring, entranced, at the joyful, innocent tableau being played out on the shale driveway. They all seemed so normal.

What had she expected? A family unit that was more frigid? Sterner? Behaviour she deemed to be typically upper class? More like her own?

A few moments later another figure appeared in the doorway. Another woman. A large, rotund older woman who was wearing a fawn-coloured uniform with puffy sleeves and a full-length starched white apron, which Helen knew to be the required dress of a Norland nanny. And in the nanny's arms was a little baby, all swaddled in blankets. Helen was too far away to see the baby's face, but she'd been told it was a boy, that he was just two months old – and that the newborn had been given the same name as his father, Theodore.

Helen watched as Franny went over to the baby and held him in her arms, cooing and smiling. She might not be able to make out little Theodore's face, but Helen could clearly see the look of love on his mother's.

Her heart suddenly felt heavy.

This could have been an advertisement for how a perfect family should be. The father only absent because he was, of course, at work.

For a few seconds Helen's view was once again blocked – this time by a passing tram. When she could see the family again, Franny was in the process of carefully passing her baby back to the nanny. She looked as though she was reticent to give him up. The nanny disappeared again before reappearing, still with babe in arms, but now also holding a wicker basket. She waited to hand it to Franny, who was bending down to give Tamara and Stanley a farewell hug.

Helen watched with growing jealousy as Franny laughed and blew kisses, all the time shooing her children back into the house.

Helen stood rooted to the spot and stared.

What a happy family.

What lovely, happy children.

And loath though she was to admit it:

What a lovely mother.

An image of her own mother flashed across Helen's mind. She could not recall one time in all her childhood when her mum had shown her such love.

Helen scratched the thought out of her head.

This was not the time for self-pity. She was here to exact her revenge.

Helen watched Franny as she started walking in the direction of the city centre.

She waited a few moments before she started following her, making sure she kept a safe distance.

When Franny stopped to chat to an elderly couple she clearly knew, Helen walked over to a newspaper stand and bought a copy of the *Oxford Mail*. She carried on following her down St Giles', past the Martyrs' Memorial just outside her hotel and along Cornmarket Street before she reached the entrance to the Covered Market.

Helen walked a little faster and lessened the gap. This would be the perfect venue to do what she had planned.

She had imagined the scenario over and over in her head: she would stop Franny and, if possible, persuade her to go for a cup of tea in a nearby café. Perhaps she would pretend she was an old university friend of Theodore's, that she had been at their wedding, but, of course, Franny wouldn't remember her as it was such a huge and extravagant affair.

It would be enough to get Theodore's wife seated – to gain her undivided attention.

And then she would tell her.

She would tell her that her husband had pretended that he was, in fact, a single man, that he had courted Helen, taken her out for drinks, and eventually taken her to bed.

She would tell her that Theodore had told her all about Oxford and his 'brother and sister', Tamara and Stanley, and that he had painted a picture of Helen and him sharing a happy-ever-after life together in his hometown.

Helen would tell Franny that she had believed him wholeheartedly. Why wouldn't she? He was a surgeon, after all. He was rich, educated and well bred.

And Helen, being naïve as she was then, had given him the one thing he was really after – her body. And not just her body, but her virginity as well.

Then would come Helen's pièce de résistance.

Because of Theo's lies, his need for sexual gratification, and her own stupidity, she had fallen pregnant with his child.

Helen knew that it would destroy their marriage.

It would destroy Theo's life – just as he had destroyed hers.

But as Helen followed Franny into the hubbub of the market, a thought kept nudging its way into the forefront of her mind.

This will destroy Franny's life too – and her children's.

Helen tried to beat away the thought, just as she tried to beat down a wave of nausea as the odour of raw meat and fresh fish hit her nostrils. She breathed in the still, dry air and coughed – it was acrid with a heavy mix of cigarette smoke and dust. Helen's eyes watered but she managed to keep her sights on Franny as she made her way through the crowds of shoppers. They were mainly housewives and, of course, academics, who seemed oblivious to everyone around them as they waited in queues, debating animatedly amongst themselves.

Helen stood outside M. Fellers & Sons, the dead fowl, rabbits and deer carcasses hanging around the shop's perimeter creating a macabre curtain and obscuring the inside. She watched curiously as Franny made her way over to a nearby fruit and vegetable stall, apologising as she went for bumping into a passer-by with her cumbersome wicker basket.

She seems so nice, Helen thought. *So polite and courteous.*

Watching how she interacted with the stallholders and her fellow shoppers, it occurred to Helen that she had not really given much thought to what Theodore's wife would be like. She had presumed she would be upper class, which she clearly was, but she didn't appear to have the attitude to match.

What was the word she was looking for? That was it. *Humble. She seemed humble.*

Well, Helen thought, leaving the butcher's and following Franny to the other side of the market, *all the more reason for her to know what her husband is really like.*

Helen joined another queue and counted her blessings she had never had to do her own shopping.

With growing curiosity, Helen watched as Franny made her way over to a beggar, an old woman who was dressed in what could only be described as rags. She saw Franny speak to her and the old woman smiled, showing yellow stumps for teeth. Her eyes, however, were the palest blue Helen had ever seen. It took her a moment to realise the beggar woman was blind.

Helen felt someone accidentally shove her from behind and mutter an apology but she paid no heed; her eyes were glued to Franny as she pressed some money into the woman's dirty, gnarled hands. The old woman reached out and Helen could not believe that Franny let the beggar touch her face with her filthy, calloused hands.

Seeing Franny walk on and join yet another long queue at the fresh fish stall, Helen slowly made her way over to her.

Now! Helen commanded herself. *Do it now!*

Helen joined the queue, just managing to beat another shopper to her place right behind Franny. She was perfectly placed to carry out her plan. Now all she needed to do was tap her on the shoulder – and tell her.

Tell her everything about the man she had married, the man she loved, the man who had fathered her three children.

Her three happy children.

Her three innocent children.

The queue seemed to go down quickly.

Too quickly.

For God's sake, just get her attention and tell her!

There were now just two people to serve before Franny.

Helen raised her hand and tapped Theodore's wife on the shoulder.

Chapter Twenty-Nine

As Helen walked out of the Covered Market she stopped and breathed in fresh air, although there was nothing fresh about it. This city that she had thought was going to be her new home seemed stuffy and hot. There was not even a wisp of wind. She wiped her brow. What she wouldn't give for a cool sea breeze. The cream Utility-style dress she was wearing felt too hot, too thick. She would have been better off in a cotton dress.

Helen forced herself to walk back down Cornmarket Street, now even busier with shoppers, scholars and street traders. Her legs felt shaky and she stopped for a moment outside a shop window that was full of headless mannequins dressed in flowing black college gowns, mortar boards and summer blazers. Helen forced herself to breathe through her mouth as she was hit by another surge of nausea. She cursed this morning sickness that she had read up about in the medical books John had loaned her. In most women it passed relatively early on, but John had told her that sometimes it lasted throughout the pregnancy and she was not to be overly concerned, unpleasant though it clearly was.

As Helen waited with a throng of pedestrians to cross the junction where Cornmarket Street ended and St Giles' began, she realised the irony that barely a month ago she had been intent on ending her pregnancy, whereas now she was worried about any problems that might prevent her pregnancy from going full term.

It seemed she was changing her mind an awful lot these days.

Reaching the other side of the road, Helen found herself in the shade, which helped to invigorate her. She felt the energy return as she strode on, knowing exactly where she was going – and precisely what she was going to do.

There would be no dithering this time.

'I've come to see Mr Theodore Harvey-Smith.' Helen spoke politely but with authority as she smoothed down her dress and smiled at the middle-aged receptionist on the enquiry counter of the Radcliffe Infirmary. 'I believe he's doing his morning rounds at the moment,' she added helpfully, 'but if you wouldn't mind fetching him as a matter of urgency, please?'

The stern-looking receptionist narrowed her eyes as she inspected the self-assured – and very beautiful – young woman now standing in front of her. Her slight northern accent told her she wasn't from these parts, although judging by the Norman Hartnell dress she was wearing and her Schiaparelli handbag, she clearly came from money.

'May I ask what the "matter of urgency" is?' the receptionist asked.

'Of course,' Helen said. 'You must tell him that it concerns his wife, Franny, and that a Miss Helen Crawford is here at the front desk, waiting.'

The receptionist picked up the receiver to what Helen presumed was the hospital's internal phone. Her voice was low and serious as she repeated Helen's request word for word.

Helen would have given anything to see the look on his face when Theo heard his former lover's name being mentioned in the same breath as his wife's.

As Helen had predicted, it took only minutes for Theodore to leave his rounds and rush to the hospital's foyer.

She stood stock-still as she watched him hurrying towards her, his white coat flapping open, a stethoscope shoved into his pocket.

His face was as white as a sheet.

'Helen!' His voice was hoarse with shock.

'Ah, Theo!' Helen put her arms out, but rather than embrace him she grabbed both his upper arms and squeezed as hard as she could. 'How wonderful to see you!' She was still holding him at arms' length, still gripping hard.

Theo threw a nervous look over to the receptionist, who was watching them both with unguarded curiosity.

'Gosh! This *is* a surprise.' He looked at Helen like a rabbit caught in the headlights of an oncoming car. 'Shall we chat outside?' The expression on his face was a plea.

Helen looked over at the receptionist and thanked her with a smile. She was genuinely grateful. This part of her plan, at least, was going perfectly.

'Yes, Theo,' Helen finally dropped her claw-like hold, 'let's go outside. It's such a beautiful day, isn't it?'

Theodore pushed his hair back nervously as he stepped forward to open the main door, allowing Helen to go first.

'What the hell are you doing here?' Theodore hissed as he guided Helen down the front steps towards a large, perfectly manicured lawn in the middle of which was a stone fountain in the shape of the Greek god Triton.

'What the hell's going on? And what the hell did you mean, it "concerns Franny"? Have you seen her?' Theodore was not even attempting to hide his panic.

'I have seen her, actually, Theo.' Helen spoke as if they were simply exchanging pleasantries. She looked at Theo.

'What … what have you said to her? Please … *please* don't tell me you've told her about … ' He paused, as if trying to find the right words. '*About us.*'

Helen let out a loud laugh, causing a few doctors who were walking past to turn their heads and look with interest.

'But there was never any "us", was there, Theo?' Helen said with more than a hint of bitterness. 'I mean, you pretended there was – and you pretended very well, I might add. But in reality there was no "us". It was all you. You. You. What *you* wanted.'

Helen stared into Theo's eyes. 'Am I right?'

Theodore looked back into Helen's green eyes, and knew he was doomed. He would not be able to lie his way out of this one.

Helen now knew everything. But that didn't bother him.

What he did care about, though, *what he was terrified might well be the case*, was whether Helen had told Franny the truth.

'Have you spoken to Fran?' His mouth was tight as he spoke, the beginnings of anger starting to show. *'Have you told Franny?!'* he demanded.

Helen looked down at Theo's hands and saw they were clenched into fists.

'I'd change your tone if I were you, Theo, otherwise I might just shout the truth out from the treetops!'

Theo's shoulders dropped in defeat.

'Just *tell me*, Helen.' He was now begging. 'Have you said anything to Franny?'

'Well, I did say *something* to your Franny.' Helen forced a smile. 'She's not at all what I imagined. Very plain – she's certainly no Lauren Bacall, but then again, you're no Humphrey Bogart either ... '

Theodore stood rooted to the spot; small splashes from the fountain were just missing him.

'I caught up with Franny in the market just now.' Helen looked about her as if momentarily distracted. 'She was shopping, as I'm sure you're aware, something she does every morning.' Helen had spoken on the phone to one of the surgeons Theodore worked with and who was also a good family friend. She had pretended to be an old school pal who wanted to pay a surprise visit. The surgeon had been particularly loquacious and disclosed more than enough information for Helen to concoct her plan down to the exact minute.

'I have to say, Theo,' Helen started to walk round the fountain, 'you really did bag yourself a saint of a wife.'

Theodore stuck to Helen's side as she strolled around the freshly cut lawn as though she didn't have a care in the world.

'For pity's sake, Helen. *Did you tell her?*' Theodore spoke through clenched teeth.

Helen stopped walking and looked straight at the man she had thought she would marry.

'As I was saying, before you rudely interrupted, Theo – I followed Franny into the market. I joined the queue she was waiting in. I even went as far as tapping her on the shoulder with the intention of telling her the truth about the man she is married to … '

Helen paused.

'But when she turned around and looked at me with those big brown eyes of hers … I simply ended up asking if she knew anything about fish, and what would she recommend.'

Helen looked at Theo and thought he was going to collapse with relief then and there.

'So, you didn't tell her? You didn't say *anything*?'

Helen shook her head.

'No, I didn't tell her, Theo. Much as I wanted to make you suffer, I couldn't do it. I couldn't make someone else suffer because of you and your lying, conniving and downright despicable behaviour.'

Theo wanted to laugh with relief.

'Oh, thank God. *Thank you*, Helen.'

Helen forced a smile to appear across her face.

'I just hope,' she said, 'that one day soon Franny realises what you're *really* like. That she finds out for herself that she shares a bed every night with a treacherous, philandering bastard that cares for no one but himself. And I hope that when she does find you out, she not only leaves you, but finds a true love to spend the rest of her life with – and that you, Theodore Harvey-Smith, grow old and very, very lonely.'

Helen could see by Theo's face that her words had sailed blithely over his head. She doubted he had taken in even one syllable of what she'd just said, and even if he had, her jibes had not in any way penetrated his conscience. That was, if he had one.

'Of course,' Helen said with a heavy dose of sarcasm, 'I'm sure a man of your intellect and education would realise that I have not travelled all the way down from the north-east of England merely to inform your lovely wife of your infidelity.'

Theo looked at Helen with the beginnings of concern.

Helen deliberately kept quiet – leaving the air loaded with the obvious question.

'So, so ... ' Theodore stuttered, 'why *did* you really come down here?'

'I came to tell you,' Helen said calmly, 'that you were wrong about something.'

Theodore's brow furrowed.

'What was I wrong about?' he asked.

'Remember how you told me – in your very serious, doctor-like way – that there was something called the "natural family-planning method" that was – how did you put it? Oh, that's right – "one hundred per cent foolproof"?'

Theodore stared at Helen, not wanting to hear what he knew was coming next.

'Well,' Helen said, 'you were wrong.'

'What do you mean, *wrong*?' Theodore's voice was raspy with nerves.

'Well, put simply, that natural family-planning method you reassured me was foolproof was not . . . '

Helen took Theo's hand and placed it on her stomach so that he could feel the small bump. His touch repulsed her, but she knew it would be the last time he would ever lay hands on her.

Theodore felt the solid, rounded bump that was pressing against the fabric of Helen's designer dress. He pulled his hand away and stared at Helen, aghast.

'Why, Theo, you've gone rather grey. I hope you're not going to faint on me, are you?' Helen laughed lightly.

Theodore looked about him as though he was seeking an escape route.

'Let's hope no one's seen you, eh?' She raised an eyebrow at Theodore before making a point of looking about her. 'Mind you, if they have, I'm sure you'll be able to make something up – you're rather good at that, aren't you?'

Theodore continued to stare at Helen.

'Gosh, Theo. For someone who normally has plenty to say, you seem to have gone awfully quiet. I'm about seventeen weeks, if that's what you were going to ask me. Well, that's what the doctor reckons. I've been given a due date of around the New Year. So,' Helen chuckled again, 'I guess if it's a boy it'll have to be Adam and if it's a girl, I'm leaning towards either Eve or January.'

Helen had no intention of calling her child either Adam, Eve or January, of course.

Theodore put his hands on his hips and leant over as if he'd just done a sprint round the block.

He looked back up at Helen. His lips were dry and his complexion had gone a light shade of grey.

'What are you going to do?'

Helen let out a loud laugh.

'I'm going to have it, silly! What else?'

Theodore looked askance.

Helen looked over at the chapel to the side of the Infirmary; it was the first time she had noticed it.

'I thought,' she said airily, 'that we could have – what do they call it these days? – *joint custody* of the child. Obviously you'll have to pay maintenance ... All these new words I've had to learn of late ... And, of course, it'll be very important that your new son or daughter gets to know his or her siblings. Especially little Theodore. I mean, they're going to be practically the same age – just ... what? Seven months between them?

'I'm actually quite glad I didn't end up telling Franny about your little dalliance while you were up north. Now that I think about it, it's going to be so much better coming from your own mouth ... And after telling Franny, you can tell Stanley and Tamara that they've got another little sibling on the way, and that although they won't be able to see their little brother or sister every day, I'll endeavour to come down as regularly as possible, so they all get to know each other.'

Helen's face suddenly lit up.

'You know what?! I can't believe I haven't thought about this until just now.'

Helen's eyes widened.

'Perhaps I can even move down here! Yes! Why didn't I think of it before? I mean, it's so much safer here for starters. No air raids. And it's not as if I'll have a job to go back to at Thompson's once I've had this little one, so I'll be free as a bird.' Helen put her hand on her stomach and painted an angelic smile on her face.

Again Theodore looked around nervously.

'Helen ... ' he licked his thin, dry lips ' ... is there no other way around this?'

'What? You don't want to see your own child, Theo?' Helen asked mockingly. 'You don't want your lovely children to know that they have a brother or sister?'

'Please.' Theodore looked as though he was about to drop to his knees and beg. 'Please, can we not just keep this between ourselves?'

Helen looked down at her watch, then back up at Theo. Seeing him like this was at least some consolation.

'Walk me to the gates,' she commanded.

Theodore did as he was told and accompanied his former lover to the huge metal gates that opened out onto the Woodstock Road.

'Theodore ... ' Helen stopped walking ' ... I'm going to stop toying with you. As much as I have enjoyed seeing you suffer, I'm afraid I've got a train to catch.'

She turned to look at him directly.

'I'm going to tell you something now and I want you to remember it for the rest of your miserable, two-faced existence on this earth.'

Theodore was staring at Helen.

Dare he hope?

'I am going to have this baby.' She spoke slowly and clearly and with the utmost seriousness. 'And I'm going to bring this baby up – on my own.'

A pause.

Theodore let out an audible gasp.

There was hope!

'You are *never* going to see the baby I have. Ever. Do you hear me?'

Helen glared at Theodore, who was nodding like a child.

'When I walk away today,' she continued, 'that is going to be the last time you ever set eyes on me. Nor will you ever set eyes on the baby that I am carrying. If you make any attempt to contact me at *any* time in the future, I will tell Franny everything. And your worst nightmare really will become reality.'

Theodore felt as though the huge black cloud that had been threatening to engulf him had just moved on.

'Do you understand?' Helen daggered Theodore.

He nodded.

'Say the words!' Helen demanded.

'Yes, I understand. I agree.' Theodore couldn't get the words out fast enough.

Helen looked at the man she had thought she loved, whom she had thought she would marry, and whom she now hated so much she was determined she would never again set eyes on him – and she turned and walked away.

As Helen strode back down St Giles', part of her was gutted. She had not had the satisfaction of seeing all her carefully laid plans carried out, but she realised that she could never have told Franny about Theo, or about the baby she was carrying. She realised that although Theo might not have a conscience, *she*, in fact, did, and because of that she simply could not devastate Franny's life or her children's.

At least, Helen thought, as she hurried across Beaumont Street, she had gained some perverse joy from seeing the fear in Theodore's eyes when he believed that she *had* told Franny – as well as the look of horror on his face when he realised that she was carrying his baby.

That would have to suffice.

Walking quickly back into the hotel, Helen looked at her watch. It had just gone ten o'clock. She felt a rush of adrenaline as she realised that if she hurried she could catch the ten-forty-five train back up north.

Striding up to the reception desk she informed them of her early departure and paid her bill. She practically ran up the stairs to her room and flung what few belongings she had into her vanity case. Not wanting to wait for a porter, Helen carried the case herself as she walked through the hotel lobby, jumping straight into a waiting taxi.

She was at the station just as the Birmingham-bound train was pulling into platform two. She might have to wait at New Street station for a connecting train up to Newcastle, and then take a rather tedious stop-start service on to Sunderland, but she didn't mind. She just wanted to go.

Stepping on to the steaming train, Helen put her case in the overhead rack and sat down in the navy cushioned seat. It didn't matter that she had come all this way and hadn't really done what she'd set out to do. She had not exacted her revenge or destroyed Theo's life. Yet something had happened to her during her fleeting visit. She wasn't quite sure what, but it had made her feel happy.

Happier than she had been in a long time.

As the train pulled out of the station, Helen put her hand on her stomach and thought about the baby she was going to have.

She knew Theo would be relieved with the trade-off they'd just done, but *she* also did not want Theodore in her life or her unborn child's.

It was, she had decided, *her* baby – like Gloria had said all those weeks ago.

'It's just you and me, little one,' she said softly. 'Just you and me. And you know what? We're going to manage just fine on our own.'

Chapter Thirty

When Peter stepped out of the main entrance of Sunderland train station he stopped for a moment and looked around him, not quite believing he was there. Seeing a taxi, he strode towards it, but sensing someone behind him, turned to find a young, dark-haired woman carrying a vanity case.

'Sorry, I didn't see you there. Please ... ' He went to open the passenger door of the taxi and smiled. He couldn't help noticing how very pretty she was, although she also looked extremely tired.

'Thank you,' she said, placing her case on the back seat. 'It's been a long journey.'

'It's always nice to get home, isn't it?' Peter said.

'Yes, it *is*.' The woman spoke the words as if she really did mean them.

Peter shut the door and watched the black Austin pull away. He looked around to see if there were any other taxis about. There were none.

'Damn it!' he cursed under his breath.

Striding down Waterloo Place and turning right into Holmeside, he spotted a double-decker bus and started running. He jumped aboard just as it was pulling away.

Looking out the window as he passed the Maison Nouvelle, he saw Kate locking up and looked at his watch. It had just gone seven o'clock. At a push, he might catch Rosie before she left for Lily's.

Getting off at Tunstall Road, Peter jogged down Valebrook Avenue and through the little wooden gate that heralded the start of Brookside Gardens, before finally reaching number 4.

Not wanting to shock Rosie by simply barging in, he knocked and counted to ten.

No answer.

If she was in, she would have come to the door by now, unless she was having a bath, or was out in the backyard.

Peter reached for his keys, adrenaline pumping around his body. His need to see Rosie, now he knew her to be so close, was overwhelming.

'Peter! You're back!'

Peter jumped as his neighbour flung open her front door.

'Ah, Mrs Jenkins! How lovely to see you.'

Mrs Jenkins was just opening her mouth to speak when Peter beat her to it.

'I'm sorry to be so rude, but I'm in a bit of a mad hurry. I don't suppose you've seen Rosie this evening?'

'You've just missed her, Peter – I heard her leave about ten minutes ago.'

'That's great. Thank you.' Peter shoved his key back in his pocket. 'Sorry, but I must dash.'

'Yes, yes, of course ... Oh ... and congratulations, Peter – on getting married!'

Peter waved his thanks as he hurried back to the little five-bar gate.

He let it clash shut and started to run, hoping he might catch Rosie before she reached Lily's.

When Peter turned into West Lawn he slowed to a walk, adjusted his tie and straightened the lapels of his overcoat. Crossing the road and making his way to the very grandiose Victorian house, he felt a little nervous. Rosie had never invited him to the bordello, or, indeed, introduced him to any of its inhabitants. He knew Kate, of course. Knew her from her past life on the streets, but had only met her properly twice since then – and both those occasions had been at the boutique.

Rosie had made it plain to him that she wanted to keep her two lives separate, and he had respected that. Tonight, though, she was going to have to make an exception. There was no way he was going to sit at home waiting patiently for her until she got back. Especially as he had only been given a twenty-four-hour pass.

Walking up the stone steps to the front door, he pressed the little brass doorbell. Within seconds he could hear the sound of footsteps and a sing-song voice shouting:

'Je vais ouvrir la porte, mon cher!'

For a split second Peter thought he was back in France, before he remembered that Lily liked to speak French.

When the door opened it was hard to tell who was the most surprised.

The pair stood and simply looked at each other.

Lily's appearance was even more outrageous than Peter had imagined. He had thought Rosie had been exaggerating when she had described her, but clearly not. If anything, she had played it down.

'Bonsoir, madame,' Peter said, taking off his trilby.

'Quelle surprise!' Lily replied, putting her hand out. *Kate had described him to a tee.*

As they shook hands Peter noticed the huge diamond engagement ring Lily was wearing. The woman was dripping with jewellery and smelled as though she had bathed in a tub of Chanel N° 5. And as for the mass of orange hair piled on top of her head – well, he had simply never seen the like before.

'I'm awfully sorry to have to call round unannounced—' Peter started to say, but before he had time to finish his sentence, Lily had ushered him in.

'We have a visitor! Detective Sergeant Miller!' she announced to the entire household.

'I'm guessing you're here to see your wife?' she asked, turning her attention back to Peter.

Before her unexpected guest had the chance to reply, Rosie came flying out of her office.

'Peter!'

She ran to him and flung her arms around him.

On hearing that Peter was there – *at the bordello* – Maisie and Vivian almost fell over themselves in their rush to see him. Closely followed by George. They were just in time to see Peter and Rosie locked in each other's arms, before the pair managed to pull themselves apart.

'Peter!' George pushed himself forward with his walking stick, his eagerness to introduce himself to the love of Rosie's life more than evident.

He stuck out his hand.

'Pleased to meet you! Very pleased indeed. I'm George!'

Peter's face broke into a wide smile. He had hoped to meet George one day, although he had not thought it would be so soon, and so unexpectedly.

'George! The pleasure's all mine! I've heard all about you.'

George laughed.

'Don't believe a word of it!' He let out a large guffaw.

'It's lovely to meet you at long last, Peter.' Lily forced a smile that ended up looking more like a grimace. 'I was beginning to wonder if you were a figment of *our* Rosie's imagination.' It didn't escape Peter's notice that Lily had stressed the word 'our'.

'Peter!' It was Kate, squeezing through the front door, which was still slightly ajar. 'You're back!' She put two skinny arms round him and kissed him on the cheek. 'How wonderful! Oh, I'm so thrilled for you both!' Kate clasped her hands together and looked at Rosie, who appeared flushed and beyond happy.

Lily cast her eyes over at Maisie and Vivian, who were loitering behind George. Seeing some of the other girls start to emerge from the back parlour, she scowled and shooed them back with her hand.

'And this is Maisie,' Lily said, stretching out her arm. 'Head of our new Gentlemen's Club – and Bel's long-lost sister.'

A big smile broke out on Maisie's face. This was the first time Lily had referred to her as the 'head' of the Gentlemen's Club. She would hold her to that later.

Peter stepped forward and shook hands. He had seen Maisie before but only from afar; she was smaller and more slender than he recalled, but now he was seeing her up close he was struck by her exotic beauty – her light brown skin, the scattering of freckles across her nose and cheeks, and the most amazing hazel-coloured eyes.

'And last but not least, this is Vivian,' Lily said, finishing the introductions.

'Fabulous to finally meet you.' Vivian stepped forward and in true Mae West form held out her hand for Peter to kiss.

Peter smiled and obliged.

'Perhaps you can meet the rest of the girls another time,' Lily added.

'Come and have a quick snifter, Peter!' George said.

George caught the look on Peter's face and knew he was about to object.

'Don't worry, though, we're going to boot you out in ten minutes,' George chuckled. 'I'm guessing you're on leave and they've not been overgenerous with the length of that leave.'

Peter's face relaxed and he smiled.

'You're right on both counts, George. I've got a twenty-four-hour pass – not a minute more.'

Peter looked at Rosie and squeezed her hand.

'Come on then!' George ushered everyone into the back kitchen. They all crowded around the kitchen table while Maisie and Vivian got the glasses from the armoire and George tipped a good measure of Rémy into each. Lily did the honours of handing everyone a drink, apart from Kate, who had got herself a tumbler of water from the tap.

'A toast!' George raised his glass and everyone followed suit. 'To the happy couple! And their not so recent nuptials!'

'To the happy couple!' everyone chorused.

As promised, ten minutes later George was ordering the newly-weds back out the front door.

'Thank you, George.' Peter leant in as the two men shook hands. 'Thank you for everything.'

'Just keep safe,' George said quietly. 'For this one's sake.' He nodded over to Rosie, who was already halfway down the steps.

When they were back out on the pavement and out of sight, Peter took Rosie in his arms and kissed her.

They stood and held each other tight – and kissed each other some more.

'I can't believe you're here,' Rosie said as they started to walk.

'Neither can I.' Peter pulled her close.

'Did you get the petals?' he asked.

'Oh, Peter, I did. *I did indeed*. I've been on cloud nine ever since.'

As they walked with their arms tightly wound round each other, they chatted away, stopping occasionally to kiss. It was as though no one else existed in the whole world.

*

The light started to filter through the blackout curtains at around a quarter to five and Rosie padded down the stairs to make tea. They had barely slept a wink, both wanting desperately to squeeze every last minute out of the too short time they had together.

'I *do* love this house,' Rosie said as she handed Peter his tea and climbed back into bed.

'I do too – now that *you're* living here.' Peter took a sip of tea. 'And there's a spare room should you relent and allow Charlotte to come back here to live,' he suggested cautiously.

'Well, that's one thing that you and Lily agree on.' Rosie gave him a sidelong glance.

'I'm not saying she *should* move back,' Peter said. 'I'm just wondering whether it might be a good idea to be able to keep an eye on her if she *is* going a little wayward.'

'I agree, to a certain extent,' Rosie said, 'but I wonder whether she might just end up going even more *wayward*, as you put it, if I did allow her to come back here to live. I mean, I'll be working all day and most evenings, so I'm not going to have a lot of time to be with her – or to keep tabs on her, for that matter.'

She was quiet for a moment.

'And I still can't face the thought of telling her about Lily's.'

Peter sensed Rosie's frustration, as well as the heavy weight of responsibility she clearly felt when it came to Charlotte. He understood. If he was in Rosie's shoes, he'd also feel a certain amount of reticence regarding Charlotte's possible return, although, having finally met Lily and George, he honestly believed that Charlotte could only benefit from their love and care. It was as plain as day just how much they thought of Rosie, and also how protective they were about her. Peter knew that they would apply the same intensity of love to Charlotte and would probably be even more protective of her because of her youth.

Rosie put her teacup on the bedside table and snuggled back up to her husband.

'I've promised Kate to take Charlotte to the boutique when she visits next. She's dying to meet her. I think it means even more to Kate because Charlotte and I are the only connection Kate has with her old life.'

'When she lived in Whitburn?'

'Mmm, when her mum was still alive.' Rosie put her head on Peter's chest. 'Before Nazareth House.'

'How old was she when she went there?' Peter asked.

'Ten,' Rosie said.

'And you don't think she'll get bothered any more by that Sister Bernadette?' Peter asked. Rosie had told him all about the nun's unexpected visit to the Maison Nouvelle, and how Kate had sought sanctuary in a bottle of cooking brandy, which was the reason she had forgotten to give Rosie his letter.

'I'm not sure, to be honest,' Rosie mused.

They were both quiet for a moment. Both thinking of the great many injustices at home and abroad.

Rosie turned her head to look at Peter's profile.

'I know there's so much you can't tell me, Peter, but you'll be careful out there – as careful as you can – won't you?'

Peter looked his wife in the eye.

'I will do everything in my power to stay safe. Alive,' Peter said. He traced her face gently with the tips of his fingers.

'I have so much to live for. Every night I lie and think of you and imagine our life together, here in this house, after the war has ended.'

He was quiet for a moment.

'But you do understand why I'm doing what I'm doing, don't you?'

Rosie pressed herself even closer and kissed him on the lips.

'I do, Peter. I really do.'

'It's unbelievable what's happening over there,' Peter said. 'Shocking.' He shook his head, stressing his disbelief. Rosie saw the look on Peter's face – the seriousness, the sorrow, and the anger. 'I thought I'd seen pretty much all sides of human nature working for the Borough, but what's happening now is far, far worse.'

Rosie put her arm across Peter's chest and felt the warmth of his skin on hers.

'Hannah tells us bits and pieces that she hears from her rabbi, you know, things that don't always make it into the newspapers. None of us know what to say. What *can* you say? This ghetto her parents are in sounds awful. How the poor girl sleeps at night, I've no idea.'

Peter had heard about the Theresienstadt ghetto and others like it, but didn't say so to Rosie.

'Hannah says it's like the Jews are being treated as though they have some terrible contagious disease.'

Peter nodded. He thought about the Jews in Paris, how they now had to wear the yellow Star of David and were banned from all restaurants, cafés, cinemas and theatres. He could feel his blood boil even now as he recalled having to stand back and watch as the Gestapo carried out a huge trawl of the city, rounding up thousands of Jewish men, women and children and herding them into the Vélodrome d'Hiver, the city's main sports stadium, before packing them all off on trains to the so-called 'labour camps', or rather, 'death camps', as they were becoming known.

'And what's truly worrying,' Peter said, 'is that if we lose this war, exactly the same will happen over here. And it won't just be the Jews, but any other race Hitler decides he wants to wipe off the face of this planet.'

Peter blew out air, sat up and pulled Rosie closer to him.

Rosie shivered at the thought.

'Anyway, enough morbid talk,' Peter said, thinking that this woman lying next to him had known her own horror during her lifetime and she didn't need burdening with more. 'I think we've got at least another hour or so before I've got to go.'

He looked at the little clock on the bedside table.

'And I don't want to spend it talking.'

Peter kissed Rosie and she responded.

And for the next hour they put aside all talk of the poison that Hitler was spreading across Europe and beyond – and instead they thought only of love.

Chapter Thirty-One

Peter had tried to persuade Rosie to say goodbye to him at the house but he should have realised that this was never going to happen. Rosie had merely laughed at the suggestion, put on her overalls, grabbed her gas mask and holdall and walked out the front door. Peter had smiled and acquiesced, and the pair had walked together into town. Rosie had waited with him until his train arrived and stayed there for a while after it had pulled out of the station. Only then had she allowed herself to cry. And cry she did.

She had then dried her eyes and walked back out into the slightly chilly but sunny morning and escaped into thoughts of the previous night as she had walked to work, choosing the longer route across the Wearmouth Bridge.

She had bumped into Helen at the main entrance and was taken aback when Helen had smiled at Rosie and wished her 'Good morning.'

Heading over to the welders' work area, she had returned to her private reminiscences. As they'd had breakfast this morning, Peter had promised to try to send her a letter or some other kind of sign that he was alive and well, but that she must not think the worst if she didn't receive anything. He had warned her that it wouldn't be long before the whole of France came under German occupation, which would, therefore, make any kind of communication nigh-on impossible.

Rosie had been able to ask him some questions about his everyday life in France, and he'd told her about some of the strange habits peculiar to the French; she was aghast to hear they ate snails, cooked in butter and garlic and served in their shells, and that the people loved nothing more than strolling along the street with a freshly baked baguette, tearing bits off and eating it as they went about their business. Rosie knew that what Peter was able to tell her was also mere crumbs, but she had been starved of any kind of knowledge of what his life was like over there – had only her imagination to fill in the blanks – so she was more than happy to have her own frugal nibble, which felt like a feast in comparison to what she'd been fed these past seven months.

Peter had also talked about his mother and how he would be forever thankful that she had forced him to speak her native tongue, but it was something Rosie secretly wished that she hadn't done. If Peter's French wasn't so fluent, he would still be here in his hometown, enjoying tea with her this evening. They could make love knowing that they could do the same the following night, and every night thereafter if they so desired – and not as though it might be their last time.

'Miss! Are yer all reet, miss?'

Rosie looked up to see Angie and Dorothy stomping across the yard towards her.

'We've been watching yer since we came into the yard 'n yer haven't moved a muscle – just staring at the ground like yer were in some sort of trance,' Angie said, concerned.

'Yes, yes, I'm fine. Honestly.' Rosie shook her head as though waking herself up. 'I think I just drifted off into my own little world for a moment.'

'Dinnit worry, miss.' Angie smiled. 'Dor's always going off into her own "little world".'

Dorothy gave Angie a scathing stare.

'It's called daydreaming, Angie, and it's meant to be good for you, isn't it, "miss"?'

Rosie chuckled as she heaved a box from the shed and dumped it on the workbench.

'Presents,' she said, 'courtesy of Helen.'

'Cor!' Angie said, striding over to the box and gaping inside. 'Eee, Dor, come and look – we've got new rods and everything!'

Dorothy gave Rosie a mock-weary look and did what her best mate asked. Secretly, though, she was relieved that Rosie was all right. For a moment, when she'd seen her there, just staring into space, she'd thought something might have happened to Peter. They didn't need another one of their gang walking around with a broken heart.

As Rosie stood up and straightened her back, she realised she'd have to be careful today. She'd had so little sleep and, as Dorothy and Angie had just brought to her attention, she wasn't at all with it. Sleep deprivation and the high she'd felt, having just spent the last twelve hours with the man she loved, made a heady combination.

Looking across the yard, her eyes focused on the rest of her squad negotiating the usual obstacle course of men, metal and machinery. As they neared, though, Rosie immediately saw that something was wrong. Polly was flanked by Gloria and Martha and looked terrible. She had dried tear marks lining her face and her eyes were puffy and bloodshot.

'Oh God, it must be Tommy!' Rosie heard Dorothy's voice behind her.

'Polly,' Rosie hurried over to see her, 'what's happened?'

Rosie looked at Gloria and Martha, who were both wearing grim expressions, but they didn't volunteer any information.

Rosie put her arm round Polly, guided her over to the pallets and sat her down. Dorothy sat on her other side, while Angie poured her a cup of tea from her flask.

Polly took it in both hands and sipped.

'They sent back all of Tommy's gear,' she said simply.

Rosie looked up at Gloria, who was standing nearby.

Martha had bobbed down on her haunches in front of Polly, her big hands on her workmate's knees.

'That doesn't mean he's dead, Pol,' she said.

Polly looked at Martha and round at the rest of the women and forced a brave smile.

'I know.' She took a deep, shuddering breath, the kind that follows a prolonged bout of crying.

'It just seems so final. If they thought he was coming back they'd have kept his stuff, wouldn't they?'

Rosie looked to Gloria, hoping she'd know more about these things, having two boys at sea.

'I believe they have a set time before they send stuff back home.' Gloria pulled up a crate next to Martha and sat down. 'It's just a formality.'

Gloria had no idea if this was the case, but sometimes white lies needed to be told.

Polly looked up.

'I'm sorry, everyone. I wish I could be braver. I feel like I'm letting Tommy down, but I just don't seem to be able to stop blubbering.'

More tears cascaded down her face.

She bowed her head.

Rosie gave her another squeeze and carefully pushed Polly's long, slightly curly hair away from her face, now wet with tears.

When the klaxon sounded out, Rosie didn't move, but instead looked up at Gloria and cocked her head in the direction of *Brutus*.

'Come on.' Gloria touched Martha's shoulder and stood up. She looked at Dorothy and Angie. 'Let's make a start.'

For the next ten minutes Rosie and Polly sat together. There were no words spoken as the riveters had started up nearby. Not that Polly really wanted to talk. There was nothing she wanted to say and nothing much else anyone could really say to her by way of comfort. It had been eight weeks since she had received the letter from Tommy's commander. Eight weeks of being pushed and pulled between two poles of thought:

Hope that Tommy was somehow still alive.

And acceptance that he was dead.

Rosie kept her arm around Polly, who rested her tired head on her boss's shoulder, tears rolling down her cheeks. Their view of the river was obscured by a frigate that had been moored by the quayside. As if to rub salt into Polly's wounds, two Wear Commissioner dock divers were getting ready to go and inspect the damage. If they had been able to see the two women's faces from one of the little port windows on their twelve-bolt helmets, they would have seen a picture of the two faces of war.

Grief and anger.

Polly had finally given up her grip on the hope she had been desperately hanging on to by the tips of her fingers. And in its place, she had handed over a free rein to grief.

Rosie, on the other hand, was in fury's hold. Anger seeping from every pore. All this heartache, sorrow, death and destruction need never have been. This madman and all his willing cohorts were not just taking land and lives – the lives of tens of thousands of men, women and children – but were also ripping love out of the very hearts of those they'd left behind.

Rosie put both her arms around Polly and gave her a gentle cuddle, wanting to make her feel better, but knowing that it was impossible. She thought about Peter and what he had said when she had told him about Tommy. It was obvious that he too thought Polly's fiancé had become yet another victim of war, and he had told Rosie that she and her squad had to be strong for each other.

'You have to be there for each other, look after each other. And,' he'd added, a stern look in his eyes, 'you have to *accept* each other's help.'

Rosie knew what he was really saying.

She pushed the thought away.

After a while Polly sat up. She looked at Rosie and mouthed, 'I'm all right,' and the two walked over to the dry basin to join the rest of the women welders. Rosie didn't question whether Polly was up to work because she knew that she wasn't up to *not* working. Building ships might not mend her broken heart, but it would help her survive.

And in these times that was about as much as they could hope for.

Chapter Thirty-Two

'Baker Street, please,' Peter told the taxi driver as he jumped into the back seat of the black cab.

Typical, he thought. There hadn't been any free taxis when he was desperate to get to Rosie, but on walking out of King's Cross with time to spare, there'd been a whole line of cabs waiting.

'Anywhere in particular on Baker Street, sir?' the cabby asked, his balding head turned slightly to his left so he could be heard through the half-opened glass partition.

'No, anywhere will do,' Peter said. There was no way he could give the driver an address because where he was going didn't technically exist. The Special Operations Executive headquarters had expanded from number 64, so that it now occupied much of the western side of Baker Street. If anyone were to ask, the properties were said to be occupied by the Admiralty or Air Ministry, or some kind of civilian company. What went on in those buildings in Baker Street was top secret, as well as surprisingly controversial. Churchill's so-called 'secret army' was still seen by many in the know as an unacceptable – 'ungentlemanly' – form of warfare.

Driving along the long stretch of Euston Road, leading on to Marylebone Road, Peter looked out the window.

'Bleedin' Jerry, eh?' the cabby said, as much to himself as to his passenger.

Peter nodded as he continued to look out at the huge mountains of rubble, dust and debris interspersed along their route, as well as countless partially demolished buildings, one of which, the cabby pointed out, was Madame Tussauds. There was no denying London had not only taken several beatings, but was being obliterated, razed to the ground, brick by brick.

There had never been any doubt from the start of Peter's initiation into this exclusive group of undercover agents that what he and others like him were doing was right, totally justified, but passing the ruins of so many once-beautiful buildings, churches, shops and family homes, Peter's resolve was made even more steadfast. Great Britain and her Allies could not lose this war. Just the thought of it made Peter feel ill. Looking at what was happening to his own country, and having seen the Third Reich in action in Paris, he knew exactly the kinds of atrocities that would be inflicted on Rosie and just about everyone else living in this once green and pleasant land.

Quite frankly, it terrified him. Much more than losing his own life.

Thank goodness Rosie understood that he had to do everything and anything he could to protect the country he loved and the people in it.

And thank goodness Rosie had people like George – and Lily – who would always be there for her, regardless of what might happen to him. He had been dreading going to the bordello and would have given anything for Rosie to have been there at home in Brookside Gardens when he had arrived last night, but he was actually quite pleased that he had ended up at the house in West Lawn. It was good to meet them all, to put faces and personalities to the names. And boy, were they all personalities, every single one of them, each in their own unique way. Lily had been even more outrageous and over the top, in both looks and behaviour, than he had anticipated. She had dominated the ten minutes they had all spent in the kitchen, and had pretty much grilled Peter about all aspects of his life to date. It had not escaped his notice that she had lost her faux French persona by the time they had all raised a toast, and by the end of their short little soirée had been speaking like the cabby presently chauffeuring him across the capital.

Meeting George had confirmed what he already knew – that he was a good man, who had helped Rosie understand the reason why Peter had joined up, and why he was putting the war ahead of his love for her. He had a sense that George knew much more than he'd let on and wouldn't have been surprised if he knew about the SOE. Judging by the description of the uniform Dorothy and Angie had found in the loft, George had clearly been high-ranking, and after Rosie had shown him George's medals, which she was keeping safe in her bedside cabinet – one of which he recognised as the Distinguished Service Order (DSO) – it was proof that he had been a very courageous man. The fact he had shoved his uniform and medals away in the dark recesses of his loft, however, said to Peter that he had also seen enough warmongering to want to forget it.

'Here we are, sir!' The cab pulled up at the bottom of Baker Street. Peter got out and paid his fare with a decent tip, which put a big smile on the taxi driver's face.

As Peter walked along the street to number 64 – an address he had visited during his initial recruitment, before he had been sent to Wanborough Manor for training – he wondered where he was going to be sent next. The circuit, code-named White Light, he had set up earlier this year had been forced to disband after there were suspicions that one of their members was leaking information to the Germans. Their suspicions had been proved right when five of his men had been arrested; they were more than likely now either dead or prisoners of war. Peter, who was the circuit leader, and one of the wireless operators had managed to avoid being captured by the skin of their teeth.

Pressing the bell at the side of the innocuous-looking front door that was the entrance to the SOE headquarters, Peter guessed there would be new identity papers awaiting him. Having heard talk about a circuit presently being set up in Bordeaux, which was where his mother hailed from and where he had spent time as a child, it seemed more than likely that the south-west of France could well be his next port of call.

Chapter Thirty-Three

Saturday 29 August

'So, that was it?' Dr Parker looked at Helen across the table as they waited for their meals to arrive. 'You just walked away … Went back to your hotel and jumped on the next train back up north?' It was the first time he had seen Helen since her trip to Oxford and he had listened intently as Helen relayed the events of that morning four days ago.

Helen nodded.

'And you're sticking to your guns? You're quite certain – you don't want anything more to do with him? Or for him to have anything to do with the baby?'

'Absolutely certain,' Helen said, taking a sip of her water. She'd forsaken her usual tipple of gin and tonic. It did not taste the same any more and John had told her that there was a school of thought that believed alcohol could be detrimental to the development of an unborn baby.

'Well, I do believe the expression *good riddance to bad rubbish* is very applicable in this case,' Dr Parker said, although he also felt that Theodore had got off very lightly. It was a brave decision by Helen, though. She had a long and difficult road ahead of her.

He raised his half-pint of bitter.

'Well, I think that is cause for a celebration in itself.'

'And let's not forget it is also your *birthday*,' Helen added, raising her glass of water.

Just then the waitress arrived with their meals and carefully placed them on the table.

Helen looked around at the restaurant, which was surprisingly full.

'I'm so glad it *is* your birthday,' she said. 'It's the perfect excuse to come somewhere like this.' They both looked around at the very plush interior of the restaurant in the Empress Hotel, one of the best eateries in town.

'And to have some decent food for a change,' Dr Parker added, popping a piece of baked cod into his mouth.

'It's a shame you don't live nearer,' Helen said. 'Mrs Westley would love nothing more than to fatten you up with all her pies and stews.'

Dr Parker knew Helen and the cook were close, much closer than Helen and her mother, which wasn't really much of a surprise.

'Do you think Mrs Westley *knows*?' he said, keeping his voice low, as an elderly couple sat down at the table next to them. He knew Helen still wanted to keep quiet about her condition for as long as possible. He'd initially thought it was because she was ashamed, but now he believed it was because she simply wanted to enjoy this time before it was spoilt, as it inevitably would be, by the judgement and malicious gossip of those she knew and those she didn't.

Helen took another mouthful of her fish covered in a parsley sauce and thought for a moment.

'I think ... ' she swallowed and took another sip of water ' ... that dear Mrs Westley might well have guessed. I mean, she's nobody's fool. It won't have escaped her notice that I've stopped drinking and smoking.' Helen had finally given up cigarettes as they seemed to make her feel nauseous. 'And I'm eating more and have put on a bit of weight. She's not said anything, though. Not that she would, but she's been fussing about me even more than normal. Checking I'm all right. Making me sandwiches to take to work, and she's always got something in the oven when I get in. Honestly, she must be queuing for hours on end to get me the choice meats she's cooking up every night. Either that or she's bribing the butcher.'

'Good,' Dr Parker said, liking Mrs Westley more by the minute. 'Give that baby all the nutrients it needs. So,' he looked at Helen, 'have you thought any more about telling your father?'

Helen nodded.

'After I came back from Oxford, I wrote to him and said I was going to come and visit him in the middle of September. I was even thinking about asking my aunty Margaret and uncle Angus if they would come and see me while I'm in Glasgow.'

'They're up in the Highlands?' Dr Parker asked, cutting up a piece of perfectly steamed parsnip.

'Yes, so I don't think they'll mind making the trip to the Clyde.'

'What do you think their reaction will be?'

'I'm not sure, to be honest.' Helen pondered for a moment. 'It's a difficult one. I think they'll be shocked, for sure, but they're a nice couple. Aunt Marg's not a bit like Mum – she'll be supportive, even if she is disapproving of my loose morals ... I guess I'm just not sure how she's going to *feel*.'

'Because she's never been able to have children herself?' Dr Parker asked. He'd got to know a little about Helen's extended family.

Helen nodded as she finished her dinner.

'What was the problem? Was it a case of her simply never falling pregnant?'

'Oh, she had no problem *falling* pregnant.' Helen sat back and dabbed her mouth with the corner of her napkin.

'She just didn't seem to be able to stay pregnant. It must have been awful for her.'

It was on the tip of Dr Parker's tongue to ask Helen if she knew how far along her aunty was when she miscarried, but he stopped. He might cause Helen to worry unnecessarily. Besides, most women lost their babies very early on in their pregnancy, certainly before they reached their second trimester.

'Well,' Dr Parker said, 'I think it's marvellous you've set a date to tell your father – and your aunt and uncle.'

'Of course,' Helen added, 'then I'll have to tell work, but I need to really think about how I'm going to approach that. I want to make sure Harold doesn't write me off. I want him to understand that I *will* be coming back after the baby is born.'

Dr Parker didn't bother to ask if Helen was sure about being a working mother. He knew nothing would keep her away from her beloved shipyard.

'It's a shame your aunty Margaret doesn't live nearer. She could have helped out while you were at work. Do away with the need for a nanny.' Dr Parker had never been keen on any kind of paid childcare, having been more or less brought up by a particularly sour-faced and very strict governess himself.

Helen looked at the man opposite her.

'You know, John, that might not be such a bad idea.' She suddenly started chuckling. 'Oh, I can just see my dear mother's face now. She'd hate it. In fact, the more I think about it, the more appealing it is – it might just drive her to take up residence in the Grand permanently!'

It was just starting to get dark by the time they left the restaurant.

'It doesn't feel right letting you make your own way home,' Dr Parker argued. He would actually have given anything to escort Helen back to her home across the river, even if it meant he had to walk all the way back to his digs in Ryhope.

'John, I'm more than capable of getting myself back home. I'm getting quite accustomed to public transport these days.' She smiled. 'I actually rather like it. Sometimes I even get off the stop before and walk along the top of the promenade and just look out to sea.'

'Well, now you're not only making me feel jealous, but also like you are depriving me of the perfect end to an evening.'

Helen nudged him playfully.

'Go on. Go and save some more lives.'

Helen started to walk away but stopped.

'And thank you, John. Not just for a lovely dinner, but for being such a good friend.'

Helen stepped towards him and gave him a quick kiss on his cheek.

'And happy birthday!' she laughed.

A tram passed them, squealing to a stop.

'Go on. Get yourself home!' Dr Parker waved his hand at the tram.

Helen hurried down the street and jumped on board.

Dr Parker stood and waited until the tram disappeared from sight before turning and making his way towards his own bus stop.

As he walked down Fawcett Street and passed the town's municipal museum, he realised that he couldn't kid himself any longer.

He had fallen for Helen.

Hard.

He had tried desperately to stop himself, but had failed.

Miserably.

He'd found Helen incredibly attractive from the moment he'd first set eyes on her at the Royal, when he'd seen her at her father's bedside. *What man wouldn't?* She was not only stunning-looking but incredibly sexy. But it wasn't her looks that had taken his heart captive, it was the person behind the perfectly made-up veneer.

They'd become firm friends these past few months. Two people who genuinely enjoyed each other's company, who laughed together, confided in each other – were themselves with each other; but did Helen's feelings, like his own, go beyond those of mere friendship?

As the Ryhope bus pulled up, Dr Parker got on, paid his fare and sat down in the only spare seat he could see.

The dilemma was, if he declared his feelings and she rejected him, it would not only destroy their friendship, but Helen would also lose one of the two people she could rely on – who really cared for her.

God, why was love so bloody complicated?

And why, he thought with a sinking heart, *did his gut tell him this was a love that could never be?*

Chapter Thirty-Four

Friday 4 September

'You two off out tonight?' Gloria looked across at Dorothy and Angie as they all pushed back their helmets and pulled off their protective gloves.

'Is the sky blue?' Dorothy said, throwing an arm up into the air theatrically.

'Let me guess,' Gloria said. 'The Rink?'

'Where else?' Angie chuckled.

Rosie stood up and straightened her back. She'd been bent over welding for just about the entire afternoon and felt like her spine was now set in the shape of a letter C. 'What about you, Martha?' she asked. 'You on duty?'

Martha nodded. They all knew that their gentle giant spent most evenings doing ARP work. 'I'll probably spend most of it drinking tea,' she said, 'not that I'm complaining.'

Apart from a glut of incendiary devices that had been dropped the previous Friday in Fulwell, when homes had been destroyed but, mercifully, no lives had been lost, the town was enjoying a respite from any more visits from Hitler's auguries of death. The theory was that Hitler needed to throw everything he had at the Soviets if he was going to succeed in taking Stalingrad.

'You don't fancy coming to the Rink tonight, do you, Pol?' Dorothy slung her haversack over her shoulder.

Polly forced a smile and shook her head.

'I don't think I'm up to the Rink at the moment, Dorothy.' Polly doubted very much she ever would be. 'But thanks for the offer anyway.'

'Just say if yer ever wanna gan out,' Angie piped up. 'Me 'n Dor will always be happy to oblige.'

'Thanks, Angie,' Polly said as they all started to make their way off *Brutus*'s deck and back down to the yard.

The women were more than aware that Polly had been really struggling since she had taken delivery of Tommy's few possessions. She was doing her work as normal, as well as any overtime going, and she would sit and eat her lunch with them all, occasionally joining in the chatter, but it was as though part of her wasn't there.

'You off to Lily's this evening?' Gloria dropped back to walk with Rosie.

'It keeps me out of mischief,' Rosie said, but they both knew what she really meant was that it kept her mind off Peter.

When they were passing the admin building, Gloria slowed down and took off her headscarf, making a great show of waving it in front of her face as if trying to cool herself. She then wiped her forehead with it before tying it to the strap of her holdall.

'Is that a new headscarf?' Rosie asked, unconsciously copying Gloria and taking off her own turban.

'What, this old thing?' Gloria turned to look at her scarf, a floral print of reds, greens and yellow. 'Nah, I've had it ages. Thought I'd start wearing it. Better than it just being shoved away in the bottom drawer.'

Dorothy suddenly looked over her shoulder and hissed at the squad's elders.

'Don't look now, but Helen's got her eagle eye on us!'

Gloria didn't look, but Rosie couldn't help it. Helen was indeed at the window.

'Oh my goodness, look at the state of you lot!'

Their attention was suddenly diverted by Bel hurrying across to join them.

'You look like you've been mining coal, not welding ships.'

The women looked at each other's blackened faces and dirty overalls.

'That's the slag,' Martha said.

Bel looked none the wiser.

'It's a black crust that forms over the weld. We have to chip if off with a hammer. Goes everywhere,' Martha explained.

Bel joined the women as they made their way to the timekeeper's cabin.

'Yet another reason I'm so glad I work in an office and not with you lot!' She sidled up to Polly.

'You all right?' she asked her quietly.

Polly nodded, but Bel wasn't convinced.

A few moments later they were joined by Hannah and Olly as they all joined the bottleneck of workers waving their time cards at Alfie.

'What are you two up to this evening?' Dorothy looked at them both. 'Now that you are officially *girlfriend and boy-friend*.'

Hannah and Olly both blushed.

'We're going to prepare for Shabbat.'

'What's Shabbat?' Angie asked, as they were all jostled forwards.

'The Sabbath,' Olly answered.

'Is that when yer can't dee owt?' Angie said.

Hannah looked puzzled. She still struggled occasionally with the north-east dialect.

Olly was just opening his mouth to answer when Alfie shouted out to Rosie:

'Can yer tell Kate I'll be in over the weekend?'

Rosie nodded.

'Has he worked up the courage to ask Kate out on a date yet?' Dorothy asked, as they were all released from the yard and were carried along by the throng of workers down to the ferry.

'Not as far as I know,' Rosie chuckled. 'But don't worry, Dorothy, you'll be one of the first to know.'

Dorothy scowled, hearing the heavy sarcasm in her boss's tone.

Gloria was just feeding Hope when there was a gentle knock on the door.

Gloria had left the front door open – it was now one of the many signs she had adopted to show Helen that she and Hope were in on their own.

'The coast's all clear!' Gloria shouted as she helped Hope guide a spoonful of baby food into her mouth.

Helen walked in, automatically looking about the flat. She lived in mortal fear that one day she would come in to find Dorothy and Angie there.

Seeing Helen's worried face, Gloria chuckled as she wiped her hands on a tea towel and walked over to give her a hug.

'Don't worry. It's Friday. They'll be dolling themselves up for their big night out at the Rink.'

Helen visibly relaxed.

'Thank God for the Rink, eh?'

Dumping her bag and gas mask by the door, she made her usual beeline for Hope.

'So, how's my little sister been today?' Helen said to Hope, pulling up a dining chair and carrying on from where Gloria had left off.

'Mmm, now doesn't this look lovely?' she said, glancing up at Gloria and pulling an expression of revulsion.

'That might look like gruel to you 'n me,' Gloria said, heading towards the kitchen, 'but it's like a gourmet feast for the bab.'

Hope took another hungry mouthful as if to prove the point.

'Ah, you've got it all to come,' Gloria shouted through from the kitchen as she got the tea tray ready and boiled the kettle.

'Mmm, can't wait!' Helen shouted back.

'Actually, John came up with quite a good idea the other night,' she added as she helped Hope hold her spoon straight and scoop more 'gourmet gruel' from her bowl.

'What was that then?'

'Get my aunty Marg down to help with the baby. She was always so lovely with me whenever she came to visit when I was a child. It's actually amazing that she and my mother come from the same stock.'

Gloria's chuckles were obscured by the scream of the kettle.

'You just wait until you have yer little 'un,' Gloria said, pouring boiling water into the teapot. 'You'll fall madly in love 'n won't want anyone else even near her, never mind looking after her, or want to leave her to go back to work.'

Helen smiled at Hope as the toddler managed to feed herself another spoonful. It didn't escape Helen's notice that Gloria often referred to her baby-to-be as a girl. It was something she felt too.

'I *am* going back to work,' Helen said adamantly. 'There's no two ways about it. Anyway, you're a right one to talk – you went back to work within weeks of having Hope.'

'Different circumstances,' Gloria said, bringing the tea tray in and putting it down on the coffee table.

Helen looked at Gloria as she poured out the tea; her hands had been scrubbed clean, but the rest of her was filthy.

'You look like you've been working down the mines,' Helen chuckled, watching Gloria pour milk into both cups. 'I'm so glad I work in the office.'

'Bel said the same thing when she saw the state of us today,' Gloria said, adding sugar to both cups and giving them a quick stir.

'She seems to be fitting in nicely in the office,' Helen said. 'Marie-Anne and her seem to have become best buddies. I'm still surprised that she wanted to work at Thompson's, though. I would have thought someone like Bel would have preferred a nice, clean – and quiet – office, somewhere in town.'

Gloria took a big slurp of her tea. 'I reckon it was just good timing – and because of Polly.'

'What? Do you think she was worried about Polly? Because of Tommy?' Helen asked gingerly.

'It would make sense,' Gloria said.

'And how *is* Polly?' Helen asked hesitantly. 'Has she heard anything more about Tommy?'

'Nothing.' Gloria shook her head sadly. 'The head honcho of his unit had all his belongings sent back the other day. She was in a right state.'

'So, they really think he's dead?'

Gloria could hear the slight tremble in Helen's voice. She put down her cup.

'I forget that you two were close as well,' she said.

Helen nodded. Tears had started to form in her eyes.

'I know everyone thinks I'm some heartless cow who just wanted to pinch Tommy off Polly on a whim, but I really *did* love Tommy. We practically grew up together. Dad will tell you. He and Arthur were best buddies and wherever Arthur went, Tommy went too.' Helen let out a sad laugh. 'Arthur used to say, "Here comes me 'n my shadow." God, Tommy adored the old man. No wonder he became a diver.'

Gloria listened quietly. She had never really talked to Helen about Tommy before.

'We may have come from opposite sides of the fence, but because Dad and Arthur were so close, Tommy and I ended up spending a lot of time together as children. I always felt like we were meant to be together.'

Helen looked at Hope, whose attention seemed to be divided between her big sister, her mammy and the novelty of trying to feed herself.

'Then when he started work for the Wear Commissioner and I started working at Thompson's, it seemed so obvious. I mean, we both had this love of the shipyards – and we knew each other really well. We were friends.'

Helen paused.

'Mum knew, of course, that I had more than a soft spot for Tommy. She was forever saying I should look for someone who was of the same social standing as myself. And I tried. I dated a few boys from well-off families, but they never matched up ... I always believed it would be just a matter of time before Tommy realised that we were made for each other.'

Helen sighed.

'And then this bloody war started – *and* Polly came along.'

Helen paused again, deep in thought.

'I was so insanely jealous of Polly when I could see that Tommy was falling for her.'

Helen looked at Gloria, her eyes swimming with a deep sadness.

'And now neither of us has got him.'

Helen brushed away a tear that had escaped and was starting to run down her cheek.

'God, listen to me getting all maudlin!' Helen sat up straight and directed her attention back to Hope, helping her scrape up the last of her food and shovel it gently into her little button mouth.

As Helen was leaving, Gloria handed her a letter from her father.

'Does Miriam know yer back in touch with yer dad?' It was something Gloria had been curious about.

'Well, she's never asked, and I've never said anything. I don't think she dares mention it after I told her I knew that she was keeping his letters from me. Besides, I think that's the least of her worries at the moment. I don't know if she's even all that bothered any more. Every time I see her – or rather bump into her when she's going out and I'm coming in – she just demands to know what I'm going to tell everyone.' Helen picked up her handbag and gas mask. 'I swear I can see smoke coming out her ears when I tell her that it's quite simple: I'm not going to tell *anyone anything*. It's my business and no one else's.'

Helen gave Hope a quick kiss on her cheek.

'See you, gorgeous. Next week if not before.' She bent down to look at eyes that never failed to amaze her. They were becoming more like her own with each visit.

'Well, I'll keep giving you the same signal at the end of the shift,' Gloria said as Helen came to give her a quick hug before heading out the door. 'If I know for sure the coast is going to be clear, the headscarf comes off. If not – or I'm not sure – it stays on.'

Helen laughed. 'Honestly, it's like the Secret Service!'

'Oh, and Helen,' Gloria said, 'thanks again for my lovely new headscarf. It pains me to wear something so nice for work.'

'Well, it does the trick. Stands out from all that grey – and all those flat caps.' Helen hurried up the stone stairs, pausing at the top to make sure the coast was clear.

'See you soon, Gloria,' Helen shouted down to the flat.

'You take care of yourself now!' Gloria called after her, but she was already gone.

When Helen left, Gloria took Hope out of her high chair and got her settled in her cot in the back bedroom. Looking down at her little girl, she was so incredibly relieved that Helen had decided to go ahead with her pregnancy, and moreover, that she seemed so genuinely happy about it. She had a lot of gumption, that girl. She had to hand it to her.

Gloria walked back down the short hallway and back into the living room. As she cleared up the tea tray, she smiled to herself, thinking of Jack's reaction when they were speaking on the phone the other day and he'd told her that Helen was travelling up to see him in a few weeks. He'd sounded like he had won the pools. Mind you, he probably wouldn't sound so jubilant when Helen told him she was expecting, but he'd get used to it. He'd have to.

She just wished Helen would let her tell him beforehand, give him time to digest the news, but that was Helen – she could be stubborn as hell when she wanted to be.

Perhaps that wasn't a bad thing, though.

It would probably serve her well in the months to come.

Chapter Thirty-Five

Monday 7 September

RYHOPE AIR RAID. THREE KILLED. FORTY INJURED.

The headline screamed out at Helen as soon as Marie-Anne placed the local paper on her desk along with her cup of tea, as she did every morning at nine o'clock.

By the time Marie-Anne was walking out the door, Helen had snatched up the phone and demanded the operator put her through to the Ryhope Emergency Hospital.

Helen listened to the phone ringing, her other hand drumming the top of her desk.

Finally, it was answered.

'Hello, this is the Ryhope Emergency Hospital, how can I help you?'

'Hello, this is Miss Crawford calling. Can you put me through to Dr Parker, please?' Helen tried to keep calm.

'Yes, miss. Please hold the line.'

The receptionist sounded young and a little frazzled.

Helen waited, listening to dead air.

'I'm sorry, miss, I don't seem to be able to locate him. Would you like to leave a message?'

'No, I don't want to leave a message!' Helen snapped. 'I want to speak to Dr Parker!'

'I'm awfully sorry, miss,' the girl sounded *very* young and even more anxious, 'but it's all rather frantic here at the moment.' She paused. 'You know … after the bombing last night.'

'Which is exactly why I need to speak to Dr Parker!' Helen had to work hard to keep her temper under control. 'Write my name down,' she commanded. 'Then go and find Dr Parker and tell him I've called. Then I want you to ring me back and tell me that you have seen him. Do you understand?'

'Yes,' the voice was submissive now. 'I'm to find Dr Parker and ring you back.'

The girl was about to hang up.

'My number!' Helen bellowed down the phone.

'Yes, of course, sorry.'

Helen could hear the girl scrabble around for a piece of paper and a pen.

'Sorry,' she apologised again, 'I'm just a stand-in today … temporary.'

Helen took a breath and gave the girl her number.

'As quick as you can,' she said.

The line went dead. There was nothing to do but wait. It was times like this Helen wished she still smoked. She looked down again at the *Sunderland Echo*.

Bloody Jerry.

Just one bloody bomb and it would *have* to land in Ryhope village. And in Smith Street, of all places. Where John had his bloody bedsit!

She read the rest of the article.

Four more bombs had landed in fields in Grangetown, some phosphorus bombs in Fulwell Quarry, and an unexploded AA shell had landed in Alexandra Road.

Helen took a sip of her tea and nearly dropped the cup when the phone rang.

'Hello!' she barked down the phone.

'Helen, it's me, John. Are you all right?'

'Oh, thank God for that!' Helen almost burst out crying with relief. 'For one horrible moment there … ' Helen's voice trailed off.

'You thought the worst.'

'Yes,' Helen said. 'I just read that Ryhope had been hit … and then when I saw it was Smith Street … '

'I was on night shift here, at the hospital,' Dr Parker explained. 'Mind you, it's been pandemonium since. As you can imagine.'

'Of course.' Helen started to breathe normally. 'All the casualties would have been brought to you … '

'You shouldn't be worrying your head about me, you know.' Dr Parker dropped his voice. 'You've got enough concerns of your own.'

'I'll jolly well worry my head about you if I want to!' Helen's tone was a mixture of anger and relief.

Dr Parker was quiet for a moment.

'Are you all right, Helen? You sound … I don't know … not yourself.'

There was silence down the phone and for a second Dr Parker thought Helen might be crying.

'Helen?'

'I'm fine. I'm fine. Honestly,' Helen tried to reassure him. 'I've just felt so ridiculously emotional this past week. One minute I feel like biting someone's head off, the next I feel like crying my eyes out. Then when I read the news and saw it was your street … well, I just panicked. I needed to know you were all right. I don't think I could bear it if anyone else I know didn't make it through this damned war.'

Dr Parker didn't say anything, but he knew Helen was more cut up than she let on about Tommy Watts. She'd told him over dinner the other night that his belongings had been sent back. Not a very hopeful sign.

'Well, nothing's going to happen to me, rest assured.'

There was another silence down the phone.

'Are you sure you're all right, Helen?' he asked.

He heard her blowing out air. She sounded as though she was in pain.

'Yes, yes, I'm fine,' she said.

'Well, you don't sound fine,' Dr Parker said, concerned.

'I've just got the most terrible bad back,' she said. 'Bloody annoying. Another one of the joys of pregnancy,' she tried to joke, but Dr Parker could hear she was still in severe discomfort.

'Mmm. I wonder whether it might be worth going for a check-up? Wouldn't do any harm,' he suggested.

'Oh, I'm fine. Probably sitting at this desk for too long every day,' Helen said. 'Anyway, I didn't call to talk about me. As long as you're all right, and you've still got a home to go back to – when you do go home, that is!' Helen could hear noise in the background. 'Go on, it sounds busy there. I'll see you later on in the week. My treat this time.'

'Well, we'll see about that. See you then.'

Chapter Thirty-Six

Wednesday 9 September

Arthur was sitting at the kitchen table. He was bent over, tying up his shoe laces, having exchanged his tartan slippers for outdoor footwear. It had just gone ten o'clock and he was getting himself ready to head out to the Town Moor to spend a few hours at the allotment.

Hearing Agnes bustle in from the hallway, he looked up to see her face barely visible behind the mound of bed sheets in her arms. Once a week Agnes would spend the entire day cleaning the house – and everything in it – from top to bottom. Just a glimpse of Agnes's face, however, told Arthur that something was up. She looked uptight. Angry.

'You all right, pet?' Arthur asked as she walked through to the scullery and dumped the sheets on the floor next to the steel dolly tub.

Agnes put her hands on her hips and stared down at the two piles of dirty laundry – one whites, the other coloureds. She didn't look at Arthur, nor did she answer his question. Instead she just stood there. Staring at the dirty laundry.

'Come 'n have a cuppa,' Arthur beckoned. He lifted the tea cosy off and felt the teapot. It was still hot.

Agnes did as Arthur bid. Abandoning the washing, she walked out of the scullery and sat down at the kitchen table. Arthur watched as she performed her usual ritual of pouring tea and a splash of milk into her cup, then tipping a measure into the saucer. Arthur took a sip of his own tea and waited. Agnes would speak when she was ready. This was the quietest time of day in the Elliot household. Polly and Bel were at work, Joe was out with the Home Guard, Pearl was round at the Tatham helping Bill with a delivery from Vaux, and Lucille and Hope were next door at Beryl's, which was where Agnes would have been had it not been her washday.

'I'm worried,' Agnes finally said.

'About Polly?' Arthur asked.

Agnes nodded slowly, then raised the saucer to her lips and sipped her tea.

'Something's happened?' Arthur prodded.

'I've just found these.' Agnes shoved her hand into the pocket of her pinny and pulled out a load of letters. 'And that's not all of them,' she added, 'there's a load more.'

Arthur looked at the carefully folded sheets of white paper.

'Letters?'

Agnes nodded solemnly and pushed them across the oil tablecloth towards Arthur.

He looked at Agnes, who nodded her head, giving him the go-ahead to read.

Arthur's gnarly hands carefully picked up the letter that was on top of the pile and opened it. He skim-read the first few paragraphs, before putting it down and picking up the next and doing the same. He unfolded each piece of paper, one after the other. He didn't need to read each and every one. The words might have been different, but the meaning was the same.

When Arthur looked up at Agnes his pale blue eyes were wet.

'Oh, Agnes.' He sat back on his chair, his hands resting on the table, his body deflated and despairing.

'There's at least another dozen, just like those. All in a pile under her bed,' Agnes said.

'Let me guess,' Arthur ventured, 'she started writing them not long after she got the letter from Tommy's unit commander?'

Agnes nodded gravely.

'Looks like she's been writing one every few days. Sometimes every day … And stopped when Tommy's stuff got sent back. She's not written another letter since then.'

Agnes picked up her saucer with both hands and brought it to her mouth.

'I don't know what worries me more … ' she said before taking a sip and putting the saucer back down. 'The fact she's been scribbling away every night writing letters that she's never going to send—'

'Or not writing any 'cos she's lost all hope our Tom's alive,' Arthur finished off.

'What should a mother wish for? That she has hope, even if it might well be a false hope, or … ' Agnes stopped, not wanting to bring even more heartache to the old man sitting opposite her.

'Or she faces the reality that Tom's dead,' Arthur said, his voice heavy with the most terrible despondency.

'Oh, Arthur, I'm so sorry. I know this is the last thing you need to hear. Me mithering on like this.'

Arthur shook his head. 'Polly's the one that we need to be thinking about. The lass has got her whole life ahead of her. I know if she was my bairn, I'd be worried sick about her.' Arthur's mind spun back in an instant to the First War, when his own daughter had got the news that the man she loved had been killed, and the soul-destroying grief that had convinced her to join him.

'I am … Worried sick,' Agnes said. 'I always knew Bel would be all right when our Teddy died because she was so angry … *So* angry … It sounds daft, but I was actually glad. Knew she just had to get it all out and she'd be all right – eventually. And she was. But Polly … she's keeping it all inside. Going on as always. Going to work, eating her supper, going to bed, but it's all festering inside of her. And I don't like it. Don't like it one bit.'

She poured herself another cuppa.

'It was bad enough the last war took her da. Poor bairn never even got to meet him. I know for a fact one of the reasons she started at that bloody yard was because she imagined her father would be proud of her.'

Tears pooled in her eyes. She put a finger and thumb under each eye to try and stop them.

'My poor girl.' Her voice was shaky. Tears started to run down her face. 'I wish I could take the pain away, suffer it for her, but I can't.'

'She's strong,' Arthur said. 'She's like her ma. Tougher than she looks.'

Agnes shook her head. 'I wish that were true, but she's not. She tries to make out she is, but she's not.' Agnes dug around in her skirt pocket and pulled out a hanky. 'When my Harry was declared missing, presumed dead, I was heartbroken. Devastated. But I had the bairns by then. I had to carry on. For their sake.'

Agnes wiped more tears away from her face.

'God, I wish I hadn't been so bloody pious and let her marry Tommy before he went.'

Arthur clasped his hands and was quiet. Grief seemed to come with so much guilt. He knew that well. Had suffered from it almost his entire life.

If.

If only.

If only he'd done different his own daughter might still be alive.

'If I hadn't been so set in me ways,' Agnes lamented, 'if I'd let them both just throw caution to the wind 'n get married, at least my girl would have been a wife, might well have started a family. Something to keep her going.'

Arthur listened.

'I know Polly.' Agnes looked at Arthur. 'She's so stubborn. So bloody single-minded. And she's loyal. She won't ever love again, you know.'

'Aye, I know,' Arthur agreed.

'And that breaks my heart.' Agnes was properly crying now, tears spilling down her face.

'My beautiful girl, never being a wife, never having little 'uns of her own ... This *bloody war*.'

Arthur let Agnes cry for a while and sat in silence.

After a while he spoke up.

'Polly can't do anything about this war, or about Tommy and what might or might not have happened to him, and yer right, if Tommy is dead, then I can't see Polly ever marrying anyone else or having any bairns of her own.'

Agnes looked at the old man, her vision now blurred from the vestiges of her tears.

'But she does have another love. A love I know you hate, but she does love them yards and it'll be building ships that keeps her going. Polly's never going to be the same – I think we both know that – but as long as she's doing what she's doing now, she'll keep going. She'll survive.'

Agnes hated to admit it to Arthur, or to herself, but she knew his words to be true.

As they both sat there in the quietness of the house, thinking their own thoughts, Agnes reflected on life's irony. She had taken Arthur in thinking that she was doing him a favour after Tommy had gone to war and left him on his own. Yet it was Arthur who had become invaluable to them all, with his calm demeanour and wise words. They needed him far more than he needed them.

And the very shipyard that Agnes had feared would threaten the safety of her beloved daughter was now looking as though it might be the very thing to save her.

Chapter Thirty-Seven

Thursday 10 September

'Is that you, Helen?'

Miriam's voice cut through the air as she shouted up the staircase.

'Who else is it going to be, Mother?'

Miriam started walking up the first flight of stairs.

'Well, it could have been the cleaner.' She purposely kept her reply light and friendly.

'At six o'clock in the evening?' Helen, on the other hand, wasn't in the mood for any kind of pretence, and didn't try to mask her contempt.

'Are you in your father's room?' Miriam was halfway up the stairs.

'I am, Mother.' Helen was standing in the middle of the back bedroom, arching her back. She'd thought you only got a bad back in the later stages of pregnancy, when you were hauling around the equivalent of a sack of coal.

'What are you doing in there?' Miriam finally reached the top of the stairs and could see Helen standing in the room ahead, hands on her hips. Her eyes fell to the pull of her skirt around her stomach. She wouldn't be able to hide her condition for much longer.

'Just having a little change around.' Helen looked around the room. She had got their cleaner to strip the single bed and box everything up. Not that there was much to pack away. Her father was not one for possessions.

'But this is your father's room.' Miriam was not happy to see the room bare. She wanted to keep up appearances.

'It's not as if he's ever going to use it again, is it, Mother?' Helen said, inspecting the empty wardrobe. 'I mean, it's not as if he's ever coming back here to live.' Helen closed the narrow wooden doors and turned the little key.

'That might be true, but that's no reason to have the room cleared.' Miriam was genuinely perplexed.

'Oh sorry, I should have told you.'

Helen turned and for the first time looked her mother in the eyes.

'This is going to be the nursery.'

Miriam's mouth dropped open.

'What?' Her voice was full of incredulity.

'The nursery,' Helen repeated. 'I would have thought you'd realise the baby will need a nursery.'

Helen looked around the room again.

'I've got it all planned in my head.'

Miriam heard her daughter's words and knew she couldn't put this conversation off any longer. Certainly not with the way Helen was starting to bust out of her clothes. She might be able to cover it up for a little while longer with the Utility-style skirts and jackets she had been wearing of late, but only for a few more weeks, at the most.

'Darling,' Miriam softened her voice and wiped the image of the nursery from her mind, 'I've been wanting to talk to you about something for a while.' She turned towards the door. 'Shall we go downstairs and have a drink?'

'I think you've already had one, Mum,' Helen said. 'I can smell the gin on you from here.'

Miriam bit her tongue. She could not get riled or she'd never get Helen back onside. And more importantly, get her to agree to her plan.

'If you want to chat to me, you can chat to me here.' Helen walked over and sat on the bare mattress.

Miriam realised she wasn't going to be able to loosen Helen up with a drink, or top herself up, so she went and sat down next to her daughter.

'You've got me worried now,' Helen said, leaning away from her mother as she spoke.

'Darling,' Miriam thought about taking Helen's hand but decided against it, 'your grandfather and I have been talking. And we really can't believe that in all seriousness you intend to have an illegitimate child – to be an unmarried mother.'

Helen felt herself bristle. 'You must know I'm never going to – how did you put it? *Get rid of it.*'

'No, I know that, darling,' Miriam said, her voice unusually calm. 'But your grandfather and I thought that perhaps it would be a wise idea, and the right time –' Miriam's eyes strayed down to Helen's stomach ' – for you to go away for a while.'

'Go where?' Helen asked, a quizzical look on her face.

'Well, your grandfather and I thought that perhaps you might want to go and stay with your grandmother's cousin.'

Helen looked at her mother.

'What, the one who's as mad as a hatter and lives in the middle of nowhere?'

'Eliza's hardly *mad*, darling. I think the word would be *eccentric*. And it's not exactly in the middle of nowhere. Eliza's got a wonderful, sprawling estate in the Ribble Valley. Near Clitheroe.'

Helen's face became serious.

'So, pray tell, what plan have you both concocted? You can't exactly send me abroad, so the next best option is to hide me away in the back of beyond, where no one knows me, with an ancient, *eccentric*, long-forgotten relative – and then what?'

'Well, we thought that you could see out the rest of your term there – during which time an appropriate *home* could be found.'

Helen was quiet for a moment.

She nodded slowly, as though digesting the idea.

Miriam felt her spirits lift.

'And then, darling, you can come back here and pick up where you left off – go back to work at Thompson's and do what you love. Your grandfather was telling me that he can see you're going to go far. Rise in the ranks. Be the first woman to run a shipyard – *in the whole of the country*, never mind just in the north-east.' This part of the argument Miriam thought was pure genius, although she had to admit that it had been her father's very clever idea to persuade Helen to do what they wanted by focusing on her ambitions, feeding into what she loved the most – her work.

'Mmm.' Helen straightened her back as she made out she was contemplating the idea. 'So, I go and stay with Eliza, where no one will know me. Obviously I wouldn't really leave the estate. I know Clitheroe's a lovely little town, but we wouldn't want anyone to see me getting as big as a bus in case they found out who I was.'

Miriam felt like cheering. She knew she would be able to solve this problem. Just like she had solved the problem of Jack and his bastard child.

'So,' Helen continued, 'I live like Rapunzel in her tower, not seeing anyone other than Eliza, of course, and her staff, who will all be sworn to secrecy – and naturally rewarded well for it.'

Miriam looked at her daughter and thought she had learnt more from her grandfather than she'd thought. Money, he'd always said, bought you anything.

'And a new *home* will be found.' Helen paused. 'I'm wondering, though – what would be best? A poor unfortunate couple who can't have their own children, like Aunty Marg and Uncle Angus.' She paused again as though in serious thought. 'Or a couple who have their own family but are more than willing to take on another child for a nice annual sum. An extra wage as such.'

'Exactly!' Miriam was finding it hard to contain her excitement. She couldn't wait to pour herself a nice congratulatory gin and tonic.

'What do you think, Mum?' Helen asked. 'A well-off but barren couple? Or a poor but ready-made family?'

'Well, I'm not sure. I guess there are advantages to both,' Miriam said. She really didn't give two hoots. It'd be the local orphanage if she had a choice.

'If I opt for the rich but childless couple,' Helen mused, 'I'm sure they would stipulate that once the baby is handed over, then that is the end of any future contact.'

Miriam nodded earnestly.

'But if we go for the penniless but pre-made family,' Helen continued, 'then I would be able to dictate if I wanted to have contact, and how often, and because they were being paid, I would be able to wield that kind of control. Come and go as I pleased. *If* I pleased.'

'Perhaps the childless couple,' Miriam suggested. Out of the two this was by far the best option. A nice, clear-cut end to the whole sorry saga. Ideally, she didn't want Helen having *any* contact with the child, just in case. Having said that, she was sure when Helen came back home she'd forget all about the baby. Would probably end up thanking her for making her see sense.

Helen stood up.

'Come on, Mum, let's go downstairs and get you that gin I know you're secretly hankering after.'

Miriam couldn't get up off the bed quickly enough. Within minutes they were in the front living room and Miriam was pouring herself a drink.

'I'll just have tonic, please,' Helen said.

Having poured both their drinks, Miriam handed Helen her tonic water.

'A toast then?' Miriam said, raising her glass.

'A toast,' Helen agreed. 'To the future,' she added.

'To the future,' Miriam said, taking a large swig.

Helen put her drink down on the sideboard and made for the door.

'You off out?' Miriam asked, thinking about her own evening. *Wait until she told Amelia.* Her friend had been right. Helen mightn't have been able to go ahead with the abortion, but she would jump at the chance of getting shot of it once she saw sense.

'Not tonight,' Helen said. 'I thought I'd stay in and carry on sorting out the nursery. I've managed not only to get a decorator, but one who can actually get his hands on some paint. Quite a find, eh?'

Miriam looked totally perplexed.

'What do you mean? I don't understand,' she asked, genuinely confused. 'There's obviously no need for a nursery now. Is there? Now that we've come to our decision?'

Miriam looked at her daughter standing in the doorway, smiling.

'Oh, Mum, you're just too easy.' Helen laughed. 'Gosh, and I used to think I was the gullible one in this house.'

She smiled.

'You don't seriously think I was going to go and live like a recluse for the next five months with a mad – sorry, *eccentric* – old woman, have my baby, and then farm the poor thing out to complete strangers?'

Helen chuckled again.

'Honestly, you do make me laugh.'

She went to leave the room but stopped and turned towards her mother, who was standing there, speechless. Helen thought she reminded her of a waxwork model, standing so still, with her glass of gin and tonic held out in front of her, frozen in the moment.

'You really don't understand, do you?' A small frown had appeared on Helen's brow. 'But I'm afraid you and dear Grandfather are going to have to understand.'

Helen took a deep breath.

Miriam was still rooted to the spot.

'You are both going to have to realise that I actually *want* this baby.'

Helen paused, letting her words hang in the air.

'I *want* this baby. And I'm going to *have* this baby. And there's nothing you or Grandfather – or anyone for that matter – can do or say to stop me.'

As Helen walked out of the room and closed the door behind her, she heard the sound of her mother's crystal tumbler being hurled across the room and smashing against the wooden panelling of the lounge door.

Chapter Thirty-Eight

Friday 11 September

'Did yer read about that place in Germany … Düssel—?'

'Düsseldorf … Aye.'

The two riveters picked up their tin trays.

'Gave Jerry a bit of their own medicine, eh?'

'Aye, 'n about bloody time.'

The two workers scrutinised the menu board for a moment.

'Sad news about Doris's son, though.'

'What? Yer missus's sister's lad? The one that's in the navy?'

'Aye.'

'What about him?'

'She got a telegram this morning. Declared him missing. She was in a right state. Came round to see the wife. Inconsolable she was. Poor woman.'

Polly was standing behind the two men as they queued up for their lunch. On hearing this last part of their conversation, she turned, gave up her place in the long line of workers, and hurried out of the canteen.

When she walked back to her squad all sitting by the quayside eating their packed lunches, she saw Bel was there with Marie-Anne.

'You all right?' Bel asked quietly as Polly sat down next to her. Agnes had confided in her about Polly's letter-writing, and she'd resolved to keep an even closer eye on her sister-in-law.

'Yeh.' Polly forced a smile.

'I thought you were getting your lunch in the canteen today?' Bel asked.

'The queue was too long,' Polly lied.

Bel gave Polly half her sandwich. 'Don't even bother arguing.'

Polly took the sandwich and forced herself to take a bite even though she didn't feel hungry; hadn't really felt hungry for what seemed like a long time now.

'So, come on, Bel. And you, Marie-Anne.' Dorothy's voice was loud, drawing everyone's attention. 'What's all the gossip?'

'Well, we put an order in for some new ribbons for the typewriters,' Marie-Anne teased.

Dorothy sighed loudly.

'Come on, there must be a few morsels you can feed us? Keep us all from dying of boredom here,' she implored.

'Well, you know Theresa?' Marie-Anne said.

Everyone nodded.

'The one who's got even more children than Angie's mam?' Dorothy nudged her friend, who simply shook her head dismissively.

'Well, she's got another one on the way.'

'Blimey, how many's that now?'

'I think this one'll make it a dozen.'

'Roman Catholic?' Gloria asked.

Marie-Anne nodded. 'Staunch.'

The women tried not to check out Bel's reaction to the news; she was still looking as slim as a pin.

'And how's *the witch*?' Angie asked.

'Yeh, we've not seen hide nor hair of her lately,' Martha chipped in, putting the lid back on her lunch box, now empty of its contents.

'She looked a bit rough today, didn't she, Marie-Anne?' Bel said. 'We reckoned she was either paying for a night on the town or had eaten something dodgy. She was as white as a sheet.'

'And,' Marie-Anne added, 'when she was dictating a letter to me, she suddenly stopped and got up and started walking round with her hand on her back. I asked her if she was all right.'

'What did she say?' Gloria asked.

'Oh, you know Helen,' Marie-Anne said, 'just snapped my head off. Said she was fine and to concentrate on my shorthand. Honestly, she's been a right Jekyll and Hyde this past week. One minute as nice as ninepence, the next a bloomin' nightmare.'

'Nothing new there then,' Polly said, forcing herself to take another bite of sandwich.

There was a general murmuring of agreement.

Gloria looked at the women and would have given anything to tell them that Helen really was not the devil incarnate they all thought she was, and that, like Theresa, she was pregnant and clearly suffering for it.

'Mind you,' Rosie said, sensing Gloria's unrest, 'she's not been giving *us* any hassle lately, has she?'

'Only because she knows she has to keep us sweet if she wants to hit a new tonnage record,' Dorothy chipped in.

Gloria would have liked to have said that it had nothing to do with tonnage, and more to do with the fact that Helen didn't want to be at loggerheads with the women any more. She would never admit it, but Gloria knew that Helen would give anything to have a group of friends like the women sitting here now.

'Anyway, how's the flat?' Marie-Anne asked. She was fascinated by the fact that Dorothy and Angie had left home and got their own place.

'We love it, don't we, Ange?' Dorothy turned to look at her best mate.

'It's brilliant!' Angie said. 'We can do whatever we want.'

'And your mams and dads were all right about it?' Marie-Anne asked, curious.

'Mine weren't bothered,' Dorothy said, 'but Ange's were a little more tricky, weren't they?'

Angie nodded. 'Aye, but they're all reet now. I still pop 'n see them every week, take them some shopping 'n help them out with the kids for the evening. That seems to keep them happy.'

'So,' Dorothy said, looking around at her workmates and at Polly in particular, 'I do believe it's time for another trip to the flicks soon. And there'll be no excuses this time. Everyone's coming.'

'Does Mr Havelock ever come to the yard?' Bel asked Marie-Anne as they made their way back to the admin office.

'Funny you should ask. He used to show his face every few weeks, but lately he's not been here at all. Probably 'cos he's getting on a bit now.'

'And what about his daughter, Miriam?'

'What? Helen's mam?'

Bel nodded.

'Actually, she's not been in for a while either.' She chuckled. 'Thank God. If your lot think Helen's bad, you want to meet her mother. She's another kettle of fish altogether.'

Bloomin' typical, Bel thought as they walked through the main door and up the stairs to the first floor. *I start work here and they stop coming.*

The klaxon sounded out the start of the shift just as she and Marie-Anne sat down at their desks.

Typing up a memo about overtime, Bel realised that her desperate need to get pregnant seemed to have been overtaken by her obsessive need to know more about her 'other' family.

She wasn't sure which was worse.

Chapter Thirty-Nine

J. Risdon & Co, High Street West, Sunderland

'Oh, this *is* rather lovely, isn't it?' The shop assistant looked at the little lemon-coloured romper suit Helen had just brought to the counter. 'Would you like it gift-wrapped?'

Helen shook her head.

'No, thank you. It's not really a present as such.'

Helen realised she should have said yes. Now the assistant would wonder why she was buying clothes for a newborn if not as a present.

The salesgirl glanced up at Helen as she popped the baby suit in a brown paper bag. This particular customer had been in the shop before. She was gorgeous, a bit like that actress in *Gone with the Wind*, and if her memory served her right, the last time she'd been in she'd bought a lovely pink sun hat for her friend's baby's first birthday.

This purchase, though, was clearly not for a one-year-old.

As Helen handed over her clothing ration book along with the exact amount of money the item cost, the young assistant noticed that the Vivien Leigh customer was not sporting a wedding ring – nor even an engagement ring.

As the bell tinkled over the door and Helen left the shop, the assistant made a private wager with herself that the baby suit the woman had just bought was, in fact, for her – and, judging by her choice, she would also guess that the woman was hoping for a girl.

*

As Helen walked back out onto the corner of John Street and High Street West, she had to stop for a moment and catch her breath. This past week she'd suffered from the odd bout of cramping pains, rather like the ones she got just before her monthlies. They hadn't lasted long, though, and she'd put them down to the changes happening in her body. She was, after all, creating another life. She was going to feel something, wasn't she?

The pain passed in a matter of seconds and Helen continued walking, holding the paper bag with her purchase in it close to her chest. She felt so excited.

She knew it was a little early to be buying clothes – some people were even superstitious about it – but she just couldn't resist. Having been in there to buy Hope a little dress and then, more recently, the sun hat, she had fallen in love with the shop; it was a veritable Aladdin's cave of babywear, toys, prams and cots.

As she turned left into Fawcett Street it suddenly occurred to Helen that, despite her recent mood swings, she was actually really happy.

'John!' Helen waved.

'That's a welcome to brighten anyone's day!' Dr Parker smiled as Helen reached him.

'Oh, John, what a lovely day,' Helen said, giving him a quick hug and kiss on the cheek.

'Yes, it is, but I'm still not happy about this being your treat.' Dr Parker opened the heavy glass-fronted door of Meng's café and restaurant.

'Well, you're going to have to remain unhappy as I'm not changing my mind. This is my way of saying thank you.' She dropped her voice as the maître d' showed them to a table for two in the far corner. 'Although I think we both know,' she said, taking her seat and putting her recent purchase on the tabletop, 'that the reason we're really here is because I just want to go somewhere nice – and I can't go on my own.'

The maître d' reappeared, handed them two menus and left.

'It would, of course, help if I actually had friends I could go out with, but at least I've got one – *you*.' Helen looked about the café, which was almost full. If they'd been any later they'd have struggled to get a seat.

'Well, this friend,' Dr Parker said, 'is more than happy to oblige. I've always been curious about this place, but never had an excuse to come here.'

The maître d' reappeared at the table and Helen ordered two scones and tea for two, which were brought to the table just minutes later.

'So, what's put you in such a *particularly* good mood?' Dr Parker asked, looking across at Helen. She certainly appeared happy, though she did look a bit peaky.

'Oh, I've been a bit naughty,' Helen said, pushing the paper bag across the table, 'and nipped into Risdon's before I met you. I just couldn't resist.'

Dr Parker took a peek in the bag and smiled.

'So, you're going to have a girl, are you?' he chuckled.

'That's Gloria's fault,' she said, 'she keeps saying *she* and *her* – she's brainwashed me.' Helen laughed. 'Anyway, boys can wear yellow, can't they?'

'Mmm.' Dr Parker took a mouthful of scone and savoured it.

'So, how's things at the hospital?' Helen asked. She was genuinely interested in what happened up at the Ryhope.

'Well, it's been busy, as usual,' Dr Parker said. 'And we had our hands full the night of the air raid.'

'Thank God they didn't hit the hospital,' Helen said. 'That would have been even more disastrous.'

Dr Parker nodded. 'I'm guessing they were aiming for Ryhope colliery.'

'And the waterworks,' Helen added.

'Anyway, enough doom and gloom,' Dr Parker said. 'Tell me about your week. You still on target for your production record?'

Helen nodded enthusiastically, but as she took another bite of her scone her face suddenly creased up in pain.

'You all right?' Dr Parker asked, concerned, leaning over the table.

'Yes, I'm fine, honestly,' Helen said, breathing out.

'What just happened there?' Dr Parker asked.

'I think it must be the baby moving,' Helen said.

Dr Parker doubted that what Helen had just felt was her baby. Certainly not something so severe.

'How often have you been having these kinds of feelings?' he asked.

'Oh, not long, it's just been this week, really,' Helen said, taking a sip of her tea and then sitting back in her chair.

'And your bad back? How's that been?' Dr Parker was struggling to keep the worry out of his voice.

'Niggling. Actually, I was going to ask you if you had any suggestions. I've tried walking around more, not sitting at my desk as much, but it seems to be there most of the time now ... But the good thing is,' Helen said, brightening up, 'I don't feel sick any more.' And as if to prove the point she took another bite out of her scone.

'And,' Helen lowered her voice, 'the part of me that was feeling very tender,' Helen glanced down at her ample bosom, 'doesn't any more. So that's a relief. No more having to lie on my back when I go to sleep.'

Dr Parker looked at Helen. He would have liked to ask her more questions, but didn't want to worry her. He would suggest when they left that she make an appointment with Dr Billingham for a check-up – just to be on the safe side.

'So, what else has been happening this week?' Dr Parker asked, not wanting Helen to sense his disquiet.

'Well,' Helen said, 'I've made a start on converting the back bedroom into a nursery.'

Dr Parker looked surprised. 'Bet you your mother's going to love that!'

Helen gave her friend a mischievous look and proceeded to tell him the events of the previous night. Dr Parker listened. Helen's mother had a lot to answer for and deserved everything Helen wanted to chuck at her, and more.

When the waitress came to clear their plates, Helen ordered another pot of tea and they continued to chat. As the conversation started to turn back to the latest war news, Dr Parker again noticed that Helen really was very pale. Was it the light? Or had she become even paler since they'd been in here?

'Sorry, John,' Helen said after a while. 'Excuse me for a moment while I go and powder my nose.'

Dr Parker watched as Helen manoeuvred her way around half a dozen tables. At one stage she appeared to grab one to steady herself.

He watched with growing unease when she stopped for a second, took a deep breath and walked on.

Something wasn't right.

As soon as Helen stood up she felt dizzy. She'd suddenly had the urge to go to the toilet and had put it down to the second pot of tea they had ordered. When she started walking, she saw stars and had to steady herself with the back of an empty chair.

As she continued walking she was hit by the most excruciating pain in her stomach. It was as though an iron fist had decided to grab her insides and not let go. It took all she could muster not to double up and make a spectacle of herself.

She stood and took a deep breath before making it the rest of the way to the ladies.

If anyone had passed her, they would have seen her face was scrunched up in pure agony.

Once she was through the toilet door she breathed a sigh of relief that it was empty.

Staggering to the mirror and looking at her reflection, she saw she'd gone a milky shade of white and her forehead was covered in small spots of perspiration.

She groaned out loud as the iron fist inside of her seemed to twist its hold. This time she had no choice but to double over.

Stumbling the few steps to the cubicle, she pushed open the door, stepped inside and closed it behind her, pulling the lock across to show the engaged sign.

As she did so, she felt something tickling her leg.

She swatted her calf, thinking it was a fly, but was surprised when she felt something wet. Turning her palm upwards, she was shocked to see that her hand was streaked with red.

Looking down, she saw blood, and another claret rivulet making its way down her other leg.

A wave of nausea was followed by another contraction of excruciating pain.

Panicking, Helen pulled up her skirt.

There was blood everywhere.

Her vision went misty.

And then she saw stars again.

Suddenly her legs felt so weak; too weak to stand.

Her whole body seemed to waver for a moment, like a building just after it's been hit by a bulldozer's swinging steel ball, standing defiant for the briefest of moments before being reduced to a cloud of debris and brick dust.

Just so, Helen felt blindsided by an invisible force.

Her whole world seemed to stop still for a second – before her knees went, and she collapsed into a heap on the tiled floor.

As gravity did its work, her head hit the side of the patterned porcelain toilet bowl and her vision changed from blurred to black.

Dr Parker looked at his watch.

Helen had now been gone a good five minutes. It seemed a long time to be in the ladies.

He shuffled uneasily on his seat.

Helen hadn't taken her handbag, so it wasn't as if she would be touching up her make-up.

Something wasn't right.

Now he was thinking about it, he'd actually felt something was amiss the moment he'd set eyes on her.

'Excuse me.' Dr Parker reached out to touch the arm of the maître d' who was just walking past him. 'This is an odd request, but I'd like to go and check on my companion, who hasn't re-emerged from the ladies. I'm a doctor,' he added by way of reassurance, 'at the Ryhope.'

The maître d' gave a curt nod of his head.

Not wasting any time, Dr Parker charged over to the washroom.

'Hello! Helen!' He knocked loudly, waited for a second, but when he didn't hear a response, opened the door and stepped into the large, rather plush ladies' toilets.

He scanned the room before seeing Helen's arm splayed out on the ceramic floor. Her black hair was just visible through the gap under the cubicle.

Dr Parker shoved the door but it wouldn't budge.

'Helen!' he shouted out, hoping to see movement, or at least to elicit a reaction, even a groan, but there was nothing. Just silence.

Dr Parker took a step back before throwing his whole weight at the door.

It did the trick and the door banged open, revealing Helen's lifeless body lying on the floor in a pool of blood.

Dr Parker immediately crouched down and checked her pulse before putting his ear to her mouth.

Thank God she was breathing, although her pulse felt weak.

He moved her head gently, inspecting it for damage. There was a gash above her eyebrow.

Dr Parker stood up and clattered his way out of the cubicle and towards the main door that led out to the café. As soon as he opened it, he saw the maître d' standing there.

'Ambulance!' Dr Parker commanded. 'Call an ambulance! Tell them it's an emergency!'

The maître d' didn't need telling twice.

Dr Parker swung round and strode back over to Helen, who was now making slightly woozy noises.

Crouching back down next to her, he checked her pulse again.

'Bloody hell,' he muttered under his breath.

Chapter Forty

Dr Parker straightened Helen's body out on the floor, before pulling her legs up and bending her knees.

Wrestling his jacket off, he covered her body, all the time alternating between checking her pulse and inspecting her for any other injuries.

He was fairly sure that Helen had hit her head on the side of the toilet bowl, as he could see a slight smear of red blood contrasted against the blue motif.

This, however, wasn't his main concern.

It was clear that Helen was haemorrhaging – heavily.

The amount of blood suggested not only that she was in the process of losing her baby, but that the bleeding was not slowing down. It had to be stopped, and quickly. And the only way that could be done was by getting her to hospital and into theatre as soon as possible.

Hearing the sirens of the ambulance, Dr Parker breathed a little easier.

Two minutes later two paramedics burst into the ladies. Thankfully, they'd come armed with a stretcher.

Between the three of them, they carefully lifted Helen on to the gurney while Dr Parker briefed them – informing them that he was a doctor, that the woman in their care was concussed, and that she was haemorrhaging internally.

They didn't need to be told where the bleeding was coming from.

*

Helen could vaguely remember hearing John's voice barking instructions at the two men in what looked like army uniforms.

The next memory she had was lying on the stretcher and turning her head to the side to see the table where she and John had been enjoying their tea and scones.

Catching sight of the brown paper bag still on the table, she flung her arm out, but it was no good, she couldn't reach it.

Her next hazy recollection was of being in the ambulance with John next to her. She thought he was holding her hand until she realised he was checking her pulse. He was speaking to her, but she couldn't really make out what he was saying.

She could hear the sirens and see flashes of blue in the corner of her eye.

It felt as though they were travelling down a bumpy road until she realised it was her own body that was shuddering and bouncing up and down on the stretcher.

Her teeth were also chattering.

She tried to stop herself from shaking, to unclench her jaw, but she couldn't.

She felt so cold.

So very cold.

Then she couldn't see the blue flashes any more – and once again the darkness came.

Arriving at the Royal, Dr Parker asked the nurse who had come out to greet them which surgeons were on duty.

On hearing Dr Billingham's name, he said a silent prayer of thanks and told the nurse to go and get him and to tell him that Dr Parker was taking a patient down to theatre and to meet him there.

'As fast as you can!' he told the nurse, who took one look at the woman shaking uncontrollably on the stretcher, and the red staining on her clothes, and knew this was no time for dilly-dallying.

The two hospital porters positioned themselves at either end of Helen's stretcher and followed Dr Parker as he led the way down a rabbit warren of corridors.

As soon as they arrived at the prep room, Dr Parker started scrubbing up and giving out orders to the two surgical nurses who had just been saying that it looked as though it was going to be a quiet night.

'What happened?' Dr Billingham came charging through the swing doors.

On hearing that it was Dr Parker who had demanded his presence in theatre, and that the patient was a pretty young woman with black hair, he'd known it was Mr Havelock's granddaughter.

'She's into her second trimester. Back pain, followed by abdominal cramps. Just started haemorrhaging badly,' Dr Parker said as the nurses helped both doctors into their white operating gowns.

'She's also got a slight concussion,' he added as he prepared the cannula. 'Looks like she fainted and hit her head as she fell.'

He looked round to see that one of the nurses was getting the drip ready.

'God, we need to stop that bleeding,' he said as the nurse stripped Helen of her clothes, now heavily bloodstained.

The swing doors flew open for the second time and both surgeons looked round to see the anaesthetist.

'As soon as you can,' Dr Billingham said, nodding across at Helen.

'She's eaten, but we'll have to risk it,' Dr Parker added. 'No time to lose.'

A few minutes later, when Helen's body had finally stopped bouncing on the trolley, she was hastily wheeled into the operating theatre.

The maître d' was carrying out his usual checks after closing up for the day – a day that had been made even more hectic than usual after the drama earlier on.

Casting his eye over the café, he returned to check the float in the till and saw that a brown paper bag had been left next to it.

Looking inside, he saw it contained a rather expensive-looking, citron-coloured baby suit.

On his way to the staff cloakroom, he stopped and put it in the lost-property box. If no one came to claim it by the end of the week, he would give it to his week-old baby granddaughter.

She'd look as cute as pie in it.

Chapter Forty-One

When Helen opened her eyes, the first person she saw was Dr Parker, sitting in an armchair at her bedside. His head was nodding forwards, touching his chest every now and again.

'What happened?' she asked. Her voice felt hoarse and raspy, and it hurt to swallow.

Dr Parker's head snapped up, and he brushed his hair away from his face. His eyes were bloodshot and tired. He reached over to the beaker of water that was on the top of the bedside cabinet and put it to Helen's dry, chapped lips.

'Have a sip,' he said quietly.

Helen did as she was told, feeling the cold water run down her throat.

'What happened?' Helen asked again. Snapshots of them being in the café flickered across her mind.

Her hand automatically went to her stomach and she felt the tug of the drip she was attached to.

Her body felt different.

And then she remembered the blood.

There'd been so much blood.

'Helen,' Dr Parker said, taking hold of her hand.

Helen looked down and thought it was the first time she had noticed John's hands. They reminded her of a pianist's hands, long and slender but strong.

'I'm so sorry, Helen,' Dr Parker continued. 'But I'm afraid you started haemorrhaging ... Badly ... And ... '

He took a deep breath.

'I'm so sorry, Helen, but I'm afraid you've lost your baby.'

Dr Parker had his eyes trained on Helen, waiting for his words to make their way through the buffer of painkillers.

He saw the moment of comprehension. He'd seen that look in the eyes of many soldiers this past year when they had come round from surgery and he'd had to tell them their worst fears had become reality.

As he looked into Helen's emerald eyes, her pupils pinpricks from the drugs she had been given, he felt a terrible pain in his own chest as he saw her heart break.

Dr Parker squeezed her hand, wanting so hard to take her suffering away, but knowing he couldn't.

Dr Parker watched as tears pooled and spilled down the face of the woman he loved.

Helen slowly turned her head away.

As sorrow racked her body and she cried from the depths of her very soul, Dr Parker kept hold of Helen's hand and allowed his own tears to fall silently.

Dr Parker stayed the night with Helen as she was consumed by her grief.

Occasionally she would stop crying and fall into an exhausted sleep before waking again.

As the anaesthetic wore off she asked more questions about exactly what had happened, and she listened as Dr Parker explained that she'd had a miscarriage, which was unusual at this stage of the pregnancy, but not unheard of.

He explained to her that they had had to operate to stop the bleeding. He didn't go into too much detail, but reassured her that they had been able to do what was necessary without damaging her chances of being able to fall pregnant again.

What he didn't say was that it was likely what had happened during this pregnancy could well happen with the next. He had a feeling that this might run in the family, recalling what Helen had said about her aunty Margaret.

That would be a conversation for another time, though.

For the moment Dr Parker just needed Helen to recover as best she could. He knew this would scar Helen emotionally, but it was knowing how badly. Everyone was different.

As Helen drifted off again, he looked at her and it hurt him to recall how happy she had been about the baby she seemed determined was going to be a girl.

That was something else he wouldn't tell her, unless she asked.

Her baby had been a girl.

When the sun started to filter through the blackout curtains, Helen looked across at Dr Parker.

'How long do you think I'll have to be kept in?'

'At least another day or two,' he told her. 'We need to keep an extra eye on you because of the nasty bash you had on your head.'

'I'll have to tell work that I'm not coming in,' she said.

'Actually, I've been thinking, and I have a suggestion,' Dr Parker said, as Helen pulled herself up in the bed. 'I know you're going to yell at me, but I rang your mother last night to tell her what had happened—'

'God, she probably got up, got dressed and went out to celebrate,' Helen said.

'But I wasn't able to get through,' Dr Parker said.

'You mean she didn't answer?'

Dr Parker nodded.

'That'll be her sleeping pills,' Helen explained. 'A bomb could land on the house and she wouldn't even stir ... So, she doesn't know?'

Dr Parker nodded again, thinking once again how similar Helen's mother and his own were.

'God, I don't think I can bear to see her.' Helen's mouth was set tight as she thought. 'Please, is there any way you can keep her from visiting?'

'Well, I had an idea,' Dr Parker said. 'Knowing you'd probably feel the way you do, I thought that perhaps *I* should go and see your mother, perhaps with your grandfather as well, and tell them what has happened. I wondered – now tell me if you think this is a good idea or not – if I should meet them at Thompson's and that way I can tell Harold that you've been taken ill with a ruptured appendix, that you're all right, but have had an operation and need to convalesce for a week or so.'

Helen took Dr Parker's hand, a hand that now felt very familiar as she had hardly let it go all night; she squeezed it with the little energy she had.

'Thank you, John, I don't know what I'd do without you.'

John squeezed it back, not wanting to let go, but knowing he had to.

Chapter Forty-Two

Dr Parker just had enough time to go back to his digs, clean up, then nip to the Ryhope to explain his absence last night, before heading back into town and across to North Sands.

By the time he entered the admin building it had just gone ten o'clock.

When he walked into Helen's office and found Harold there with Miriam and Mr Havelock, he politely asked Harold if he could first have a private word with Helen's mother and grandfather.

'Of course, of course! Just get Marie-Anne to come for me when you're ready. There's a pot of tea over on the side there. Please, just help yourself,' he said, leaving the room and shutting the door firmly behind him.

As soon as Harold had gone Dr Parker went over to Miriam, who was standing by the large glass window, looking out at the office workers beavering away on their typewriters and comptometers.

'Hello, Mrs Crawford.' He put his hand out. 'I'm not sure if you remember me – from the Royal? When your husband was ill?'

Miriam gave him a limp handshake.

'Yes, of course, although it's a period of my life I prefer to forget,' she said, wandering over and sitting in a chair by the side of the desk.

Dr Parker turned to Mr Havelock, who was ensconced behind Helen's desk as though this was his domain and no one else's. He was smoking a thick Cuban cigar. He half pushed himself out of the leather swivel chair and shook hands.

'We've never met,' Mr Havelock said, his grip vice-like and belying his fragile physique, 'but I have heard about you from various sources.'

'First of all,' Dr Parker said, pulling a metal chair from the corner of the room and sitting down, 'thank you both for coming here. I thought it would be the best place to meet, all things considered—'

'John, isn't it?' Miriam interrupted, her voice sharp and impatient.

Dr Parker nodded.

'Why don't you just tell us what this is all about? And why my daughter is not here with us now – at work?'

Dr Parker looked at Miriam's perfectly made-up face and her blonde, slightly curly, bobbed hair, and thought how she didn't look at all like her daughter.

'I'm afraid your daughter,' he said to Miriam, before directing his attention to Mr Havelock, 'has been unwell. Very unwell. She started haemorrhaging last night and had to be operated on to stop the bleeding, but she is now out of theatre and is recovering at the Royal.'

Dr Parker looked at two shocked faces. 'I'm so sorry that you've only just got to know, but I did try to ring you, Mrs Crawford. Unfortunately, though, I wasn't able to get a reply.'

Mr Havelock gave his daughter a scathing look.

'So, is my granddaughter all right?' He looked at Dr Parker, who could see genuine concern on the old man's face.

'Yes, she's fine ... Well, as fine as can be—' Dr Parker said.

'So, what happened?' Miriam snapped, no discernible concern or compassion on her face.

'She's had a miscarriage, I'm afraid,' Dr Parker said simply.

Miriam's face lit up as she jumped out of her chair.

'Really? A miscarriage? She's lost the baby?' Miriam walked over to Dr Parker and put both her manicured hands on his shoulders. She stared at him, needing him to confirm what he had just said.

'Yes, Mrs Crawford. She has, indeed, had a miscarriage and lost her baby.'

Miriam looked as though she was about to burst into song she was so happy. Instead, she hugged Dr Parker with all her might. Tears of joy in her eyes.

Dr Parker had to fight the urge to push this horrid woman away.

'Well, I can't lie,' Mr Havelock had also stood up on hearing the news, 'this is the best news I've had all year. Thank goodness for that.' He moved around the desk and – to Dr Parker's continuing disbelief – shook his hand.

'Well, all things for a reason, eh?' Mr Havelock wasn't even trying to disguise his satisfaction at the latest turn of events.

Dr Parker suddenly felt trapped. He badly needed to get out of this small office and away from the two mad people in it who were now beaming from ear to ear. It was as though he was in some strange, warped dream.

'Well … anyway … ' Dr Parker stuttered, taking a step back. 'Helen asked me to tell you both what had happened. Obviously, she's not up to having any visitors, and has specifically asked that her wishes be respected. She's hoping to be discharged tomorrow – Monday at the latest – so she said she will see you when she gets back home.' Dr Parker started pulling at his tie; all of a sudden he felt as though it was strangling him.

'Just like my sister!' Miriam suddenly declared. She had walked round to the front of the desk and was pulling open the bottom drawer.

'Sorry?' Dr Parker's voice was scratchy. His throat felt dry as a bone.

'Helen obviously takes after Margaret, my sister,' Miriam explained, taking out the half-bottle of whisky she knew Jack had kept stashed away when this office was his.

She looked at her father, who was lighting up a fresh La Corona cigar and puffing on it in earnest. He nodded whilst doing so.

'Did they ever find out why?' Dr Parker asked, his eyes darting from Miriam, who had located two tumblers from the top of one of the metal cabinets and was splashing whisky into them, to Mr Havelock, who was now intermittently puffing out small balls of smoke.

'No idea,' Mr Havelock answered. 'Didn't stop her trying though.'

Dr Parker stepped back so that he was in reach of the door.

'Drink?' Miriam raised the half-bottle of whisky. Dr Parker replied with a shake of the head.

'I thought the best way round all of this,' he said, watching as Miriam chinked glasses with her father, 'would be to tell Harold, and anyone else who might want to know, that Helen had a ruptured appendix and had to be rushed into hospital and operated on. As a result, she'll be recovering for a while, so will probably be off work for a week or thereabouts.'

'Excellent idea,' Mr Havelock said, putting his cigar down in the ashtray. 'Very well done,' he added, whilst rummaging around in the inside pocket of his jacket.

Dr Parker stared at the old man, who was making him feel as though he was back at boarding school being commended by his headmaster.

'So ... ' Mr Havelock continued talking as he proceeded to take out his chequebook, before patting the top pocket of his jacket and pulling out a gold-plated Mont Blanc fountain pen. 'You enjoying it up at the Ryhope?' he asked, opening the chequebook and scrawling in it.

Dr Parker nodded, thinking that 'enjoying' wasn't a word he would have used for the operations and amputations he had to carry out on the increasing numbers of wounded soldiers that ended up under his care.

'Yes, sir,' Dr Parker said, 'doing what I can to help.'

He was just about to make his excuses and leave when Mr Havelock stopped scribbling, ripped the cheque from its stub, and waved it in the air.

'Here,' he said, 'I hope you'll find this is enough for what you've done for my granddaughter. And ...' he paused and looked Dr Parker in the eye ' ... for keeping quiet about the awful predicament she got herself into – which now, thank God, has ended up resolving itself.'

Dr Parker opened his mouth to speak, but nothing came out. He stared at the cheque, making no attempt to step forward and take it from Mr Havelock's hand. He jumped as Miriam leant over the desk and snatched if off her father to present to him.

'No, no, please, I don't need any kind of payment for what I've done.' Dr Parker couldn't keep the abhorrence he felt out of his voice. 'I did what I did for Helen because I'm a doctor – and because I'm her friend.'

He knew he had to get out of the office and quickly, before he said something he might regret.

'I'm afraid I'm going to have to go now,' he said, his hand flailing behind him and finding the knob of the office door. 'I'm expected back at work in ... ' he made a show of looking down at his wristwatch ' ... half an hour, so I really must dash.'

Mr Havelock and Miriam stared at the peculiar young man, with his mop of blond hair, who wasn't grasping the very generous cheque with both hands and clicking his heels.

'If you can apologise to Harold on my behalf, please, for leaving in such a dash.' Dr Parker opened the door. 'And I'll tell Helen you were both asking about her – and that you'll see her when she's back home.'

And with that Dr Parker turned and walked out the office, closing the door behind him, before hurrying down the stairs and out into the yard as fast as he could, desperate to put as much distance between himself and those two monstrous people.

Marie-Anne stood by the side of Bel's desk, pretending to explain something to her.

In reality, the pair were watching the mime being unwittingly performed by the three men and one woman presently milling around in Helen's office.

'So you don't know why Helen's not in today?' Bel asked; like a skilled ventriloquist, she barely opened her mouth.

'No idea, but I've got a feeling we'll find out soon,' Marie-Anne muttered under her breath.

They both watched surreptitiously as Harold left, closed the door behind him, and headed back to his own office.

'Must be something serious, though. I can't actually remember a time – ever in fact – when Helen hasn't turned up for work. To be honest, I can't even remember a time when she's been late.' She looked at Bel, whose eyes were fixed on the scene being played out on the other side of the large glass panels that divided Helen's office from the rest of the administration department.

'So, that's Mr Havelock sitting in Helen's seat?' Bel asked, even though she knew exactly who it was.

'Yes,' Marie-Anne said. 'He looks different from the photos in the paper, doesn't he?'

Bel nodded, although she was actually thinking he looked pretty much the same as the day she'd seen him outside his home in Glen Path.

'He looks older,' Marie-Anne whispered. 'The head and shoulders shot they always use in the *Echo* must have been taken a good ten years ago.'

'And obviously that's Helen's mother, Miriam Crawford?' Bel asked. Again, she knew exactly who it was.

'Yes, people call her the "ice queen" behind her back. She's apparently a total and utter cow. All sweetness and light on the outside, but hard and totally ruthless on the inside. Heartless, apparently.'

'Honestly, Marie-Anne, you should write your own gossip column.' Bel threw her friend a half-smile, showing she was very much enjoying being the recipient of her friend's inside knowledge.

'She used to pop in quite a bit when Mr Crawford was here,' Marie-Anne said, pretending to look at a notebook and turning over the page. 'But since he's gone, I've heard she spends most of her time at the Grand. You know what they say, *while the mice are away ...* ' She paused. 'Odd couple, though.'

'What, Miriam and Jack?' Bel said.

Marie-Anne looked at her friend in surprise. Only those who knew Mr Crawford ever called him Jack.

'Oh, look!' whispered Bel.

'Looks like they're celebrating something,' Marie-Anne said.

Making out that they were discussing a letter that Bel was holding up in front of her, the two women watched, entranced, as Miriam put her hands on Dr Parker's shoulders and embraced him. She then went over to Helen's desk, opened up the bottom drawer and produced a half-bottle of whisky. Mr Havelock, meanwhile, was lighting up a cigar, smiling from ear to ear.

They looked on as Dr Parker edged towards the door.

'Looks like he can't wait to get out of there,' Bel said. 'I didn't realise he was a doctor.'

'Me neither,' Marie-Anne said. 'Every time he's been here Helen always refers to him as Mr Parker. I would have thought she'd want everyone to know she was stepping out with a doctor.'

'Mm, you would have thought,' Bel mused.

'Oh, look,' Marie-Anne said suddenly. 'Looks like the good doctor is making his escape.'

They both watched as Dr Parker quickly left the office and, without a backward glance, practically ran down the stairs to the yard.

'Not bad-looking, though,' Marie-Anne said.

Dr Parker's level of attractiveness had not been of any interest to Bel. Her eyes had been pinned solely to the man who was her father – Mr Havelock.

Watching his every move.

Scrutinising him.

'Oh, I'm being summoned,' Marie-Anne murmured quietly, as she walked quickly over to Miriam, who had her hand in the air and was beckoning her over.

'So, Helen's had a – what was it you said, Marie-Anne?' Dorothy asked.

'A ruptured appendix.' Marie-Anne took a sip of her tea, followed by a big bite of her sandwich. She was starving. It had been all systems go since Harold had told her that Helen had been taken ill and would be off, probably for the next week or so.

'But she's going to be all right?' Gloria asked. She had been sitting quietly, taking in every word Marie-Anne and

Bel had told her about this morning's impromptu meeting. She had a horrible feeling she knew exactly why the whisky had been brought out and why Miriam and Helen's grandfather had been so jubilant.

She prayed she was wrong.

'Sounds like she's going to live to tell the tale,' Bel said, looking across at Polly, who had been listening but had not said anything during their midday conflab in the canteen.

'My old neighbour had that,' Angie said, swallowing hard on her sandwich. 'Nearly died, he did. Apparently yer appendix gans bad with loads of pus 'n infection 'n it all just bursts inside of you. It can poison yer to death if they don't get it out fast enough.'

'Blimey, Doc Ange here,' Dorothy said, mouth open in astonishment.

'How long's she going to be off for?' Rosie said, knowing the chain reaction that would occur if Helen wasn't at the helm. As much as she hated to admit it, their reviled yard manager was very good at her job.

'Harold reckoned it's gonna be a week or so before she's back,' Marie-Anne said.

Rosie grimaced.

'Exactly.' Marie-Anne dropped her voice. 'Which means it's going to be chaos. Harold's a nice enough boss, but he's bloody hopeless. Couldn't organise a booze-up in a brewery.'

'So, she's still in hospital?' Martha asked the question on the tip of Gloria's tongue.

'Sounds like it,' Marie-Anne said, before polishing off her sandwich.

Gloria forced herself to eat her own lunch.

It was the most she could do to stop herself from getting up and making a dash straight for the hospital.

*

'Well, young lady.'

Helen looked up to see Dr Billingham by the side of her bed.

'I've just come to give you a quick check-over.'

Helen looked at the doctor who had been going to take her baby away back in July.

How ironic he had ended up doing the job six weeks on.

'You're a very lucky woman,' he said as he moved around the room, checking the clipboard at the end of her bed, and the saline solution that was to be her last one.

Helen felt like slapping him; probably would have if she'd had the strength and he had been nearer. 'Lucky' was about the last thing in the world she felt at this moment in time. She had never felt more dreadful in her entire life. Had never before been cursed with this all-consuming darkness that seemed to have invaded her body and mind since John had told her she'd lost her baby.

'You were lucky – very lucky,' Dr Billingham continued, as though he had read Helen's thoughts and was determined to disprove her.

'*Lucky* that you were out with John when you started haemorrhaging. *Lucky* that he got you here and into theatre as quickly as he did – otherwise, young lady, and I hate to have to tell you this, but you might not have been here today.'

Helen looked at Dr Billingham.

She would have liked to tell him that she wished she wasn't here now – that she wished more than anything she had died with her baby right there on the tiled floor of the ladies' powder room.

Chapter Forty-Three

'Polly seems quiet,' Marie-Anne ventured as she and Bel made their way back to the admin building. They were both hurrying as the winds were whipping up and there was a faint drizzle.

'I know. It's not good,' Bel agreed. 'I've known Polly since I was five years old and I've never known her to be so withdrawn.'

Marie-Anne pushed the entrance door open, breathing a sigh of relief to be out of the wind and rain.

'People are always asking me if there's been any more news,' she said. 'Everyone here loved Tommy,'

'I know. I can tell by the way people talk about him whenever he's mentioned,' Bel mused as they made their way up the stairs.

'And everyone really feels it for Polly, you know?' Marie-Anne added. 'They mightn't say it, but they think it. God, I know I do, and I've only really just got to know her.'

They reached the top of the stairs and made their way through the double doors.

'I think it was because everyone got a little carried away with their romance. It was just so lovely.'

'I know,' Bel agreed sadly. 'I never thought Polly would fall in love. She was so … how can I describe it … so *dismissive* of blokes in general. Like she really didn't have the time of day for them. And then she met Tommy and all that changed in an instant.'

They walked into the open-plan office, which was still quiet as there was another five minutes before the end of the lunch break.

'You know,' Marie-Anne confessed, 'sometimes me and the other girls would watch the pair of them chatting down in the yard – they were just so clearly head over heels in love with each other. I think we were all a little envious, not in a bad way, but like ... ' She paused for a minute. 'Like we were watching what we hoped would happen to us one day.'

The two women were quiet for a moment.

'Do you think there's any chance he might be alive?' Marie-Anne asked.

Bel's face turned solemn and she shook her head.

'I don't reckon so.'

She paused.

'It's so hard to know the right thing to say. Should I encourage Polly to keep hoping? Or is it better that I try and help her accept that Tommy's gone and he's never coming back?'

The door opened and the first batch of office workers sauntered back in from their lunch break, bringing an end to any more talk about Tommy.

Marie-Anne went over to speak to them about what needed to be done by the end of the shift.

Bel sat down and put a clean sheet of paper into her typewriter, ready to start typing up the pile of memos on her desk. She looked out the window and could see the drizzle had turned into fully formed rain. What a day it was turning out to be. Her heart hurt for Polly – and she felt for Helen as well. No one had seemed that bothered about her well-being, nor that she'd undergone an emergency operation. It couldn't have been nice. And if what Angie said was true, she could have died.

Was she feeling this sorry for Helen because she knew they were related? Because she had seen Mr Havelock and Miriam today? *Her father and her sister.*

It still felt strange calling them that – even in her head. As she had watched them when they were in Helen's office this morning, she had been taken aback by how similar in looks she was to them. Even though Mr Havelock was old – *very old* – she could still see herself in him. And she could definitely see herself in Miriam. They had the same short, slightly curly blonde hair, narrow build and pale complexion. If she plastered herself in make-up and did her hair the same as Miriam's, it would be like looking in a mirror.

Bel suddenly jumped.

The phone on Marie-Anne's desk was ringing.

Bel might finally have got used to the yard's horn blaring out, but phones were still a novelty to her. She looked around for Marie-Anne and saw her making her way back to her desk.

'Good afternoon, J.L. Thompson and Sons,' Marie-Anne trilled into the receiver. Bel listened, as her friend had told her that she wanted Bel to start answering the phone and taking messages.

'Sorry, madam, would you mind repeating that? I didn't quite catch what you said there. It can get very loud here.'

Bel looked across at Marie-Anne. She knew this was her friend's ploy whenever she'd been caught on the hop and wasn't sure what to say.

'Ah, yes, I can hear you now.' Marie-Anne looked over at Bel, raising both her eyebrows dramatically. 'You'd like to speak to one of our secretaries here. What did you say her name was?' Another wide-eyed look across to Bel. 'Miss Thornton. Miss Rosie Thornton? Yes, if you could just hold the line a moment I will see if I can find her.' Marie-Anne paused. 'And may I ask who's calling, please?'

Marie-Anne had a pencil in hand, poised over the notepad on her desk.

'Mrs Willoughby-Smith, deputy head at the Runcorn School for Girls in Harrogate.'

Now it was Bel's turn to stare wide-eyed back at Marie-Anne.

'Thank you. If you'd just hold the line, please, I'll just see if she's available.' Marie-Anne put her hand over the receiver and raised her shoulders at Bel as if to say, *'What should I do?'*

Bel scribbled furiously on a piece of paper and held it up to Marie-Anne.

Rosie ring her back!

Marie-Anne took her hand off the receiver.

'I'm awfully sorry, Ros— Miss Thornton is over in the drawing office, but she should be back in the next ten minutes or so. Can I take a number and get her to call you back?'

Bel watched as Marie-Anne jotted a number on her notepad before saying her goodbyes and hanging up.

'Well,' Marie-Anne said, 'this day just keeps on getting stranger and stranger. Why would Mrs Deputy Head think Rosie worked as a secretary? And why's she got the deputy head of some posh girls' school ringing her up?'

Bel looked at Marie-Anne. Although the pair had become close since she had started working at the yard, she was still careful about what she told her, especially when it came to the women welders – and even more so when it came to Rosie.

'I'll explain later,' Bel said. Now it was she who was stalling. 'Let me go and get Rosie. Will it be all right for her to come up and use the phone?'

'Of course,' Marie-Anne said, 'providing you tell me later what's *really* going on?'

Bel avoided the question and hurried off.

*

Bel found Rosie hunched over a weld. She hated being in the yard when it was so busy, and so loud. At least, though, the rain had stopped.

'Rosie!' Bel yelled before nervously tapping her on the shoulder and standing back, fearful one of the sparks from the weld she was doing would land on her bare arms or, worse still, on her only decent dress.

Rosie stopped welding and turned around. On seeing it was Bel she pushed her helmet up. Her face was dirty and sweaty.

'What's up?' she shouted.

Bel bent down so that her mouth was near Rosie's ear.

'The deputy head from Charlotte's school's just rang up.' Bel paused, waiting for the words to sink in.

Rosie's face changed instantly. She reached over, flicked her welding machine off, dumped her mask on the steel flooring of the deck she had been working on, and stood up.

'Marie-Anne said you would ring her straight back,' Bel shouted, again into Rosie's ear.

Before she had time to say anything else, she saw Rosie look over to Gloria, who had spotted Bel's arrival. Rosie made a sweeping motion with her hand over the area where the rest of her squad were working and Gloria nodded. Bel guessed that was sign language for Gloria to take the reins and keep an eye on the women.

Rosie then cocked her head at Bel and marched off across the deck and down the long sloping metal gangplank to the yard. Bel had to jog to keep up. When they reached the admin offices and had shut the door behind them, Rosie looked at Bel, her brow furrowed with worry.

'Is Charlotte all right?'

'Sorry, Rosie, she didn't say. She just rang and asked to speak to you. I think she's under the impression you're a secretary here. But,' Bel added quickly, 'Marie-Anne didn't say that you weren't. Just said that you were in the drawing office and would call back in ten minutes.'

Rosie bounded up the stairs two at a time; Bel jogged up them one at a time.

As she walked through the double doors, Marie-Anne was there to greet her, or rather to usher her into Helen's office.

'Use the phone in here. There's more privacy,' Marie-Anne said as she pushed the piece of paper with the name of the deputy head and the telephone number into her hand.

Rosie didn't need to be told twice. Marie-Anne closed the door behind her and stood guard – not that anyone would dare go into the boss's office without permission.

Bel went back to her desk so as not to draw attention to the second drama of the day unfolding within the confines of the yard manager's office. Once again it was like watching a silent movie as she observed Rosie stooping over the desk as she dialled the number she had been given. She stood motionless for a moment, presumably waiting for someone to answer. All of a sudden Rosie's body straightened and Bel could see her face become animated as she spoke. There were another few moments when Rosie stood perfectly still, the receiver pressed against her ear.

Then Bel saw Rosie's overall-clad body sag in what looked like utter relief. She watched as she pulled up the metal chair that Dr Parker had sat on earlier, and flumped down as though exhausted. She continued to listen intently. As she did so her free hand went under her chin as though she was deep in thought, and Bel was reminded of a picture she had seen of a famous bronze sculpture of a naked man in exactly the same pose.

She watched as Rosie began to talk. Her face was no longer etched with worry – but anger.

When Rosie stepped out of the office she looked flushed.

'Thanks, Marie-Anne, I really appreciate that,' she said. 'And I really appreciate that you didn't put her right about me being a secretary.'

'That's all right,' Marie-Anne said. She was hoping for more of an explanation but it was clear she wasn't going to get one. That was Rosie, though. She'd always been a bit of a dark horse.

'Oh, and can you sign me off on Wednesday, please. With a question mark over Thursday.' It wasn't a request, but a statement.

'Of course,' Marie-Anne said.

That was all they needed – Rosie off as well as Helen.

Rosie stomped across the yard, up the gangplank and back to work. For the next three hours she worked fast and furiously, her energy driven by her ire.

'Everything all right?' Gloria asked when the klaxon finally sounded out the end of the shift and they could all speak rather than lip-read.

'No,' Rosie said, causing Polly, Martha, Dor and Angie to look at their boss. It wasn't often they saw her mad, and it was clear that at this moment she was positively seething.

'What's wrong?' Polly asked.

'That little sister of mine. Charlotte!' Rosie said through clenched teeth.

'What's she done?' Martha asked.

'I think it's a question of what *hasn't* she done!' Rosie fumed.

They all started making their way off the deck and down the gangplank. Bel was at the bottom, waiting for them.

'Is everything all right, Rosie?' she asked, a worried look on her face. She'd had to evade Marie-Anne's questions and wanted to ask Rosie what she should tell her, especially as she knew something was up and that Rosie had lied about her position at Thompson's.

Rosie let out a sigh. 'The school's been trying to contact me and not only has Charlotte not given them my new address like I told her to, she's given them a completely false one!'

'Eee, never!' Angie was gobsmacked.

'But why would she do that?' Polly asked.

'Because she's been up to no good and the school want to speak to me about her behaviour, from what I can gather. The deputy head didn't want to chat on the phone, so I'm going to have to go down there and see if I can sort this out … You all right taking charge while I'm gone?' Rosie looked across at Gloria as they all got their clocking-off cards ready for Alfie.

'Of course,' Gloria said, handing her card in first.

As they all boarded the ferry, Bel sidled up to Rosie.

'Marie-Anne's been asking questions,' she said quietly.

'I thought she might. She's a lovely girl, but such a nebby-nose,' Rosie said.

Bel chuckled.

'She's a more refined version of Muriel.'

Rosie laughed for the first time.

'That's a good way of putting it.'

'But, I do think that – unlike Muriel – Marie-Anne can keep her mouth shut when need be,' Bel volunteered.

'Well, it's not that Charlotte's going to boarding school is some great secret. It's just something that I don't like to broadcast,' Rosie said. 'I don't mind her knowing, as long as she keeps it to herself. And if she can keep up the pretence that I'm a secretary should the school ever ring again, I'd be eternally grateful.'

Again, Rosie didn't elaborate on the reason for her saying she was a secretary rather than a welder, but Bel guessed why. She was sure Rosie must have spun some sort of yarn as to how she could afford Charlotte's fees and that her being a secretary was part of that story.

As the women shuffled off the ferry, which was rammed with workers all eager to get home or to the pub, Rosie said her goodbyes and weaved her way through the throng to catch her bus to Tunstall Road. Martha was the next to go, jumping onto a tram headed for Villette Road, where she intended to drop by to see Hannah before getting ready for her ARP duties. Dorothy and Angie managed to snake their way single-file through the crush back to Foyle Street, both champing at the bit to return to their digs and get ready to dance the night away at the Rink – while Polly, Bel and Gloria allowed themselves to be buffeted along by the current of workers heading towards the east end, all three of them lost in their own thoughts as they made their way to Tatham Street.

Chapter Forty-Four

When Rosie arrived at the bordello she felt as though she could have fought with a feather. Seeing the look of thunder on her face as she walked through the front door, three of the girls who were gossiping at the bottom of the stairs quickly fell silent.

Heading straight for her desk in her office in the front room, Rosie sat down, flung open one of her ledgers and threw herself into the bookkeeping. She intended to get up to date with the bordello, as well as the Gentlemen's Club, which had been a little slow to take off, but which had become much more popular of late. Maisie was doing a good job, not just of managing the place, but of promoting it too.

Half an hour later Rosie heard the front door creak open. There was hardly a sound as it shut, which told her that it was Kate back from the Maison Nouvelle. Rosie jumped up from her desk and stuck her head round the office door just in time to catch her at the bottom of the staircase.

'Kate, I need to pick your brains,' Rosie said, coming out of the office.

'A cuppa in the kitchen?' Kate looked at her friend, sensing that something wasn't quite right.

They walked into the kitchen to find it empty.

'Goodness, I can't believe there's no one else here,' Rosie said, but as soon as the words were out of her mouth, they both turned their heads as a sudden blast of laughter and chatter escaped from the back parlour.

'I think I spoke too soon,' Rosie said as she put the kettle on to boil.

'Rosie! Kate! *Mes chéries!*' Lily came blustering into the kitchen with a glass of wine in one hand and an unlit Gauloise in the other. She was followed by George, who had a copy of Evelyn Waugh's *Put Out More Flags* under his arm. Rosie noticed he seemed to be leaning heavily on his walking stick.

'Come and sit down, George,' Kate said, pulling out a chair. She too had clearly seen that he needed to take the weight off his bad leg.

'Thank you, my dear,' he said, grimacing a little as he sat down.

'You all right?' Rosie asked. 'Your leg looks like it's giving you some gyp?'

'No, it's fine.' George put his book on the kitchen table. 'Just done a few laps of the town this afternoon with my future wife here.'

'Of course, it's all *my* fault!' Lily butted in. 'Dragging my *future husband* around the shops. But what my betrothed fails to mention is that most of the shops we went to were for his benefit. His suit's getting that tatty he'll be starting to look like a bleedin' beggar off the streets before long.' Lily looked across to Kate. 'No offence, my dear.'

Rosie looked at Kate. She was immaculately dressed and her thick, dark brown hair was cut into a perfect short bob with a blunt fringe. As always, she was wearing one of her signature little black dresses, which never looked sombre, just stylish. The transformation her friend had undergone never ceased to amaze her.

'We spent more time in that bookshop on Fawcett Street than anywhere else. I thought I was going to die of boredom,' Lily said.

'Clearly you didn't,' Rosie said. 'Far from it.'

Lily pretended not to hear and sat herself down at the head of the table and lit her cigarette. 'Anyway, you two look like you're up to something.'

'We may have just wanted to catch up,' Rosie said. Seeing George start to push himself out of his chair, she stood up. 'Stay there, George, I'll get it.' She threw a reprimanding look over at Lily, before going over to the armoire and retrieving a bottle of single malt and George's favourite whisky glass. She poured him a good measure, handed him the tumbler, and put the bottle of Glenfiddich on the table.

'So, come on, spit it out,' Lily demanded, pulling the ashtray towards her. 'What's up?'

Rosie poured the boiling water into the teapot and carried it over to the kitchen table.

'I need Kate to sort me out with an outfit,' Rosie said.

'Ooh, you off gallivanting somewhere?' Lily asked, a quizzical look on her heavily made-up face.

'Not that kind of an outfit,' Rosie said, looking across the table at Kate, who she knew had a variety of second-hand clothes at the boutique.

'I need something that's conservative.' She paused. 'Something you would imagine a secretary from quite a well-to-do background might wear if she's going somewhere important.'

'So, it's not a social occasion?' Kate asked.

'No, more business,' Rosie said.

'You going incognito somewhere?' Lily looked intrigued. She took a sip of her wine; as she did so her face suddenly became animated.

'You're going to Charlotte's school!'

The lack of a denial from Rosie told Lily, George and Kate that this was indeed the case.

'Well, that sounds rather ominous,' George said, a concerned look on his face. A look mirrored by Kate.

Rosie stirred the pot of tea, trying to keep her anger at bay.

'What's she done?' Lily demanded, stubbing out her cigarette.

'God, Lily, you always think the worst,' Rosie said.

'Let me guess,' Lily shot back, 'you don't actually know what she's done. You're only going to find out when you get there. I'm guessing they've asked to discuss it with you in person.'

Rosie glowered at Lily.

'Well, Charlotte's not stupid,' Lily said. 'If she gets herself expelled, you won't have any choice but to have her back here.'

'Oh, I don't think Charlotte would go that far,' Kate said. 'I mean, getting expelled is serious. Isn't it?'

George nodded. 'And it might scupper her chances of being accepted into another school.'

Rosie looked at the three people around the table and thought that they all talked about Charlotte as though they knew her. In a way they did, even though they had never actually met her before.

'I'm really, *really* annoyed at her,' Rosie admitted. She sat down, deflated, as Kate got up and poured them each a cup of tea and added a splash of milk.

'I told her to tell the school I've moved and to give them my new address and she did as I'd told her – but, clearly knowing she was in trouble, she decided to give them a false address.'

Lily sucked in air, pulled out another Gauloise and sparked it up.

'The school's been writing me letters and not getting any response,' Rosie continued, 'which is why the deputy head rang me this afternoon at work.'

'Oh dear,' George said, gravely. He knew that Rosie had told them she was a secretary at Thompson's, but had never thought the school would ever have reason to ring her there.

'Did they find out you were a welder – and not a secretary?' he asked.

'No, thank goodness. But only because Marie-Anne answered and didn't let on,' Rosie said.

'I hate to say this,' Lily blew smoke up to the ceiling, 'but you're going to have to bring that girl back home. And sooner rather than later. She's clearly going off the rails and if you don't get her back on track, like George says you mightn't even be able to get her into the Church High School up the road. They won't want to be taking on troublemakers.'

Rosie took a sip of her tea. She knew she couldn't run away from this problem for much longer.

There was a moment's thoughtful silence before the quiet was broken by the kitchen door swinging open.

'So sorry we're late, Lily!' Maisie sounded bright and cheery. She was followed by Vivian, wearing a red fishtail dress that Kate had made and which was an exact replica of the one worn by Mae West in *I'm No Angel* – Vivian's favourite film.

'We got held up,' Vivian said in her near perfect American drawl. 'Those men can talk!'

Lily waved her hand about, signalling the pair to sit down.

'That's not a problem,' she said, 'work comes first. Besides, it's given me a chance to catch up with Rosie.'

Lily took a sip of wine and looked around the table. She took a deep breath.

'I just wanted to get you all together to tell you that George and I have finally set a date for our wedding!'

'Hurrah! At last!' Kate said.

'That's great news!' Maisie said.

'Fabulous.' Vivian shot her best friend a look. They were particularly pleased as they knew the marriage would give Lily, and therefore her business interests, a façade of respectability.

'And the date is?' Rosie asked.

'Saturday the nineteenth of December,' George answered, raising his whisky glass and taking a drink.

'Ooh, how exciting! A winter wedding!' Kate said.

'So, where are you going to have it?' Maisie asked.

'The registry office in John Street, followed by a good old knees-up at the Grand!' Lily said.

Maisie's and Vivian's eyes widened with excitement. This was clearly going to be a no-expense-spared wedding.

'We put the deposit down this afternoon, so there's no bailing out,' George declared, looking across at Lily.

'So, that's why you've both been doing laps of the town today?' Rosie asked.

'Exactly,' Lily said.

'As long as you weren't trying on any wedding dresses,' Kate said.

'Heaven forbid!' Lily said in mock earnestness. 'There's only one shop I'll be going to for my dress!'

'Only the best for the future Mrs Macalister,' George said, winking at Kate.

'So,' Kate said excitedly, 'I've got three months to create the most amazingly extravagant wedding dress ever!'

'Yes, *ma chère*, let's sit down when we've got shot of this lot – ' Lily threw a mischievous look at her audience ' – and then I can tell you exactly what kind of dress *I* would like to get married in, and you can tell me exactly what *you* think I should have.'

Kate's face shone with excitement as she pushed her chair back and stood up.

'I'll just go and get some of my bridal magazines. I've been collecting them since Bel's wedding.' Kate hurried out of the room.

Everyone chuckled.

'Well, that's Kate in seventh heaven from now until Christmas,' Rosie said, taking a sip of her tea.

'But let's not forgot George here,' Maisie said. 'What will the groom be wearing on the big day?'

'What about your old officer's uniform?' Vivian asked.

George shook his head. 'Oh no, my dear, there'll be no uniforms at our wedding. I think we've all had enough of war.'

Rosie looked at George. She thought of the medals in her bedside cabinet, and his freshly pressed uniform hanging up in Dorothy's and Angie's wardrobe.

'Lily's forcing me to splash out on a new suit. We must have been to every tailor in town and after much deliberation in each and every one of those shops,' he cast Lily a sidelong glance, 'my betrothed has picked out one that is to her liking from Blacketts.'

'And a bleedin' good choice it is, if I say so myself,' Lily said, sipping her wine.

'And what about the guest list?' Vivian asked. 'How many people are you inviting?'

George coughed and poured himself another whisky.

'Let's just say it's as long as my arm!' he declared. 'Actually, both of my arms!'

Lily tutted.

'Well, the maximum allowed at the Grand is a hundred. So, that's exactly how many invites will be going out, which might sound like a lot,' Lily shot a look of reprimand at George, 'but actually isn't. Not when you consider that all the girls will be invited, and a handful of our regulars. Then there's all George's old cronies, some of *my* old cronies from London, and we'll be inviting all your women welders,' Lily looked at Rosie, 'and, of course, Charlotte will be invited too, which means we might finally get to meet her, especially as she won't have to miss any school since she'll be on her holidays.' She paused. 'Providing, of course, that she's still at the school.'

Maisie and Vivian saw the frosty looks exchanged between Lily and Rosie and guessed that Charlotte had – yet again – been the topic under discussion before their late arrival.

'And,' Lily looked at Maisie, 'invites will be going to Bel and her family, and Pearl, *Gawd help us* ... Vivian dear, just give us the names of anyone you might like to bring along – family or otherwise.'

'Here we are!' Kate nudged the kitchen door with her back and staggered in with a pile of magazines she could barely see over.

She dumped them in the middle of the table.

'I think that's our cue to exit,' George said, picking up his book and his drink. He was followed out by Rosie, Maisie and Vivian.

Kate had opened one of the magazines and had her pencil and drawing pad to hand by the time the kitchen door swung shut.

Chapter Forty-Five

After picking Hope up from Beryl's, Gloria hurried back home, but rather than go down to her basement flat, she went round to the main entrance and rang the bell to Mr Brown's.

Relieved that the old man was happy to babysit Hope, she then raced up the road and jumped on a bus to the Royal.

Once there, the receptionist gave Gloria directions to where Helen was.

Keeping her fingers firmly crossed, and her eyes peeled so that she did not bump into Miriam should she be visiting, Gloria hurried up the stairwell and along the corridor before arriving outside Helen's room. Putting her ear to the door and listening for voices inside, Gloria felt confident that there was no one else there. Knocking lightly on the door, she opened it a fraction and looked in.

Helen turned her head to see who was there.

'Gloria!' She pushed herself into a sitting position.

'You all right me visiting like this?' Gloria asked straight away.

'Yes, yes, of course,' Helen said, plumping up her pillow with her free hand; her other was still hooked up to a drip.

Gloria stepped tentatively into the room.

'I was worried yer mam might be here. Or yer granddad,' she said, still looking concerned.

'No, no,' Helen said, her voice croaky. 'I gave John strict instructions to tell them that they were not to visit. They are the last people on earth I would want here now. And I think they probably know that.' She gestured to Gloria to come in and sit down on the chair by the bed. 'Besides, they're probably both out celebrating,' she added bitterly.

Gloria thought this might well be the case after what Bel had said.

'So, tell me what happened?' Gloria said, sitting down and looking at Helen's unnaturally pale face.

Helen's chest rose as she breathed in, trying to fight back the tears, but it was no good, there was no stopping the grief.

Tears started to run down her face.

She opened her mouth to speak the terrible truth but couldn't.

The most awful, heart-rending wail came in the place of words, and it was all Gloria needed to hear.

She got up, perched herself on the side of Helen's bed and put her arms around the young woman whose desolation was so painfully clear.

For a good while, Helen sobbed her heart out, all the while clinging to Gloria as though she were a life buoy without which she would surely drown.

Chapter Forty-Six

Tuesday 15 September

At the end of the shift Rosie had a quick word with Gloria about what she wanted the squad to do while she was gone, before reassuring Marie-Anne that her second-in-command was more than capable of cracking the whip and maintaining their work output. Rosie also told Marie-Anne that, if it was possible, she would only take the *one* day off, and that she'd try her hardest to be back on Thursday. Rosie knew Marie-Anne was under pressure. With Helen off on the sick, and Harold being Harold, her responsibilities had suddenly jumped from those of head secretary to acting manager.

Rosie had wanted to hang back and chat to Gloria as she had seemed unusually quiet and a little down these past few days, but there wasn't time. She had too much to do. She resolved to make time when she returned.

Leaving her squad amidst a chorus of 'Good luck' and 'Hope everything's all right', Rosie hurried home to get changed, and then went to Lily's. She spent an hour or so on the balance sheets, as well as on her own personal finances. She now had three incomes – her day job at Thompson's, her share of the bordello's profits, and the income from the flat Gloria rented, although that was minimal and was something Rosie viewed more as an investment.

She also wanted to think through her strategy for her meeting with Mrs Willoughby-Smith – to work out the best way to handle the situation, even though she had no idea just how serious Charlotte's misdemeanours had been.

'Rosie, can I come in?' Kate's quiet voice followed a timid knock on the door.

Rosie waved her in.

'I've got your outfit,' Kate said, sliding her thin frame around the door. 'But I have to say, it pains me to have to give you something so *brown* and so *boring* to wear.'

Rosie laughed as she got up and walked around her desk to take the skirt and jacket from her friend.

'This is perfect,' Rosie said, holding the freshly pressed tweed ensemble out in front of her. '*Brown* and *boring* is just perfect.'

'Ah, *ma chérie*.' Lily swung open the office door and walked into the room, heading straight for the desk and pouring herself a glass of cognac that Rosie kept in a crystal decanter for clients. 'The costume – or *déguisements*, as the French would say!' she declared, before taking a sip of her brandy.

'C'est répugnant,' she added, looking at the offending suit, which Rosie had laid across the back of the armchair.

'I'm guessing the French lessons are going well?' Rosie said, deadpan, making Kate chuckle.

'Mais oui,' Lily agreed, equally deadpan.

Rosie and Kate exchanged amused looks.

'I'll be getting off ... Loads to do,' Kate said. 'Alfie's asked me to take in his grandmother's skirt for her. He claims she's shrinking.'

'Ah, *Alfie*,' Lily said, turning and narrowing her eyes. 'That's all I hear these days – *Alfie, Alfie, Alfie*.'

Kate looked at Lily with a genuinely perplexed look on her face.

'The lad can't help it if he's not a dab hand at sewing.' Rosie came to Kate's aid. 'And as Kate has already explained, Alfie lives with his grandmother. No parents to speak of, so he has to go somewhere to get his clothes mended and altered.'

Lily walked around Rosie's desk, pulled out the top drawer and retrieved the packet of Gauloises she kept stashed away there.

'Mmm, as long as it's just Kate's skills of seamstressing that the boy's after – and nothing else.'

Kate tutted as though the very idea that Alfie's interest was in anything other than her ability to sew was totally absurd.

'Well,' Kate said, leaving the room, 'I hope it goes all right tomorrow.'

'Thanks, Kate,' Rosie smiled, 'and thanks for sorting me out with something to wear.'

After Kate had left, Rosie looked at Lily, who was lighting up her cigarette.

'Why do I get the feeling that there's something on your mind – and that I'm about to find out exactly what it is.'

'You're a mind-reader, *ma chérie*,' Lily said, going over to the desk and tapping her cigarette in the ashtray. 'I do indeed have something on my mind. That something being Charlotte and your meeting tomorrow.'

Rosie walked back around her desk, shuffled the balance sheets into an orderly pile and put them in the bottom drawer.

'Why do I now feel I might just be about to get a lecture?' Rosie said, closing her personal accounts ledger and putting it in the middle drawer.

'*Ma chère*, I'd never *lecture* you,' Lily said, taking a draw on her cigarette.

Rosie let out a mocking laugh.

'I would just like to offer you some advice,' Lily added. Her tone was unusually serious.

'I'm not bringing Charlotte back home,' Rosie said, as she went over to pick up her second-hand outfit.

'I wasn't going to suggest that,' Lily said, watching Rosie as she got ready to leave.

'All I wanted to say to you ... ' she followed Rosie out of the office ' ... was that when you are in your *meeting* with Miss Deputy Head tomorrow, looking like some spinster matron from *Tom Brown's Schooldays*, don't get into the role-play so much that you forget who you are.'

Lily put her hand on the front door and opened it, but not enough for Rosie to leave.

'And most of all, don't forget that your little sister has no one to fight her corner – other than you.'

Rosie turned and looked at Lily.

'So, whatever Charlotte may or may not have done, you make sure you have her back.'

Lily opened the door wide.

'Because you are the *only* person that girl's got.'

Chapter Forty-Seven

Wednesday 16 September

The next morning, as the train pulled out of the station, Rosie looked at her watch, a delicate gold one, the only possession she had of her mother's. Normally it brought her comfort and warm memories, but not today – today all she could think about was the tedious six-hour round trip to Harrogate, and how having nothing to do with either her hands or her head was going to be pure purgatory.

Since Peter's fly-by-night visit, she had been working flat out to keep any worries about where he was, what he was doing, and whether or not he was still alive, to a minimum. She was actually pleased Helen was driving them all so hard in her determination to hit the production target as it meant any angst-ridden thoughts were banished by the job at hand.

Today was the first time since Peter's departure that she had been forced to sit and confront the many unwelcome thoughts and feelings she was doing such a good job of running away from.

Looking out of the window at the lush green countryside, Rosie also wondered how long she could shy away from the conundrum of what to do with Charlotte. She had to admit to herself that, practically speaking, it would be so much easier if her little sister was back home. The fees at the Sunderland Church High School would be cheaper.

There would also be no more trooping to and from Harrogate. And, as much as Mr and Mrs Rainer loved Charlotte to bits, they were both getting on and neither was in the best of health.

But then, the other side of the argument was equally convincing. More so. For there was no getting away from the fact that if Charlotte came back, it was inevitable that Rosie would have to tell her about Lily's – and that was something she really could not envisage doing.

Which brought Rosie's mind back to the present day – and what exactly it was that her sister had done to require the deputy head to request this meeting.

'Yeh!' Dorothy had jumped onto a nearby cleat and had her arms raised in the air as though she was standing on a rostrum acknowledging a roaring crowd.

The end-of-day klaxon had just blared out, which was one reason for Dorothy's jubilation – the other was that they were all going straight to the cinema from work.

Gloria arched her back and looked up at Dorothy. Seeing Jimmy, the head riveter, staring from across the deck, the two raised their eyes to the heavens above.

'Enjoy yer night out at the flicks,' Jimmy shouted over to Gloria with a playful grin on his face.

'What we going to see again?' Martha asked as Dorothy jumped down.

'*The Man Who Came to Dinner*,' Angie said.

'Please don't tell me it's one of those sickly-sweet romantic films you two love so much,' Gloria said as she went round checking all the machines were off.

'Nah, it's a comedy,' Angie said, looking across at Polly, who was quietly packing up her haversack. Angie and Dorothy had purposely chosen something funny to go and see in the hope of cheering up their workmate.

'It's got Bette Davis in it,' Dorothy chipped in as she got out her treasured Elizabeth Arden lipstick.

'We've not got time for that!' Gloria scolded Dorothy. 'You're not on the pull tonight, so there's no need to bother with the war paint.'

Dorothy defiantly put a smear of Victory Red on her lips and blew Gloria a kiss.

'It's bad enough we're not going home to change, never mind being forbidden to wear any make-up!' she pouted.

'Yeh, we're gonna look a right sight, gannin to the flicks in our dirty overalls, looking like chimney sweeps,' Angie said.

'Well, it's either that or not going at all,' Gloria said, cocking her head in the direction of the gates, showing Dorothy, Angie, Martha and Polly that it was time for the off. 'Martha's got to get back fer her ARP duties 'n I've got to pick up Hope by eight.'

As the women made their way over to the main gates, Gloria dropped back to speak to Polly.

'You all right?'

Polly looked at Gloria and forced a smile.

'I think so ... I just feel so ... I don't know how to explain it.' She thought for a moment. 'So *lifeless*.'

They parted for a moment as they walked around a huge coil of thick metal chains.

'Thank God I have to come to work every day as I swear I think I would struggle to get out of bed.'

Gloria thought of Tommy's letter and how he had been wise to stress how proud he was that Polly was a shipyard worker.

'Well,' Gloria said, 'there's no shortage of work, that's fer sure. When you're having to get through what you're going through, you've just gorra do whatever yer can to keep going.'

Polly squeezed Gloria's arm.

'Thank goodness I've got you lot.' She looked ahead at the rest of the squad, all waving at Bel, Marie-Anne, Hannah and Olly, who were patiently waiting for them at the timekeeper's cabin.

'I think we all need each other,' Gloria said. As she spoke she thought of Helen lying in her bed at home – alone. She wished more than anything that she could go and visit her, but that was never going to happen. She'd have to wait until Helen was well enough to come round to the flat.

'Hey, Alfie!' Dorothy shouted over the chatter of workers as they all handed in their clocking-off cards. 'How's Kate?'

Alfie blushed.

'You better ask her out soon,' Dorothy said.

'Cos yer gonna run out of clothes for her to fix,' Angie piped up.

'Leave the poor lad alone,' Marie-Anne reprimanded as they all chuckled.

'Which cinema are we going to?' Bel asked as they made their way up the embankment to the main road.

'The Bromarsh,' Angie said. 'Near to where I used to live.'

'Before she moved up in the world,' Martha guffawed.

'So, have you two met any of your neighbours yet?' Marie-Anne asked.

'Just the auld lady below us,' Angie said. 'She's dead posh, yer knar, stinks of lavender, 'n speaks ever so, but she's always friendly.'

'And better still,' Dorothy added, 'she's deaf as a post.'

'Yeh,' Angie butted in, 'so me 'n Dor can make as much noise as we want.'

'What about the bottom flat?' Bel asked.

'That belongs to some bloke, but me 'n Dor think he must be away at war 'cos he's never there.'

When they all reached Dame Dorothy Street they turned left.

'I wonder how Rosie's got on?' Hannah piped up.

'I dinnit blame her little sister for playing up, mind you,' Angie said. 'I mean, who wants to be stuck in the middle of nowhere doing lessons all day long?'

'As if living here with bombs being dropped on us willy-nilly and spending nine hours a day welding is such a great alternative?' Dorothy jibed.

'Well, I just hope she's back tomorrow so I don't have to play schoolmarm to you lot for another day,' Gloria said, before adding casually, 'Any idea when Helen's going to be back, Marie-Anne?'

'God, I'd be the last to know.' Marie-Anne let out an exasperated laugh. 'Soon, I hope. If you hear someone snoring in the cinema, it'll be me. I'm knackered. I didn't realise just how much Helen did, to be honest. When she does come back I'll be coming out with you two,' she looked across at Dorothy and Angie, 'and painting the town red to celebrate.'

'Careful what you say,' Martha said in earnest, 'them two will hold you to that.'

'Too right we will,' Dorothy said.

'Yeh, we'd have a right laugh. The three musketeers!' Angie said.

Everyone groaned, apart from Marie-Anne, who didn't seem too deterred by the prospect.

When they finally reached the Bromarsh another chorus of groans sounded out when they saw the queue.

'It's always like this,' Angie said.

'Did you know this was actually the town's first ever cinema?' Olly piped up.

Everyone shook their head.

'It was built in 1919 and was called Black's Picture Palace. Then it was taken over by the Marshall Brothers, who renamed it Bromarsh – which is sort of an anagram of their name.'

'What's an anagram when it's at home?' Angie asked.

They all shuffled forward as the queue started to go down.

As Marie-Anne explained what an anagram was, Gloria's mind started worrying about Helen again. The poor girl had been so distraught when she had seen her in the hospital. Gloria had pleaded with her to let her tell Jack what had happened, but Helen had been adamant. She didn't want her father to know anything.

How could she get it through Helen's head that her father loved her unconditionally?

If only Jack knew what had gone on, he'd be here like a shot. He could have been with Helen now, instead of her being on her own. She'd even put off seeing him – again – making out she couldn't take the time off work.

The chatter was momentarily put on hold while they all paid for their tickets and shuffled into the cinema, filing into a row that had enough empty seats to accommodate them all. They continued chattering away until the curtain went back and the screen flickered to life.

The movie was, as promised by Dorothy and Angie, a comedy, and the audience were soon chortling away. But when a romance developed between lovelorn secretary Bette Davis and a local reporter played by Richard Travis, Gloria thought she heard snuffles alongside the chuckles.

She was proved right when she looked down the row and saw Polly standing up and apologising as she made her way along the line. She was followed by Hannah, who had been sitting next to her.

'I'm so sorry, Hannah.' Polly was standing outside the main entrance, wiping tears away from her eyes with the cuff of her overalls. 'Please, you go back in and enjoy the rest of the film.'

Hannah took Polly's arm and started walking. 'No way! I should be thanking you. What a dreadful film!'

'I know,' Polly let out a half cry, half laugh, 'and I end up crying over it.'

'Which proves it was a bad film,' Hannah said. 'It was a comedy and it made *you* cry – and it bored *me* to tears!'

The pair chuckled and Polly wiped her wet cheeks.

'I wish I could just buck myself up. It's been nearly three months now – eleven weeks to be exact.' She let out a sad laugh. 'But I can't.'

'Perhaps you just need to feel like this for a while,' Hannah mused, 'before you can "buck yourself up". *Feeling* is the hard part. If you try and avoid it, that's when things go wrong – in your head and in your body ... Well, that's what my rabbi told me when I first came over here. I got terribly sick and was having the most awful headaches and he talked to me – a lot – and he made me talk to him – *a lot*. And he said I had to feel all the things I was feeling, you know, about leaving Czechoslovakia, my home, my family, my friends. And gradually my headaches got less and less and I stopped feeling sick.'

Polly thought about Hannah's words as they walked along North Bridge Street.

'I feel *so many* things – *all the time*,' Polly said. 'I feel so angry about this war. Angry that Tommy signed up when he was reserved occupation – even though I understand why he did. I feel so sad every time I hear that someone else has been killed – or gone missing. Honestly, I feel like crying even though I don't even know the person. I feel like I spend most of my time trying *not* to cry.' Polly let out another bitter laugh. 'I keep thinking about Teddy as well and then I'm angry and sad all over again.'

Polly was quiet for a moment as they passed a group of sailors coming across the bridge.

'And then I feel so frustrated that I have no idea what has happened to Tommy. And the chances are I'll never know.'

They were now halfway across the bridge, and they both automatically went over to the thick iron balustrade and stood and looked out at the River Wear – its watery surface barely visible due to the chaotic clutter of overhanging cranes, ships, steamers, colliers and cobblers. Even the air felt dense, with an early-evening fret seeping in from the North Sea.

'You must feel that too?' Polly looked at Hannah. 'The anger. The not knowing. With your mam and dad?'

'I do,' she nodded. 'But I guess I'm lucky in that I have my faith. I believe that the soul lives on even when the body dies. I believe that if my mother and father have died, their spirit will always be with me. That helps me. I talk to my rabbi. And, of course, Aunty Rina. And I have people around me who help me even though they probably don't realise it.'

Polly knew Hannah meant the women welders.

As they carried on walking and talking, Polly found herself crying again, but this time she didn't stop the tears, letting them drip down her face. When they started down High Street East, Polly's tears came to a natural end and it was then she realised where Hannah had brought her.

Vera's.

Entering the café, they saw two faces behind the counter immediately light up.

'Welcome!' Rina hurried over to her niece and her workmate and embraced them both. She saw the tear marks on Polly's face and understood why Hannah had brought her here. She went to shut the door and turned the sign to show that they were now closed for business.

Vera had also seen the marks of grief on Polly's face.

'I think a nice cuppa is what's called for,' she said, flicking the tap down on her bronze water urn, releasing a cascade of steaming water into a large ceramic teapot.

'And a piece o' cake to build you two up. There's not a pickin' on either of ya.'

As they all sat down at one of the tables in the empty café to drink their tea and eat their cake, Vera thought that now would be a good time to tell Polly about the little boy who would come with his grandad to the café, scruffy and red-faced, and always starving. How she had watched him grow into a young man who, like his grandad, claimed to love her bacon baps more than anything else in the world. How she had seen that the young Tommy's passion for this town – and, of course, its shipyards – had never waned and he had dedicated his life to both.

She would tell Polly how all those who knew Tommy spoke about him with such obvious pride – he was 'our diver lad' who had gone to pull bombs off the bottoms of boats, to save the country he loved and, even more, the people he loved.

Vera would tell Polly all of this in an attempt to fill the huge hole in the poor lass's heart – a void the old woman knew that Polly would always have.

For Vera knew there were such women in this life, herself included, who loved only the once.

Chapter Forty-Eight

Thursday 17 September

When Rosie returned to work the day after her trip to Harrogate, she was, as she had anticipated, bombarded with questions.

'So? How did it go?' Dorothy demanded, as they all walked over to the quayside to have their lunch.

'Yeh? How's Charlotte?' Martha asked.

'Wot was it she done wrong?' Angie said.

'And what was Mrs Willoughby-Smith like? She sounded a right battleaxe on the phone.' This last question was from Marie-Anne.

Rosie looked at their expectant faces as they all settled down to eat their packed lunches.

'Well, it didn't go the way I thought it would,' Rosie said, glancing at Polly and thinking the poor girl looked washed out.

'Does this mean yer letting her come back home, miss?'

Rosie looked at Angie and had to suppress a chuckle. She had been full of it since she'd moved into George's flat. She was even giving Dorothy a run for her money in the gobby department.

'No, Angie, she's definitely *not* coming home,' Rosie said, pouring herself a cup of tea from her flask. 'Charlotte's at one of the best schools in the country – and according to Mrs Willoughby-Smith she's doing really well in all her subjects. Extremely well.'

'So, what's the problem?' Gloria asked.

Rosie sighed.

'It would appear that Charlotte has been in a fight with one of the other girls in her year.'

'Really?' Dorothy said, almost choking on her sandwich.

'That's awful,' Hannah said, looking shocked.

'I hope she came out of it on top, miss?' Angie's face was deadly serious.

'She did come out of it "on top", Angie. Perhaps a bit too much so,' Rosie said, a little wearily. She had taught Charlotte how to defend herself. She knew how to throw a decent punch as well as where to kick a bloke if he ever got funny with her. Rosie hadn't, however, expected her sister to use what she'd been taught on her own gender.

'But no one was seriously injured, were they?' Gloria asked, concerned. Any kind of violence always disturbed her.

'I don't think there was any blood drawn,' Rosie said, 'but it sounds like the other girl pulled out a clump of Charlotte's hair and Charlotte retaliated by punching her in the stomach.'

'Oh. My. God!' Dorothy couldn't contain herself.

'What caused the fight?' Martha asked. She had been listening intently while munching her way through two rounds of sandwiches.

'That's something I never really got to the bottom of,' Rosie said. 'Charlotte said the girl had been picking on her – but wouldn't say why – and that the other girl had been the one to lash out first.'

'And let me guess,' Bel chipped in, 'the other girl said the same thing about Charlotte?'

Rosie nodded, taking a bite of corned-beef and potato pie she'd got from the canteen. She'd been too tired this morning to make sandwiches.

'Don't they suspend or even expel pupils for that kind of behaviour?' Marie-Anne asked. Her previous job with a particularly affluent local family had given her an insight into how the other half lived.

'Yes.' Rosie washed down her mouthful of pie with a glug of tea. 'As Mrs Willoughby-Smith was at pains to point out. She said the only reason Charlotte was presently sat in her classroom learning how to *conjugate a verb in Latin ...'*

Everyone looked baffled.

'Don't ask!' Rosie laughed. 'I also have no idea what that means. But anyway, the only reason she said that Charlotte wasn't being expelled – or given a suspension at the very least – was that they were aware that Charlotte came from one of the most heavily bombed towns in the country and the other girl came from London. And because of that, she said, they were prepared to make an exception, providing there wasn't a repeat performance any time in the future. She told me that she had given Charlotte a good talking-to and she suggested that I do the same and teach her the "Christian values as written down in the Gospel according to Matthew".'

'Eee, she sounds a right stuck-up cow,' Angie said.

'I think that might well be a good way of describing Mrs Willoughby-Smith,' Rosie said. 'She actually quoted the exact verse word for word, which basically amounted to, if someone slaps you then you must turn the other cheek.'

'Wot, so yer can get whacked again on the other side of yer face?' Angie's mouth dropped open in a display of sheer disbelief.

'It's what posh people like to say, Ange,' Marie-Anne explained.

'So, what did you say?' Polly asked, puzzled.

Rosie let out a bitter laugh.

'I have to say I think I may well have added oil to the fire.'

'Why?' Martha asked, biting into an apple.

'I think I might have been a bit brusque.' Rosie's mind skimmed back to yesterday afternoon and feeling uncomfortable in her tweed suit as she sat in the oak-panelled room.

'And?' Dorothy said, eager to hear what Rosie considered 'brusque'.

'I told her that as Charlotte had lost both her parents when she was just eight years old, it had fallen on my shoulders to bring her up in a way I saw fit. That one of the most important lessons I've instilled in her is never to lie – and I believed Charlotte had told the truth when she said she hadn't started the fight. And the second most important lesson I have taught her is to always stand up for yourself.' Rosie could feel the anger welling up inside her as she relayed yesterday's tense face-off with the school's deputy. 'And if someone strikes you – or pulls out a clump of your hair – then you fight back. And that I most certainly won't be telling Charlotte to *turn the other cheek*.'

'Bravo!' Dorothy shouted more loudly than she had intended, causing some of the caulkers to look over at her.

'Hear! Hear!' Bel chipped in. She had been relentlessly bullied at school.

'Yeh, good on ya,' Gloria said.

'I might have also said,' Rosie added, a little shamefaced, 'that it would be a dire state of affairs if we as a country had decided to turn the other cheek with Hitler and allowed him to just come on over and stomp all over us.'

Dorothy clapped her hands.

'Hurrah for Rosie!'

Rosie looked at Dorothy and the rest of the women.

'I don't know about cheering me, Dorothy. I don't think my attitude helped much.' Rosie thought about Mrs Willoughby-Smith's pursed lips and clipped words as she had brought the meeting to a close.

'I think I might have marked Charlotte's card even more than it already was. Especially as I could tell that the deputy's alliance was clearly with this other girl, who, Charlotte told me afterwards, comes from a very well-to-do family, and whose father is some kind of politician.'

'I hope you don't mind me asking,' Marie-Anne said, 'but why don't you want to bring Charlotte back here?'

Everyone looked at Marie-Anne. She was the only one of them who didn't know about Rosie's 'other' life at Lily's. And, therefore, the only one who didn't know the real reason behind Rosie's refusal to let her sister come home.

Rosie seemed stuck for words.

'Well, it's obvious, isn't it?' Martha said, coming to the rescue. 'It's like what that Mrs Willoughby-what's-her-name said. She doesn't want her here because of the bombings. Look at what happened in Ryhope the other week.'

Rosie smiled at Martha, thankful for her intervention.

'Anyway, enough about Charlotte,' she said, 'I'm sure it'll sort itself out.'

They were all quiet for a while as they ate their lunch.

'Have you heard when Helen's coming back?' Rosie's question was directed towards Marie-Anne, whose face immediately lit up.

'Yes! She rang me for an update today. She said she'd definitely be back on Monday – possibly before. Thank goodness.'

'Marie-Anne, you must be the only person who's glad to have her back,' Dorothy joked.

'Only because it makes my life easier. I can understand why you lot don't want her about, though.' Dorothy had filled her in on all the wrongs Helen had committed against the women welders, Polly in particular.

'Well, that's all water under the bridge now, isn't it?' Gloria tried to make her voice sound upbeat.

'Is it?' Dorothy sniped back.

As the afternoon shift got going and they were all once again immersed in their own world of sparkling arcs of molten metal, bereft of chatter and, therefore, with nothing to listen to but their own thoughts, Rosie reran the events of yesterday.

She felt she had done little to calm the waters regarding Charlotte's situation. Actually, she felt she'd done quite the opposite and instead had poked the hornets' nest – more than once. And any good her dowdy conservative attire might have done helping her to ingratiate herself with the school deputy had been obliterated by her sharp words. She might as well have gone to the meeting in her overalls and with her hair in a turban.

As Rosie burnt metal into submission, the anger she'd felt within the confines of that musty room came flooding back. Anger about the way Mrs po-faced Willoughby-Smith had talked about Charlotte, and even greater anger that the behaviour they were trying to instil in Charlotte was the antithesis of the way Rosie felt her sister should conduct her life.

Rosie sat back on her haunches and looked at her perfectly straight weld. She might have sounded convincing to Angie that there was not a cat in hell's chance she would consider having Charlotte back, but Rosie had to admit – much as she hated to – that she did, in fact, have her doubts about Charlotte's continued education at the school.

And now, on top of everything else, she had another nagging worry to add to the many others concerning her sister.

Neither girl had been forthcoming about what it was that had riled them both so much that they had gone at each other hammer and tongs.

They were clearly hiding something.

What had Charlotte's fight *really* been about?

Chapter Forty-Nine

Friday 18 September

'Are you sure this isn't a bit early to be going back to work?' Dr Parker had a concerned look on his face.

'Yes, I'm sure,' Helen said. 'It's not as if I'm out in the yard, like Gloria, doing physical work. I'll be sitting behind a desk, putting up orders, telling people what to do. The most strenuous activity I'll be doing is lifting up the bloody phone! Now stop treating me like I'm one of your patients and try and catch that young waitress's attention to give her our order. It shouldn't be hard, she's been giving you the glad eye ever since we came in here.'

Dr Parker looked over at the pretty blonde waitress in her black short-sleeved dress and frilly white apron tied tightly around her waist, accentuating her petite but womanly figure. He raised his hand and smiled and she hurried over, her pocket-sized notebook in one hand, a pencil in the other.

'Tea for two, please,' he said. 'And two scones.'

'Not for me,' Helen interrupted. 'Really, I'm not hungry.'

The waitress scribbled in her pad and smiled sweetly at Dr Parker before returning to the counter, ripping the page from her pad and handing it to the matron-like woman behind the display counter.

'You should try and eat plenty,' Dr Parker said. 'Build yourself up.'

'God, John, now you're beginning to sound like Mrs Westley. She's done nothing but nag me to eat and shove liver and kidney casseroles and any kind of red meat she can get her hands on in front of me. She even tried to get me to eat some black pudding, which she knows I hate.'

Dr Parker chuckled. He had met the cook the day after Helen had been discharged from the hospital and had instantly taken to her, in part because she had sat him down and fed him the most delicious pie and pea supper, but mainly because it was obvious by the way she fussed over her that she adored Helen.

'Well, she's not daft,' Dr Parker said. 'That's exactly the kind of food you need to be eating. Plenty of iron.'

'Will you please take off your doctor's hat for one minute and just go back to being my friend?' Helen laughed sadly.

'All right, no more nagging,' Dr Parker agreed as the waitress arrived with a tray and carefully unloaded a pretty Garrison pottery teapot, two matching cups and saucers, a little jug of milk, and a small plate on which there was a large scone filled with a good dollop of jam and cream.

The young girl's eyes kept flicking to Dr Parker and when he finally looked up to thank her, she gave him a beguiling smile.

'Well,' Helen said after the waitress had gone, 'I don't think it's just the scone that's been offered to you on a plate.'

Dr Parker could feel his face flush.

'You should ask her out on a date,' Helen said, pouring out their tea and adding a splash of milk.

'If I promise to stop being doctor, will you also refrain from being matchmaker?'

Helen laughed. 'Agreed. Anyway, it's better for me if you remain single, because as soon as you *do* start courting, there'll be no way you'll be allowed to go out for tea with me.'

Dr Parker looked at Helen.

Why would he bother going out with another woman if he'd simply end up spending every minute thinking about the woman he was with now?

'So,' Dr Parker leant forward and put his hand on Helen's, 'tell me, how have you been since I saw you last?' His tone was serious, and it was clear he wanted a truthful answer.

Helen took a sip of tea, partly because she was thirsty, but also because it helped to keep the tears at bay, which just seemed to come out of nowhere.

'Honestly?' Helen said. She could feel the sting at the back of her eyes and she blinked hard and took a deep breath.

Dr Parker nodded. He looked into her emerald eyes and saw such deep sadness. Her outward appearance of bravado and smiles didn't fool him.

'In a word,' Helen said, 'wretched. More wretched than I've ever felt in my entire life.'

Dr Parker squeezed her hand gently.

Helen took another sip of tea and swallowed the tears that had once again tried to break free.

'It's like there's death everywhere.' She kept her voice low. 'All those people that died when the *Laconia* got hit.' Dr Parker nodded sadly. More than a thousand lives had been lost when U-boats had struck just off the coast of West Africa.

'And,' Helen continued in an even lower voice, 'the bits and pieces that have been coming out about all those poor Jews – *all those children* – being treated like animals.' Helen had to stop. She closed her eyes for a moment and took a deep breath.

'I can't stop thinking about it. And then I keep thinking about Tommy. It's just so unfair. Tommy never did anything even remotely nasty to anyone. Even when we were little. I miss him. And lately, I seem to be missing him more.'

'Do you think that's because it's looking likely that he's no longer alive?' Dr Parker consciously avoided using the word 'dead'. He looked down at Helen's hand, covered partially by his own, and he had the urge to take it, lift it to his mouth and kiss it. He wanted to tell her that there was death. Too much death in all of their lives. He had seen the life leave too many men under the glare of operating-room lights. But there was also love.

Helen couldn't say any more. Her throat was constricted. It actually ached with the effort of keeping back the grief that she knew was desperate to escape – to make itself heard.

'Come on, eat your scone,' she finally managed to say. 'And then tell me about work. I want to hear about what you've been doing this week.'

Between mouthfuls of scone and sips of tea, Dr Parker told Helen about the recent batch of wounded soldiers that had been admitted to the hospital. He purposely kept the conversation light, telling her about some of the characters he'd come across, the pranks they played on the nurses, even about a few romances that had blossomed.

Helen listened, enjoying the reprieve from her own thoughts, her own world, even if it was just for a short while.

When they were preparing to leave, Dr Parker once again asked if Helen thought it wise to be going back to work so soon.

'I think I might go mad if I don't,' Helen said. 'Just coming here with you for a cup of tea has made me feel so much better. I can't bear the thought of spending another day at home. It feels like a mausoleum. Besides,' she said, 'when I spoke to Marie-Anne yesterday it was obvious she's run ragged and struggling. Harold should have stepped in while I was away, but he's pretty hopeless. He should really retire. Anyway, when I told Marie-Anne I'd be back on Monday and may well come back before then, I could almost hear her praising the "good Lord" and doing an Irish jig around my office.'

Dr Parker chuckled.

'I take it your hard-put-upon secretary is from the Land of the Blarney?'

Helen nodded. 'Even if she didn't speak, you'd know. Long curly ginger hair. Pale. Freckles. Sea-blue eyes.'

Helen got out her handbag and pulled the little saucer on which the bill had been placed towards her.

'My treat,' she said, pulling out her purse.

'Please,' Dr Parker said, trying to take the bill from Helen's grasp. 'I can't allow the woman to pay. It goes against every bone in my body.'

'Well,' Helen said, 'it'll just have to.' She opened her purse and put five shillings on the silver dish, which included a generous tip.

'Besides, if I pay,' Helen added, 'the young waitress will know we're not a couple, and you can come back and ask her out on a date.'

Dr Parker forced an unconvincing laugh.

'Just look at that lovely dress,' Helen said as they walked out of the Holme Café.

Dr Parker looked at the pastel pink wedding dress that was displayed in the window.

'The seamstress here,' Helen pointed at the Maison Nouvelle sign above the shop, 'is incredible. There's nothing she can't do with a needle and thread – and her designs …

Amazing. She's shown me a few and they are wonderful. If we win this war—'

'*When*,' Dr Parker interrupted.

'*When* we win this war,' Helen corrected herself, 'she's going to be huge. You mark my words.'

As they turned and walked back down Holmeside, Helen looked at the museum. 'Remember that night?'

Dr Parker nodded, knowing exactly which night Helen was referring to. The fateful night she had left the charity do and had unwittingly been targeted by Theodore, who had followed her out, slowly reeled her in, and landed her good and proper.

'I often think of that evening,' Helen said. 'Do you remember that you were a real gentleman and offered to walk me to the Grand?'

Dr Parker nodded.

'I often think that if I'd have said yes, my life would have been so different. I'd never have ended up going out with Theodore – and none of this awfulness would have happened.'

Helen took Dr Parker's arm as they strolled to the bus stop on Fawcett Street, both lost in their own worlds, thinking of what life might have been like if only Helen had said yes.

Helen lay in her bed and let the tears roll down her cheeks. She knew her eyes would be puffy in the morning, but she didn't care.

When she had been discharged from hospital, she had made a resolution not to shed another tear over her baby – she had cried enough. She had sobbed so much during the two and a half days she'd been in the Royal, she'd believed she had no more tears left.

But she did.

There seemed to be a bottomless well of the damn things. After being driven from the hospital, she had walked back through her front door and cried.

She had gone to her bed and stayed there for two days and cried.

She had come downstairs and eaten whatever Mrs Westley had put in front of her and cried.

She had walked into the room that she had intended to be her baby's nursery and sat on the bare mattress and cried so much she thought her head was going to explode.

And today, when she was with John, she'd felt like crying – really crying – but, thank goodness, she'd manged to stop herself. She might have lost just about everything else, but she was determined to hang on to her dignity.

The only time she didn't feel like crying was when she saw her mother, which wasn't often. Her mother had put on a display of concern, but it didn't wash with Helen any more, although it did make her wonder how many occasions in the past her mother had put on the same false mask and she had believed the pretence.

Helen had told her mother, 'The joy in your eyes belies the words coming out of your mouth, dear Mama,' before adding that she thought it would be best all round if they simply avoided each other. Every night since she had heard her mother quietly slip out to the Grand, no doubt to continue celebrating her sudden and unexpected turn of fortune.

Helen was glad she was going back to work. She needed to hear the chaotic cacophony that was the sound of the shipyards – she needed to hear life, *feel* life, to be a part of life. She felt as though she was drowning in death – and as much as she would have preferred to have been sucked under, she knew that was not to be.

Her baby had been taken from her – dragged from her very being – but she had been washed ashore.

Chapter Fifty

Two weeks later

Friday 2 October

When all her squad had sat down at their table in the canteen, Rosie rummaged around in her haversack and pulled out half a dozen white envelopes. Like a seasoned croupier she dealt one card to each of the women presently tucking into their lunch.

Dorothy immediately dropped her knife and fork and snatched up her card. Inspecting the front of the envelope on which her full name had been written in swirling calligraphy, she quickly opened it and pulled out a gold-embossed wedding invitation.

'Oh. My. God!' she declared. 'Cinderella is going to the ball!'

All the other women had also stopped eating and were opening up their envelopes.

'Cor.' Angie was agog. 'We're being invited to *your* Lily's wedding, miss?' she asked Rosie in disbelief.

'It's also *your* landlord's wedding, don't forget,' Rosie said, looking at all the surprised faces.

'What? We're being invited to both the wedding *and* the party afterwards?' Martha was also staring slightly open-mouthed at the thick white card she was holding carefully in her hand.

'That's what the invite says,' Rosie answered, suppressing a smile.

'Blimey, they're having the after-do in *the Grand*!' Polly exclaimed.

Rosie looked at Gloria, who was staring down at her invite. She looked up.

'A week before Christmas. I don't think I've ever known anyone to get married then.'

Rosie chuckled.

'Well, that's Lily for you. God forbid she does anything that may be in the least bit conventional.'

'This,' Dorothy declared, waving her invitation in the air and nudging Angie, 'is going to be the best Christmas ever!'

The rest of the lunch break was spent excitedly discussing every aspect of the Yuletide nuptials in between mouthfuls of fish pie. Dorothy was so excited she looked like she was going to burst. Rosie felt as if she was on some kind of quiz show, with question after question being fired at her, each one demanding an instant response. When Hannah and Olly turned up later with their packed lunches, they automatically took a joint step back as five ecstatic faces loomed at them and broke the latest news.

The two lovebirds, as they were now known, were clearly chuffed to pieces at being given an invitation as a couple. Olly's Cheshire-cat grin said it all, while Hannah admitted she was particularly excited about seeing the Grand because of what she had heard about its colourful history and artistic interior design.

During the flurry of chatter, Rosie kept a discreet eye on Polly. She had actually put off handing out the invitations for fear of causing her more heartache. A wedding might be a *cause de célébration*, as Lily had declared the other night when dishing out the invitations to the girls at the bordello, but for Polly it could only be a reminder of the love she had lost. The wedding she would never have. Watching her now, smiling at Dorothy's and Angie's high jinks and animated discussion on what they were – and were most *definitely not* – going to wear, it didn't appear as though the wedding invites had pushed the knife in any further. Or was that because the blade of grief had already gone as deep as it could go and there was no more damage to be done?

As Dorothy debated what she and Angie should wear and just about every other aspect of what promised to be a rather grand wedding, Polly again forced herself to smile, determined that no one should guess her true feelings – should see her broken heart.

She used the past tense as her heart did indeed feel as though it had now broken. The actual breaking had been a slow process – delayed by the hope that Tommy might still be alive. Somewhere. That some day she might see him again. But when she'd received the letter about his gratuity pay that morning, what little hope she had hung on to had been yanked away from her.

Seeing her workmates' jubilation over Lily's forthcoming nuptials, she wished more than anything that she could participate more in their excitement. Feel that lightness of being. But how could she when all she was able to think about was her own wedding – the one that *she* should have been planning and looking forward to with Tommy.

She had never been one to wear her heart on her sleeve, but more than anything she did not want her workmates to know how she honestly felt for the simple reason that she did not want to see their happiness turn to sadness on seeing her pain.

She didn't want her misery to infect their joy.

*

'You all right? About this wedding malarkey?' Rosie asked Polly as they all headed back into the yard. The temperature had dropped and the wind was whipping up.

Polly forced a smile and nodded. Rosie thought she looked on the verge of tears and realised that the blade of grief hadn't, in fact, gone as deep as it could go.

'Lily said to tell you that she won't be offended if you decide you're not up to coming,' Rosie said.

Polly shook her head vehemently. 'What? And miss out on a knees-up at the Grand? You've got to be joking.' Her words were jovial, but her voice sounded shaky. Polly stopped to put the invitation into the side pocket of her haversack. As she did so, an official-looking document poked out and Rosie couldn't help but see the heading typed in big bold black lettering: payment of war gratuity.

Polly noticed that Rosie had seen it.

'It's notification of Tommy's pay,' she explained, sadly. 'Apparently they pay it even if someone is missing or a prisoner of war. Tommy obviously told them to give it to me if anything were to happen to him.' Polly stopped speaking for a moment. 'I feel like giving it away – probably would, but Ma would kill me!'

Rosie could see Polly was struggling to keep it together. She looked at the rest of her squad, who were walking on ahead, still chattering away nineteen to the dozen.

'I'm guessing you got it in the post this morning?' Rosie asked.

Polly nodded.

'Perfect timing, eh?' Rosie said. She saw that Polly was subconsciously touching the top pocket in her overalls, where she kept her engagement ring. 'And there's me handing out wedding invites!'

Polly let out another sad laugh. 'I wouldn't have minded – I mean I don't mind, really … It's just so ironic because

Tommy told me he was saving every penny of his pay for our wedding.'

'Oh, Pol,' Rosie said, putting her arm round her workmate and pulling her close, 'I'm so sorry. I really am.'

Helen was smoking at the window overlooking the yard, watching the women welders as they made their way back to SS *Brutus*.

God, they all looked so bloomin' chummy!

They had clearly had some good news as Dorothy was practically dancing across the yard and even Martha looked animated and was moving her great big arms around as she nattered away to Gloria. Polly didn't look too chirpy, though. Mind you, that wasn't surprising. Gloria kept her informed on any updates regarding Tommy and there still hadn't been a word.

Helen stubbed out her Pall Mall. She had started smoking again, much to John's disapproval. She was just about to turn back to her office when she saw Rosie putting her arm around Polly and comforting her. She felt a bolt of unrestrained jealousy.

'Sorry, Miss Crawford.' It was Marie-Anne shouting across to her from her desk. She had the black Bakelite receiver pressed into her chest.

'You've got a call,' she said, pointing down at the phone buried in her bosom.

Helen turned and walked back into her office.

'Hello, Miss Crawford speaking,' Helen said in the usual hoity-toity voice she used on the phone when she didn't know who it was or it was someone she didn't like.

'Helen, it's John!'

'Are you all right? You sound harassed.' Helen immediately picked up that he was in a rush.

'Yes, sorry ... I am ... I'm just about to go into theatre. Bit of an emergency with one of our recent recruits.'

Helen had got used to John calling his patients 'recruits', as though they had signed up to being at the Ryhope.

'No idea who the poor chap is ... not that that's so unusual.'

Helen knew her friend was anxious as he had a tendency to ramble when he was worried or under pressure.

'Not that you need to know any of this.' He paused. Helen could hear shouting in the background. 'I just rang to say I won't be able to meet up with you this evening. This looks like it's going to be an all-nighter.'

'John, don't worry,' Helen said. 'Saving the life of some "poor chap" is a little more important than meeting me for a cup of tea and a piece of cake. Now, go and save a life!'

Helen heard more panicked shouts and the phone went dead.

After she put the phone down, Helen did something she would never normally have done and she offered up a prayer for the 'poor chap' with no name.

Please let him live, she silently pleaded.

It was as though lately she couldn't bear the thought of anyone else being deprived of life.

Chapter Fifty-One

The Ryhope Emergency Hospital

Two days later

Sunday 4 October

'So, *please* tell me you saved the "poor chap" from the other day?' Helen looked at Dr Parker. 'Actually, scrap that. *Only* tell me if he's alive. I don't want to know otherwise.'

Dr Parker glanced across at Helen. She had finally got her colour back – and her figure. She looked more stunning than ever.

'Well, we operated on him – and he did make it through.' Helen noticed that John always used the plural when he talked about performing surgery. He had told her that any kind of operation was a team effort. Helen thought how totally different he was compared to Theodore, who had openly boasted about his prowess as a surgeon as though he were the Saviour himself.

'But?' Helen asked. 'I can tell there's a "but" coming.'

Dr Parker grimaced.

'*But,*' he said, 'it's still very touch-and-go. He's got round-the-clock care, but to be honest, I think it's fifty-fifty whether he makes it.'

The pair were strolling at a snail's pace around the hospital grounds. They had their arms linked, as was their custom whenever they walked anywhere together.

Dr Parker had caught their fractured reflection in one of the large windows criss-crossed with anti-blast tape, and had been reminded of the film *The Wizard of Oz* and of the way Dorothy had linked arms with her companions – the Scarecrow, the Lion and the Tin Man: totally platonic.

As he only had an hour to spare, and because Helen knew her friend craved fresh air whenever he got the chance to leave the confines of the hospital, she had suggested they spend the short time they had together simply walking around the grounds, chatting.

Helen smiled at a couple of soldiers in wheelchairs, who were chatting and smoking. Their faces lit up and they gave her a salute and a wink.

'So, the other day when we spoke briefly on the phone – when it all sounded rather chaotic, to say the least – what was happening?' Helen had become increasingly curious about John's work at the hospital. Even more so after he'd saved her life.

'Ruptured spleen, causing massive internal bleeding. If we hadn't got him into theatre there and then he'd have been a goner for sure.'

Helen shivered. Perhaps someone had been listening to her prayer.

Helen looked at another soldier who was hobbling on crutches, a rolled-up cigarette in one hand. His left trouser leg had been pinned up, revealing a gap where the lower part of his limb should have been.

'Nice day,' he said to Dr Parker as he lurched past, swinging his lower body forward.

'It is indeed, Danny,' Dr Parker replied.

Helen smiled.

'How can he be so cheery?' she whispered when the one-legged solider was out of earshot.

'I really have no idea,' Dr Parker mused. 'Danny's just applied for a desk job with the War Office. Says if he's not fighting, he's got to be doing something to beat Jerry.'

They walked on in silence.

'I guess that's what they call an indomitable spirit,' Dr Parker said.

'Well,' Helen said, 'don't you be getting any ideas about going off to the front line to work in any of those field hospitals you've been telling me about, or sailing off on one of those hospital ships that are being bombed even though they're not supposed to be.' She glanced at him and caught a look in his face she couldn't read.

'You hear me?' she said. 'You're needed here ... And I don't just mean as my one and only friend.'

Dr Parker looked at Helen.

'You have Gloria.'

'Ah,' Helen said, 'Gloria's more than a friend.' She laughed. 'Strange though this may sound – considering she is, after all, my father's secret lover – Gloria's more like the mother I never had and always wanted, if that makes sense?'

'Perfect sense,' Dr Parker said.

He looked forward to meeting Gloria one of these days.

Chapter Fifty-Two

One week later

Sunday 11 October

'Bloody Nora!' Lily exclaimed as she flailed her arms around, hurrying everyone down to the bordello's make-shift air raid shelter in the basement.

'Come on! We've not got all day!' she bellowed at two of the girls and their clients as they stood chatting in the hallway.

'George!' Lily shouted over half a dozen heads. 'Can you get Kate down here *now*. Drag her away from her precious Singer before I have a bleedin' coronary.'

Lily stomped across the hallway and flung open the heavy oak door so that it banged against the wall.

'And you can get your head out of those ruddy ledgers too!' she shouted at Rosie, who was still sitting at her desk, her head bent over a balance sheet.

'Coming.' Rosie stood up and hurried out of the room. There were certain times you didn't argue with Lily and this was one of them.

Five minutes later – just before the grandfather clock in the empty parlour room struck nine – everyone was safely ensconced in the basement, though the atmosphere was unusually tense. A few weeks back a bomb had dropped just a quarter of a mile away from their front door.

'Like a tin of bloody sardines!'

Rosie could hear Lily's voice somewhere in the middle of the packed basement. She peered over heads and could see what looked like an orange bird's nest bobbing about. A few minutes later they heard a series of muffled explosions directly followed by tremors that pulsated underfoot. It was a sure sign the bombs that had just landed were near. Rosie manoeuvred her way over to the small drinks cabinet to find George acting as barman.

'Brandy?' George asked.

Before Rosie had time to answer, Maisie was by her side.

'Yes, please, George. Make it a large one,' she said, her voice strained.

'They'll be all right.' George read Maisie's mind, repeating what he always said to calm her concerns about her ma, her sister and her niece. 'They'll have got to the shelter in time.'

'George, you always say that!' Maisie snapped, before reining herself in. 'Sorry, I know you're right. I don't mean to be sharp. It's just ... It's just ... '

George smiled. 'It's just you care – loath though I know you are to admit it – and when you care, you worry. Now take your drink and go and rescue Lily from the Brigadier. You know how she feels about being so close to him. Heavens knows what she'll say or do to the poor man with the mood she's in at the moment.'

George splashed brandy into another tumbler and handed it to Rosie.

'I think this may well be payback for Munich and Saarbrücken,' he said.

'Do you think so?' Rosie asked as she took the proffered drink.

'I do. And I believe there'll be more. Hitler may be concentrating on Russia and North Africa, but he's not so busy that he's averse to a play of tit for tat.'

'I don't suppose you've heard any more from your chums about life over the Channel?' Rosie asked quietly.

'The Resistance are still holding their own over there,' George said, hoping the truth of what he had heard did not show on his face: southern France was just about to fall to the Axis. It would put operatives like Peter in even more danger.

Rosie took a sip of her drink. She knew George only told her what she wanted to hear, but it didn't matter, it still gave her comfort.

Chapter Fifty-Three

The following day

Monday 12 October

'Where's Martha?' Rosie's voice could not hide her panic when she saw Dorothy, Angie, Gloria, Polly and Hannah arrive for work without the group's gentle giant.

'Don't worry,' Hannah said. 'She's fine. She was up most of the night doing her ARP duties. She had no sleep and her mam and dad have refused to let her come to work.'

'And rightly so,' Rosie said, relieved. 'And are you all right?' She looked at Hannah, whose childlike face looked wan, her olive skin almost translucent.

'Yes, I'm fine. But I feel so sad,' she admitted.

Dorothy stepped forward and wrapped her arms around Hannah.

'It *is* sad,' she said.

Helen was in her office when Marie-Anne brought in her cup of tea and the *Sunderland Echo*.

Reading the headline: two children dead, she turned down the blinds, shut her office door and cried.

'You and yours all right?' Marie-Anne asked as soon as Bel came into work. The bombs had dropped in Hendon, just a half a mile from Tatham Street.

'Yes, thank God. Yours?'

Marie-Anne nodded solemnly.

Neither of them mentioned the two children, four women and one man who had not survived the air raid, nor the twenty homes that had been totally razed to the ground – nor the school on Valley Road that had been reduced to rubble.

From the moment the klaxon sounded out the start of the day's shift, every man and woman at Thompson's shipyard worked flat out, as did every other worker in every other shipyard, engine works, factory, ropery and colliery on both sides of the river.

Their actions spoke louder than their words.

They would not be beaten.

Chapter Fifty-Four

Four days later

Thursday 15 October

'Sod it!' Helen said, putting her coat back on. 'I'm sick of us having to hide out in your flat every time I come to visit.' She marched over, grabbed Gloria's coat, which was hanging up on the back of the door, and gave it to her before walking over, easing Hope out of her high chair and swinging her onto her hip. The little girl gurgled with excitement, sensing the sudden change of mood.

'We're going to the museum. It's open late tonight.'

'Are you sure?' Gloria asked, still standing in the same spot in the middle of the lounge, clutching her coat. 'I mean … someone might see us?'

'Well, if they do, they do. I'm tired of all this sneaking around like we've got something to be ashamed of. If anyone sees us, they can think what they want. And in the unlikely event someone we know *is* walking around the museum at the same time as we are, then for all they know we've simply bumped into each other.' Helen opened the front door. 'We *are* work colleagues after all. Now come on!'

Gloria quickly put her coat on, grabbed her gas mask and handbag and followed Helen and Hope out the front door.

Within minutes they had walked the few hundred yards from Gloria's flat, across the Borough Road, and arrived at the grand, pillared stone entrance of the municipal museum.

Helen put Hope down once they got through the main doors and held her little hand.

'This is her first visit to the museum,' Gloria said, looking down at her daughter, who was staring about her in awe. 'And I have to admit, it's been years since I came here.'

'Well,' Helen said, 'we don't have to actually *look* at the exhibits, it's just nice to go out for a change. I overheard Bel say the other day that she was taking her daughter to Backhouse Park with her sister – Maisie, I think her name is.'

Helen pushed open one of the thick glass swing doors and held it back while Hope toddled through.

'It was the first time I really felt resentful that I couldn't do the same with Hope.'

'Wouldn't that be nice,' Gloria sighed, 'you taking Hope out while I stay at home with my feet up.'

The two women and toddler walked around the large, musty-smelling room, ambling past miniature models of ships from the days of wood and sail. It was Helen's favourite exhibition.

'Talking about being open about everything … ' Gloria said as Helen took Hope and showed her HMS *Venerable*, a particularly famous Sunderland-built ship. 'Perhaps it's time to be open with yer dad about what's been going on.'

Helen's head snapped round.

'No way, Gloria. That's something he's never going to know about.'

She turned her attention back to Hope, who was stretching out her arms, demanding to be picked up.

'I want to forget that part of my life now. And if Dad gets to hear about it, it'll always be there. At least when I chat to Dad I can pretend everything's the way it was.'

They both knew, though, that nothing would ever be the way it was, no matter how much Helen might try to pretend – or forget.

Looking at Helen as she hoisted Hope onto her hip, Gloria was just thankful that even though Helen had lost her own baby, she still wanted to be around Hope and clearly loved her as much as, if not more than, before. She just wished the girls at work could see Helen now and realise she wasn't the Wicked Witch of the West they all imagined her to be.

'So,' Gloria said as they looked at old photos and maps, 'how's John?'

'Oh, he's practically working round the clock at the moment. I went up to see him the other day at the hospital. He only had an hour spare, so we just had a walk around the grounds.' Helen moved Hope onto her other hip. 'It really brings it home to you, seeing all those young men in wheelchairs and with missing limbs.' As they meandered around the rest of the large exhibition hall, Gloria listened as Helen told her about John's most recent batch of 'recruits'.

'John seems a really nice bloke,' Gloria said. 'And Marie-Anne says he's rather dishy as well?' Gloria looked at Helen, trying to gauge her reaction.

Helen laughed. 'Marie-Anne finds everyone dishy! Well, anyone who is male, available and aged between twenty and thirty. Anyway,' she changed the subject, 'how are all your lot?'

Gloria had got used to Helen's attempts at sounding casual when it came to asking about the women welders. She might be good at hiding any feelings she was harbouring for her doctor friend, but when it came to her curiosity about her workmates she was not quite so successful.

'I think they were all a bit shaken by the bombing on Sunday,' she said.

Helen nodded sadly. 'And Polly. How's she coping? I'm guessing she's not heard anything?'

Gloria sighed. 'I think she's coping, but that's about it. She got his gratuity pay the other day, which knocked her back.'

Helen's heart sank. 'Do you think that means they've resigned themselves to the fact that Tommy's definitely dead?' Just saying the words brought tears to her eyes.

Gloria nodded.

Seeing the sadness that Helen normally kept under wraps come to the fore, she squeezed her arm.

'Come on, let's go 'n get a nice cuppa at mine.'

Helen wiped a tear that had escaped the corner of her eye. 'I don't know what I'd do if I didn't have you, Gloria,' she said as they stopped in the main foyer so that Hope could climb onto the back of Wallace, the town's famous stuffed lion.

'Nothing's gonna happen to me,' Gloria said. 'Yer stuck with me whether you like it or not.'

Chapter Fifty-Five

The following day

Friday 16 October

'So, what are you two up to tonight?' Gloria said, swinging her haversack across her shoulder and looking across at Dorothy and Angie. 'No, let me guess – the Rink?'

'Actually, Glor,' Dorothy said with great satisfaction, 'you're wrong.'

All the women welders looked at the squad's 'terrible two' with surprised expressions on their faces.

'We're gannin on a double date,' Angie informed them all, taking off her headscarf and ruffling her shoulder-length blonde hair.

'And where are your dates taking you?' Rosie asked.

'We're meeting them in the Burton House,' Dorothy said, 'and as it's just opposite you, Gloria—'

'We can pop round 'n see ya!' Angie chuckled

'You can if yer want to,' Gloria said, 'but you won't get an answer, because there won't be anyone there. *I'm* also going out tonight.'

Now it was Dorothy's and Angie's turn to look intrigued.

'Ohh,' Dorothy said, 'and where are you gallivanting off to?'

'Hope and I are going to see an old friend of mine,' Gloria informed them.

'Old as in *old*, or old as in you've known her ages?' Dorothy asked.

'Both,' Gloria said, adding, 'Mrs Crabtree is old, *very old*, and I've known her most of my life. She's just moved back to Hendon. Actually, she's just moved into a house down the road from Polly on Tatham Street.'

'Really?' Polly asked, curious. 'Whereabouts?'

'Right at the bottom end. Number two.'

'I know the one,' Polly said. 'I thought there was a family living there?'

'There was. Still is. They've just gone to stay for a while with relatives in Whitby.'

'I'm guessing they're sick of the bombs,' Rosie said.

Polly nodded.

'They've got five young 'uns. I think they got fed up hauling them off to the shelter every five minutes.'

They all started to make their way to the timekeeper's cabin, where they were joined by Martha who had been riveting all afternoon with Jimmy's squad, which was one man down.

'You on ARP duties tonight, Martha?' Rosie asked.

'I am, but I'm pretty sure it'll be quiet. We got a bashing on Sunday. We never have two in the space of a week,' she said.

'Don't tempt fate,' Gloria said, looking up at the admin offices. There was no need to take her headscarf off tonight as she knew Helen was going to Ryhope to see John.

'Yes, Martha, don't tempt fate,' Angie said. 'We dinnit want our night spoiled, do we, Dor?'

Dorothy chuckled as she started rummaging in her bag for her time card.

'You at Lily's?' Gloria looked across at Rosie.

'No, I'm not,' she said, looking at the women. '*I'm* also going out tonight.'

'Really?' Dorothy said, shocked.

'Eee, miss, yer never gan out,' Angie chipped in.

Rosie laughed.

'I know.'

'So, where yer off to?' Gloria was equally curious.

'Lily thought it was time we all had an evening out together. A bit of a "powwow" is what she said.'

'You, Lily and George?' Polly asked.

'*And* Kate, Maisie and Vivian,' Rosie added.

'Where yer all gannin?' Angie managed to beat Dorothy to the question they were busting to know the answer to.

'The Palatine,' Rosie said.

'Cor! It's dead posh there, isn't it!' Angie exclaimed.

'That's Lily for you,' Rosie said. 'Only the best.'

The women's banter continued as they entered the bottleneck of workers all in a hurry to leave work.

It was Friday after all.

When the end-of-shift klaxon sounded out Helen quickly tidied up her desk, grabbed her handbag and gas mask and shut her office door. She had no intention of working late tonight, but she also didn't want to get caught in the usual Friday crush. She lit a cigarette and stood at her usual spot by the window. Seeing the women welders walking over to the gates, their clocking-off cards to hand, all clearly excited about either going home or going out, Helen felt the familiar stab of envy.

As soon as the queue at the timekeeper's cabin had gone down, Helen hurried out of the empty administration building, across the yard and through the main gates. Walking quickly, she made it home within a quarter of an hour. After changing her clothes and putting on a new red dress she had bought herself, then quickly touching up her make-up and pinning back her victory rolls, she was back out the door. A tram journey into town was followed by a half-hour stop-start journey by bus to Ryhope. As was usually the case when her mind was free to wander, her thoughts strayed to the baby she might have lost – but whom she could not let go.

By the time the bus arrived at the stop just outside the hospital on Stockton Road, tears were pooling in Helen's eyes. She was used to it, though, and had a handkerchief to hand. Carefully dabbing away any tears that had started to trickle down her face, she stepped off the bus. Looking at her watch, she saw it had gone half-past seven. The black-out meant she could barely see a few yards in front of her, but she knew her way well enough now not to have to get out the little electric torch she kept in her handbag.

When she was halfway down the long path that led to the entrance of the hospital she could make out John's silhouette as he waited for her on the front steps. She could see his profile as he stared up at the night sky, which wasn't as dark as normal due to the illumination afforded by a full moon.

'Now that's true beauty,' Dr Parker said, before drawing his attention back down to earth and looking at Helen.

Like this woman before me, he instinctively thought.

'It is,' Helen agreed, as she gave her friend a hug.

Their embrace seemed to last a fraction longer than usual, and Helen found herself momentarily loath to break free. She looked up at Dr Parker's face. He seemed uncannily serious.

'So,' Dr Parker said, reluctantly letting go of Helen, 'where to?'

'Well, I think it's either the Railway Inn – or the Railway Inn,' Helen laughed.

'So, how come *I* have the pleasure of your company tonight, not Gloria?' Dr Parker asked as he put his pint of beer and Helen's gin and tonic down on the small round table they had managed to commandeer before the pub got too busy.

'She's seeing an old friend of hers,' Helen said, lighting up a cigarette. She didn't add that she had rearranged her usual Friday night with Gloria in order to be here, as it was rare for John to get a few hours off in the evening. Especially on a Friday night.

'They going anywhere nice?' Dr Parker asked, taking a sup of his beer and loosening his tie.

'No, the friend – Mrs Crabtree – is pretty ancient. She's just moved into a house at the bottom of Tatham Street. The old woman's from the east end originally. She moved out to South Hylton when she got married, but now her husband's gone, she's decided she wants to spend her final years where she was born and brought up, or at least that's what Gloria reckons anyway.' Helen sipped her drink. 'The old woman's desperate to meet Hope, so Gloria said she'd take her round there tonight.'

'And tell me about Hope. How's she doing?' Dr Parker asked. He knew how important the little girl was to Helen, and how close they'd become.

The next hour was spent deep in conversation, their chatter mainly about what had been happening at work. Dr Parker listened and chuckled as Helen told him she thought she might well lose her right-hand woman, Marie-Anne, to Rosie and her gang of welders.

'She never used to even venture into the yard before Bel started, and now the pair of them are out there every chance they get,' Helen said indignantly.

Dr Parker looked at Helen. He knew she was only joking, and that Marie-Anne would never forsake her warm office job for the gruelling, dirty work of a welder, but behind the jocularity he could see that Helen was envious of her secretary and the fact she had made friends with the women welders.

'She's even started to go out on an evening with Dorothy and Angie,' Helen's emerald eyes grew wide, 'to the Rink!'

Dr Parker almost choked on his beer as he let out a loud laugh.

'A den of iniquity if ever there was one!' he said in mock outrage.

Helen scowled across the table at her friend.

'No good will come of it!' As soon as the words were out, she too burst out laughing.

'Oh my goodness, I sound like some Bible-bashing old spinster!'

Dr Parker again looked at Helen and thought she was even more beautiful when she laughed.

The pair continued to chatter. Helen's heart sank when she realised they'd both finished their drinks and she saw the time. John had to be back at the hospital by nine.

As if reading her thoughts, Dr Parker looked up at the clock behind the bar.

'Why does time go so quickly?' he asked.

'Come on,' Helen said, putting her coat on, 'I'll walk you back.'

'Isn't that meant to be my line?' Dr Parker joked as he stood up and picked up their two empty glasses. Helen waited until he had taken them to the bar. As they left, the landlord shouted out cheerio to them both.

'You've gone quiet,' Helen said as they walked back to the hospital. 'What are you thinking?'

'Oh, nothing really,' he lied.

Dr Parker glanced at Helen, who had linked arms with him as soon as they had left the pub. He had been in turmoil all evening, trying to find the right time to ask Helen if she would like to accompany him to a dance next week at the village hall. But he had struggled with how to ask her, and, even more, with how to ask her in such a way that she would understand that he wanted her to accompany him as his date – not purely as a friend.

They walked in silence for a short distance.

'Anyway,' Helen chirped up, 'you haven't given me an update on our "poor chap" yet?'

Dr Parker smiled. Ever since he had told Helen about his patient with no name, who had nearly died several times over, she had never once failed to ask how he was doing. It was as though, to Helen, he'd come to symbolise hope. At the start of every shift, Dr Parker dreaded coming onto the ward and finding the man's bed empty.

'Remarkably, he's still hanging in there,' Dr Parker said.

'Good,' Helen said. 'I've a feeling he's going to make it.'

Just as they reached the hospital grounds it started to drizzle. Dr Parker looked up at the sky, which was clouding over.

'I'm guessing you've not got an umbrella stashed away in that handbag of yours?'

Helen shook her head.

'Let me fetch you one? I'm sure I've got one somewhere.'

Helen looked up at the sky and could feel spits of rain speckle her face.

'All right,' she said, secretly glad their evening was not quite at an end.

'Anyway,' Dr Parker said, 'it'll be nice for me to show you where I work.'

Opening the door, Dr Parker let Helen walk through first, before gently taking her by the elbow and guiding her down the corridor.

'Nearly there,' Dr Parker said as they came to a set of swing doors. Above it was a sign that read 'Post-Operative Ward'.

'Don't be put off by the matron; her bark's worse than her bite.'

He pushed open the door, putting his arm out for her to go first.

Seeing Helen, the matron's mouth opened, but before she had time to ask her what on earth she thought she was doing visiting at this time of night, Dr Parker appeared.

'It's all right, Mrs Rosendale. She's with me,' he smiled, causing the matron's face to soften.

As Helen let Dr Parker take the lead and walk through the ward, she tried not to stare at the dozen wounded soldiers who were either lying unconscious in bed or were propped up, their legs or arms, or both, in plaster casts.

'Hey! Bonny lass!' one of the men called out.

Helen looked to see a young man, his head bandaged and his arm in a sling and hoisted up in a pulley. She smiled at him, before noticing that the bed next to him had been stripped bare. The sheets had been balled up at the bottom of the mattress. Whoever had occupied that particular bed had either recovered enough to leave, or else had died. She feared it might well be the latter for John normally told her if he had been able to send any of his recruits 'packing'.

'I think I've died 'n gone to heaven!' one of the soldiers, who was playing a game of solitaire, shouted out.

'Enough of the cheek, Sergeant Perivale,' Dr Parker reprimanded.

Helen winked across to the soldier.

'That may be, Sergeant Perivale, *but I'm no angel*!'

There was uproar from the men who were awake, and a few groggy exclamations from those who were just waking up.

'Don't forget I work in a shipyard,' she whispered to Dr Parker.

As Dr Parker showed Helen through to his consultation room, the men quietened down.

While he started to search for the umbrella, Dr Parker's mind could only think about the dance at the village hall. This would be the perfect chance to ask Helen – might well be his only chance. He was hopeless on the phone at the best of times. Besides, when he asked her, he needed to see her face, determine her reaction. See with his own eyes if she understood he wanted to take her there as his date.

'There it is!' Helen stepped around the piles of paper and files that littered the floor.

'Honestly, John, I've never seen such chaos!' She grabbed the umbrella that was hanging exactly where it should be – on the hatstand in the corner of the room.

'Oh, that's great!' Dr Parker looked at the umbrella held triumphantly in Helen's hand and then at Helen. For the briefest of moments their eyes locked. Dr Parker felt his heart pumping hard. He stepped across the room towards her. All logical thought went out of his mind. At that moment all he wanted to do was simply to take Helen in his arms and kiss her.

As he reached her, Helen dropped her arm – and the umbrella. She looked up at her friend, whose face she knew so well, whose brown eyes she had looked into so many times these past months when she had been distraught and desperate, when she had nearly died, and, more recently, when she had started to feel the stirrings of happiness – something she had thought she might never feel again.

'Dr Parker!'

The slightly panicked voice of the matron made them both jump back.

'Sorry to interrupt,' Mrs Rosendale looked from the doctor to Helen, 'but one of your patients is coming round.'

Hurrying back onto the ward, Dr Parker made a beeline for the wounded soldier, who was clearly in distress and was thrashing around in his bed, shouting out unintelligible words.

As Dr Parker reached the bed, he checked the man's pulse, and felt his forehead whilst telling the matron to prep ten millilitres of morphine.

The soldier had tossed his bed sheets off in his tussle with consciousness and Helen could see he was bandaged around his torso.

'This, my dear, is your "poor chap",' Dr Parker said, all the while keeping his eyes on his patient. 'He's been like this since he was brought in. In and out of consciousness. Semi-lucid.'

'Can I do anything to help?' Helen asked, just as the matron arrived with a sterile wipe in one hand and a syringe in the other.

'Could you hold down his other arm, please?'

Helen hurried to the other side of the bed, her heart thumping as she grabbed the soldier's arm, which was flailing around.

'Keep him still if you can,' Dr Parker said. His voice was commanding but not harsh. He quickly took the antiseptic swab from the matron, wiped the soldier's bare arm, and carefully injected him.

The matron took the empty syringe and hurried off, leaving Helen and Dr Parker on each side of the bed.

'You can let go now.' Dr Parker looked across at Helen, who was still pushing down on the man's arm, even though he had stopped trying to punch his invisible opponent. 'You did a good job there.' He smiled at her.

'You don't fancy a job as a nurse do you?' he joked, looking back down at the man, who was now starting to relax. His body had stopped thrashing around and his shouts were now reduced to incoherent mumbles.

Helen smiled back at Dr Parker.

'*So*, this is our "poor chap"?'

'It certainly is,' Dr Parker said. 'He's a fighter – that's for sure.'

Helen looked at the man, whom she felt she knew thanks to the regular updates she had been given by Dr Parker these past couple of weeks.

And then she looked more closely.

Dr Parker glanced up at Helen and noticed that the expression on her face had changed.

He saw her hand gently brush the man's hair away from his eyes, which were flickering open as he tried desperately to fight the effects of the morphine.

'Tommy?' Helen's voice was barely a whisper.

'Tommy!' She put both her hands around the man's unshaven face.

'Is it you? Tommy?' Helen's mouth was close to the man's as she gently repeated his name.

The man's eyes flickered open but only momentarily. He tried to say something but he couldn't get his words out.

'Tommy. It's me!' Helen gasped in disbelief.

'It's me … Oh, thank God!

'You're alive!'

Chapter Fifty-Six

'Oh, Tommy, I can't believe it – *you're alive*!'

Helen held the face of the man whom she had only just recognised – who looked very different from the one who had left to go to war.

He was a shadow of his former self, but it was Tommy!

The man she had known since they were children.

The man she loved.

It was Tommy.

Her Tommy.

And he wasn't dead.

'Tommy. You made it! You made it!' Helen repeated, still not quite believing it.

As Tommy fought to open his eyes, he took Helen's hand and put it to lips that were dry and cracked and kissed it, before his head sank back into the pillow.

'You're back home now, Tommy,' she told him, tears pouring down her face. There was so much she wanted to say to him. The words were bubbling up, desperate to escape and tell him how distraught she had been thinking he was dead, how much she loved him, how much she wanted him – that they could have a wonderful life together.

As Helen's tears fell onto Tommy's face, his eyes opened wide.

'Is it you? Is it really you?' he said, a wide smile spread across his gaunt face. 'I've waited … so long.' His voice was raspy. He swallowed hard.

Helen could hear Dr Parker asking the matron to bring some water.

'I'm here, Tommy.' Helen was holding his hand, squeezing it. 'I'm here. I've always been here for you. I always *will* be here for you.'

She was crying with happiness.

Tommy wanted *her*.

She felt euphoric.

'Oh, Tommy, I love you,' she said breathlessly.

Tommy's eyes flickered shut.

He started mumbling again, trying to talk.

As Helen gently held his hand and put her ear to his mouth, she listened intently to what he was trying to say.

Finally she heard.

Tommy's voice was croaky and frail, but there was no mistaking what he was saying.

'Polly ... *My Pol* ... How I've missed ya.'

He smiled again, his eyes still closed.

'Ah Pol ... ' his voice was now slurred with the effects of the opiate ' ... there's not been a day gone by when I've not thought about yer ... '

The morphine was winning the battle.

Tommy slowly slipped into a pain-free slumber.

Helen's heart, which had just soared to the highest Heaven, now plummeted back down to earth and shattered into a thousand pieces.

Tommy. Her true love. Her first love.

He was alive.

But he didn't want her.

He wanted Polly.

He had always wanted Polly.

Helen looked up to see John's face, watching.

'*So*, this is Tommy,' he said.

He kept his voice strong, his face impassive, as his own heart broke.

'Mrs Rosendale, can you keep an eye on him, please? If he wakes, try and get some liquids down him. That would be great. Thank you. He should be all right for the next few hours. If there are any problems, get Dr Kayne, I believe he's also on duty tonight. I should be back in a couple of hours at the most.'

The matron nodded, glancing at the young woman who was standing stock-still by the side of the bed, staring down at the patient they now knew was called Tommy.

Dr Parker walked around the bed, gently touched Helen's arm and guided her out of the ward. The other patients watched but didn't utter a word.

When they finally made it out of the hospital and were standing on the front steps of the main entrance, breathing in the fresh night air, Helen turned to Dr Parker.

'God, I feel like the stupidest woman on this planet!'

She looked into her friend's eyes, but could not read them.

'You're not stupid at all, Helen,' he tried to reassure her. 'Just overwrought ... And you've had one hell of a shock.'

He paused.

'I do think, though, that we need to get a message to Polly to tell her that her fiancé is alive.'

The word 'fiancé' felt like another slap in the face.

Helen took a quivering intake of air.

'Of course,' she said, nodding her head and wiping her tears away. 'Polly ... Of course ... Gosh, she's going to be beside herself. She's not going to believe it ... *I* can't believe it! This really is the best news ever.'

She started down the stone steps.

'I'll go now and tell her ... I know where she lives.'

Dr Parker caught Helen's arm to stop her leaving. She looked in a daze. It was clear she was in no fit state to go anywhere by herself.

'I think that sounds like an excellent idea,' Dr Parker said, 'but you're not going on your own. I'm coming too. They can manage without me for a few hours.'

Helen looked at Dr Parker and didn't argue.

'If you think they can spare you? And Tommy's all right?'

'There are other doctors they can call on if needed. And don't worry, Tommy's going to be fine. He's made it this far, I don't think he's going to give up now.'

He smiled at Helen. She seemed so bereft. So lost. Almost vulnerable.

'Now wait here while I go and get our coats and your handbag,' he said. 'It's not exactly warm this evening.'

He looked up at the sky. It was still spitting rain.

Helen watched as Dr Parker turned to go back into the hospital.

'And the umbrella,' she shouted out after him. 'Don't forget the umbrella!'

Dr Parker turned to see Helen giving him a smile, a weak one, but a smile all the same.

'You must think I'm a prize fool,' Helen said to Dr Parker as they sat on the bus back into town.

Dr Parker looked at Helen and for once was at a loss for words. He was reeling himself from shock, not only that his patient was *the* Tommy Watts, but at the intensity of feelings that Helen still harboured for the man she had once loved.

Clearly still *did* love.

Helen linked arms with Dr Parker as they sat next to each other in the single-decker bus slowly making its way along unlit roads.

'Talk about making a complete spectacle of yourself,' Helen said, resting her head on his shoulder.

Dr Parker looked at Helen as she closed her eyes.

'Don't be so tough on yourself,' he said. 'I think it's hard when you love someone and that someone doesn't love you back.'

Half an hour later the bus pulled up at the stop at the top of Toward Road. Helen had been dozing, thinking about what had just happened. The more she thought about it, the more mortified she felt by her actions. It was as though she had seen Tommy as her salvation. She had desperately wanted to believe that if he was hers, he would miraculously make everything go back to the way it had been before.

God, hadn't she learnt anything from her disastrous relationship with Theodore? She'd thought Theo too had possessed such magical powers. That he would change the way she felt. She had looked through the warped reality of Alice's Looking-Glass and seen her very own knight in shining armour – someone who was the answer to all her problems.

And now here she was doing it all again.

'I think the next stop is ours.' Dr Parker turned his head slightly as he spoke quietly to Helen. He too had been lost in his own world, rerunning the evening's events – his mind dragging him back to the moment he had gone to kiss Helen while they had been looking for the umbrella. He was sure she had realised what his intentions were, and yet she had not recoiled. *Was it possible that she would have kissed him back?*

God! Get with it man! Dr Parker scolded himself. *What did it matter now?*

After seeing how Helen had been with Tommy, it was clear there was no room in her heart for anyone else – even if the heart of the man she still loved belonged to someone else.

Seeing their stop approaching, Dr Parker and Helen both sat up straight, unlinked their arms and got ready to get out of their seats and leave the quiet hub of the bus.

'Do you know what number Polly lives at?' Dr Parker asked.

'I don't, but I know it's opposite a sweet shop halfway down Tatham Street, just a few doors down from the Tatham Arms, where Bel's mam works,' Helen said, looking out the window and seeing only darkness where she knew Mowbray Park to be.

She looked back and focused her attention on Dr Parker.

'Thank you, John.'

'For what?' he said.

'For everything. For always being there for me. For coming with me tonight.'

Dr Parker was just about to tell Helen that it was nothing when they suddenly heard the all too familiar wail of the air raid sirens starting up.

'Oh, I don't believe it!' Helen said. 'Not tonight of all nights!'

Hearing the warning and seeing the first flash of searchlights criss-cross the skies, the bus driver pulled over.

'Most of these houses – ' he pointed to the three-storey Victorian terraced homes that faced the park ' – have cellars. Otherwise there's the Palatine a bit further down. They've always got plenty of room in their basement – and from what I've heard it's been well kitted out.'

Everyone hurried off the bus.

'The Palatine?' Helen said.

Dr Parker let out a loud laugh.

'I might have guessed! Come on then!' He raised his voice to be heard above the sirens, now blaring out at full volume.

They both walked quickly down the road.

'It's probably just a false alarm,' Helen shouted, but as soon as her words were out, there was another familiar sound – the drone of a German bomber.

And it was getting louder.

Chapter Fifty-Seven

The Luftwaffe pilot of the Heinkel He 111 bomber cursed as he flew through yet more clouds. Just over an hour ago the skies had been clear and the moon bright. Now it was cloudy and drizzly, making visibility poor.

'Verdammt!' Leutnant Karl Mayer cursed again as his vision was obliterated by thick patches of mist and fog. His sentiments were echoed by his bombardier, Unteroffizier Hans Fischer, sitting cramped up next to him in the aircraft's trademark glass nose.

'Gott sei Dank!' Leutnant Mayer shouted out his relief as the skies suddenly cleared and he was gifted an unobstructed view of what he knew to be the 'Biggest Shipbuilding Town in the World'.

Seeing the snake-like curves of the River Wear, Leutnant Mayer glanced across at Unteroffizier Fischer just as he flicked the switch to open the bomb bay doors. The Heinkel immediately lifted, having become lighter after successfully unleashing its consignment – three 500-kilogram bombs. Seconds later they heard the boom of the first explosion, then the second, but not a third. One of the bombs must have failed to detonate.

Leutnant Mayer thought of his own family in Dresden and prayed that the high explosives had hit their intended targets – and not any of the long lines of homes that seemed to cling to the hems of the town's revered shipyards. When he had originally looked at the aerial map of the town, he had whistled aloud. His Kommandeur had nodded, having read his thoughts.

'Ich weiss,' he'd said. *'Sie lieben ihren Werften so sehr, dass sie praktish in ihnen wohnen.'* ('They love their shipyards so much they practically live in them!') They had laughed, but their joviality masked a deep concern. They were both family men. They hated the thought of innocent women and children being killed in their own homes. This was not what they had signed up for.

As Leutnant Mayer directed the Heinkel towards the North Sea he felt a surge of happiness. In a few hours he would be back in Germany. He was due leave – a forty-eight-hour pass at the very least. He couldn't wait to see his wife, Ingrid, and their two young children, Gerald and Elke.

Just as they were flying over the mouth of the harbour, though, he and his co-pilot were momentarily blinded by the glare of a searchlight, then deafened by the furious rat-ta-tat sound of the AA guns as they opened fire. Their gunner and radio operator returned fire, but it was too late.

Seconds later Leutnant Mayer felt the plane jolt and knew they'd been hit. He looked down at the dashboard, which had lit up like a Christmas tree.

In the corner of his eye he saw the orange flicker of flames. He looked ahead again. Both propellers had frozen. His crew were deathly silent as the engine laboured and the Heinkel took a nosedive towards the dark runway of the North Sea. He knew the water would be like concrete when they hit it.

Leutnant Mayer's last thoughts were of his wife and children. He knew he would never see them again – not in this world anyway.

Chapter Fifty-Eight

'Yer didn't fancy being cosied up in the shelter with your bloke then?' Angie shouted into Dorothy's ear as they made their way out of the pub.

'God, no!' Dorothy looked at Angie with horror. 'I'd have died of boredom!'

'Yeh, same here. Dull as dishwater mine was.'

The air raid sirens had sounded out a few minutes earlier and the two women had said their goodbyes to their dates in the lounge bar of the Burton House hotel.

'Shame Gloria's not in,' Dorothy shouted out.

The two women looked across the road.

'I know – her shelter sounds all right, as far as shelters gan. She said Mr Brown always keeps it stocked up with biscuits 'n wotnots.'

The two women dithered for a little while, as people hurried past them.

'Let's go to Tavistock House. Where Polly and Bel always go.'

'The geet big house round the corner?' Angie said.

Dorothy nodded, took her friend's arm, and the two started walking.

Turning the corner into Back Tatham Street, Angie suddenly pulled Dorothy to a halt.

'I've got something in my shoe!' Angie shouted out as she bent over. 'It's digging right in.' Hopping on one foot, she took her shoe off and shook it. A small stone dropped onto the pavement.

'Ange, we're in the middle of a bloody air raid!' Dorothy shouted in her friend's ear.

'I can't help it if I've gorra geet big boulder in me shoe!' Angie hollered back.

Dorothy had just opened her mouth to speak again when the sirens were blotted out by the deafening drone of an aircraft engine. Seconds later there were two almighty explosions – one immediately after the other. The two friends screamed and grabbed each other. Their terrified cries were obliterated by the sound of shattering glass, and the crashing torrent of smashed brickwork. They clung to each other as the air around them was instantly saturated with asphyxiating black smoke.

They stayed clutching one another until a deathly quietness descended.

It was only when the air cleared enough for them to see the vague outlines of people and buildings that they knew for certain they were still of this world.

Angie and Dorothy finally let go of each other when the ghostly calm was broken by the shouts of the ARP wardens, and the ringing of bells signalling the approach of the fire engines.

'It's still there!' Dorothy shouted out, pointing at the house where they believed their friends to be sheltering.

'Eee, thank God for that!' Angie mumbled. She felt as though she'd had the stuffing knocked out of her.

Dorothy turned to look at Angie and saw that they were now wearing what looked like identical grey dresses.

They also had the same grey hair – and their faces had been plastered with a similar ghoulish grey make-up.

Angie spat some dirt out of her mouth and stared at the bombed building that she knew to be Moore's warehouse.

Hearing the approach of the fire engine, they watched as it swung into Tavistock Place.

'Bloody hell, Ange, I think we had our guardian angel looking after us there!'

Angie nodded, still not able to find the energy to speak.

Catching the flash of blue lights in their peripheral vision, they turned to catch sight of an ambulance heading towards Tatham Street.

They looked at each other.

'Gloria and Hope!' their grey faces mouthed at each other.

Turning their backs on the bomb site that was Tavistock Place, they started to run as fast as their shaking legs would allow.

Chapter Fifty-Nine

When Gloria heard the air raid sirens start up, she panicked.

'Bloody typical,' she cursed under her breath. 'The one night I go out 'n there's a bloomin' air raid.' If she'd been in her own home, she'd simply have grabbed Hope and gone straight to the shelter in the back garden.

Picking Hope off the lounge floor, where she was having an imaginary tea party with an old teddy bear Mrs Crabtree had given to her, Gloria hurried into the kitchen, where she found the old woman making a fresh pot of tea.

'You've not got a shelter out back, have you?' Gloria asked, knowing it was unlikely as most of the terraces along the street had concrete yards as opposed to gardens.

Mrs Crabtree shook her head, putting the kettle back onto the range, then bending down to scoop up her ginger tabby, which had spent the entire evening either nestled up in her lap or weaving in and out of her bandy legs.

'Teddy!' Hope wailed. Gloria jigged her daughter on her hip, trying to placate her.

'Teddeee!' Hope's wails were starting to match those of the siren. Realising her daughter would not rest until she was once again in possession of her new toy, she went back into the lounge and grabbed the one-eyed brown teddy bear.

Coming back into the kitchen, Gloria found the old woman standing in the middle of her small kitchen, stroking her beloved pet, trying to keep it calm.

'Come on, I'll get our coats and gas masks. We'll go to the public shelter,' Gloria shouted; not only were the sirens loud, but Mrs Crabtree was also almost deaf.

The old woman shook her head.

'Too far!' she shouted back.

As soon as she spoke, the ginger tabby leapt from her arms and darted into the lounge.

'The cupboard under the stairs!' Mrs Crabtree pointed a gnarly finger towards the hallway, before shuffling past and heading into the lounge to fetch the cat.

Gloria stood for a moment, unsure whether to risk the hike to the shelter, which she knew would probably take them a good five minutes to get to, probably longer with an old woman and a fourteen-month-old toddler in tow.

For God's sake, make yer bloody mind up! Gloria chastised herself; she didn't feel able to think with the noise of the sirens.

Just get in the cupboard!

Coming out of the kitchen and into the tiled hallway, Gloria pulled open the small wooden door under the staircase. She carefully stepped down onto the dropped floor, shielding Hope's head so that she didn't hit it on the door frame.

Once her eyes adjusted to the darkness she felt a modicum of relief; it was bigger than she had anticipated. Turning round, her foot knocked something and she looked down to see a candle and a box of matches.

Putting Hope down, she lit the candle and looked around. There was easily enough room for the three of them.

Spotting a blanket and cushion neatly stacked in the corner, Gloria realised that Mrs Crabtree never bothered with the public shelter. This here was her own Make Do and Mend air raid shelter. As Gloria moved the flickering candle slowly around, she noticed a little mound of rags – the old woman had even made a makeshift bed for the cat.

'All right, sweetie.' Gloria tried to make her voice light as she bobbed down on her haunches. Hope was clutching the teddy bear to her chest.

'We're going to play a game.' Gloria looked into Hope's eyes and saw both uncertainty and the beginnings of fear.

'We're going to stay here for a little while. Like hide and seek.' Gloria looked at Hope but she still looked unsure and a little scared.

Gloria stepped towards the small door that she'd left ajar.

'Mrs Crabtree,' she shouted out, 'are you coming?'

There was a moment's silence.

'I'll be there in a moment, pet!'

Gloria could hear that Mrs Crabtree was still in the lounge and by the sounds she was making was clearly trying to coax the ginger tabby out from some hard-to-get-to hiding place.

'Just leave the cat!' Gloria shouted back. 'It'll be fine!'

There were more *'Puss, puss ... '* sounds coming from the living room.

'They've got nine lives,' Gloria shouted out, louder this time.

There was more silence.

'I've got her!' Mrs Crabtree's triumphant voice finally sounded out.

Her words, though, were immediately followed by a deafening blast that shook the very foundations of the house.

Gloria instinctively dropped down on her knees to cover her daughter's body with her own, just as a shower of bricks rained down on her back.

Chapter Sixty

'Come on!' Dr Parker shouted above the deafening sound of the sirens and the bomber's engine. Grabbing Helen's hand, he dragged her towards the hotel. It was only a few hundred yards away, but the bomber's shadowy presence was already passing over them, thudding its way over the town, hauling its metal wares of destruction across the cold October sky.

'Bloody hell!' He looked around him, frantically searching for some semblance of shelter.

And then he heard it: the whistling of the bomb as it cut through the air, piercing through the sound of the sirens.

Automatically pulling Helen to the side, he wrapped her in his arms, covering her head with his hands. The earth around them shuddered in shock as 500 kilograms' worth of explosives hit the ground, filling the air instantly with a thick veil of dust.

Seconds later he felt Helen's body instinctively jerk when the earth underneath them juddered yet again as another explosion racked the town.

The deafening booms and the two huge clouds of grey told them that both bombs had landed near – very near.

Squinting through the ash- and dirt-filled air, he saw the bright lines of the tracers shooting upwards into the sky, and the snatch of a swastika painted on the side of the bomber, caught for a split second in the poking finger of a searchlight. There was an immediate burst of ack-ack fire. The lone bomber disappeared into the dark folds of the night sky, but a sudden flare of flames illuminated its flank once more. Dr Parker saw the tail of the aircraft upend, and he followed its descent as it spiralled towards death and a watery grave.

Helen lifted her head and looked around her. She blinked hard, trying to adjust her vision to the flurries of dust and ash that seemed to be floating around her like grey snowflakes.

'Please, Helen, go to the shelter!' Dr Parker demanded again.

'They've hit the east end!' she said, panicked, ignoring his plea.

'Helen ... ' Dr Parker shouted to be heard, placing both his hands firmly on her shoulders. 'I need you to get to the hotel's shelter!'

'Where are you going?' Helen's eyes were darting around her. Their world had switched in an instant from order to complete bedlam.

'To see if they need help with any casualties.' Dr Parker leant towards Helen so as to be heard without shouting.

'I'm coming too!' Helen said.

'No, you're not.' Dr Parker flashed her a look that said this was not up for debate. He grabbed her arm. He was sure the hotel entrance was around the corner. 'Just until the all-clear,' he said, looking up at the skies, fearful of seeing yet more harbingers of death.

Helen pulled back.

'Come on!' He tugged her in the direction of the hotel, but she wasn't having any of it.

'There's an ambulance!' she cried out as a flashing blue light became visible.

Dr Parker looked at Helen and knew this was a fight he was not going to win.

He let go of her, stepped off the kerb and waved his arms frantically at the ambulance.

Seeing him at the last minute through the darkness of the blackout, the driver screeched to a halt.

'I'm a doctor! I work up at the Ryhope,' Dr Parker shouted through the window.

The driver leant across and pushed open the door.

Dr Parker clambered in, followed by Helen.

The two men looked at her, but before they had time to object, she shouted, 'Get going!'

The ferocity of her voice made the driver jump and he slammed the ambulance into first gear.

'Where did they land?' Helen demanded.

'Hendon,' the driver said, as they turned right down Borough Road.

'Where in Hendon?!' Helen barked her question.

Dr Parker looked at Helen and saw the growing panic etched across her face.

'One hit Laura Street at the junction with Murton Street, but didn't explode ... The second Tavistock Place ... And the third ... ' The driver pulled the wheel round as he turned right.

'Here ... ' he shouted, his eyes focused on the road. *'Tatham Street.'*

'Oh my God!' Helen's face went pale. 'Gloria! *Hope*!'

Dr Parker took her hand.

'We'll find them.' He tried to sound reassuring, but looking ahead, his heart sank.

It was like driving through the gates of Hell. There were men, women and children wandering about, their faces blackened and their hair grey with dust. They saw people running in or out of homes along the long stretch of terraced houses. The air raid warning had come too late; it was clear people hadn't been able to make it to any of the nearby shelters.

The ambulance steered around an abandoned tram, all its windows shattered.

The further down the street they drove, the more frenzied the atmosphere.

Two elderly spinsters, both dressed from head to toe in black, came out of their front door looking dazed and confused. Helen looked at the shattered windows and saw it was the sweet shop.

She looked across the road, where she knew Polly and Bel lived. Thank God the houses there were still standing and intact.

Suddenly the ambulance jammed on its brakes as a skinny blonde woman stepped out onto the road without looking and hurried across the cobbles; she was followed by a portly man of around the same age.

As they neared the end of the street, Helen caught sight of a man in a tweed suit desperately clawing at the rubble of a partially demolished house. She saw what looked like a half-buried tricycle next to him. His face looked manic as he desperately flung bricks and stones to the side.

The ambulance was forced to a halt by the amount of broken furniture and debris strewn across the road. Helen jumped out, her legs shaking, followed by Dr Parker. Two medics appeared from the back carrying a stretcher, while the driver strode over to talk to an ARP warden.

'Casualties at the south end,' he shouted out, looking at Dr Parker and then at the medics.

Helen felt sick to the pit of her stomach.

That was where Mrs Crabtree lived!

Dr Parker looked at Helen and read her thoughts.

This time he didn't say anything; instead they both hurried down the street, their way hindered by piles of rubble. As they arrived at the end of Tatham Street, Helen stared at the space where two houses had once stood. There was now only a twenty-foot-wide crater. Rescuers were sifting frantically through the ruins for survivors.

'Over here!'

Helen looked to see the two medics making their way over to a couple of ARP wardens who were hauling the body of young lad from underneath a stack of bricks. Dr Parker raced over, ordering the men to put the boy on a stretcher while he examined him. Helen caught sight of the lad's head, his thick brown hair crusted with blood and dust, as he turned to look up at Dr Parker. *Thank God, the poor child was still alive.*

The two wardens moved out of the way and it was only then that Helen saw the bigger of the two was, in fact, a woman.

'Martha!' Helen shouted out.

Her voice was lost in the shouts for help, the sound of people crying and the continuous lament of the air raid siren.

Martha was wearing a blue denim overall, not dissimilar to the one she wore for work, a pair of wellington boots and a dome-shaped tin hat.

'Martha!' Helen shouted again, picking her way across the ruins.

This time Martha heard her name being called and looked around. Her eyes widened when she saw who was trying to catch her attention.

'Helen! What are you doing here?'

'I'm looking for Gloria and Hope!' she shouted, her eyes darting about, hoping to see mother and child on the war-torn street.

'Won't they be at home?' Martha asked, puzzled, not only as to why Helen thought they might be here, but why Helen would be looking for Gloria and Hope at all.

'No, they were going to visit an old friend. Mrs Crabtree. She lives in one of these houses.' Helen looked around at the buildings on both sides of the road. As well as the two that had obviously taken a direct hit, there were others that looked on the verge of total collapse.

Panic shot through Martha. 'Let's find them!'

The two women started asking the growing swell of people arriving at the scene if they knew where a woman called Mrs Crabtree lived.

'She's an old woman,' Helen said to a man in a three-piece suit, who looked dazed and had a gash on his head. 'She's just recently moved into one of these houses.'

The man thought for a moment before shaking his head.

'Sorry pet,' he said, before wandering off up the street.

'Helen!' Martha was waving at her. She was towering over a small old woman.

Helen rushed over. 'Are you Mrs Crabtree?'

'No, hinny, I'm not her,' the old woman said, viewing Helen with her pale blue eyes.

'But I know who she is, pet,' she added, shuffling around unsteadily. 'She's just moved into number two.' The old woman pointed an arthritic finger to one of the three-storey Victorian terraces.

It reminded Helen of the inside of a doll's house – only a doll's house that someone had just stamped on.

'Oh my God.' Helen hurried towards the half-demolished house with Martha just a pace behind.

Chapter Sixty-One

'Gloria!' Helen shouted as loudly as she could, trying to outdo the air raid sirens but failing.

'Gloria!' Martha's voice boomed behind her as they both made their way over the uneven blanket of red bricks leading to the partially destroyed doll's house.

Helen heard what sounded like the gentle trickle of a brook; looking for the imaginary stream, she instead found a burst water pipe.

Stopping for a few seconds, she scanned every part of what was left of the house. There was no roof to speak of. Nor attic. No third floor whatsoever. The second floor now had a view of the stars. Helen spotted the brass knobs of a bed poking through the remnants of the collapsed ceiling.

When her eyes dropped to the ground floor, her heart sank. *Please, God! Let them have made it to the shelter!* If anyone had been inside when the house had tumbled around their ears, it would be a miracle if they were still alive.

'Martha!'

Martha and Helen turned round in unison to see Dorothy and Angie, covered from head to foot in grey shrouds of dirt, jogging down the street towards them.

They stopped in their tracks.

'Oh my God!' Dorothy said, looking at the demolished houses.

'What yer deein'?' Angie shouted through the tannoy of her hands, hoping upon hope that the answer wasn't what she thought it was going to be.

'Looking for Gloria and Hope!' Martha shouted back.

Angie's and Dorothy's faces dropped.

'They might be trapped!' Martha shouted, although she had been working as an ARP warden long enough now to know that if there had been anyone in this house, the chances were they wouldn't be coming out alive.

'We'll help!' Dorothy shouted out as she started to make her unsteady way over the first mound of bricks. Angie followed. Helen waved her hands at them both, signalling them to halt.

'They might have made it to the public air raid shelter. Or there's a chance they went back to the flat!' Helen shouted out. 'Can you go and check?'

Dorothy and Angie stopped in their tracks. They knew it made sense. They nodded and put their thumbs up to show they would.

They were both so worried about Gloria and Hope they didn't think to wonder why Helen was there, or why she was just about to walk into a death trap – to risk her own life for those she barely knew.

'I bloody well hope she's at the shelter.' Angie threw her best friend a sidelong glance. 'Anywhere but there! I can't see *anyone* getting out of that in one piece.'

Dorothy's face was desperately serious.

'Gloria's not daft. She'll have got to the shelter.'

'*If* she had time! *We didn't!*'

'Oh, come on and shut up!' Dorothy said, tears springing into her eyes as they both started to run. They prayed that they'd find their friend and the little girl they had helped bring into this world in the middle of another air raid just fourteen months previously.

After Dorothy and Angie left, Helen looked across at Martha.

'You stay here!' she shouted, before turning and making her way over bigger and bigger mounds of masonry, stumbling a few times as she went, although the obstacles underfoot did nothing to lessen her haste.

Sensing movement, Helen stopped for a brief moment and snapped her head to the side to find Martha just yards behind her. The two women looked at each other. Helen opened her mouth to tell her to go back, but before the words were out, Martha shook her head from side to side as she too stumbled clumsily across the debris-strewn ground.

Helen carried on making her way towards what had once been the front door of the house, but instead of walking through an actual doorway she passed through a cloying veil of smoke and dust. She gagged immediately and automatically put her hand to her mouth. She felt a weight on her shoulder and turned to see Martha's outstretched hand holding what looked like a handkerchief. She took it and pressed it against her nose and mouth.

Her heart was pounding, but her mind was as clear as day.

She had one aim, and one aim only. Nothing was going to stop her. *She had to get to Hope!*

She might have lost her own baby, but she was damned if she was going to lose her little sister as well.

Helen knew she would sacrifice her own life for her sister, and with that realisation – the acceptance that death could well be near – any fear she might have felt left her.

'There!' Helen heard Martha's loud but muffled voice.

She looked behind to see Martha pointing to a large gap in the wall.

Helen's eyes were stinging and her vision blurred, but she was just able to make out the faintest shape of a body.

It had to be Gloria.

And if it *was* Gloria, there was no doubt that Hope would be there too.

Helen clambered across more dirt and debris, climbing over an upturned bookcase and nearly falling in her desperation to get to the figure, who appeared to be crouched down on all fours. *Was it Gloria hunched over Hope?*

'Gloria! Gloria!' she was screaming as she reached out.

Suddenly she jumped back in shock as her touch caused the lifeless body to slump over onto its side.

It was Mrs Crabtree.

In her arms was her ginger tabby. It was alive, but showed no willingness to move. Far from it. Its eyes glowered at its potential rescuers and its hiss told them to let well alone.

'Mrs Crabtree?' Martha shouted through a piece of rag she had tied around her face.

Helen nodded, beyond relieved it wasn't Gloria and Hope.

They both looked around, straining to see or hear any signs of life.

Helen pointed back to the way they had come in, but just as they stepped forward there was a loud cracking sound as if some giant door in need of oiling was being slowly pulled open. They both looked up in horror as a huge wooden beam dropped down. Helen felt herself being propelled backwards. It took her a second or two to realise it was Martha's hand yanking her from behind.

Falling backwards, she braced herself to feel the pain of landing on broken bricks, but her fall was broken by Martha's bulk. Straining her head forward she saw the wooden beam was just inches away from them. She would have been lying under it had it not been for Martha.

Rolling off and putting her hands and feet on the glass-strewn floor, Helen looked at Martha, who was pushing herself into a sitting position.

'Are you all right?' Helen asked, scrutinising her for any sign of injury.

Martha nodded, her eyes trained on the scene of devastation all around them, still hunting for Gloria and Hope, but seeing only chaos and thick grey swirls of dust.

Both women stood up unsteadily.

Sensing that the back of her head was wet, Martha's hand instinctively went to wipe away what felt like water dripping down her neck. When she looked at her hand it was red.

And then they heard it.

Just after the tone of the ARP siren changed from undulating to a monotone, sounding out the all-clear, Rosie and Martha heard another wailing noise, only this one was human.

Helen and Martha looked at each other.

'Hope!' Martha said.

They both scrambled around the remnants of a coffee table and an upturned armchair and headed for the doorway, of which only the frame was left.

'Maaaammeee!'

'Oh my God! There!' Helen pointed to a small wooden door that was lying on top of what looked like a heap of rubble under the staircase.

They had walked straight past it on coming into the house.

Helen's heart was beating so fast she thought it was going to explode.

Hope was alive!

'We're coming, sweetie,' Helen cried out.

Martha nudged Helen aside, took the small wooden door in both hands and threw it towards the gaping hole of what was now the entrance to the kitchen.

As she did so, Helen saw the bloody wound on the back of Martha's head.

'Maaammee!' Hope cried out again.

And then they saw Hope's tear-stained little face, completely caked in thick dirt and dust that had acted as a perfect camouflage, faultlessly blending her in with the deathly grey landscape around her.

On top of her – also well camouflaged – was Gloria.

But there was no movement or sound.

No sign that Gloria was still alive.

Chapter Sixty-Two

'Here we are, sweetie ... Your aunty Martha's here to see you as well ... ' Helen tried to keep her voice calm as she carefully stepped around the mound of bricks and mortar that had encased mother and child.

'We're going to get you out of here,' she promised. 'Everything's going to be just fine.'

Finally, she reached Hope, whose little cherub-like face was stricken with terror. On seeing Helen it crumpled and she started crying.

'It's all right, sweetie. Everything's going to be just fine,' Helen cooed, stroking Hope's face. Helen looked at Gloria's inert body, which had saved Hope, but also trapped her.

Knowing what needed to be done, Martha carefully took hold of Gloria's upper body and lifted it just a fraction so that Hope could stretch her arms up to her sister.

''Elen,' she whimpered. It was the first time Hope had ever said Helen's name.

Tears stung Helen's eyes and she blinked hard.

Thank God she was all right.

'Come here, cheeky Charlie.' She half laughed, half cried with relief as she eased Hope from under Gloria's dead weight.

Once freed, Hope hooked her chubby little legs around Helen's waist, and wrapped her arms around her neck.

'It's all right. You're safe now,' Helen said.

Helen looked at Martha, who had a grave expression on her face.

'Can you turn her over?' she asked, putting her hand on the back of Hope's head to prevent her from seeing anything.

Still on her haunches, Martha bent over Gloria.

Shards of glass and bits of rubble tumbled off as Martha carefully turned Gloria so that she was on her back.

Helen stifled a sob as Martha started clearing Gloria's eyes, nose and mouth of dust, before putting her ear to her chest.

For what felt like an eternity, Helen stood stock-still, staring, not daring to even breathe.

Suddenly Martha's head shot back up, her eyes wide.

'She's alive!' she shouted. 'She's alive!'

Helen gasped for air. Tears immediately started streaming down her charcoal-smeared face as she watched Martha force Gloria into a sitting position and start gently slapping her in an effort to bring her round.

Gloria suddenly inhaled a huge gulp of air and started coughing.

Helen felt her legs start to go with sheer relief.

'Gloria!' she shouted.

In a daze, Gloria looked at Martha, who was checking her pulse and scrutinising her head and body for any sign of bleeding or injury. She then slowly turned her face and stared up at Helen and Hope, who was still clinging to her big sister like a little chipmunk, her head buried in Helen's neck.

'Hope! Is she all right?' Gloria's voice was gravelly and hoarse.

Helen nodded. 'She's fine, Gloria. Fine.'

Hearing her mother's voice, Hope twisted her face round.

'Mammee!' she called out.

Gloria looked around her for the first time, and then up to the ceiling. Bits of plaster had started to drop down. The ceiling looked as though it was about to collapse any minute.

'Please,' Gloria begged. 'Get … Hope … out.'

Helen looked up nervously at the huge gap in the ceiling above them. It was bowed and sporadic sprinkles of dust and rubble kept drizzling down. They had to get out of this very precariously stacked house of cards. And fast.

'We're not leaving you,' Martha said, brushing the remaining debris off Gloria and staring down at a thick metal girder that was lying over her friend's legs.

Helen looked at Gloria's lower half and saw that she was trapped.

'No, we're not leaving you, Gloria,' Helen said, stepping carefully over to Martha and inspecting the bloody gash on the back of her head.

'But *you* are, Martha,' she ordered, teasing Hope's body from her own.

'Hope, darling,' Helen said, giving the little girl a kiss, 'your aunty Martha's going to take you now, and your mammy and I are going to follow.'

And without further ado, Helen handed Hope over. Martha looked at Gloria and then at Helen, wanting to argue the case that *she* should be the one to stay and help Gloria, when there was another cracking sound and an avalanche of tiles and bricks showered down, missing them all by inches.

'Get her out of here!' Helen yelled at Martha through the chaos. 'There's no time!'

She looked up at the ceiling. There was now an ominous grating noise coming from above.

'Go!' she shouted, desperation in her voice. 'Now! Before the whole building goes down!'

Martha hesitated for a fraction of a second before jigging Hope around so that she had a secure hold on her, and turning to make her way along the rubble-strewn hallway.

Reaching the entrance, she stepped onto Mrs Crabtree's front door, which was lying flat on the ground, providing a gangplank over the debris and leading her and her human cargo to safety.

Hope's forlorn face stared over her rescuer's shoulder as she watched her mammy and her sister disappear from view.

Chapter Sixty-Three

When the air raid sirens sounded out, Lily sighed dramatically.

'And I was so looking forward to my dessert,' she exclaimed, looking around the table at her nearest and dearest.

'I hope it's not going to last long,' Kate said. She didn't need to say why. Everyone knew she was itching to get back to the bordello to work on Lily's wedding dress.

'It's probably just a false alarm,' Vivian said, with just a slight suggestion of an American accent; she kept her full-on Mae West impression to the confines of Lily's.

'Let's hope so,' Maisie said. During the last air raid attack her heart had turned over when she'd heard the bombs had landed just a few streets away from Bel's and Lucille's front door.

'Don't worry, hon,' Vivian drawled, reading her friend's thoughts. 'Lightning never strikes twice. Well, very rarely anyway.'

Rosie looked at Vivian and Maisie, then at Kate, and finally at Lily and George. She wondered what it would be like if Charlotte was also here. Would she like the people who had become a strange, dysfunctional kind of family? Or would she be repelled by the nature of the business in which they all worked? Was she even old enough to be told about the kind of work they were all involved in?

Not long after they and the other diners and hotel guests had made it down into the extremely well-supplied cellar, they heard the bombs land, and felt the ground shudder underfoot. No one said what they were thinking. They didn't have to. It was obvious. Rosie noticed Maisie becoming increasingly agitated. She could empathise. All her women welders lived in the east end.

Just over half an hour later when the all-clear sounded out, Maisie was one of the first to leave the relative comfort of the hotel basement, followed by Rosie.

'Where did they drop?' Maisie grabbed an ARP warden heading towards Hendon.

'Tatham Street, Laura Street and Tavistock Place,' the man told them, his face grave. 'It's bad by all accounts.'

Rosie and Maisie took one look at each other.

'We'll see you back at West Lawn,' Rosie shouted back as she and Maisie broke into a run.

Neither needed to say where they were going or what they dreaded finding when they got there.

'I'll just have a quick fag,' Pearl told Bill, speaking loudly to be heard over the air raid sirens that had just started up.

'Probably a no-show,' she said, walking round and sitting on the other side of the bar. She had just poured herself a large Scotch.

'See yer later!' she shouted over to the last couple of regulars to leave.

Walking back across to the bar after locking up, Bill looked at Pearl; she didn't seem in much of a rush to go down to the basement.

'Gerra move on, you two!' Ronald's voice shouted up from the depths of the cellar. 'We're just about to deal here!'

'Hold yer horses, we'll be down in a minute.' Pearl took another drag on her cigarette.

'Go on then, twist my arm,' Bill said, grabbing a glass from the side and pouring himself a good measure.

'Well, dinnit blame me if a bomb drops on us,' Pearl laughed.

Bill had just pulled up a stool next to Pearl when the bombs did drop. And although they didn't land on top of them, they weren't far off.

'Jesus!' Pearl grabbed the side of the bar, feeling as though the earth had just moved underneath her, which it probably had.

The noise of both explosions, one immediately after the other, was deafening and terrifying.

Bill did a quick scan of the pub. Everything was still in one piece.

'So much fer a "no-show",' he said.

Pearl stubbed out her cigarette and downed her whisky in one, before jumping off her stool.

'Isabelle 'n Lucille!' was all she said.

Bill hurried ahead and unbolted the front door.

Looking down the street to her left, Pearl could just make out that two of the houses opposite the Education Architect's Offices had been obliterated. Looking over the tops of the houses to her right she could see another plume of destruction. She guessed by the location of the billowing smoke that Tavistock Place had taken a hit. Panic kicked in. Bel and Lucille always took shelter in the basement of one of the big houses there.

Hurrying across the cobbles, coughing because of the sudden dryness of the air and the spreading smoke, Pearl kept her eyes fixed on the front door of number 34. She didn't notice an ambulance slam on its brakes to avoid adding to the number of casualties; her mind was elsewhere. It was nearly ten o'clock. Lucille would normally have been in bed at this time. Bel would be drinking tea and chatting to Polly if Joe was on Home Guard duty. The chances were they'd not have had time to get themselves round to Tavistock Place – fingers crossed.

Standing on Agnes's front doorstep, Pearl took a deep breath. She felt Bill behind her, his hands on her shoulders.

She banged hard on the door.

'Isabelle! LuLu! You in there!' Pearl shouted at the top of her lungs. Her heart felt as though it was hammering its way out of her chest. She heard footsteps before the front door swung open.

'Ma!' Bel said. She had a tight hold of Lucille, who had her coat on over her nightdress. Polly, Agnes and Arthur stood in the hallway behind them.

'We're just leaving for the shelter!' Bel picked up Lucille and stepped out of the house, looking around her at the growing mayhem.

'No, yer not,' Bill said, as Agnes, Arthur and Polly followed. 'Looks like Tavistock Place's just taken a hit. You're all coming to the pub.'

No one argued.

'What about Beryl 'n her two lasses?' Arthur asked; like Lucille, he too had his coat on over his nightclothes.

'It's all right, Arthur,' Agnes said, taking him by the elbow, 'they're visiting relatives in Shields.'

Hurrying across the road and into the Tatham, they all just about managed to squash into the cellar, although Ronald grumbled quietly about having to forsake his game of poker.

'I hope Gloria and Hope are all right,' Polly worried.

Bel gave her a questioning look.

'She was off to see an old friend who's just moved in down the road,' Polly explained.

'With Hope?' Bel asked, instantly worried.

As soon as the all-clear sounded out, everyone climbed out of the cellar and made their way round to the other side of the bar.

'We're going to find Gloria,' Polly said.

'And Hope,' Bel added. 'LuLu, you stay with your two nanas while Mammy goes and sees a friend quickly.'

'Be careful,' Agnes told them both, as she hauled her sleepy granddaughter onto her lap.

'Aye, watch yerselves,' Pearl added as Bel and Polly hurried out of the pub. She would never say it, of course, but she was beyond relieved that it had been the end of the street that had been bombed and not the middle.

Bill grabbed a bottle of whisky he kept for personal use from under the counter.

'I think we all need one of these,' he said, sloshing the Scotch into each glass and handing them out.

No one argued.

Chapter Sixty-Four

Seeing Martha turn and gingerly make her way out of the skeleton of the house, Helen turned her attention to Gloria.

'Right, time to get *you* out of this hellhole!'

Clambering around the mound of rubble so that she was behind Gloria, Helen clamped her arms around her friend to gain as much leverage as possible, before using her own bodyweight to pull Gloria from under her stone counterpane.

'Argh!' Gloria was clearly in agony.

'I'm stuck!' She twisted her head round. 'This place is going to go any minute. Please, Helen, leave me! Get out while you can!'

Helen didn't say anything, but kept on pulling.

Gloria's face blanched. Something metallic was cutting into her left leg.

'Please, Helen!' Gloria begged. 'Go! What'll happen to Hope if neither of us makes it out?' She cried out in pain again as Helen continued to jerk her backwards.

'Take care of Hope! You'll make a brilliant mam!' Gloria bit down on her lip, the pain making it hard for her to speak. 'Hope *adores* you.'

Helen puffed as she desperately tried to pull Gloria out. She felt as though she was in a tug of war, only her opponent was invisible – and much stronger than her.

'As much as I adore Hope,' Helen spoke through gasps, 'I don't want to be her "mam", thank you very much!'

She pulled again. This time there was a slight movement.

'I'm quite happy being her big sister.'

She pulled again.

Again there was another slight shift.

'Did I ever tell you I always wanted a sister?' Helen spoke through a rush of air.

'Just a few dozen times!' Gloria laughed and cried out at the same time. She felt as though someone was slowly piercing her left leg with the blade of a knife.

'Come on! One more time!' Helen shouted.

Gloria pushed back as hard as she could, as Helen pulled with the last shred of strength she had left.

Screwing up her eyes, making her world go black, Gloria felt the most unbearable, searing pain, and let out the most ear-splitting cry of agony.

And then, suddenly, she felt a jolt as her leg jerked free.

'Thank God!' Helen cried out as she toppled backwards.

Gloria wasted no time in dragging her legs out from under the metal beam.

As they both struggled to their feet, they froze in terror as they heard the house let out a deep groan.

'Come on, Gloria! We've got to go!' Helen looked down at Gloria's left leg, and felt herself gag. It was a bloody mess.

'Put your arm around me,' she ordered. Gloria hooked her arm around Helen's neck as they both staggered down the hallway.

Glancing at her friend, Helen thought she looked like she was on the verge of passing out.

'Stay with me, Gloria!' she shouted.

Gloria's head nodded forward and Helen felt herself bow under the weight. Her whole body was shaking with nerves and exhaustion.

'Gloria!' Helen shouted.

Gloria's head came up off her chest.

'I'm here,' she mumbled.

As they stumbled towards the front door, Mrs Crabtree's home gave up the ghost.

Letting out another deep, sorrowful lament, the ceiling finally caved in.

Seconds later, the walls followed suit.

Chapter Sixty-Five

When the all-clear siren sounded out, Hannah and Olly were the first to leave the sanctuary of the synagogue's basement. They'd heard that Tatham Street and Tavistock Place had been badly hit.

Hurrying along Ryhope Road, Hannah prayed aloud:

'Please let everyone be all right!'

Turning right down Gray Road and passing the rear entrance of the Sunderland Church High School, Hannah's mind flickered to Rosie. She had always agreed with Rosie's decision to keep Charlotte in Harrogate. Even more so now.

Crossing over Toward Road, they heard the clanging bells of the fire engines in the distance.

'I hope Martha's being careful,' Hannah said, glancing across at Olly.

'She'll be fine.' Olly tried to sound reassuring, although he had got to know Martha well and was under no doubt that when it came to helping others, the idea of being careful would be the last thing to cross her mind.

After a few minutes they reached the end of Gray Street and turned left onto Suffolk Street, passing St Ignatius Church, where they had all gathered just under a year ago to see Hope baptised. The streets now were beginning to fill with people emerging from their homes or walking back from wherever they had sought sanctuary.

'Is that Dorothy and Angie?' Hannah asked Olly as she spotted two women walking ahead of them.

'It's hard to tell,' Olly said. Not only was it dark, but the two women in front of them were covered from head to foot in grey soot.

'Dorothy! Angie!' Hannah shouted out.

The two women turned around. Hannah gasped. She had never seen them looking this dirty at work, but more worryingly, she had never seen them looking so dejected.

'What's happened?' Olly asked, seeing that Dorothy and Angie also had identical tear marks running down their ashen faces.

'Please don't tell us it was Polly's house?' Hannah felt her stomach turn.

'No, no, we passed their house. It's fine,' Dorothy said, tears welling up.

'And Tavistock Place where they go for shelter?' Olly asked. 'Is that all right?'

Dorothy and Angie both nodded.

'It's Gloria and Hope!' Dorothy blurted out.

'What do you mean?' Hannah asked, her stomach turning over. 'Gloria's flat's on the Borough Road?'

'She was visiting some auld woman she knew from way back,' Angie said. 'At the bottom of Tatham Street. Where the bloody bomb dropped.'

'And she had Hope with her,' Dorothy said, forcing back more tears.

'Ó můj bože!' Hannah broke into her mother tongue.

'The house is a wreck!' Tears had started to fall down Dorothy's face.

'We saw Martha 'n Helen outside what's left of it,' Angie said.

Hannah looked confused at the mention of Helen, but didn't say anything.

'Were Gloria and Hope in there?' she asked, her voice barely a whisper.

Dorothy looked at Angie.

'We think so. Helen told us to check the flat and the public shelter—'

'That's where we've been,' Angie said, 'but they weren't there. We can't think of anywhere else they might have gone.'

'Come on,' Olly said, squeezing Hannah's hand. 'Let's go and see if they've found them.'

They hurried down Suffolk Street and then under the railway bridge that heralded the start of Tatham Street, where they slowed down, shocked by the surreal scene that greeted them.

ARP wardens and residents were digging in the rubble of the two houses that had been completely razed to the ground. The building opposite was all but demolished. People were wandering around, crying and shouting out the names of loved ones, random fires were being put out by the auxiliary fire service – then, amidst the pandemonium, they spotted Bel and Polly.

'Over here!' Dorothy shouted out.

The women all hurried towards each other.

'Have you seen Gloria and Hope?' Bel asked. Her face was gaunt with worry.

'We think they're in there,' Angie said.

'In the house?' Polly said in horror.

Dorothy and Angie nodded.

All of a sudden they heard someone shouting.

'Bel!'

They all looked around to see Maisie and Rosie jogging towards them.

'Thank God, you're all right!' Maisie grabbed hold of her sister and gave her a bear hug.

'Where's Lucille? Is she all right? I went to the house but no one was there.'

'Yes, yes, she's fine. She's with Ma and everyone in the Tatham,' Bel said.

'What about Gloria and Hope?' Rosie asked.

Her answer was met by silence as Hannah, Olly, Dorothy, Angie, Polly and Bel all looked towards the shell of the house in front of them.

'We think Martha's in there too,' Dorothy said.

'And Helen,' Angie added. They'd almost forgotten about Helen.

'Well, we better get in there and get them,' Rosie said, matter-of-factly, as she started to climb over the mammoth mound of bricks that led to the house.

They all started to follow when suddenly they saw Martha's distinctive figure staggering unsteadily out of what had once been the front of Mrs Crabtree's home.

She had Hope in her arms.

Chapter Sixty-Six

Martha hesitated for a fraction of second, before she turned away from Helen and Gloria and carefully stepped over the masonry that was covering the mosaic tiles of Mrs Crabtree's hallway.

Her pace was slow as she felt a little unsteady and she was fearful of falling with the babe in her arms.

She could feel Hope's chin on her shoulder and knew she was looking back at her mammy and her sister.

She could also feel blood trickling down her neck from where she'd bashed her head.

As Martha walked through what had been the entrance to the house, and along the front door that was lying flat on the ground, she looked ahead of her.

She blinked hard.

Her vision had become blurred. Either that or the weather had turned misty.

She blinked hard again.

Was that Rosie? What on earth was she doing here?

And was that Dorothy and Angie behind her?

And Polly?

Blimey, the whole squad was there. Even Hannah and Olly.

Martha felt the strangest urge to laugh.

Rosie looked like Boadicea going into battle with her cohorts behind her.

The urge to chuckle, however, ended abruptly when she realised she was losing her balance.

Come on! Martha ordered herself.

Instinct told her to put the child down. They were a good few yards away from the house. They were safe now.

Martha carefully lowered Hope to the ground.

As soon as she did so, she felt her legs buckle, followed by a jarring pain as her knees hit hard stone.

How strange that everything seemed to be happening in slow motion.

She caught a glimpse of Hope standing by her side as the rest of her body went down, just like a tree being felled.

Rosie reached Martha at the same time that Bel reached Hope.

Bel swung the little girl up into her arms and immediately started inspecting her for any obvious wounds. Maisie looked at the house. She'd seen plenty like it in London. She grabbed Bel's free hand and led her carefully over the rubble, wanting to get as much distance as possible between themselves and the building before the inevitable.

'Martha can you hear me?' Rosie squatted down, willing the group's gentle giant to respond. But there was nothing. She looked out for the count.

'Můj bože!' Hannah cried out on seeing the huge bloody gash on the back of her friend's head. She knelt down and put her skinny arms around Martha's broad shoulders.

'Dorothy! Angie!' Rosie looked up to see two grey, panic-stricken faces. 'Get help!'

The pair immediately turned and started making their way back over the ruins, waving their hands and shouting at a medic tending a girl on a stretcher.

'Gloria's still in there,' Polly said to Rosie, staring at the house.

'And Helen,' Hannah added, looking across at Olly.

'Come on,' Rosie said, standing up. 'Before the whole lot comes down!'

Rosie, Polly and Olly had only managed to take a couple of steps forward when they heard a loud crack, followed by the sound of falling debris.

Then a huge billow of dirt filled the air and obscured their vision.

Dr Parker looked around him.

Still no sign of Helen.

'You're going to be fine,' he said to the young girl lying on the stretcher. She was in shock and had some pretty deep cuts that would need a few stitches, but from what he could tell she had escaped serious injury – unlike some of the people he had tended to this past hour.

He'd heard there were at least a dozen people missing – including an entire family who lived in one of the houses that had been hit. The death toll was going to be heavy, there was no doubt about that. He just begged whatever God might be up there that Gloria and Hope weren't part of that count.

'All right, lads.' Dr Parker looked up at the two wardens, who didn't look much older than the girl on the stretcher. 'Get her to an ambulance. When she's at the Royal, tell them to check for any internal injuries. Just in case.'

'Over here!'

Dr Parker looked up to see two women, both grey from head to foot, waving their arms frantically at him.

Spotting two medics leaving the back of an ambulance, he signalled for them to follow him before clambering across the rubble to the women.

'Hurry, please! It's our friend. She's collapsed,' one of the young women told him as they hurried towards the half-demolished house.

Dr Parker realised the two women were taking him to where he had last seen Helen.

This must be Mrs Crabtree's house – or rather, *what used to be her house*.

'Is Gloria all right? And Hope?' he asked.

It took Dorothy a second to realise the man they were asking for help was the blond-haired bloke they'd seen with Helen at the yard.

'Hope's all right,' Dorothy said.

'But Gloria's still in there,' Angie added.

'Do you know where Helen is?' Dr Parker asked.

The two women exchanged looks and Dr Parker felt his stomach turn.

'She's in there as well,' the women said in unison.

Dr Parker started to stumble across the debris towards the house just as a cracking noise sounded out through the night air.

Rosie, Polly and Olly were the nearest to the house.

Dr Parker was just a few yards behind them.

And Dorothy and Angie a few yards behind him.

They stopped in their tracks – helpless to do anything other than watch in horror as Mrs Crabtree's house creaked into submission and the last remaining ceiling caved in.

'Noooo!'

Dr Parker's voice echoed through the cloud of dirt and destruction that had enveloped them.

Why hadn't he made her go to the shelter!

Why had she walked into a bloody death trap?

But he knew why.

Hope.

And Gloria.

A surreal stillness filled the air as the dusty grey shroud started to disperse.

He stared ahead, wishing more than anything in the world he could go back in time, wishing he could rewind the events of this evening – wanting more than anything to change destiny.

Anything to keep his love alive.

Chapter Sixty-Seven

They stood there – all of them.

All dreading what they would see when the smog lifted.

All standing statue-like, not deigning to move as the air slowly started to clear.

And then the faded outline of two figures appeared.

'Gloria?' Rosie said tentatively, not quite believing her eyes.

'Helen!' Dr Parker shouted out.

Neither Helen nor Gloria moved – both in total disbelief that they had escaped the deluge of death by seconds.

Both women were squinting, trying to keep the dust from their eyes.

Gloria was leaning heavily on Helen, her arm around her neck. Behind them lay a six-foot mound of bricks and mortar, over which lay a huge wooden beam.

'Gloria!' Rosie yelled again as she rushed forward and grabbed hold of her friend.

Having been released from Gloria's weight, Helen suddenly felt her legs go and Polly arrived just in time to catch her.

'Helen! Are you all right?' Dr Parker reached the woman he loved. 'Have you any pain anywhere?' he asked, scrutinising every part of her, looking for signs of any kind of injury.

Helen shook her head.

'Do you feel wet anywhere?'

Another shake of the head.

He turned to the young woman with the long chestnut hair, who he guessed was one of the women welders since she was wearing dark blue overalls scattered with pinhole burns.

'What's your name?' he asked

'Polly.' She put her arm around Helen's waist to better support her weight. She could feel Helen's strength ebbing fast.

'Polly, do you think you can manage to get Helen over to one of the ambulances?'

'Yes, no problem,' Polly said with more confidence than she felt.

'Get the medics to check her over. I'll be there in a minute.' He took one last look at Helen before turning to Gloria, who was now being held up by Rosie on one side and Olly on the other.

This time there was no need to ask any questions as he could see she was injured, and her contorted face told him she was in agony.

'Don't worry, Gloria, we'll get you something for that pain in a minute.'

Dr Parker's head snapped around.

'Here!' he shouted over to two ARP wardens.

As soon as they arrived, they got on either side of Gloria, taking her from Rosie and Olly.

'Give her a shot of morphine as soon as you get her to the ambulance,' Dr Parker said.

'Hope?' Gloria managed to spit out her daughter's name through the pain.

Dr Parker looked to Rosie for an answer.

'Yes, Glor, she's fine,' Rosie reassured. 'Hope's fine. Bel's got her.'

'Martha?' Gloria said through gritted teeth.

'She's going to be fine too,' Rosie said, even though she had no idea if Martha was, in fact, going to be all right.

Gloria's body sagged and she let the two strapping young men take her weight.

'Can you go with her, Rosie?' Dr Parker asked. 'Shout if you need me.'

Rosie looked anxiously over at Martha, who was being attended to by two auxiliary army medics. Hannah was by her friend's side and had been joined by Olly.

'Don't worry, I'll see to Martha,' Dr Parker told Rosie as he headed over to the woman he had heard so much about from Helen – how she was stronger than most men, and that she had saved one of the workers last year when a metal plate had landed on his leg.

'Hello there, Martha,' he said, dropping down on his haunches and giving her a quick once-over. 'I'm Dr Parker. How are you feeling?'

'All right,' Martha said.

'We've got her sitting up,' one of the medics said, 'but weren't sure whether or not to move her.'

'Má strašný střih … cut … *na zadní straně hlavy* … head.' Hannah was struggling with her English. The shock had catapulted her back to her native tongue.

So this was Hannah. The group's little bird. The one Helen felt the most guilty about.

'Well, let's have a look,' he said, gently turning Martha's head.

'Cut' was somewhat of an understatement.

Signalling for the medic to hand over his khaki bag, Dr Parker found what he needed and started to clean up the gash on Martha's head as best he could.

'Do you know where you are, Martha?' he asked, pulling out a bandage from the bag.

'A bomb site. Tatham Street.'

'Can you tell me how you hit your head?' Dr Parker started carefully wrapping Martha's head in a bandage, being mindful not to make it too tight.

'I fell backwards.' She didn't mention she had hit her head whilst pulling Helen out of the way of a falling beam, and therefore hadn't been able to break her own fall.

'All right,' he said, having done what was needed. 'I think we'll get you a stretcher and these two medics can get you over to the ambulance.'

Martha let out a puff of laughter.

'I think I can manage myself.'

Proving her point, Martha slowly got to her feet, guided by Hannah and Olly.

'See?' she said.

Dr Parker smiled.

Helen hadn't been exaggerating.

'Is Hope all right?' Helen asked as Polly helped her over the ruins.

'Yes, she's fine,' Polly said. 'Martha got her out and then Bel took her.'

'Took her where?' Helen panicked.

'Just off this blasted bomb site.' Polly forced a laugh. She could see Helen was in shock. Her whole body was trembling, and she was looking about her as though she wasn't quite sure where she was, which wasn't really surprising as even *she* didn't recognise Tatham Street, and she'd lived here her whole life.

'We'll see her in a minute,' Polly reassured her.

'See,' she pointed over to the ambulance. 'They're just over there. The medics'll be checking her over. Not that there's anything wrong with her,' Polly was quick to add, seeing the look of alarm appear on Helen's face. Polly knew that Helen and Hope were sisters, but she had no idea they had ever met each other – never mind become so close that Helen would risk her life for the little girl. *And for Gloria as well.*

'How are you feeling?' Polly asked.

'Yes, yes, I'm fine. Absolutely fine,' Helen said as though the question was quite ridiculous.

'That's good,' Polly said as they finally reached a part of the road they could actually see. Polly looked at Helen in her ruined red dress, her face smeared in soot, her hair a mess, and thought she looked anything but fine. It was the first time since she had got to know her that Polly had felt even a sliver of compassion for her.

'So, tell me what happened?' she asked.

'Well,' Helen started, not knowing where to start. 'The sirens went off … then the bombs dropped.'

'Didn't you make it to a shelter?' Polly asked.

'No, John and I got in an ambulance.'

Polly guessed John was Dr Parker. There had been speculation at work that the two were courting, but Polly sensed they were just friends.

'Why did *you* get in the ambulance if the sirens were still going?' Polly could understand why Dr Parker had done so. It was his job to save lives. But Helen?

'Hope and Gloria,' Helen said as though it was obvious. 'I knew they were visiting Mrs Crabtree and that she lived at the bottom of Tatham Street.'

'But the bombs had just dropped,' Polly said. 'There might have been more coming … '

'Exactly,' Helen said, looking ahead, her eyes searching for Hope. 'I had to make sure Hope was alive. That she was safe.'

Polly looked at Helen. She was finding it hard to tally the person she was now talking to with the one she had been unable to abide for the past two years.

'But you put yourself in danger – terrible danger – going into that building.'

Helen looked at Polly, but didn't say anything.

It was then that Polly realised that she and Helen weren't so dissimilar for she would have done exactly the same for Lucille and Bel.

'There she is,' Helen said, her eyes trained on Hope, who was sitting on Bel's knee and was being fussed over by a very beautiful woman of mixed race.

As soon as Hope saw Helen she put her arms out.

''Elen,' she cried out.

Bel looked surprised at seeing Hope's reaction to a woman she had no idea the little girl had met, never mind formed such an obvious attachment to.

Bel stood up and took Hope over to Helen.

'Are you all right to take her?' Bel asked.

'Yes, of course, I'm fine. Thank you, Bel,' she said as Hope swapped the comfort of her former childminder for that of her big sister.

'How's my brave little girl?' Helen inspected Hope. It was only now, seeing Hope with her own eyes, that Helen felt reassured that she was, indeed, safe and well.

Bel touched Polly's arm.

'I'm going to nip back to the Tatham with Maisie and tell them that everyone's all right.'

Helen looked up. *So the coloured woman was Bel's sister*.

'Good idea.' Polly smiled.

Seeing Gloria, Helen hurried over to her friend, whose feet were barely touching the ground thanks to the two medics on either side of her.

'Give your mammy a quick kiss,' Helen told Hope as she lifted her towards Gloria.

Hope clasped her mother's face in her pudgy hands and gave her a kiss.

'Let's get her sat down,' one of the medics said, looking around.

'Here!' Dorothy shouted out. She was carrying a dining-room chair from one of the nearby houses. Behind her was Angie with a stool.

Patting the chair, Dorothy looked at the medics and flashed them both a smile.

'There we are,' she said, shooting Angie a look, 'if you can both just lower Gloria down.' The two young men did as they were told while Angie put the stool in front of the chair.

Gloria tried unsuccessfully not to grimace in pain. Every part of her body felt as though it had been battered.

'Eee, I could get used to this,' she said through gritted teeth as one of the medics started to tend the wound on her leg, and the other rolled up Gloria's sleeve to give her a shot of morphine.

Polly looked at Helen and thought she appeared unnaturally pale. She was also shaking badly.

'Come on, Helen, let's sit down here,' she said, guiding her by the elbow to the back of the St John's ambulance.

Helen sat down with Hope still clinging to her like a baby koala bear.

'Look!' Angie pointed to the ground by Helen's feet.

They all stared at the sudden appearance of a ginger tabby that had started to weave between Helen's legs.

'Well, I never,' Gloria said, amazed not just by the cat, but by the fact that she was already starting to feel the instant effects of the morphine.

'Pussy!' Hope stretched her arm out in an effort to stroke the cat.

Helen looked at Gloria.

'I'm sorry,' she said, her face now deadly serious. 'We found Mrs Crabtree in the lounge.' Helen shook her head, not wanting to say the words.

'She didn't make it?' Gloria said.

Helen shook her head again.

Gloria looked at the cat, now settling itself at Helen's feet.

'She might have done were it not for that damned cat.'

As Martha, Hannah and Olly slowly made their way across the rubble, they were closely followed by Dr Parker, who was purposely lagging behind to keep an eye on Martha, unsure as to whether she was as with it as she purported to be. It was only when they neared the ambulance that he saw Helen. Hope was cuddled up on her lap – *and was that a ginger cat at her feet?* Polly was sitting next to her on the back step of the ambulance, and Gloria was resting on a chair next to them, her injured leg raised on a stool.

Standing around them were Rosie, Dorothy and Angie.

'Martha!' Dorothy screeched on seeing them approach. She flung herself at her friend and gave her a hug.

'Are you all right?' Polly asked. 'God, you went down like a bag of hammers.'

Martha nodded.

'Are you sure?' Rosie held her by her shoulders and inspected her for a moment before embracing her.

'Eee, Martha, yer really *are* a proper hero!' Angie said.

'She certainly is!' Gloria said. 'Come here!' She beckoned her workmate over to where she was sitting. The medic stood up, having finished bandaging her leg.

Going over to her friend, Martha bent over her and hugged her hard.

'I can't thank yer enough,' Gloria said, looking at Martha as she straightened up. Tears were rolling down Gloria's face. 'I really thought me 'n Hope were gonna die in there. You really are one very brave woman.'

Martha looked at Gloria and then at Helen. She looked exhausted, and even though her face was smeared with dirt, Martha could still see she was ghostly white.

'Actually,' Martha said, looking at the woman about whom they never had a good word to say, 'it's *Helen* who was the brave one.'

Helen looked up as Martha spoke.

'It was Helen who went searching for Hope and Gloria,' Martha continued, 'who went into the house even though you could see it was just about to collapse.' Martha's eyes fell momentarily onto the little girl who had miraculously escaped unscathed and was now playing with her sister's black hair without a care in the world.

'It was Helen who got Hope and made me leave with her, and who stayed to help Gloria even though there was a good chance she'd get buried alive.'

Helen was looking at Martha. Tears had started to sting her eyes. She felt Gloria reach out and take hold of her hand.

Rosie, Polly, Dorothy, Angie, Hannah and Olly looked at Helen, realising that if it hadn't been for her, they would have been pulling the body of their beloved workmate from under a mound of rubble, and there'd have been a good chance that Hope's lifeless body would have been found next to her.

'So,' Martha said, 'I think we should all really be thanking Helen.'

The women were all nodding, not sure what to say.

Rosie spoke first.

'What you did there was incredibly brave, Helen. I don't think we'll ever be able to thank you enough.'

Helen batted away the compliment.

'Agreed,' Polly said, looking at Helen, who was in the process of handing Hope over to her mother.

The women all stared at Polly and then at Helen. Never in a blue moon would they have predicted the two arch enemies would be sitting within half a mile of each other, *never mind speaking to each other.*

'Oh my goodness!' Helen suddenly blurted out.

She stared at Polly.

'I can't believe I forgot!'

Everyone was looking at Helen.

'What?' Polly asked, a worried look on her face.

Tears fell freely from Helen's face as she looked at Polly.

'I've got the best news ever for you!' Helen took a deep breath.

'It's Tommy! He's alive!'

Polly stared at Helen. A look of total confusion on her face. Not daring to believe the words she had just heard.

Seeing her disbelief, Helen nodded.

'It's true! He's alive! I've seen him with my own eyes!'

Helen heard one of the women gasp.

Polly still seemed incapable of speech.

'He's *here*, Polly!' Helen said. 'He's back!'

'He's alive?' Polly's voice was practically a whisper. As though she didn't even dare speak the words, never mind hope that the man she loved more than anything in the entire world was not dead.

'He's up at the Ryhope.' Helen was staring at Polly, trying to make her understand that this was real.

Polly got to her feet.

Helen stood up, although every muscle in her body told her to sit back down again.

'He's in a bad way, Polly,' she told her quickly. 'Sounds like he's been through the wringer. But he's all right. He's going to be all right.'

Helen looked up and found the person she was looking for.

Dr Parker stepped forward.

'He's been in and out of consciousness,' he told Polly. 'He's lost a lot of weight and he needed an operation.' Everyone was now listening with bated breath. 'He lost a lot of blood, but he's still in one piece.' Dr Parker wanted Polly to know what to expect – and also that he hadn't, like so many of the soldiers that ended up on his table, lost any limbs.

Polly was nodding – taking in everything that she was being told.

'He just gained consciousness a few hours ago,' Dr Parker said.

'And,' Helen looked at Polly, 'he was asking for you. Saying he had waited so long to see you.'

All the women – not just Helen and Polly – now had tears in their eyes.

'We were on our way to tell you,' Helen said, 'when this happened.' She looked around at the surrounding devastation.

'I've got to go and see him!' Polly said.

'See who?'

It was Bel, accompanied by Maisie.

'Tommy!' Polly turned to her sister-in-law and grabbed her by the shoulders.

'He's alive, Bel. He's alive!' She was crying and laughing as she hugged Bel.

'He's up at the Ryhope,' Rosie said to Maisie.

'Are you thinking what I'm thinking?' Maisie asked.

Rosie nodded.

Maisie turned to Polly. 'George'll take you up there in his car. He always keeps a secret stash of petrol for emergencies.'

Polly's face lit up. She looked around at the women, and then down at Gloria and Hope.

'Well,' Gloria said, 'what yer waiting for?'

*

They all stared at Polly and Maisie as they hurried off.

'That's amazing news,' Bel said.

'I can't believe I forgot to tell her straight away,' Helen said.

'Well, I think you had a good excuse as to why it skipped your mind,' Dr Parker said with a smile.

'I do think, however,' he added, 'that it's high time we got Gloria and Martha to the hospital. I'd like to see those wounds properly cleaned and stitched up as soon as possible … And I know you're not going to like it, but the pair of you are going to have to spend at least one night in the Royal. Gloria, you'll probably need two. That leg is going to need to be rested.'

Martha looked over to Hannah and Olly, who read her thoughts.

'We'll go and see your parents,' Olly promised.

Martha opened her mouth to speak.

'And, *yes*,' Hannah said, 'we'll tell them that you're fine and they're not to worry.'

'But nothing we say,' Olly chuckled, 'will stop them rushing up there faster than the speed of light to see you.'

Gloria glanced at Hope and then at Bel.

Helen caught the look and anticipating what Gloria was going to ask Bel, she stepped forward and gently eased a sleepy Hope out of her mother's arms, jiggling the floppy little girl onto her hip.

'*I'll* look after Hope. She is my sister after all.' She smiled at Bel. Not for the first time she thought that Bel reminded her of someone but couldn't quite put her finger on who it was.

'Are you sure?' Gloria said.

'More than sure,' Helen said, looking down at Hope.

'Well, if you need anything,' Bel said to Helen, 'you know where we are.'

Helen smiled and nodded her thanks.

'Right,' Bel said, looking round at the rest of the women, 'I'm going to go and tell Arthur the good news. God, he's going to be over the moon!'

As everyone shouted their goodbyes, Bel turned and hurried back to the Tatham.

'Will it be all right you staying at mine?' Gloria asked Helen, thinking about Miriam.

'Of course it will be.'

'Well, the front-door key's under the mat,' Gloria said. 'You know where everything is so just make yourself at home.'

The women all stared at Helen and Gloria.

There was a silence, broken by Dorothy, who couldn't contain her excitement and curiosity.

'So, you two are friends?'

Helen looked at Dorothy but didn't say anything.

Gloria chuckled.

'I would have thought you had worked that out by now, Dor!'

For once Dorothy was at a loss for words.

At least now she knew why Gloria was always sticking up for Helen.

'You know,' Rosie said to Helen, 'none of us will ever forget what you did this evening.'

Helen looked at Rosie – her face becoming serious.

'I'd have done anything for this little girl.' She looked at Hope, whose head was now heavy on her shoulder.

'And for Gloria. I don't know what I would have done without Gloria these past few months.'

The women looked puzzled but knew not to ask.

Rosie smiled. She was glad Gloria's and Helen's friendship was now out in the open. She'd guessed a while back but hadn't known for sure until she'd seen them coming out of the museum the other night.

'But, I'm afraid to tell you – ' Rosie looked at Helen, her face deadpan ' – that whether you like it or not … '

She paused and allowed a smile to break through.

' … you have just made yourself some friends for life.'

'Friends. For life,' Martha agreed.

'Friends!' Dorothy and Angie said in unison.

'Which means we're here for you too, if ever you need it,' Hannah added.

Helen looked at the women and forced back tears.

For once, though, they were tears of happiness.

Looking at Rosie, Martha, Dorothy, Angie and Hannah, there was so much she would have liked to have said, but she didn't.

Instead she looked at Gloria and then back at the women.

'Well, looks like I'm stuck with you all, doesn't it?' The slight quiver in her voice betrayed her true feelings.

She took a deep breath, before a mischievous look spread across her face.

'But don't think this means I'll be giving you any slack at work.'

She paused.

'We've got a target to hit, you know!'

They all burst out laughing.

Chapter Sixty-Eight

'You two feeling all right?' Rosie asked.

She was perched on the narrow bench in the back of the St John's ambulance that was making its way up through the town to the Royal.

Martha was sitting bolt upright next to Rosie, a bandage around her head, and Gloria was sitting on the stretcher opposite, her wounded leg stretched out in front of her.

'I'm more than fine,' Gloria said. Her voice was a little slurred due to the painkiller she had been given.

'I'm more than fine, too,' Martha said, 'although I wish they'd given me whatever it was they gave Gloria.'

'It's because you've got a head injury,' Rosie said. 'You sure you're feeling all right?'

'Yes, I'm all right. Honestly,' Martha said with a smile.

Rosie nodded.

'Well, after what's happened this evening, my mind's made up. That's for sure.'

Gloria and Martha stared at Rosie with puzzled looks on their faces.

'Charlotte,' Rosie said by way of an answer.

'Ahh,' Gloria said.

'You're not going to let her come back?' Martha said.

'No way,' Rosie said. 'Not in a month of Sundays. Certainly not until this war is over. Not after tonight.'

She was quiet for a moment.

'I have to admit, though, I was dithering and wondering whether to have her back home, but not any more. No way, José!'

Gloria laughed.

'Well, I don't blame ya. In fact, I think me 'n Hope will move to Harrogate. It'll be a damn sight safer.'

Rosie looked at her workmate and knew she'd never leave her hometown – bombs or no bombs.

As Dr Parker walked up Tatham Street with Helen and Hope, who was now fast asleep in her sister's arms, he didn't think it was possible to love another woman as much as he loved Helen.

He took his jacket off and draped it around her shoulders.

'What a night, eh?' he said.

'Not one we'll be forgetting any time soon, that's for sure!' Helen laughed.

When they reached the top steps to Gloria's basement flat, Dr Parker looked at Helen.

As their eyes met Helen had a flash of memory of earlier on in the evening when they had stood just like this.

John had been about to kiss her. She was sure of it.

Helen waited with slightly bated breath as John bent his head towards her.

She closed her eyes slightly and waited to feel the touch of his lips on her own.

But when she felt nothing, she opened them again to see his head moving to her side to give Hope a tender kiss on the forehead.

'There's one very lucky girl,' he said, looking at the sleeping child in Helen's arms.

'And she's got one very brave big sister.' He smiled and gave Helen a kiss on her cheek before turning and heading back to Tatham Street.

It was going to be a long night.

Chapter Sixty-Nine

As Polly and Maisie hurried along Salem Street it seemed that the whole of the east end was up and half of them were out on the street, either heading in the direction of Tatham Street or chatting to neighbours on their doorsteps.

Turning right at the bottom and onto Mowbray Road, Maisie and Polly walked as fast as they could, dodging people and jogging when they got the chance. They ran across the wide breadth of Ryhope Road, watching out for any more ambulances and fire engines.

The further they walked, the quieter it became, and by the time Mowbray Road turned into Tunstall Vale, there was barely a soul to be seen.

'You all right?' Maisie asked breathlessly, glancing across to Polly. She looked as though she was in a different world.

'Yes ... Yes ... I think so,' Polly said. They turned the corner into Briery Vale Road.

'I can't quite believe it ... don't think I'll believe it until I see him,' she added as they crossed the road onto West Lawn. She rarely came to Ashbrooke. Never had much reason to come this far out of town. She had forgotten just how upmarket it was here and how grand the houses were.

'Here we are!' Maisie said, jubilantly. She was exhausted. And her feet were killing her. *Thank God she hadn't put on her high heels this evening.*

Maisie opened the small gate and Polly followed, looking up at the huge three-storey mid-terrace.

So, *this was Lily's*. This was what a *bordello* looked like. They'd all known about Lily's for almost two years – since they had come to Rosie's rescue that night her uncle had attacked her – but none of them had ever been here, not even Bel, *and her sister lived and worked here*. It was a place they all knew about, were all secretly madly curious about – especially Dorothy and Angie. *God, they'd have given anything to be here now.*

Maisie banged on the front door and seconds later it was flung open. Lily's face was a mixture of worry and anger.

'Where's Rosie?' she demanded before either Maisie or Polly had time to draw breath.

'Is Rosie all right?' It was George.

'Has something happened?' Kate pushed through Lily and George.

'She's fine,' Maisie said. 'Absolutely fine. There's nothing to worry about.'

Lily's face immediately relaxed.

'Well, come in!' She moved to the side. 'Can't have you both standing there on the doorstep like two little street urchins, can we?'

Maisie looked at Polly and rolled her eyes.

Stepping into the hallway, Polly almost gasped in awe at the unadulterated opulence of the place.

'Maisie, thank goodness you're back!'

Polly and Maisie looked up to see Vivian hurrying down the stairs.

'I wish you hadn't just gone running off like that. You've had us all worried sick.' She reached the bottom of the stairs and went to give her friend a hug. 'Did you find Bel and Lucille? Are they all right?'

'Yes, thank goodness, they're fine,' Maisie said. 'Although a couple of Rosie's squad had a bit of a hairy time of it all.'

Everyone looked, wanting to hear more.

'I'll tell you all later, but right now there's something far more pressing that needs addressing.' She looked at Polly, who still hadn't uttered a word. 'And which requires your services, George.'

George looked at Polly and back to Maisie with a question on his face.

'Polly needs you to take her to the Ryhope – *tout de suite*,' she added, looking at Lily and seeing her smile at her attempt to speak French. 'For Polly here has just had the most marvellous news.'

She paused for dramatic effect.

'Her fiancé, Tommy Watts, is alive!'

'Oh, that's the most wonderful news!' Kate rushed over and flung her arms around Polly. 'I'm so happy for you!'

'Formidable!' Lily declared. *'Une raison de célébrer!* Come into the parlour!'

Maisie looked at Lily and thought she'd already had a few. She'd obviously been fretting about her golden girl and quelling her anxiety with a few brandies, as she was wont to do.

'No, Lily,' Maisie said, glancing at Polly, who was looking more than a little bewildered. 'We've got to get Polly to the Ryhope – now. Polly doesn't want to sit around hobnobbing with us lot when the love of her life who she thought was dead is very much alive and just up the road.'

'Well, now you put it like that,' Lily said, turning around to face George. 'What are you waiting for? Chop, chop!'

George was already at the stand by the front door getting his jacket and scarf.

'Come on, my dear,' he said to Polly, 'we best get you there and pronto!'

Polly's eyes lit up.

'Thank you, George! You sure it's all right?'

'All right?' George said, raising his eyebrows. 'It's an absolute pleasure!'

And with that he gave Lily a quick kiss and, aided by his walking stick, made his way carefully down the front steps.

'You've made an old man very happy tonight,' he told Polly as he opened the front gate and let her go through first. 'I've not had an excuse to take this old girl out for a spin in ages!'

As he opened the passenger door for Polly, he heard Lily shouting out:

'Drive carefully, George!'

George guffawed.

'As if I'd do anything else!'

As Polly climbed into the passenger seat of George's little red MG, she looked up to see Lily, Kate, Maisie and Vivian all waving and shouting out their good wishes from the top step.

When George turned the ignition and the engine died as soon as it started up, Polly thought for an awful moment that the car wasn't going to start, but on the second try the engine spluttered to life.

Fifteen minutes later George was pulling up outside the Ryhope Emergency Hospital.

'Well, here we are, my dear,' George said. 'Go and give that fiancé of yours a big smacker!'

Polly gave George a hug, jumped out of the car and ran as fast as her legs would take her to the main entrance.

George sat, the engine still running, and watched as Polly disappeared through the revolving doors.

He wanted to savour this moment.

It wasn't often these days you got to hear some good news.

And this was good news.

Bloody good news.

Chapter Seventy

'I've come to see a patient,' Polly said, leaning on the front reception desk. 'A Tommy Watts. He's been unconscious and has just woken up. I'm his fiancée.' Polly rushed the words out.

The middle-aged receptionist looked at Polly in her grubby overalls, her long brown hair clinging to her red, sweaty face, and she knew there was no way she could tell her to come back during visiting hours. Sometimes exceptions had to be made.

'He's been looked after by Dr Parker,' Polly said, fishing around in her top pocket for her engagement ring. Finding it, she put it on.

'Ah,' the receptionist looked up, 'if it's Dr Parker it'll be the post-operative ward.' She stood up and pointed towards the corridor on her right.

'Just follow your nose until you get to the end and then take a left. Keep going for about a hundred yards and you'll be there. It'll be signposted.'

'Thank you ... Thank you,' Polly shouted out as she hurried down the corridor and out of sight.

Polly's heart was beating like a drum as she rushed down the windowless corridor. She slowed down as she passed a couple of nurses and two doctors, who couldn't help but stare at the overall-clad woman hurrying past them.

Finally, Polly drew to a halt when she reached her destination, but only for a second. Pushing open the swing doors and walking straight onto the ward, her eyes scanned the dozen or so beds.

'Excuse me, miss?'

Polly looked round to see the stern face of the ward matron.

'Sorry,' Polly said, 'I've come to see Tommy Watts. I'm his fiancée.'

Polly looked to her right and that's when she saw him.

As though in a dream, she walked to his bed. Tears had started to fall unchecked down her face.

When she reached him she realised he was asleep.

She stared at the man she loved, the man she thought she had lost for ever, and she simply looked at him, savouring the moment.

It was real.

Tommy *was* alive.

Sensing movement behind her, Polly looked round to see Mrs Rosendale approaching with a chair. She put it down gently next to the bed; her finger went to her lips to show Polly that she must be quiet.

'Is he going to be all right?' Polly whispered to the matron, who nodded her reply.

Polly sat down, and gently took Tommy's hand in her own and kissed it.

For half an hour she sat there, her eyes not once leaving Tommy's face.

And then she leant over and kissed him gently on the lips.

'I love you, Tommy Watts,' she whispered into his ear.

As she did so, she saw his eyes flutter open.

'Is that my Pol?' His words were barely audible.

'It is,' Polly said, choking back tears and squeezing his hand.

Tommy put his free hand on top of Polly's. As he did so his fingers felt the ruby engagement ring.

'It *is* – it's my Pol,' he said, a smile stretched across his face as he managed to keep his eyes open for a few seconds.

'I thought I'd never see you again,' he mumbled.

'I didn't think I was going to see you again either,' Polly said.

Tommy was fighting to keep awake.

'Polly, do you still want to be my wife?'

Polly smiled, leant over and kissed him again.

'Of course I do,' she whispered in his ear.

For a moment she rested her face against his.

This is not a dream, she told herself.

This is real.

'Well,' Tommy said, his sparkling hazel eyes fluttered open, allowing him to look at the woman he loved, 'I think we should set a date. Soon. Very soon. I think we've waited long enough.'

'I do … I do too, Tommy,' Polly said, kissing him again, and smiling through her tears.

Epilogue

The late cross-country service from York finally pulled into Sunderland station just after 11 p.m.

The air raid that evening had caused delays on all the trains passing through the town, but thankfully this was the last one. The stationmaster could go home as soon as this batch of passengers had disembarked and gone on their way.

Watching the dozens of tired travellers haul luggage and sleepy children onto the platform, the old man looked on as they all made their way in dribs and drabs up two flights of stairs, through the barriers, and out into the cold but clear October night.

One of those passengers, who didn't look at all tired, was a fourteen-year-old girl.

She was dressed in a school uniform that the stationmaster didn't recognise. It certainly wasn't from these parts. She was struggling with a large suitcase that was bursting at the seams and looked as though it weighed the same as, if not more than, the young girl who was carrying it.

Seeing that she was alone – and thinking that he wouldn't have liked his own bairns to have been travelling alone this late at night – he stopped her as she reached the barrier.

'Can I just check your ticket, pet?'

The young girl dumped the suitcase down and scrabbled around in her bag for a few moments before producing her ticket.

'Ah, Harrogate,' the stationmaster said, peering over his half-moon spectacles. 'You visiting relatives?'

The bright-eyed young girl shot him a look and shook her head fiercely.

'No, I *live* here,' she said, taking her ticket back off the old man.

'This is my home.'

Welcome to

Penny Street

where your favourite authors and stories live.

Meet casts of characters you'll never forget,
create memories you'll treasure forever,
and discover places that will stay with
you long after the last page.

Turn the page to step into the home of

Nancy Revell

and discover more about

The Shipyard Girls...

Dear Reader,

The background image used on the cover of *Courage of the Shipyard Girls* is an original photograph taken the day after the bombing of Tatham Street on 16 October 1942. I can only imagine the kind of courage needed on that awful evening and during the ensuing days, weeks and years as those affected dealt with the loss of their homes and their loved ones.

In total, fourteen people were killed – tragically seven of those were children. I believe the bravery of those who lived through this air raid, as well as other bombings throughout the length and breadth of the country, is truly inspirational.

Whatever fears or hardships, tragedies or losses you, dear reader, may have to deal with, now or at any time in the future, I sincerely hope that you too are able to find the courage to simply carry on.

Until next time.

With love,

Nancy x

HISTORICAL NOTES

To mark the 80th Charter Year of Soroptimist International of Sunderland, its members have commissioned and provided funding for a piece of public artwork which pays tribute to the hundreds of courageous, hardworking and inspirational women who worked in the Sunderland shipyards in World War One and World War Two.

The commemoration came about thanks to Suzanne Brown of the Sunderland Soroptimists, who read the first instalment of *The Shipyard Girls* and, like myself, was both enthralled by the real-life women who stepped into their men's steel toe-capped boots and got to work repairing and building ships, but also outraged that they had more or less been forgotten.

During World War Two, *seven hundred women* worked in the Sunderland shipyards – then the 'Biggest Shipbuilding Town in the World' – women, who, at the drop of a hat, swapped their pinnies for overalls and signed up to become welders, riveters, platers, crane drivers and labourers. Work previously only deemed suitable for men.

These women were under no illusion about the kind of back-breaking work they were letting themselves in for. They often did twelve-hour shifts, six days a week, in all kinds of weather. They worked in harsh and hazardous conditions, with scant regard for health and safety – only then to return home to cook, clean and care for their families.

They also had to contend with constant air strikes by Hitler's Luftwaffe, as the world-famous shipyards, (which produced a quarter of Britain's merchant shipping at the time), were a strategic target for German bombers. Without the shipyards, there would have been no cargo vessels for the essential transportation of vital food, fuel and troops. The country, quite simply, would have been forced to surrender.

These women chose to undertake such difficult and often perilous jobs in the yards, not only because they needed to work, but also because they wanted to be a part of the war effort.

And all the while they were living with the fear that the men they loved might not make it home from the frontline.

It is thanks to Suzanne and the Sunderland Soroptimists that these remarkable women who played such an important role in a crucial period of our history will never be forgotten. The contemporary artwork will overlook the River Wear where the women worked and it will stand as a lasting legacy to the real Shipyard Girls, becoming part of the city's heritage for years to come

I personally hope other towns and cities in the UK, who also had women working in the shipyards during World War One and World War Two, will also follow suit.

Turn the page for a sneak peek into my new novel

Christmas with the Shipyard Girls

PROLOGUE

Gibraltar, 21 June 1942

Tommy looked up at the darkening sky. Its palette of yellow and orange mixed with an array of blues reminded him of the huge oil paintings that Arthur had taken him to see as a child in the town's museum. His grandda had told him that a person could learn a lot about the world by simply looking at these depictions of days gone by and far-off lands, but all Tommy had wanted to do was run out of the musty-smelling exhibition room and look up at the *real* skies and stare out at the real sea.

'Here you are,' a soft woman's voice drew his eyes away from the oil-painted sky. 'Let's get this around you.'

Tommy looked at the pretty face of the nurse as she bent over his stretcher and tucked a blanket tightly around his body. She nearly lost her balance a few times as the lifeboat bobbed about in the choppy waters.

'Help's on its way,' she reassured. Tommy felt her palm on his forehead. Her hands were icy cold but cooling against his own hot brow.

'You're cold,' Tommy mumbled.

The nurse smiled but didn't say anything. Tommy looked at her familiar white pinafore emblazoned with the distinctive emblem of the Red Cross and he suddenly realised that he didn't know her name. Hers was the only face he had seen during his spells of consciousness. He'd heard the living and the dying since he'd been hauled on board the hospital ship, but hers was the only face he'd seen, or at least remembered.

Turning his head to the side Tommy looked out at the Atlantic Ocean that was now covered in a layer of black oil from the ship's fractured fuel tank. He could just make out the ship itself. It's white painted flank slowly disappearing beneath the surface.

'Here! Over here!'

Tommy felt the lifeboat sway as two dark figures got to their feet and started shouting and waving their hands. He craned his neck.

'See, I told you.' The nurse put her cold hand on his forehead once again, before easing a thermometer into his mouth. 'They've come to get us.' Tommy heard the Yorkshire Dales in her accent.

There was lots of movement, shouts and cries of jubilation as a ship's grey bow ploughed towards them, a sense of euphoria spreading through the packed lifeboat as salvation approached.

Tommy watched as the nurse took the thermometer out of his mouth and looked at it. Her face looked sombre. 'And not a moment too soon,' she muttered, grabbing the side of the boat, unsteadied by the swell created by the approach of their rescuers.

'Come on,' she put her arm around Tommy's shoulders and helped him to sit up. 'I want you to be one of the first off.'

Tommy's body was shaking and his teeth were chattering but he didn't feel at all cold.

'Listen!' A man's voice next to him suddenly shouted.

The excitement died down.

And that's when they all heard it.

The ominous drone above them.

Looking up, they saw a lone bomber thudding its way across the sky. Its target obvious. There were no other ships within sight – other than the one coming to their rescue.

'Please, God, no!'

Tommy saw panic and alarm on the young nurse's face as she made the sign of the cross.

Turning his vision back to the sky's oil-painted canvas he could just make out the bomber's metal underbelly releasing its innards and the outline of three giant-sized bullets as they careered through the air, see-sawing ungainly before smashing into the sea. Three white mountains of frothing angry sea water erupted one after the other, causing Tommy's world to suddenly turn upside down. Air was replaced by water; the burning heat that had been consuming his body for weeks now, extinguished in an instant.

A familiar quietness followed. It was the sound of silence that Tommy knew well and had lived much of his life with.

An instinctive feeling of relief surged through him; he was where he belonged.

His body had stopped shaking; his arms and legs felt strong and fluid as they stretched out and swam back up to the surface. Breathing in air he looked around.

He saw the upturned lifeboat. Two men had managed to climb on top and were trying to pull someone out of the water. His vision blurred as another angry wave washed over him. Blinking he caught sight of the nurse. She was gasping for air. Tommy could see her arms were trying to keep her afloat, but her clothes, like dead weights, were dragging her under.

Tommy started swimming, punching through the surface of the sea and battering his way to get to her. She disappeared under the water again, but re-emerged, coughing and gulping for air.

He had to get to her.

He powered through the water.

His arms pulling his body forward, his legs kicking furiously. He was nearly there. Just a few more strokes and he'd be able to grab her.

Another wave pushed him back, but only for a second.

Coming up for air, he scanned the surface of the turbulent waters.

He couldn't see her.

Panic coursed through him.

He swung his head around, frantically treading water, but she was nowhere.

Taking a huge gulp of air Tommy upended his body, diving underneath the waves and back into the quiet watery underworld. Through stinging, blurred eyes he spotted her.

You can't have her! His whole being screamed as though the sea was his foe.

Swimming, pulling water back with every ounce of energy he possessed, Tommy desperately tried to reach her.

Seeing him, her eyes widened.

Tommy saw the look of desperation as she reached out to him with splayed hands.

No!

He saw her mouth open and knew what she was about to do.

Don't breathe!

But it was too late.

Her mouth formed an oval shape, her body jerked the once, before a mass of bubbles started streaming around her pretty, young face.

She began gasping, sucking in water instead of air. As she did so, her body began convulsing.

Please God! No!

Tommy strained every muscle as he tried to grab her. Frantically, his arms dug deep into the darkening waters, dragging himself down after her.

But then the writhing stopped. Her body became still. Tommy saw the red cross of her white uniform fluttering like a flag in a gentle breeze.

Still he tried to reach her, but her body was now sinking. Fast.

Tommy swam deeper, still snatching at water as he tried to grab her, refusing to give up.

Suddenly the nurse's head tilted upwards – her brown hair swirling about her face like Medusa – her eyes stony-dead.

It was too late.

And then Tommy's own world went black.

When Tommy was hauled into the wooden lifeboat, spewing sea water and retching death from his lungs, he looked at his rescuers but did not see their faces.

For many weeks after, whether in a sweat-soaked semi-consciousness or in a deep medicated slumber, the only face he could see was that of the young Red Cross nurse.

As the ship he was on rocked its way across the Atlantic, so did his mind similarly crash back and forth.

Like the swell of a strong current he would often find himself sucked back to memories of his former life, encased in his canvas suit and twelve-bolt helmet, immersed in the murky waters of the River Wear.

Occasionally, as though elevated by strong winds and high waves, his mind's eye would surge upwards, escaping reality, catapulting itself into a future devoid of warmongering and death. It was then he would see a vision of Polly's smiling face, and he would imagine their life together. He clung to that image, but it was never long before it began to fade and in its place, like an image in a photographer's developing tray, the grey, lifeless face of the Red Cross nurse would slowly emerge.

The weeks spent crossing the Atlantic passed in a vague, dream-like haze. Tommy heard snatches of conversations, always about either love or war; always in a constant cloud of cigarette smoke.

He heard medics coming and going, soldiers near him either vomiting with sea sickness or crying out in a delirium of agony. Occasionally someone was carried out on a stretcher and did not return.

As the ship crossed the seas, the stench of death seemed to become increasingly more odorous and might well have ended up suffocating them all, had they not reached their homeland when they did.

Then the undulating wash of the Atlantic was replaced by the jarring feel of the army first aid truck on terra firma.

On the second day of October, Tommy was stretchered out of the makeshift ambulance and into a building he guessed by the smell of antiseptic and the blur of white coats was a hospital.

'Have we a next of kin for this one?'

Tommy heard the polished tones of an educated man as he was wheeled along a narrow windowless corridor.

'I'm afraid not, Dr Parker. We don't even have a name yet.'

The front of the trolley buffeted a pair of swing doors open.

'Over here, please!' This time it was a woman's voice. She sounded old and stern.

Tommy managed to open his eyes. He had guessed right.

'Can you tell us your name?' Dr Parker was bent over him.

As the two men manoeuvred him onto the bed Tommy tried to speak.

Tommy... Tommy Watts! The words were as clear as day in his mind, but they seemed to lose their way before reaching his mouth. Instead he listened as the familiar broad Scottish accent of the driver explain that any identification he might have had was now probably lying on the bottom of the Atlantic.

'We only knew to bring him here 'cos one of the lads heard him shouting in his sleep. Recognised the accent straight off.'

'Well, at least he's home,' Dr Parker's voice became distant as he moved on to the next patient.

If the doctor had turned around, he would have seen the beginnings of a smile on the face of the patient with no name.

He'd made it.

He was home.

WHICH SHIPYARD

1. WHICH OF THESE CHARACTERISTICS BEST DESCRIBES YOU?

a) Pragmatic

b) Loyal

c) Kind

d) Resilient

2. WHICH WORD WOULD YOUR FRIENDS MOST LIKELY USE TO DESCRIBE YOU?

a) Independent

b) Stubborn

c) Caring

d) Confident

3. WHICH PAIR OF SHOES ARE YOU MOST LIKELY TO WEAR?

a) Comfortable heels

b) Work boots

c) Sensible flats

d) The latest fashion

4. YOUR PERFECT EVENING IS...

a) A night alone with your dashing beau

b) Tea with close friends

c) A quiet night at home with your family

d) Dinner at a high-end establishment

GIRL ARE YOU?

5. IF YOU WEREN'T WORKING AT J.L. THOMPSON'S, YOU WOULD BE...

a) An owner of an independent business
b) Doing nothing else – working at the shipyards is your dream
c) A stay at home mother
d) A lady of leisure

6. IF YOUR FRIEND IS GOING THROUGH A TOUGH TIME YOU WOULD...

a) Take it upon yourself to fix the problem
b) Rally the girls and find a solution together
c) Comfort and care for her
d) Tell her to pull herself together

7. COMPLETE THIS SENTENCE: FRIENDSHIP IS...

a) Very rare and something to cherish
b) What keeps you strong
c) All around you
d) Found in the most unlikely places

THE SHIPYARD GIRLS

Mostly A's – You are Rosie Miller **(née Thornton)**
You are determined, fiercely loyal and independent.

As the squad's leader, it's your job to keep everyone in line and you're really rather good at it. You're organised and your friends look to you for guidance and support. You're the anchor of the group and despite having troubles of your own, you never let them get in the way of helping a friend in need. From tough beginnings, your hard work and perseverance will see you succeed in the end.

Mostly B's – You are Polly Elliot
You are passionate about your heritage with strong morals and a stubborn edge.

No one will ever get in the way of your dreams. Your strength and determination will ensure that you always get what you want but you will never sacrifice your integrity to do so. You're loyal to those you love, and your friends know they can rely on you to get them through the toughest of times. Just remember to put yourself first once in a while.

CHARACTER QUIZ ANSWERS

Mostly C's – You are Gloria Turnbull
You are a kind, caring but no-nonsense woman.

As the eldest welder, you are the squad's mother hen. Your friends look to you for comfort and you welcome them with open arms and a cuppa. You're patient and calm, but you're not afraid to put your foot down when people step out of line. If you're ever on the wrong track, don't fear; the path to true love never did run smooth and it will all be worth it in the end.

Mostly D's – You are Helen Crawford
You are strong, resilient and never let anything get in your way.

A rare beauty, you are often misunderstood. People judge you by your affluent upbringing but beneath the surface there is a heart of gold. Although it takes people a little longer to break through your walls, once they do they have a friend for life. Your friends admire your strength and ability to overcome any misfortunes that come your way. You may get knocked down a few times, but your resilience will see you through.

HAVE YOU READ
They worked for their country, their families, and for each other . . .
The Shipyard Girls
Nancy Revell
THE SUNDAY TIMES BESTSELLING AUTHOR
With their men at war, they must turn to each other . . .
Shipyard Girls at War
Nancy Revell
THE SUNDAY TIMES BESTSELLING AUTHOR
The war rages on but their friendship is stronger than ever
Victory for the Shipyard Girls
Nancy Revell
THE SUNDAY TIMES BESTSELLING AUTHOR
Join the Shipyard Girls

THEM ALL?

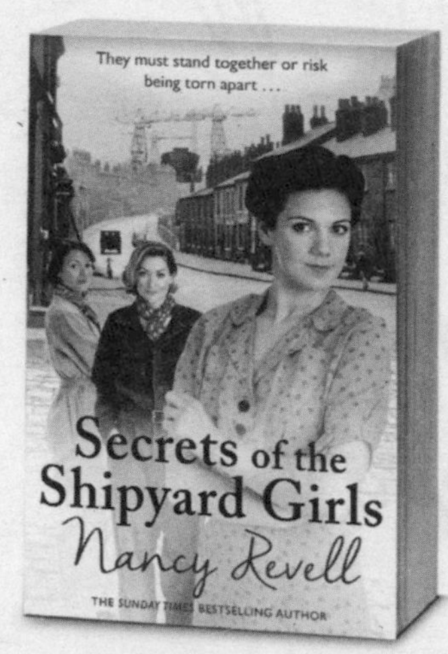

through love, life and war…